PRAISE 1

Tom Clancy fans open to a strong female lead will clamor for more.

— DRONE, PUBLISHERS WEEKLY

(Miranda Chase is) one of the most compelling, addicting, fascinating characters in any genre since the *Monk* television series.

— DRONE, ERNEST DEMPSEY, AUTHOR OF THE SEAN
WYATT THRILLERS

(*Drone* is) the best military thriller I've read in a very long time. Love the female characters.

— SHELDON MCARTHUR, FOUNDER OF THE
MYSTERY BOOKSTORE, LA

Superb!

— DRONE, BOOKLIST, STARRED REVIEW

A fabulous soaring thriller.

— *TAKE OVER AT MIDNIGHT,* MIDWEST BOOK
REVIEW

Meticulously researched, hard-hitting, and suspenseful.

Expert technical details abound, as do realistic military missions with superb imagery that will have readers feeling as if they are right there in the midst and on the edges of their seats.

Buchman has catapulted his way to the top tier of my favorite authors.

Nonstop action that will keep readers on the edge of their seats.

M L. Buchman's ability to keep the reader right in the middle of the action is amazing.

The only thing you'll ask yourself is, "When does the next one come out?"

The first...of (a) stellar, long-running (military) romantic suspense series.

I knew the books would be good, but I didn't realize how good.

Buchman mixes adrenalin-spiking battles and brusque military jargon with a sensitive approach.

13 times "Top Pick of the Month"

DRONE

A MIRANDA CHASE THRILLER

M. L. BUCHMAN

Buchman Bookworks

Other works by M. L. Buchman: *(* - also in audio)*

Other works by M. L. Buchman:

Contemporary Romance (cont)

Where Dreams
Where Dreams are Born
Where Dreams Reside
Where Dreams Are of Christmas
Where Dreams Unfold
Where Dreams Are Written

Science Fiction / Fantasy

Deities Anonymous
Cookbook from Hell: Reheated
Saviors 101

Single Titles
The Nara Reaction
Monk's Maze
the Me and Elsie Chronicles

Non-Fiction

Strategies for Success
Managing Your Inner Artist/Writer
Estate Planning for Authors
Character Voice

Short Story Series by M. L. Buchman:

Romantic Suspense

Delta Force
Delta Force

Firehawks
The Firehawks Lookouts
The Firehawks Hotshots
The Firebirds

The Night Stalkers
The Night Stalkers
The Night Stalkers 5E
The Night Stalkers CSAR
The Night Stalkers Wedding Stories

US Coast Guard
US Coast Guard

White House Protection Force
White House Protection Force

Contemporary Romance

Eagle Cove
Eagle Cove

Henderson's Ranch
Henderson's Ranch

Where Dreams
Where Dreams

Thrillers

Dead Chef
Dead Chef

Science Fiction / Fantasy

Deities Anonymous
Deities Anonymous

Other
The Future Night Stalkers
Single Titles

ABOUT THIS BOOK

A US Air Force C-130 transport plane, bearing top secret cargo, lies shattered in the Nevada desert at Groom Lake.

China's prototype fifth-generation jet fighter goes missing.

Far above, a US supersonic, stealth drone flies a very lethal Black Op.

The CIA, the US military command, and the secretive National Reconnaissance Office are all locked in a battle for control of the nation's future.

Miranda Chase, the National Transportation Safety Board's air-crash savant, lands in the center of the gathering maelstrom.

Burdened with a new team and a polarizing personality, she must connect the pieces to stay alive. And she must do it before the wreckage of her past crashes down upon her and destroys US-China relations forever.

PROLOGUE

Flight 630 at 37,000 feet
12 nautical miles north of
Santa Fe, New Mexico, USA

THE FLIGHT ATTENDANT STEPPED UP TO HER SEAT—4E—
which had never been her favorite on a 767-300. At least the
cabin setup was in the familiar 261-seat, 2-class
configuration, currently running at a seventy-three percent
load capacity with a standard crew of ten and one ride-along
FAA inspector in the cockpit jump seat.

"Excuse me, are you Miranda Chase?"

She nodded.

The attendant made a face that she couldn't interpret.

A frown? Did that indicate anger?

He turned away before she could consider the

possibilities and, without another word, returned to his station at the front of the cabin.

Miranda once again straightened the emergency exit plan that the flight's vibrations kept shifting askew in its pocket.

This flight from yesterday's meeting at LAX to today's DC lunch meeting at the National Transportation Safety Board's headquarters departed so early that she'd decided to spend the night in the airline's executive lounge working on various aviation accident reports. She never slept on a flight and would have to catch up on her sleep tonight.

Miranda felt the shift as the plane turned into a modest five-degree bank to the left. The bright rays of dawn over the New Mexico desert shifted from the left-hand windows to the right side.

At due north, she heard the Rolls-Royce RB211 engines (quite a pleasant high tone compared to the Pratt & Whitney PW4000 that she always found unnerving) ease off ever so slightly, signaling a slow descent. The pilot was transitioning from an eastbound course that would be flown at an odd number of thousands of feet to a westbound one that must be flown at an even number.

The flight attendant then picked up the intercom phone and a loud squawk sounded through the cabin. Most people would be asleep and there were soft complaints and rustling down the length of the aircraft.

"We regret to inform you that there is an emergency on the ground. I repeat, there is nothing wrong with the plane. We are being routed back to Las Vegas, where we will disembark one passenger, refuel, and then continue our flight to DC. Our apologies for the inconvenience."

There were now shouts of complaint all up and down the aisle.

The flight attendant was staring straight at her as he slammed the intercom back into its cradle with significantly greater force than was required to seat it properly.

Oh. It was her they would be disembarking. That meant there was a crash in need of an NTSB investigator—a major one if they were flying back an hour in the wrong direction.

Thankfully, she always had her site kit with her.

For some reason, her seatmate was muttering something foul. Miranda ignored it and began to prepare herself.

Only the crash mattered.

She straightened the exit plan once more. It had shifted the other way with the changing harmonic from the RB211 engines.

———

Chengdu, Central China

AIR FORCE MAJOR WANG FAN EASED BACK ON THE JOYSTICK of the final prototype Shenyang J-31 jet—designed exclusively for the People's Liberation Army Air Force. In response, China's newest fighter jet leapt upward like a catapult's missile from the PLAAF base in the flatlands surrounding the towering city of Chengdu.

It felt as he'd just been grasped by Chen Mei-Li.

Never had a woman made him feel like such a man. Fan hadn't known that he could be taken past the ultimate peak so many times in a single night. More than once he'd half feared that his given name would come true and he would die collapsed upon her—his fellow test pilots often teased him about his first name, Fan, meaning "mortal."

Of course, never before had he been with a woman who cost a week's salary. It would take at least a month to hide enough money from his insipid wife—now revealed to be so much less skilled than he'd thought—to buy another night with Mei-Li, the beautiful red gem.

Perhaps if this flight went well, he would get a promotion from *Shao Xiao* to *Zhong Xiao*—major to lieutenant colonel—and the money that came with it could simply never be revealed to his wife.

It was possible. After all, Lieutenant General Zhang Ru was his wife's uncle. Hadn't he lifted Fan from the officer corps to be a test pilot, and introduced Fan to his own niece and encouraged her to become his wife?

Uncle Ru personally had chosen him to be first in the Chinese Air Force to fly the new J-31—a great honor indeed.

Each successive flight in the long week of testing had built neatly on the one before. Today he had finally been given permission to truly test the J-31's limits.

And now Uncle Ru had arranged his night in heaven with Chen Mei-Li.

Fan had felt truly *immortal* when he stepped up, flipped aside her robe, and entered her from behind this morning as she'd been bent over to set their breakfast table—white rice scattering wide at her surprise. Steamed buns had fallen upon the blue-and-white floor tiles depicting ancient gardens and elegant courtesans, each pork *baozi* exploding in slow motion like a tiny bomb.

Forevermore, the fiery blend of ginger, sesame, and five-spice would season his memories of that purest sexual perfection.

In the moment of that crashing release like no other, he had indeed entered *Tian* and become Yǔdi the Jade Emperor taking Mazu the Jade Empress right up her heaven-perfect ass. He hadn't been Wang the prince (as his surname meant) or even king—he'd been a god.

For the gift of last night alone, he would do anything his uncle asked.

As the first Air Force pilot to fly the J-31 *Sǔn,* Gyrfalcon in the English that Uncle kept pushing him to learn, he would also have a pilot's bragging rights for a long time to come. That too he owed to Honorable Uncle Ru.

The twin Chinese-made WS-13E engines delivered 200 kN, over 46,000 pounds of thrust, all driven straight into his aching member as a single roar of glory. The sixteen-meter-long fifth-generation fighter jet leapt for the heavens. It was only the fourth fifth-gen jet fighter in the world—and personally he felt Russia's Sukhoi Su-57 was overrated. Besides, the Russian jet was still no more than a prototype, so the J-31 was the third of the new breed (he didn't count the J-20, even though it had flown first, because with the arrival of J-31, the two-year-old jet was already obsolete).

The two American fifth-gen aircraft were, sadly, very impressive. Now it was time to put them in their place.

The Gyrfalcon looked ungainly on the ground, more wing than plane. The shapes were all wrong when compared with the PLAAF's other aircraft. But like the American F-35 Lightning II that had been the inspiration for the superior Chinese engineers, its looks didn't matter. It did indeed fly like its namesake, the largest of all falcons.

"Crossing five thousand meters, Mach 0.9. All systems nominal," he continued his running report. He wouldn't radio it in, because the foul Americans would be listening with their satellites even here in Chengdu, a thousand kilometers from any border. It was also why they were testing here rather than in Shenyang so close to the American listening posts in South Korea and Japan.

Instead of broadcasting back to base, he was to keep a running commentary of the test flight for the internal cockpit recorder. All of the sensors attached for this test flight would record far more information than he could ever grunt out against the brutal g-forces, but they wanted him to make the verbal recording anyway.

No, *Uncle Ru* had wanted that. And he was the one who had ordered radio silence despite the advanced encryption systems on his radio.

Why?

Think, Fan. Think like the leader Uncle Ru is grooming you to be.

Ah!

His silence would be so that no other commander could get any information ahead of Uncle Ru.

He *was* a very wise man and Fan still had much to learn from him. Fan would capture as much as he could, then make sure the tape was delivered only into his uncle's hands.

"Flight is smooth," at least compared to the Russian RD-93 engines with fifteen percent less power that had been in the prototypes.

The J-31 didn't offer the stable ride rumored on the ever-so-similar American F-35 Lightning II, but it was the first production model delivered to the People's Liberation Army

Air Force, and for now, the seventy-million-dollar aircraft was all his.

"Impressively clean transition through Mach 1." Normally the transition was a hard shake, like taking his CFMoto 650 motorcycle down an untended dirt road.

He detailed the differences from the Shenyang J-16 (copied from the Russian Sukhoi Su-35—with all of its engine problems that had almost killed him in testing) and the Chengdu J-20 (China's first homegrown supersonic stealth aircraft—except for some "acquired" details from the American's own stealth jet program).

Every single time he broke the sound barrier, it amazed him how noisy it was to fly beyond the transition. The arrowed tip of the jet's nose cracked the air, which the hard chines of the stealth hull split into sections for smoother supersonic flow. The roar of the mighty engines, rather than being left far behind, was transmitted through the hull and couldn't be outrun.

"Mach 1.5 at ten thousand meters. Preparing for agility tests."

Chen Mei-Li had grown up inside the state-sponsored gymnast program for eighteen years. Now too old to compete at twenty-one, she had brought her lithe form and all of that incredible agility to the bedroom.

The jet felt just as responsive, and he was just entering his prime.

The J-31's design was primarily for air-to-air combat. Intended for lower altitudes than the bombers, it delivered exceptional maneuverability even at supersonic speeds.

He started with a simple twist—flying in a straight line and rolling the aircraft sideways wing over wing. S-turns and loops became second nature as he learned the feel of the jet's behavior at supersonic speeds.

He finally aimed straight up and opened the afterburners wide. The jet drove into the sky until there wasn't enough air for its engines to push against. He gradually slowed until, for an instant, he hung suspended with his momentum wrung dry, perfectly balanced: twenty kilometers into the sky on 46,000 pounds of thrust.

He held out a fist with only his pinkie finger raised toward the satellites that circled in space.

"Your dick is smaller than this, America!"

He half hoped that their cameras were powerful enough to see his gesture. They knew nothing of the meaning of power.

Maybe he would quietly remove some funds from his private savings account and celebrate this flight in Chen Mei-Li's arms. He'd tell his wife he was needed at the base for debriefing. Or maybe he would just take his wife as masterfully as he had Mei-Li this morning.

Finally toppling, the jet plunged downward, ramming back into the thicker atmosphere. At Mach 1.7, nearing the aircraft's top speed, he leveled out close above the vast patchwork pools of Sichuan Basin rice farms. He imagined the cracking sonic boom rolling over farmers and their wives as the newest jewel of the PLAAF rushed by so close overhead. Perhaps the sheer power of the Gyrfalcon would cause the farmers' daughters to orgasm at his passage.

Fan carved a hard turn and raced into the foothills of the Hengduan Mountain Range. They started abruptly to the west of Chengdu, building rapidly until they crested over seven thousand meters in the fearsome Gongga Shan. Far taller than any puny peak in North America, it rose only fifteen hundred meters less than mighty Everest.

The next stage of the test was to ease deeper and deeper into those valleys and gorges to test the jet's agility against the real world. If India became an enemy rather than a tenuous ally, the battle could well occur in the Himalayas.

Low-level high-speed flight was the greatest adrenaline ride there was. He flung himself into the testing range, rattling the mountains themselves with his flight. An area covering thousands of square kilometers had been cleared of indigenous hill tribes and it was strictly for pilots to test new aircraft to the limits.

Rumors said that the American pilots didn't need to touch the controls. That they could steer their flight with simple motions of eyes and head. Where was the fun in that? Wang Fan could feel the Gyrfalcon vibrate and shudder just like a woman as it submitted to his commands.

Slewing around a peak that rose a thousand meters above him, he volleyed hard from right to left to avoid the next. At eighteen hundred kilometers an hour, he covered a kilometer every two seconds. The peaks of the Hengduan Range crowded very close together at that speed.

Unable to fully catch his breath despite the pressure suit that compressed his legs and lower torso to force blood to reach his brain, he stopped his audio narration and left the instrumentation to record his actions. Uncle Ru had been a great pilot in his day. He would understand.

Fan raced into the Daxue Range, the highest part of the Hengduan. How easy would it be to climb over that last snowy crest onto the Tibetan Plateau and at long last fully subjugate those rebellious primitives with a fleet of jets like this one?

Not on today's planned mission, but someday he'd take them down just as he had taken—

Close by the icy edifice of mighty Gongga Shan, so proud in her glacier-shrouded glory, a shadow fell over his cockpit. One moment the sun had been shining strong from the southeast, then it had blinked out.

He twisted to look aloft. A needle-shaped plane with a broad delta wing blocked the sun. The heat of anger flashed through him. No one was supposed to be using the test range other than himself. Who dared presume?

Mottled gray, it had an unusually long nose spike that must help crack the supersonic air apart. Smooth lines sleeker than even the finest woman.

The fuselage was too slender to hold a pilot.

It must be a drone!

It certainly wasn't AVIC. The Aviation Industry Corporation of China might be one of the largest companies in the world—one tiny division manufactured the magnificent J-31 Gyrfalcon—but he knew their drones. Unless it was some other division of AVIC trying to show him up? No. China's first supersonic drone, *Dark Sword,* was still in the early stages of development.

And the mockup didn't look like this one at all.

The same fifteen-meter length as his jet but it was no configuration he'd ever seen before.

He held his heading until he was close enough to the glaciers of Gongga Shan to see down into individual crevasses. He slammed aside at the last moment, hoping that the drone would overfly its course into the mountainside. No such luck. It eased in closer until it flew directly above his head. Less than twenty meters away, it seemed to fill the sky.

Flipping his KLJ-7A radar from beyond-visual-range to close-in mode revealed...nothing. Impossibly, though he was close enough to read the markings—if there had been any—it barely registered as more than a patch of turbulent air. Its stealth was already a generation or more ahead of the J-31's.

Nothing he tried could move it from its position directly above his cockpit. He slammed through maneuvers that he didn't know he had in him: twists, rolls, and aborted dives.

The J-31 behaved magnificently.

But the drone mirrored his moves with unreal perfection.

At first he thought it was simply locked on to his aircraft for guidance. Except there were moments when it made small, unpredictable adjustments that meant somewhere there was a pilot in active control—a pilot with reaction times like none he'd ever seen in an entire career of dogfights. Fan had made test pilot because of his own exceptional reaction speed, but he couldn't match the drone's pilot.

And for the first time since Mei-Li had heated his blood until he'd thought it might turn to steam, he felt a cold chill.

Uncle Ru must be told of this, but the radio returned nothing except static when he ignored orders and tried it. The drone was blocking his transmissions, which wasn't supposed to be possible.

The drone wasn't Chinese.

And it wasn't Russian. Especially not a thousand kilometers into China.

It must be American—and it was hunting him.

There was no weapon he could bring to bear on something flying closer than his own shadow.

As if reading his thoughts, the drone pulled ahead of him. He heard no sonic boom as it passed, though he should have. Stealth and boomless? Formidable indeed.

At Mach 1.79—two thousand one hundred and forty kilometers per hour at this altitude—it descended abruptly to ten meters in front of him. Less than a hundredth of a second ahead.

The precision of the move astonished him for a moment too long.

Wang Fan tried to turn aside, but it was too late—too late the moment the drone started its move. He knew that he'd never make lieutenant colonel and that he'd never again bury himself in the glory of Chen Mei-Li.

The turbulent air of the drone's supersonic wake shattered his plane as surely as flying into the ground.

Wang Fan reached for the emergency handle but didn't pull it, knowing that even ejecting couldn't save him now. Today his name—the Mortal Prince—would come true.

The last thing he ever saw was the drone twisting aside to reveal a final look at the icy crevasses of Gongga Shan straight ahead.

He would leave no more impression on its mighty edifice than a pork *baozi* splattered on a blue-and-white tile floor.

———

CIA, Langley, Virginia

CLARISSA REESE SAT ALONE IN A SECURE OBSERVER'S ROOM

three stories beneath the New Headquarters Building. She watched the massive avalanche as it continued to bury any sign of the Shenyang J-31 and its pilot deeper and deeper. The Chinese would never find it there.

Her pilot, deep in a Nevada control bunker, had flown his drone into formation with the J-31 when the high peaks were blocking all of the Chinese surveillance satellites. From that moment on, only the closest inspection would reveal the drone as anything other than an oddly dull reflection off the J-31—because nothing else could be that close to a supersonic craft performing high-g maneuvers. The Chinese would believe that right down to their boots.

Her source had alerted her to, and a CIA analyst had confirmed, the escalating series of J-31 tests over the last few days, giving Clarissa enough time to have the drone flown deep into China the night before. That had allowed her to pick the place and time of the meet up. Those three minutes of the close-in flight had offered alarming information regarding the J-31's true capabilities.

The Chinese had started from stolen plans for the F-35 Lightning II and they'd done a fine job of copying it. By theft and massive effort, they had closed a technological advance that should have taken them another decade to achieve. Like the Japanese of the '70s and '80s reverse engineering electronics and personal computers, the Chinese were now the masters of copying American ingenuity.

There'd been no detectable transmission by the pilot for the forty-seven minutes they'd been tracking the jet since its departure from Fenghuangshan Airport in Chengdu. Once in formation, the drone had blocked the J-31's radio frequencies but left the instrumentation reporting systems active.

She imagined the horror of the Chinese as they watched their precious jet run wildly out of control—the pilot's attempt to save his life—then disappear.

The force of the jet's impact with the mountainside had guaranteed that nothing bigger than a rivet would survive. The final crash had again been timed to be wholly out of view from any satellites other than the CIA's own USA-224 KH-11 keyhole sat—an Earth-facing copy of the Hubble Space Telescope and one of the four active real-time capable craft. Actually, the Hubble was a space-facing version of the earlier KH-11.

The drone certainly detected no emergency locator signal on a close flyby.

She spoke into the secure link to the Nevada control bunker that had remained silent throughout the flight.

"General Harrington, bring it home."

"Yes ma'am."

She closed the link.

Freezing the best image of the avalanche from the drone's final pass on her screen, she tried to see any sign of the Chinese plane. There wasn't even a hint of its ultimate resting place. No blemish of a fuel explosion on the face of the pristine fall of ice. It was simply gone.

The Shenyang J-31 hadn't had enough fuel to reach a border, so their military would be forced to cross off a possible defection. It had simply behaved chaotically, as if the pilot was fighting for his life against a failing aircraft that then disappeared forever up the narrow mountain valley. No search would find any evidence until it fell out the bottom of the glacier decades or even centuries from now.

Clarissa would make sure her operative at Chengdu convinced Lieutenant General Zhang Ru that it was a fault with the plane. The next time Ru was in the operative's arms, she'd drop a hint of trouble that the pilot had "happened to mention to her" during their night together. It would lay the seeds of doubt. Perhaps of something he had discovered— though been vague about—not wanting to shame his commander by pointing out the jet's flaw.

Yes. That should work nicely. And the highly detailed volume of classified information the pilot had divulged into the former gymnast's recording equipment would be for Clarissa's people alone.

Should the operative cry for the lost pilot on Ru's shoulder or shouldn't she?

The girl would know; she was perfect.

Chen Mei-Li's coach had made it easy to recruit the lovely gymnast at the last Olympics. He'd struck her to the ground (just out of sight of international television) for placing a single tenth-point off the gold to a meticulously drugged Russian wind-up doll.

That the bastard also had made himself her personal-and-private coach—in a way wholly unrelated to gymnastics —had only made Clarissa's job all the easier. Mei-Li had proven an unslakable hunger for revenge on the institutions of her native country.

She claimed she was more than willing to offer her body to that end and had twice refused Clarissa's half-hearted offer of an extraction—not that she'd have actually done it.

Mei-Li was an exceptional resource who would be impossible to replace.

Clarissa had cemented the Chinese waif's undying gratitude by arranging for the coach's car to crash horribly before the games had ended.

For strictly personal reasons, she'd used a well-place Agency med-tech to ensure his death was slow and exceedingly painful. Too sad for him that he'd lost the ability to scream.

Clarissa purged all records of the drone and satellite session from the observation room's secure server's memory —one of the many advantages of holding a director-level clearance—then checked that there were no stray strands from her trademark white-blonde ponytail. The slick look combined with her five-ten height before donning heels said, "Mess with me at your own peril." She hadn't had to prove it more than two or three times before her reputation preceded her.

Men were always thrown off balance when she turned and they saw the rest of her hair. It wasn't some neat, short, athletic ponytail. Instead her hair went thickly wavy where it passed her shoulders on its way to the middle of her back. In 2001, a *Journal of Experimental Psychology* article—read between sessions of teenage slavery on her father's office couch—concluded that men perceived long hair as a sign of sexual health.

The day of her father's death—that she wished in retrospect had been ten times more painful than the coach's —she'd begun growing it out in earnest. No longer was her hair bobbed short to avoid it being a handhold, but neither would any of the imprudent minions who dared cross her path ever get to touch it. She only let it down for *very* special occasions.

With a sharp clack on the marble floors, her high heels heralded her approach as she strode toward her top-floor office. In the world of low-profile women, it announced that the CIA's Director of Special Research was on her way and everyone should fear her. As well they should; she'd just set the Chinese fifth-generation jet program back by years.

Enemies were all to be erased with maximum prejudice. Her country was all that mattered. Lovers? Occasionally. Friends? Who had the time?

1

THE DEBRIS FIELD OF THE C-130 HERCULES TRANSPORT PLANE lay strewn across the high desert of the NTTR.

Miranda had only handled two other crash investigations in the Nevada Test and Training Range and neither had been so near the highly sensitive base at Groom Lake, better known as Area 51. There were only three National Transportation Safety Board inspectors cleared to work inside the NTTR and she must have been closest. But she'd never been so near to Groom Lake itself.

Here be aliens! Tante Tanya might have teased her. Her childhood governess, who had raised her on the family island after her parents' deaths, seemed to enjoy doing that for reasons Miranda could never fathom. She'd learned how to tell when Tanya was doing so—she always affected an overexcited tone, which was a helpful cue—but the logic remained elusive.

From aloft in the UH-1N Huey helicopter that had met her at the Las Vegas airport, Groom Lake was a dirty-white salt flat that probably hadn't seen standing water since the last ice age. It lurked in a narrow valley deep in the heart of the largest and most secure testing area in the US military—the NTTR filled most of southern Nevada.

The mountains blocked Groom Lake from casual view, but the real security was its massive hangars. Everything was kept inside during daylight hours as much as possible, with aircraft only slipping out of their secret dens in the darkness of the night. Like raccoons or vicious wombats, the nation's most lethal aircraft emerged from their secret burrows of Groom Lake—the ultimate testing place.

There, just beyond the low notch in the hills where the C-130 had crashed, the U-2 and SR-71 Blackbird spy planes had been developed. Secretly acquired Russian jets were extensively tested in dog fights flying out of Groom Lake. The F-117 Nighthawk—the first operational stealth fighter in history—had also been developed at Groom Lake before eventually moving to the nearby Tonopah Testing Range Airport once it was operational to make way for other projects. Now all of the Nighthawks were stored at Tonopah, outdated barely out of their second decade by the relentless advance of American ingenuity.

How mundane to have a C-130 cargo transport crashed at the very border of the top secret area. It was one of the most common military aircraft in the US and indeed worldwide with over sixty operator countries flying more than two thousand aircraft in total.

The juxtaposition could almost make Miranda smile.

Except she had *hated* airplane crashes ever since one had killed her parents when she was thirteen. Each time she struggled not to recoil from the mangled metal, the shattered airframes, and the vivid red splatters of fluids that had once been inside human bodies, instead forming a rapidly browning crust on every surface.

The C-130's inverted-T tail section lay at the northeast end of the area. Usually the empennage survived mostly intact—which was why flight data recorders were mounted there. Not this time. It was barely recognizable.

A single Allison T56 engine stood tall, planted nose down into the soil like an ostrich with its exhaust port raised to the sky. At twelve feet, two inches long, it should not have been the highest remaining part of the thirty-eight-foot-tall, ninety-seven-foot-long airplane—but it was. The hull, where it hadn't crumpled or shattered, had been pancaked as if a giant had stepped on it.

Was it down because of something she'd done? That she'd missed? She had only worked on three other C-130 crashes.

The C-130A Hercules loss on the Cannon Fire in 2002 had been straightforward. The brutal math had caught up with the forty-five-year-old airframe when it was dropping retardant on a wildfire. One jolt too many from the sudden unloading of seven tons of fire retardant on the stress-cracked wing-box cross members had caused the wings to catastrophically fold upward and break off. The crew had never stood a chance as the wingless fuselage had rolled in mid-flight and crashed inverted into the wilderness at a hundred and forty-six knots.

The additional crash of a fifty-seven-year-old PB4Y-2 *Privateer* thirty-one days later had caused a panic in the Forest Service. Mass inspections for microfractures had revealed significant issues in a wide variety of airframes, which ultimately led to the grounding of all thirty-three remaining Type I firebombers—those capable of delivering over three thousand gallons. The groundings, which had followed from her initial investigation, had greatly impacted the wildland firefight for years, with devastating losses to wildfire until the capacity loss of the large firebombers could be replaced with helicopters and smaller aircraft.

The planes had been her concern, but the damage of those unchecked fires weighed on her still.

One of the other two C-130s she'd investigated for the National Transportation Safety Board had also had a mechanical issue. Improper inspection of a propeller had led to the blade breaking off and arrowing into the fuselage, which had destroyed the aircraft in midair. The last C-130 had also been on a fire, where the pilot and his guide had failed to account for the possibility of a microburst and been slammed fatally into the ground through no fault of the plane.

But maybe she had missed something. Maybe more had died here in the Nevada desert because she hadn't...

She noticed her hands were clasped together so tightly that they hurt.

Or maybe it was just another crash, Miranda. Don't wrap yourself in a cloak of Jewish guilt—at least not until it's warranted. How many times had Terence, her first mentor at the NTSB, given her that instruction?

He was right. Catholics don't know anything about guilt. Her people had it down to a science since losing the Garden of Eden. Would Eve take it back if she could? Remain in paradise rather than lose the beneficent care of God her father to the harsh reality of—

She cut off the thought. God had *not* died in a plane crash. Except He had. Her belief in a Supreme Being had died the same day her parents had fallen from the sky. She stared out the window, forcing herself to keep her hands separate. Palms down. On either thigh.

The UH-1N Huey helo that had met her at McCarran International Airport in nearby Las Vegas flew directly over the wreck—as if he *wanted* to disrupt the evidence—to set down beside a Humvee parked too close to the eastern edge of the debris field.

Were his actions mere neglect, the cause of so many wasteful actions? Or was there malice or intent involved? A thousand times she wished she was better at discerning others' emotions.

All irrelevant.

Focus on the next steps.

2

"WHO THE HELL ARE YOU AND WHAT ARE YOU DOING IN THE NTTR? This is a secure area. No civilians." The two-star general didn't even wait for her to get clear of the Huey's pounding rotor blades.

No black smoke or carbon stench of fire from the wreck.

It was so unusual for such a violent crash that it startled her out of her normal investigation process.

No visual sign that it had burned at all. The sharp bite of kerosene on the air confirmed that plenty JP-8 jet fuel had been freshly spilled, but it hadn't been ignited.

Miranda had been about to ask the second half of that question herself, though with a bit more tact: "Why have you sent for an NTSB inspector?" The military only called upon the National Transportation Safety Board for the most difficult or sensitive investigations. Now her pro forma question for military crashes had been made irrelevant and it threw her off balance.

"Well?" The general snapped it out like she was one of

his junior officers. Two did indeed hover nearby. Seven more were spread out on the desert landscape, forming a wide perimeter around the plane.

The general's forward-weighted posture invaded her personal space—which she knew was larger than most people's—and was paired with a narrowing of eyes. Wouldn't more widely opened eyes be more appropriate? Entering a conflict situation should call for maximizing visual acuity.

The New Zealand Maori war dancers made a particular point of this in their demonstrations. She'd witnessed a show after assisting their Transport Accident Investigation Commission with a particularly ugly crash of a DC-8 cargo plane well past its proper retirement age.

It turned out that the plane had suffered severe salt corrosion in its pitot tubes making the airspeed indicator wildly inaccurate on a simple landing at Rotorua Airport in New Zealand. Instead of landing, they'd flown into the lake and plowed into a large, fully loaded tourist boat. She was able to prove that it wasn't pilot error or a maintenance error —at least not based on standard practices. New service recommendations had been made and adopted.

The Maori dancers at a hotel one night had shown the faces their ancestors had traditionally made to scare their opponents: eyes wide, tongue extended, a startling yell as they raised their spears.

Man was the only predator she knew of who typically reduced his visual acuity by squinting and decreasing light intake during an attack.

All the general had achieved with his tirade was to arouse her curiosity.

"Why are *you* here?" Miranda had never before seen a two-star general dressed in combat fatigues guarding a pile of airplane wreckage.

His snarl indicated that hadn't been the correct response.

Start from the beginning. One of her basic survival rules when dealing with people.

She held out her ID while trying to regroup. Miranda always approached crash site investigations in an unvarying manner. Her mentor had helped her develop her own style of approach that had served her on hundreds of mishaps and accidents.

Here in the NTTR, they were already being forced to shift. She knew herself well enough to know that could fast become a problem if she didn't correct the patterns.

Spheres. It's all about the spheres.

But first she had to deal with the general.

As he inspected her ID, her attention again drifted to the single upright T-56 engine. It was unnatural. She'd seen a thousand engines in a hundred different attitudes, but never this one. What could have caused—

No! Don't look yet! Don't conjecture! Start with the facts. Yes, remembering that, she felt better.

"Miranda Chase," the general read aloud as if doing so might make her ID less authentic. "National Transportation Safety Board, Two-C. What's Two-C?"

"I-I-C. It's not a Roman numeral. Investigator-in-charge."

"What's the NTSB doing here?"

"I was on a flight from LA to DC, but my plane was turned around. Only a top priority request to the NTSB would cause this. Your helicopter also arrived to meet me. I must conjecture that the two events have a similar root cause. If the order wasn't yours, I don't know whose it was. I'll start now." There. That was taken care of. She stepped up to the general's Humvee and placed her knapsack on the hood.

Miranda extracted and donned her vest. Across the back it announced NTSB in shoulder-wide bright yellow letters. Even the smallest standard-issue vest was too large on her so she'd had one custom made—someday her country would understand that women now worked for a living. As she didn't expect it to happen soon, she erased the thought as a waste of mental focus.

The numerous front pockets were already pre-filled with recorders (she always carried two plus spare batteries), flashlights, gloves, evidence bags in four sizes, and, in an oversized pocket, a tablet computer enabled for precise L5 band GPS tagging of every image she took with a localization accuracy of thirty centimeters. Four markers and three pens—arranged in order by increasing wavelength of their color—and a paper notebook. She could always trust paper.

"What time did it come down?" She didn't like saying the word *crash*—too sharp, as if it had points like a medieval mace. Its late Middle English origin was particularly appropriate for the metaphor, which pleased her.

The general growled before answering, "At 0507 hours and 19 seconds."

"Good." Thirty-three minutes before sunrise and now it had been just two hours and eight minutes since the impact. That was better than most impact events—some of which she couldn't reach in days, or sometimes weeks for planes downed and lost in a wilderness area.

It was also an atypical degree of precision that she appreciated and her team would confirm when they recovered the FDR—assuming the airframe wasn't so old that it didn't carry a flight data recorder. Typically, the military installed black boxes on their aircraft only during service-extension upgrades when they changed over to digital cockpits.

Even then, the recorders were often set to auto-wipe in the event of a crash so that the information couldn't fall into enemy hands. Pilots were supposed to disable the erase function for service over friendly soil, but bitter experience with an F-22 Raptor, a crash that she'd never been able to properly resolve the causes for, had taught her that didn't always happen.

3

THE GENERAL SEEMED RELUCTANT TO RETURN HER ID.

Miranda had to reacquire it with a bit of a yank so that she could hang it from the front of her vest. By having everything in precisely the right place, she would bring a minimum of her own entropy to the severely entropic nature of an airplane crash—the ultimate state of disorder.

She checked. Everything present and accounted for.

She started to check again, but caught her right hand with her left and pushed it down to her side. It really was a foolish habit, but she was having trouble breaking it.

"Could you see that the rest of my team joins me as soon as they get in?"

"You are not authorized for this area. You and your kind don't belong here. Now turn your pretty little ass around and—"

"I'm one of the three IICs in the whole agency cleared to top secret sites such as Groom Lake—a fact you can clearly see on my CAC." She once again removed her ID wallet from

her vest and pointed to the Common Access Card on the
other side. He inspected it as if it was a bomb that might go
off in his hands.

While he read it, she mulled over the reference to her
"pretty little ass." It had no more relevance to the
investigation than her being five-four and having brunette
hair. She never understood why men had so much trouble
focusing on what was important—like the debris field
behind her.

A class at the NTSB had included statements of what
constituted sexual harassment. Had he grabbed her ass,
she'd definitely know what was going on. But the phrase,
with no contributing tonal or expression shifts (he still had
narrowly squinted eyes), didn't appear to be about her
sexuality or lack of it.

Perhaps he was the one who should have taken the class
and not her.

He pulled out a phone and flashed the barcode across
the bottom of her card. He glanced at his display, then the
card, then back to his screen without actually looking at her
—which she appreciated.

"Fine." He practically threw her ID wallet at her. "Go
ahead. Do your worst."

She returned her ID to the front of her vest so that her
NTSB ID faced outward, and was careful to keep her other
hand firmly at her side. Now, with everything in place, she
could finally begin.

"Spheres," she set her starting point.

"What was that?" the general snapped.

"*Musica universalis,*" she explained. When his scowl
shifted, apparently to confusion, she ignored him. She

supposed that confusion was an improvement over aggression.

The Music of the Spheres—the Music of the Universe.

Terence had suggested that she find her own formula for approaching a crash site. She wasn't one to take it all in big gulps the way her mentor did. He would look at a thousand yards of wreckage and, nine times out of ten, focus right in on the problem.

But the other ten percent, where the details had him stumped, was where she shone. Details had a certain beauty to them. Minute details fit together like a mosaic, slowly interconnecting until they formed a complete picture—a wholeness that had great internal beauty, even when it was a shattered aircraft.

Pythagoras had formulated the *musica universalis* while contemplating the harmonies of motion demonstrated by the sun, moon, planets, and stars—each celestial object attached to a successive crystalline sphere, centered upon the Earth, to explain their separate motions across the sky.

Miranda had found it far more useful to turn it inward. Instead of looking up at the motion of the stars, she had tunneled it inward to forge her own method of crash investigation. She supposed that made her methodology into a meta of a meta. Though Pythagoras' imagination had cast his spheres as real and concrete as the marble columns of the ancient Athens Agora marketplace. So she'd made an inward meta of an outward misguided conclusion which...

Time to begin.

Environment Sphere (the outermost layer): They were well inside the high-security border of the NTTR. It made missile attack unlikely. A collision or training accident was a possibility, but her initial inspection from the air only indicated a single aircraft. A lone aircraft—mechanical failure or pilot error was the most likely cause. Which was conjecture, but each model had its uses in guiding the investigation as long as she was careful not to allow such models to bias her observations.

Observational clarity superseded methodology superseded conjecture.

Intriguingly, it constituted science in reverse. Science had started with a theory of powered flight and, after centuries of struggle, eventually achieved it.

But when that flight lay shattered upon the ground like this poor aircraft, the scientific process became reversed. Evidence of destruction, observed, then reverse-engineered through a variety of modeling systems, could create a theory of what had happened.

Proof first, then theory later in so many respects.

She noted that thought down on the back page of her personal notebook. She hadn't considered it that way previously and wanted to preserve the concept for the next time she lectured at the NTSB Training Center.

Weather Sphere: Clear sky.

Miranda glanced around, but no members of her NTSB Go Team had arrived yet. She'd want a full assessment from a weather specialist but for now she pulled a handheld weather station from its pocket and held the device aloft for thirty seconds before pressing hold and checking the readings. Four thousand four hundred and three feet above sea level, plus or minus thirty feet. She'd learned to round such numbers off to ease communications with others less concerned about precision—four thousand four hundred feet...plus.

Ambient temperature eighty-nine degrees Fahrenheit, hot for early June at two hours and—she checked her watch —seventeen minutes after sunrise, but not out of the normal range.

Wind speed, at least here at the surface, light and variable averaging eight-point-three knots.

She noted down the humidity though it was rarely relevant.

None of which excluded possible wind shear or other events at altitude; it was simply a data point. She eyed the few puffy altocumulus clouds in the ten- to twenty-thousand-foot levels, moving lazily across the sky. Weather—unlikely cause.

"Don't you want to know what happened?" The general was looking over her shoulder and she did her best to pretend he wasn't there.

"If you knew what happened, I wouldn't be here." It had to be something truly exceptional and unknown for her to be called, yet somehow that simple logic escaped the general.

The general harrumphed but didn't speak again.

Terrain Sphere: They stood on a slight rise that offered a good view of the area. It explained why the general had parked here.

Groom Lake lay in the distance, barely visible as a patch of salt white in the vast brown of central Nevada. Tiny boxes were clustered near midfield, which would be the massive hangars and facilities of the military base. The hills here were soft rolls rather than hard humps or even sharp ridges that she'd previously observed during her two prior NTTR investigations, both near Yucca Mountain to the southwest.

From the arriving helicopter, she'd made note of the most obvious debris radius—atypically small.

The C-130 at the Cannon Fire had left a five-hundred-foot impact zone where the wings had come down and burned and a seven-hundred-and-twenty-foot debris field where the inverted fuselage had descended. And *that* had been a constrained spread for that class of aircraft, its expanse limited by the forest and rough terrain of the Sierra Nevada Mountains.

The debris field here appeared to be little longer than the aircraft itself. It implied a steep angle of impact that would contain the crash rather than spreading it over vast stretches of desert. No high terrain; in fact, most of the area astern was a wide pass between low hills. Terrain—unlikely cause.

The Overview Sphere. This was a difficult step in her system. It was her first real look at the crash, but the amount of hidden information was overwhelming.

She needed the details to see the big picture, but this was the big picture without the details. She tried squinting her eyes, which did seem to decrease the flow of information and allowed her to observe more overall.

Jagged shards of jet were strewn beneath the hot desert sun. Twists of metal that had once been wings.

The hull caved in down its entire length, again the image of the giant's foot crushing it flat. (The giant from *Jack and the Beanstalk* had given her terrible nightmares as a little girl and it seemed he wasn't done with her yet.)

No sign of any cargo. Her first impression from the air

had been correct—as unusual as it might be, the single upright engine was indeed the highest point remaining. She made a note for Tony to do a soils analysis when he arrived to help estimate angle and force of impact.

Head down against a sudden blast of wind, she began photographing the site from this small rise. The wind built hard and fast, soon backed by the hard whine of a Lycoming T53 turboshaft—probably a UH-1Y Huey helo—but she didn't want to look toward the approaching aircraft and inaccurately overlap her images.

"Goddamn it! No photographs." The general shouted at her over the roar of the landing helicopter. If it was still flying, it wasn't her problem.

She ignored both the helicopter and the general until she'd completed her first series. Only then did she see his shadow beside her feet on the soil—with his handgun raised shoulder high and pointed at the back of her head.

Apparently he had reverted to aggression.

How curious. Like Plato's shadows on the cave wall, the allegory that shouldn't be able to actually affect her.

At least her mind was curious; her body couldn't seem to recall how to breathe as the adrenaline slammed into her system.

4

MIRANDA TURNED VERY SLOWLY; SHE'D NEVER FACED A WEAPON before.

She could shoot one well enough, though she'd never enjoyed it particularly. Living in a very isolated area as she did between assignments, it was occasionally necessary to put down an injured animal herself. It still made her cry every time. So beautiful and free in life, then—*bang!*—gone forever. Just like every victim in a plane crash she'd been unable to prevent.

"I said no goddamn photographs. Now give me that thing." He tipped the weapon slightly to indicate her tablet.

The pumping adrenaline made her even more hyperaware of details than normal. Every bit of grit shifting under the sole of her boots was a moment of individual assessment until she came face-to-face with the tiny black hole at the end of the barrel, which seemed to expand until it filled the world.

Now her heartrate was escalating toward panic and her palm went sweaty holding the tablet.

She glanced over the barrel at the scowling general's face. This time when her eyes refocused on the tip of the barrel, the black hole had returned to its normal size—small, black, and utterly void of feeling.

Before she could decide on the best course of action, a tall blonde came toward them from the landed helicopter—slightly behind the general's field of view. She could have blindsided him easily. Instead, she scuffed her boot loudly by kicking a thorny scrub brush.

The general flinched and redirected his aim at the newcomer, which caused the blonde to do little more than arch an eyebrow.

"Now isn't this just so interesting." Her accent was thickly Australian. She remained at perfect ease as she circled around to stand close beside Miranda.

The handgun tracked her closely.

"Now general, I don't want to be telling you your job, but is this really the best course of action? First, if you do manage to shoot me, there will be a whole mess of paperwork just pilin' up higher than Uluru—that's the big red rock at the center of Australia, by the by, just in case you're not from around about there—which is a lot of paperwork. Shooting a civilian is very bad form. Even worse, firing on the IIC of the NTSB Go Team investigating your crash would make your motivations appear maybe a tiny bit suspect to people. People you probably don't want suspecting things about you. However, far more importantly, me former mates in the SAS—that's the Australian Special Air Service, not my Brit brethren—would be sorely

disappointed if I was to let either of those scenarios happen."
She stood as casually as if she was chatting with a friend.

Miranda inspected her more closely.

She was five-ten and looked remarkably fit. Which
would be fitting for the SAS. Australian Special Operations
might not be Delta Force, but they were very elite military.
Miranda had no idea what she was doing here, but the
woman appeared far better prepared to deal with a weapon-
bearing general than she herself was.

Her hands—Miranda always noticed hands—were
strong and had a wide variety of calluses. The most
prominent were on the webbing between thumb and
forefinger. Miranda tried flexing her own hand through
several positions that different tasks might require, but none
of them seemed likely to create such a mark. Unless...

Miranda formed her hand as if she was firing a pistol.
Yes, each shot would make the weapon buck against the
webbing between thumb and forefinger, which matched the
observed data. Just how much did someone have to shoot to
create a callus there? Obviously, this woman could answer
the question.

"So, mate. I'm asking myself, 'Holly'—that's my name, so
it's how I typically address myself—'Holly, should you break
one or both of the general's hands as you take his weapon?'
For the moment, you may consider that an idle question
while you consider the next part. As an extra add-on service,
I'd be glad to shoot you with it after I rip it from your
bleeding fingers. Just a graze, mind you, so that you could
claim you struggled manfully before a Sheila took away your
personal weapon and spanked you with it."

The general's expressions shifted through a wide range

during Holly's speech. The anger appeared to dissipate, replaced by suspicion and several other emotions that Miranda couldn't identify. But at Holly's final threat, the anger had definitely returned.

Miranda looked at her watch.

Her motion had the general returning his aim to her own chest.

Not her best move.

But she saw that they'd already wasted eleven minutes since she should have started her investigation—which would never do. She pushed the barrel aside and stepped into his personal space. He stumbled back.

She'd have to remember this tactic.

He snapped off the safety with a sharp click as if that was somehow more threatening than the black hole at the end of the barrel.

It was.

She began swallowing compulsively.

Maybe this wasn't her best idea after all.

But, damn it, there had to be limits. She ignored the weapon and followed through with the initial impetus that had sent her forward. Bending down, she photographed an object that she'd spotted when looking down at her watch. It had been partly under the general's boot.

"What's that?" He didn't lower his aim, so it was now pointed where her head had been. Failure to track her as a target? Reverting once more from aggression to confusion. She really didn't understand people. Or perhaps he was just a pile of inconsistencies, shifting before she could analyze one moment from the next.

Miranda selected a pair of needle-nose pliers from her

vest and delicately lifted the disk of metal, shaking it lightly
to clear the dirt. Then she held it up in the general's face, just
inches away.

"Hey!" he stumbled back another step, his weapon
swinging down to point at the ground.

"*This* is the dial card for an aircraft's analog compass."

The helicopter that had delivered the blonde former SAS
soldier and a man who remained in the background took off
again, forcing Miranda to shout.

"Normally I would ask myself what force could possibly
move such an object so far from its point of impact.
However, now that you've stepped on it, I must ask if it was
bent by the force of the crash and thrown this far. Or, if
your interference with the site has misplaced and damaged
what may have been a key piece of evidence in my
investigation. Now move your vehicle back fifty meters and
leave me alone. And tell your pilots to *stop* flying over my
crash site."

She turned away and carefully bagged the compass dial.

It took her three tries as her hand was still shaking with a
fury she was unused to. The fear...had been too familiar; an
emotion she'd worked very hard to leave behind. Apparently
not.

The fact that the dial face had come from a Sikorsky UH-
60 Black Hawk and had been sitting in the desert for at least
fifteen years based on the scaling and edge corrosion was of
little relevance to her. It made her point. Besides, she didn't
have one of this generation in her collection—bent or
otherwise.

While she bagged it, a staff sergeant ran up with a piece
of paper and handed it to the general. It had only three lines

and made the two-star nearly apoplectic before he threw it at her.

Holly snatched it in mid-flutter and handed the message to her.

To: Major General Oswald Harrington – NTTR
Extend all access to NTSB agent.
ALL!

There was a code designation for a signature that she didn't know: *CJCSGDN.*

She checked. The name tag stitched over the general's right breast said Harrington, so she'd assume this was addressed to him.

Holly, whoever she was, read the message over Miranda's shoulder, then Miranda handed it back to the staff sergeant as the general leaned forward until his face was only inches from her own.

"Get one thing straight, Ms. IIC. This crash investigation is top secret, code-word classified." He'd had eggs, a banana, and strong coffee for breakfast. She could use a cup of tea at the moment.

He turned away and began stalking off toward his other guards, who had watched everything from a distance.

"General?"

"What?" He snarled back at her.

"You didn't give me the code word."

He looked around the site for a moment before snapping out, "Amber!" and walked away.

"He totally just made that up," Holly whispered in her ear.

"Really?" Miranda had just accepted the word at face value.

"Maybe he's a fan of *Jurassic Park,*" Holly sounded as if she was ready to giggle.

Miranda had heard of the movie, but never seen it. She could only presume that it had something to do with petrified tree sap. "It doesn't matter if he made it up on the spot. He is the senior military leader on a military crash, so this investigation is hereafter code-word classified."

"Sure thing. No worries. I'm Holly."

"Hi, Holly. Do you know where the rest of my Go Team is?"

The Australian pointed at her own chest.

"No! I mean *my* team."

Why weren't they here yet?

5

HIGH OVER THE BERING SEA, LIEUTENANT COLONEL HARVEY Whitmore circled his MQ-25 Stingray refueling drone. M for multi-mission, Q for unmanned, and he tried not to give a shit that no matter what you called it, the Stingray was just a fucking drone. It was hard. Sure, the eggheads preferred UAV—unmanned aerial vehicle—but he wasn't an egghead; he was a pilot.

Or he had been. And that was the hardest part.

Not making the astronaut corps, he could deal with that. It had always been a major dream, but he knew the odds sucked with the thousands who applied. But being permanently grounded after seventeen years and thirty-seven days in the jets made flying a UAV just plain gross. Still, it was better than flying some damn desk.

Accepting that it was a drone and doing nothing to defend it to others as being a "real plane" had cut down on most of the teasing that actual pilots could dump on him. Only in the dark of long sleepless nights did he ever contemplate his fall from hotshot air jock to a refueling boomer—so named because it stuck out a refueling boom like some lame jet fuel teat for real pilots to feed on.

Squadron commander to drone pilot in under ten minutes totally sucked.

Now he sat in a Groom Lake bunker the size of a small shipping container and remotely flew his drone. There was a reason they were called coffins. All the guys he used to fly Hornets with were now moving on to Raptors and Lightnings—man but he'd love to have flown the F-35 Lightning II stealth fighter.

But a suit failure during a high-altitude ejection had blown one of his eardrums. The hearing aid had fixed any deficiency, but scar tissue made it so that his right ear couldn't equalize quickly to pressure changes. Even low-level domestic runs could be agony. Punching supersonic aircraft up to sixty thousand feet just wasn't ever going to happen again.

Of course flying remotely was way better than flying nothing. Only recently approved for purchase by the Navy, the Stingray tanker he'd been flying for the CIA from Groom Lake had its points. For two years before the first one was even ready for Navy testing it had been his. Even now there were only three Stingrays in operation—one here, one based in Elmendorf, Alaska (that he was currently piloting), and the last one out of Ramstein in Germany (also remotely piloted from here). He'd made lead pilot in a painfully small program but at least it was a form of flight. Sort of.

Ever since the WWI box kites, Whitmores had flown for the US military. Grandpa had gone down in 'Nam. He'd come home as little more than a skeleton from four years as a POW, but died in a VA hospital from liver failure before Harvey was born. Dad had eaten it in a training mishap.

But still Whitmores flew.

Until suddenly he couldn't.

No son either.

Just a girl that his long-ago ex-wife had made without him. He hadn't even done anything wrong. He'd been riding hard in an F-15E Strike Eagle over Afghanistan when she'd decided to fuck a dentist instead of him. Bitch.

The drone aerial tanker, which looked like little more than a fat fuel bladder with a turbine engine, could dump sixteen thousand pounds of JP-5 jet fuel into a mated aircraft in under a minute.

Manned aerial tankers normally had a crew of three: two pilots facing forward and the boom operator who sat at the far stern, facing the incoming aircraft for refueling purposes. The Stingray had two pilots who flew remotely from a flight control station inside a secure coffin. But when refueling the top secret aircraft, he was the only one authorized to view the rear camera in order to line up the refueling boom.

He might be flying a drone, but what slipped toward his Stingray—straight out of the forbidden airspace to the west—almost made him forget about what his life had become.

He wasn't really supposed to even look at the crazy aircraft he refueled, but the moonlight was plenty bright. Besides, he had to look to steer the refueling boom.

Okay, he was supposed to look, but he wasn't supposed to *see*. Or even think about what he saw. And the brass wondered why it was called the US Air *Farce*.

The bird that sidled up to his aircraft to nurse a quick twenty-five hundred gallons of fuel from the Stingray's boom-shaped teat was like nothing he'd ever seen before. At least not until last night. He'd been hoping to see it again—wished to hell he could ask someone what it was.

The slender delta-winged needle fired the imagination with a hundred questions.

Like why fifteen meters of aircraft had a lower radar signature than a plastic Frisbee? And just where had it gone and what had it done there?

No question that someone else at Groom Lake was the pilot, but who was it? Chuck who played shortstop on their interdepartmental softball team or maybe some babe he'd slept with?

It could be anyone.

Last night, in this same spot high over the Bering Sea, the unidentified drone had arrived from the east and departed to the west. Now it was returning by the same route. He didn't have to still be a top fighter jock to know that his location was exactly on the best route from Nevada to central China. The flight path would just nick Russia's Kamchatka peninsula, but pass well north of the Koreas. If it had only been going to coastal China, it would have returned last night instead of spending a full day in-country.

Damn but that was the kind of cool-as-shit mission that he really missed.

The real question as he watched it mate up and guzzle down his fuel: how fast could that aerial hotrod go?

"I feel the need. The need for *speed!*" Maverick had it totally right in *Top Gun*. And here Harvey was poking along at three hundred knots in his lump of a refueling drone. Worse, his ass was still parked on the ground and it was his

Stingray that was doing the cruising, even at a lazy three-double-zero.

"Time," as his mom said after hearing about Dad's death, "definitely time to embrace the suck."

Two weeks later, she had. Right out the end of a shotgun.

6

MIKE MUNROE STEPPED UP TO THE TWO WOMEN AFTER THE general was out of hearing range.

"What is wrong with you two? Are you *trying* to get shot?"

Holly, the blonde Australian who had been on his flight —apparently asleep from the moment she hit the seat until the helicopter's skids touched the ground—arched an eyebrow at him. Clearly practiced to put men in their place, he didn't bother reacting to it.

The petite brunette on the other hand ignored him completely as she carefully labeled the scrap of metal she'd bagged.

"I mean seriously. The man had a revolver."

"That's not a revolver. It's an M17; a Sig Sauer P320 to civilians. Nice upgrade from the M9 your Army boys used to carry," the Australian was emphatic.

"He was going to shoot you."

"Not with a revolver, he wasn't, mate. Because he didn't have one."

Mike considered kneeling down and pounding his forehead on the sandy soil.

"You're NTSB?"

The blonde turned her back on him to show the NTSB emblazoned across the back of her vest that he probably should have noticed sooner.

"How'd you get here from Australia?"

"Decided to hop a 'roo and try something new. ATSB, Australian Transport Safety Board, sent me over for cross training."

"Here," he tossed her a tube of sunscreen. She was fair-skinned enough to burn in minutes. She tossed it back right at his face. Only his quick reaction time managed to save his nose. Normally women appreciated his thoughtfulness.

She then pulled out a ball cap as if that would save her ears, neck, and other exposed areas. She made an unruly ponytail through the loop of the cap. The woman looked as if she'd hacked off her hair with a knife. Maybe the big one strapped to her thigh.

Her cap was yellow and green and announced the Australian Matildas.

"Who are they?"

"Hallo! Best soccer team in Oz? Well, not yet, but they will be. Catch a clue, pretty boy. There'll be a quiz at end of week."

"It's already Saturday." And dammit, that reminded him that he'd had a hot date lined up for this afternoon: 5K run, dinner at Basta, and hopefully some serious sex afterward. At least he had before they'd mobilized him out of Denver a couple hours ago. He checked his cell. No reception. No way to reach her. Alejandra—even her name was sexy—was gonna be pissed, probably past recovery. This sucked in so many ways.

"Better get studying then, hadn't you?" Holly was enjoying herself too much at his expense, so he ignored her.

The brunette was drifting away, turning back toward the wreck. "Excuse me, is one of you Miranda Chase?"

The brunette turned back to look at him with narrowed eyes. Then she opened them incredibly wide—but not as if she was surprised. More as if she was seeing how wide she could make them. She didn't speak; instead she tapped her badge.

He glanced down and read her name.

Mike held out a hand. "Hi. I'm Mike Munroe, your operations and human-performance investigator."

"You're not Evelyn," Miranda narrowed her eyes again. Was she angry that he wasn't?

He made a show of glancing down at himself. "No, I don't seem to be. At least not today."

"He could be an Evelyn," Holly inspected him from head to toe as if he was a dead fish. Usually ladies liked what they saw when they looked at him. Alejandra certainly had.

"I'm not." He waited a moment longer before withdrawing his unshaken hand.

"Where's Evelyn?"

"I wouldn't know."

"You sure you're not Evelyn?" Holly's smile was only about one degree of separation from being a sneer. Kind of like being less than six degrees of separation from Kevin Bacon, only even more pathetic.

Miranda pulled out her cell phone and tried placing a call.

"There's no signal out here," he sighed once more about the loss of Alejandra.

"Plenty of signal," Miranda said staring at her phone, "but you're right. No connectivity." Next she extracted a DF loop from her vest.

He remembered from training that it was used for locating black boxes—not his part of an investigation.

After a few moments of tinkering, she tucked it away. "There's no signal from the black boxes. Though there is plenty of cell phone signal, I simply can't connect to it. It must be the Groom Lake encrypted network."

"Groom Lake? Like Area 51 and aliens?"

"Where the hell did you think we were, mate? The Great Barrier Reef?"

Mike ignored Holly. He hadn't noticed what direction they'd flown him from Vegas. He'd climbed aboard thinking it was just another crash in the desert.

He and his dad had always kept up on Area 51. It was the thing they did together and was still some of the best memories of his childhood. Mom was always "tolerantly amused" but wanted nothing to do with "such nonsense," so it was seriously exclusive Dad-time for him.

He'd never really bought into it and he suspected Dad didn't either, but it had meant that a lot of Saturday afternoons were spent on the living room couch with a couple of root beers, watching *Mystery Science Theater 3000*. They'd laughed together over the goofy comments of the host and two puppets as they watched old science fiction B-movies like *This Island Earth* and *Santa Claus Conquers the*

Martians. And they never missed an episode of *The X-Files*, even when Dad finished an episode passed out on the couch —wiped out by his hours as a longshoreman.

Mike's first major crush as a kid had been Dana Scully on her search for aliens and he was still partial to smart redheads.

Miranda tucked away the DF loop and pulled out a satellite phone with the trademark fat antenna.

"Where's Evelyn?" Miranda asked as soon as the phone was answered.

Between that and the general, she really had to work on her people skills.

"Maternity leave? And where's my structural specialist?"

Holly raised her hand.

"Not you. Where's Tony?" Miranda asked into the phone. Another pause. "He retired? When? Wait. Maybe he told me about that."

"So you're a structural specialist?" He asked softly enough to not disturb Miranda.

"I'm not from back o' Bourke."

"Back of where?"

"Seriously remote town up against the edge of the Strzelecki Desert. I think you call it a hillbobby."

"Hillbilly?"

"Right. One of them. That's not me. I'm more of a saltie."

"A *Saltine?*" Mike went for the tease. He knew enough Strine to know what she meant.

"A *saltie*. A croc! Hallo? Six meters and a thousand kilos of armored nasty with teeth. Just like me," Holly made a show of snapping her teeth at him, leaning in close enough as she did so to send him stumbling backward to protect the end of his nose.

"Cut that out!"

"Don't be thinking 'Ooo, she's a hot blonde Sheila with a sexy accent from Down Under.' You won't like what happens to you if you start thinking things like that."

Hard *not* to think of her that way, because she definitely was. Holly was also well steeped in the Ozzie attitude that a good jibe made for a thousand laughs.

"And don't use Down Under. It's rude just because you blokes are in the Northern Hemisphere."

"You're using it."

"I'm from there. We get to. You don't. Besides, you really need better boots."

He looked down at his Rockport walking shoes—good for most terrain. "What's wrong with these?"

She bent down to pick up a rock and zinged it nonchalantly to the side. He didn't think anything of it until he saw a rattlesnake racing out the far side of the puff of dirt that had erupted on the stone's impact.

"Snakes?" He looked down again quickly to see if one, or a whole *Indiana Jones* nest of them, was circled around ready to attack.

"Easy, mate," her grin was wicked. "Not like it's a taipan or a common death adder. It's not even a red-bellied black snake. Maybe you're a close relative: a yellow-bellied white-boy snake? That's just a quiet little rattler out for some sun. Young one by its looks."

He wondered how fast he could get knee-high boots made of armored saltie. Maybe taller. How high could a striking snake bite? Knee? Thigh... He swallowed hard and tried not to wince his legs together. He decided against asking Holly.

"Haven't actually seen a rattler before. Way more interesting than you, bucko." She jabbed a finger into his chest. He'd have stumbled back if he hadn't feared stepping on some hidden cobra or lethal scorpion or who knew what.

"Where did you learn about aircraft structures?" Mike desperately needed a subject change.

"Well, I know more about blowing them up, but I can't do that anymore."

"Why not?"

"Shh. We're on deck."

Miranda hung up and pocketed her phone. She did the eye-squint, then eye-wide thing one more time, as if she was clearing it out of her system.

"Structural." She asked the Australian without making it a question.

"I know a fair amount about engines as well. You see, sometimes—"

"And you?" Miranda cut Holly off, which Mike could actually like her for.

"Mike Munroe, human factors and operations specialist. I'm the one who's going to go convince the general that dragging you two off to a firing squad really isn't his best option. At least not yet." He considered holding his hand out in greeting again, but she preempted the move by turning back to the wreck.

"Okay." She went through a quick ritual of tapping every pocket on her vest and cargo pants without looking at either of them.

"You're with me," she appeared to be talking to the

blonde Australian. Maybe.

Before following, Holly stuck her tongue out at him. She'd definitely be paying for that. Miranda though, she was a seriously odd duck.

Even back in training, he'd heard Miranda Chase stories.

"Best investigator the NTSB has ever seen."

"Crazier than a hologram of flying batshit."

"Heard she went through over a dozen team members in her first year."

"Pray you never work with her, dude. Just pray."

He'd imagined that his first assignment with an investigation with the NTSB would have a somewhat more rational start. Instead he'd landed straight in the fire.

Mike took a moment to study the view before going to calm down a two-star general—which was going to be a first if he pulled it off.

The white salt flats of Groom Lake lay nestled deep in the broken lands along the eastern side of Emigrant Valley and close by the low but rugged Groom Range. This really was too cool for words even if he had to put up with the weirdo of a lead investigator and a structural specialist with the sense of humor of an Australian guttersnipe.

Dad was going to die when he heard Mike had been assigned here. But the wreck was code-word classified. Could he even mention it next time they spoke? Probably not. That really sucked.

Mike was most of the way to the general, already had his casual greeting smile in place, when he realized that Miranda Chase had a satellite phone. He should have borrowed it to call Alejandra. Too late now.

"Hi, I'm Mike Munroe." It was time to get to work.

7

"LADY, ANY TIME I NEED A SHEILA TO TAKE DOWN A PISSED-OFF general for me, you're my gal."

The blonde Australian walked as if she owned the desert. But she did it silently and didn't appear to even disturb the light soil as she did so, unlike the clumsy general who had clearly bent the old compass dial.

Perhaps she wasn't really there.

Miranda had certainly had enough conversations with her dead parents. Of course they rarely answered back.

"I wasn't 'taking him down'," Miranda explained. "I simply required an expedient method to demonstrate that it's the evidence that has importance, not some preconceived security concerns." Even to herself that sounded pompous. She'd never developed the knack of making her own team comfortable. She'd known Evelyn and Tony for so long that they'd understood that about her and ignored any awkwardness. But now there were new people and how were they going to react to her?

"Either way, you rocked it, girlfriend."

Girlfriend? Even after five years, she'd never have thought of Evelyn that way. And here Holly was using it in their first five minutes.

She had no experience to judge such a statement by. There weren't exactly a lot of women on the family island to be girlfriends with. Even ashore for school, she'd never fit in. Her last girlfriend had been...Cindy in eighth grade, who'd ultimately had no patience for a mourning Miranda whose parents had just been blown up over the Atlantic. In retrospect, Cindy hadn't been all that great a friend *before* her parents died either.

Finally returned to the point where she'd been trying to start this investigation twenty-three minutes ago, Miranda focused on the next sphere.

Scope of Debris Field: It started—

"Whoa! Someone really flattened that poor bugger, didn't he? Looks like a pancake run over by a road roller." Holly's whistle of surprise forced Miranda to look three more spheres inward and actually study the fuselage.

Holly's description was not far wrong. The round tube of the fuselage, normally fifteen feet high, had indeed been pancaked flat so that only one or two small portions rose more than five feet above the desert.

"It's not explosives; there's no peeling back around the edges of the skin breaks. No centerline of impact. Instead of being bent down in the middle—which would be bloody hard to do in the first place—it's all bulged out at the side, making the top cave in. And that's even harder to do. Seriously. It's like it was slapped down from the top, but without ever being touched. Never seen anything like that before."

Miranda hadn't either. "Where did you learn about airframe structures?"

"Libya was a lot of it. Colonel Gaddafi should have won that mess like a piece of piss instead of getting a well-deserved bayonet up his lecherous bum. He certainly had the military force, whereas the rebels started with little more than sticks and stones. Me and a couple of my mates went in and made sure that Gaddafi's aircraft didn't work so well."

"You blew up planes?" Miranda's skin went cold despite the day's rising heat.

"You don't think that Gaddafi's Air Force went from three hundred and fifty combat capable aircraft to one-fifty total, including puddle jumpers and trainers, all on its own, do you? We got to where we were splitting them up in different ways, just to see how the airframes collapsed. Did you know that if you set up a MiG-25 just right, you can slice it from the cockpit back to the engine exhausts just like a sawmill slicing the length of a log? *Plonk!*" She made a show with her hands of the two halves of an aircraft tipping over sideways in opposite directions.

Miranda swallowed hard and staggered aside. Looking away didn't help, because all she could see was the wrecked C-130. The Australian had destroyed planes? On purpose? Her whole life was about putting them back together and Holly had...

It took all her strength not to be sick.

The woman had to go away.

She couldn't be here.

Miranda couldn't face—

A young man with Vietnamese features stepped right in front of her.

"*You're* Miranda Chase? Oh my God! I can't believe it." He grabbed her hand and began shaking it. "I'm Jeremy. Jeremy Trahn. Systems specialist. I can't *believe* I'm on your team. When the security guy driving me here told me who I was meeting, I didn't believe him. No way, just no way. But here you are. I've read every single one of your investigation reports." His English was accentless and so fast that it was hard to follow.

Her hand was still tightly clasped between the two of his.

"All the way back to that first Cessna 152 that flew into the powerlines by Boeing Field in Seattle and ended up dangling upside down for hours. I've taught you everything I know. No. Wait. Everything I know I've taught... You know what I mean. I'm— I'm...speechless."

"All evidence to the contrary," Holly remarked drily from somewhere behind her.

Miranda's attempts to recover her hand weren't working.

"It's amazing. I've been so hoping to just meet you or even attend one of your lectures. And now here I am assigned to your team. This is too perfect to be true. I'm Jeremy. Jeremy Trahn. Did I already say that? I'm just so excited to be here that I can't begin to tell you. Such an honor to—"

Holly reached out and casually took Jeremy's forearm.

"Ow! Hey!" His clasp relaxed suddenly, as if his nerves had been switched off.

Miranda recovered her hand and Holly let the man go.

"I think she got the idea, mate."

"Sorry, it's just—" Jeremy wrapped his other hand

protectively over where Holly had seemed to barely touch his forearm.

"Honor and privilege and all that rot." Holly turned to Miranda. "So I'm guessing that you're some kind of hot shit crash girl in addition to facing down generals. I seriously like that. Want to get married? Not that I'm into girls, but I bet you're a gas to hang around with. What are *you?*" She addressed the last to Jeremy.

"Systems specialist: electrical, fuel, hydraulics, you name it," he rebounded with his full enthusiasm even as he rubbed at his arm. "Oh and weather. I'm always fascinated by the interaction of processes whether it's electronic, fuel-based, or even atmospheric conditions. MIT at sixteen for computer systems. Though I went to Princeton for a double doctorate: fluid dynamics and advanced system topology modeling. Then I—"

Holly reached out toward his arm again.

Jeremy clutched it to his chest and stopped talking.

Miranda managed a breath.

"So, boss lady. What's next?"

Spheres. Miranda needed something even a little familiar to grab onto. She looked around seeking the next sphere. Not the oddly flattened fuselage. Not the upright engine plowed nose first into the ground.

Not these strange people, none of whom she'd worked with before. Tony had retired? Evelyn was pregnant? Were these people her new team?

But she didn't know them!

Didn't know their skills or how best to apply them. What if—

Focus, Miranda. You know how to do this. You began reading

NTSB reports at thirteen to understand what happened to Mom and Dad.

She looked at Jeremy, his eyes alight with the passion of investigating plane wreckage. For him, too. Even she could see it. But for him the wreckage wasn't a dark burden, heavily awash in a murky gravy of guilt and doubt, but rather an intellectual pursuit of great fascination. It was such a different view.

As was Holly's, but Miranda couldn't think about someone who had intentionally *destroyed* airplanes. At least not right now.

"Perimeter," she managed to grasp onto the next sphere. "We need to define the perimeter of the debris field."

8

"RIGHT." JEREMY RUSHED OVER TO THE SUPPLIES DUFFLE THAT he must have brought with him. He rushed back with small green flags on half-meter wires and handed them each a fistful.

Miranda slipped hers into a thigh pocket on her pants. The familiar weight was the start of her next sphere of the investigation.

Depending on the scale of the debris field and the type of terrain, it would sometimes take two or three circuits to define the outermost edge of wreckage. This one looked so compact, she felt as if she could draw a circle around it all by herself without fear of missing anything.

Many investigators moved directly to the key elements: the wreckage, the black boxes, the cockpit that was the origin of so many problems. But they often missed the small details, only backtracking if they needed to—by which time so many of them had been obliterated. Miranda worked from the outside in, careful to miss nothing along the way, no matter how apparently trivial upon first inspection.

She walked toward the wreckage, occasionally picking up the line of General Harrington's fading boot prints in the powdery soil, until she found the first piece of the aircraft. The small curve of red plastic would be the lens of the marker light on the tip of the right wing. It had landed barely ten meters from the end of the wing itself. She pulled out one of her green stakes and stabbed it into the soil. The tiny plastic flag fluttered weakly in the breeze. They'd have to hurry. The wind was picking up and might soon hide evidence they needed.

The three of them spread out in a line with her closest to the aircraft, then Holly and Jeremy in a line perpendicular to the heart of the craft. It would be better to have four, but she'd rather have Mike keeping the general out of their way than walking the desert with them.

They stood close enough to have overlapping fields of vision, far enough apart to cover as much ground as possible.

She turned to face right, parallel to the wreckage.

Holly and Jeremy turned left, noticed what she'd done, and turned to match.

Miranda always walked wreckage in a counterclockwise direction. She'd observed that most Westerners, upon entering a church or museum walked clockwise. Muslims, perhaps from their traditions of walking counterclockwise during the Hajj to Mecca—seven times around the massive black-shrouded shrine of the Kaaba—tended to do the same in other public places. Walking counterclockwise forced her and her team's Western sensibilities out of their normal modes of perception, thus heightening awareness.

As the walk began, one part of her mind watched the ground and one part watched the wreckage. She tried to focus wholly on the walk, but her inner thoughts were already cataloging the overall layout.

One, two, three, four...stop at five paces. Turn back to see if something had been hidden from view, perhaps by landing to one side of the low desert scrub. Holly, being at the center, was the call leader.

"Anything?"

At her and Jeremy's negatives, Miranda led them closer to the center of the crash. Four steps later she found an outboard aileron trim tab and staked it.

Both port side engine cowlings remained sufficiently intact to indicate there'd been no engine explosion on this side.

Holly called the turn and they once more stepped five times, then stopped and inspected the area. This time it was Holly who found a piece of something. She staked it and they shifted the line back outward before proceeding.

The twenty-foot-tall rudder snapped off and folded up like a piece of paper into neat quarters.

Five more paces. A piece of scrap metal that might be from the hull.

The horizontal stabilizers that stuck out to either side of the tail were bent down at a very unlikely angle, like the downbeat of a grey goose rather than the soaring spread of a vulture.

Five more paces...

In less than an hour they had a small line of green flags marking the outlines of the debris field. And she had made a hundred observations of the next sphere. Even though she'd done her best not to look ahead, she'd failed. There was something strange about this wreck.

"Well that's odd," Jeremy was looking over their circle. Odd enough to curb even his effusive eloquence.

In addition to her own observations, the size of the perimeter was *very* unusual. With only a few minor exceptions, the debris field was no more than ten meters longer or wider than the intact plane had been. It was also symmetrical—nothing had been cast particularly more to one side or the other.

"I've seen roadkill Down the Alice what covered more ground than this." Holly saw it as well.

While Miranda didn't believe that even in Australia could there be a dead animal that covered an area forty meters long and fifty wide, it made Holly's point. Miranda had certainly seen wrecked Cessna light planes with debris fields twice this size.

Debris Field Sphere: She'd seen enough of the wreckage during the walk to skip that sphere for now. Typically, key evidence was scattered widely across an expansive site; not in this case. Because it encompassed such a confined space, their inspection could wait for the moment.

Wreck Exterior Sphere: Second to last.

She finally allowed herself to turn and fully contemplate the wreckage.

"I spoke with the general," Mike said as he joined them, interrupting her thoughts before they had any chance to form. He apparently took joy in stating the obvious. They'd seen him standing beside the general for the entire duration of the perimeter walk.

"And..." Holly growled at him.

Mike's smile said that he'd just gotten exactly what he wanted, though Miranda couldn't imagine what.

"He said that all they touched were the five bodies they removed: two pilots, navigator, flight engineer, and loadmaster. He said it was traveling empty, returning from a delivery run. Though he declined to say what he was delivering."

"And why did it take you so long to figure that out?"

"Well, he's not exactly a warm guy. And with you and Holly making him madder than a hatter, it took some doing to calm him down."

"He already had his M17 aimed at her before I came along," Holly sounded ticked about that.

"A general pointed a gun at you?" Jeremy was horrified. "Why did he do that?" His degree of idol worship had not detectably diminished over the last hour and didn't seem likely to be altered if she addressed it, so she didn't bother.

"General Harrington was angry before I arrived," Miranda recalled. "Finally being ordered to cooperate seemed to tip him over some edge."

"So you just went out of your way to make it worse," Mike was laughing.

And people wondered why she rarely talked.

She considered pointing out to him that "madder than a hatter" was a historical reference to mental insanity among nineteenth-century hat makers probably due to mercuric nitrate poisoning from the felt curing process and was therefore an inappropriate description for the general's fury. He hadn't appeared the least bit addle-brained as he'd aimed his weapon at her face. So what would the proper form be? Mad as one of Holly's

Tasmanian Devils perhaps? A breed indeed know for a high degree of intolerance.

Miranda opened her mouth, then closed it without speaking. She'd long since learned it was best when she kept such thoughts to herself.

She turned back to the wreckage.

Almost as if she'd cued him, Jeremy began discussing the etymology of "madness in hatters" with Mike.

"Tell me you weren't just thinking that yourself. Please," Holly whispered.

"And if I was?"

"Hmmm. As long as you unload it on Mike, you won't find me complaining, mate." Then she switched topics in mid-breath. "It doesn't look right, does it? I can't put my finger on quite why."

Holly, who up until that moment had seemed to jitter at the edge of Miranda's vision, had shifted to a quiet, solid form.

Miranda understood this quieter woman far better than the outspoken Australian. Perhaps the soldier *had* served a purpose destroying Colonel Gaddafi's airplanes, but to have said she'd destroyed planes for a living, and to say it so lightly, still rankled deeply.

"Also, where are the military inspectors?"

Miranda noted that when she glanced at Holly, she instinctively narrowed her eyes in question. What genetic-survival trait that represented still eluded her.

"Look at them. They've got nine guards standing about looking bored out of their skulls. I don't know where they found you, but the NTSB hauled my bum out of a training session at the Boeing plant in Everett, Washington. That new

777 wing is like nothing we've ever seen. Between the titanium wing box at the center, the composite construction, and the folding wingtips, it's really something. Even compared to the 787 it's a major step ahead."

Miranda had thought the same herself when she'd inspected the prototype.

"But the military crash inspectors can be no more than a 'roo hop away at Nellis Air Force Base. They should be all over this."

Whatever her past—Australia special Ops to ATSB to NTSB—Holly's assessment was accurate. There was something about this wreck that was indeed unique in her experience. But she couldn't see what it was either.

So think of something else and let that question answer itself with time. There were other, more pressing matters.

Like what had she been thinking, facing down the general like that? It was certainly the first time she'd stared down the barrel of a firearm.

No. That wasn't the right question.

The right question was *why* had she ended up staring into the bottomless hole of the general's M17? Not the meta-why that Mike Munroe seemed so focused on—as if it was somehow her fault that the general had aimed his weapon at her. That was something she still didn't understand.

But the *concrete* why. The facts were now forming a word cloud almost as clearly delineated as the crash itself: a general standing guard, plus nine armed guards, no military crash inspectors, an order from an unknown source of sufficient urgency that she hadn't simply been told to take the next flight back but had instead had a seventy-three percent loaded commercial aircraft turned back to deliver her. The speed with which a team arrived, even if none of them were her team. There was something very urgent here...and very wrong.

"It's making my Spidey sense tingle."

She had no idea what Holly was referring to. Yet she was right. Whatever Spidey senses were, her own weren't happy at the moment either.

For perhaps the first time, she questioned whether the answers she needed would indeed be somewhere here on the floor of the high Nevada desert. If not, where else could she look?

9

AT DUSK, A HUEY UH-1N HAD ARRIVED TO TRANSPORT Miranda's Go Team to a barracks at Creech Air Force Base. Creech lay in the southeast corner of the NTTR. Set among rugged mountains, the three runways of the air base formed a triangle on the perfectly flat valley floor. Originally the base for much of America's nuclear bomb testing, it was now the center for drone missions. Rows of coffins commanded most of the large attack and reconnaissance drones. Half of the UK's MQ-9 Reapers were flown by an RAF team stationed at Creech.

Miranda had held her patience while Mike arranged for a secure conference room off the DFAC—what the Air Force called a dining facility. As soon as the doubled door was closed and the team seated, she pulled up a map of the crash site on her tablet. Jeremy hooked it up to the room's systems and the image shone on the four big monitors arranged corner-to-corner to make a single screen.

The four of them had taken over a thousand

photographs in the last nine hours. They'd also placed over three hundred numbered orange flags and collected the GPS coordinates on every remaining piece of the aircraft larger than a compass dial.

"It has—had a digital cockpit," Jeremy began. "Wiring and mounts for both the Flight Data Recorder and the Cockpit Voice Recorder in the tail section, but no recorders on the mounts. Not that there was all that much left of the mounts either."

"Someone had already nicked them." Holly tipped back in her chair with her crossed feet propped on the table. Her plate piled up with four massive slices of pizza.

Mike had teased her about eating for two.

She'd replied that he was as well: him and his ego.

For herself? Miranda had been the only one to take a salad after the long arduous day in the baking sun. Again she didn't fit in, though she didn't know why this still continued to surprise her after all these years.

"Fresh marks on the mounting bolts," Holly explained with her mouth full. Miranda had been researching the curious ground impact patterns of various pieces of the aircraft and hadn't heard about that.

"Mike?"

"Holly tipped me off on that. I talked to the general again. He needs more practice at lying. No question that his people took the recorders, but he wouldn't admit that in a full-on court-martial. He did say he knew the cause of the crash. Made some scathing remarks about you not caring about the truth."

"Which was?" Miranda wondered if Mike's need to draw out a statement of fact was time he spent thinking before speaking. She did recall the general claiming to know the answer, which she'd dismissed as irrelevant. The wreckage told the true story.

"Pilot error. Stall at too low an altitude to recover."

Holly snickered, "And me mum was a 'roo herder."

Miranda pulled up the crash modeling software she'd been feeding information into on and off through the afternoon and plugged in the numbers. "Stall speed is—"

"A hundred and fifteen miles an hour," Jeremy leapt in. "Uh, sorry, I don't have the stall speed altitude and loading corrections chart memorized. But one-fifteen is a good working number." It earned him a smile from Holly and shrug from Mike. He would need to learn that something other than the personnel involved were relevant. Knowing the aircraft's performance characteristics as well as the pilot could be useful during interviews. And the number was close enough for this simulation, so she didn't correct Jeremy.

"Even a hard stall can be recovered in five hundred feet by a skilled pilot under most conditions. We'll assume it wasn't a high-speed stall as that would be very unusual for... Tony?"

When no one answered, she looked up to see where her personnel specialist was. But he wasn't here. Oh he'd retired. Her new—

"She's talking to you, Evelyn," Holly aimed a piece of pizza at Mike.

"Is that your middle name?" Jeremy asked with all seriousness.

Mike sighed before answering her, "Pilot was an Air Force Major with over thirteen thousand flight hours.

Copilot a captain with only a few less years and hours." His job was personnel and he seemed to know that part at least.

A high-speed vertical stall ending in impact would require a steep dive of the airplane. Continuing down until too close to the ground before attempting a recovery. The resultant crash would be belly first—which did fit the crash —as the wings lost all lift due to the sudden change of direction creating an extreme angle of attack. However, the belly landings were not typical of the violence of the crash they'd witnessed today. It certainly didn't explain the flattening effect on the fuselage.

Miranda tapped a thousand-foot flight level into the model (appropriate for the distance from the Groom Lake runway), set the ground's hardness to nine (the same as diamond), and clicked Run.

The software simulated a C-130 Hercules in a nose-high, low-speed stall at a thousand feet up and slowing below 115 mph.

Imminent Stall pulsed in red on the screen. A buzzer would have sounded in the cockpit too loudly to be ignored. The digital cockpit upgrade that had replaced the old dial instruments with glass screens and far more sophisticated readouts would also have reported verbally, "Low speed. Low speed." Then "Stall-stall. Stall-stall."

In the simulation, she left the four, six-bladed propellers turning fast but with the blades mostly feathered— appropriate for a low-speed stall.

Stall, flashed on the simulator.

The nose of the aircraft dropped suddenly, dipping below vertical as the wings lost sufficient lift to keep the plane aloft. At a sixty-degree angle below level flight, the dive was steep enough for the wings to recover lift. The inherent airworthiness of the Hercules would have required only a light pull on the control wheel to return to level flight.

She didn't enter the command to indicate the pilot had made any corrections.

Ground Impact Imminent had time for seven agonizing one-second flashes.

The speed gathered during the fall created enough lift that the plane struggled to recover itself, achieving a forty-five-degree downward dive before—

Ground Impact.

The simulator crumpled the nose and snapped off the wings. As the hull slammed into the ground, the empennage broke free and the primary wreckage spread for a thousand meters.

Changing the ground's hardness to a four, not unreasonable for a silicate sand mixed with organic earths, made little difference—the aircraft tumbled more, but still the debris would have spread far and wide. Also, the plane would have remained far more intact.

Again starting at five hundred feet.

Again at...

"Not a stall," Holly observed in a dry tone and bit down on another slice of pizza.

"Not a stall," Miranda agreed.

10

Night had fallen by the time Harvey watched the MQ-45 Casper stealth drone—just like the one he'd refueled last night over the Bering Sea—roll into the Groom Lake hangar designated 33B. There wasn't a 33 or 33A. In fact, at Groom Lake, where everything was very orderly, the next highest numbered hangar was 24. This building was a complete anomaly in the middle of a base that was known for its anomalies.

Major General Oswald Harrington had asked Harvey to join him to "discuss something"—Air Force parlance for "you really fucked up this time, Harvey." Lowly boomer-drone pilots never had anything to do with the general other than saluting whenever he happened to pass nearby.

This so didn't look good.

With no other options, he'd followed where the general led. He'd expected at best the general's office and at worst a firing squad. Instead he'd ended up here, inside Hangar 33B.

Groom Lake was like Las Vegas—what happened here,

stayed here. There was camaraderie in isolation and plenty of good times to be had.

The beer and the grub were top notch, better than any Vegas hotel. The baseball games were fierce—he played first base for the USAF *Remotes* unmanned aircraft flight team and two days ago they'd thrashed the Lockheed Martin *Technicians* 9-4. Pending no mission, they'd take on the USAF *Fire Heads* (munitions specialists) in two days, who were a tough bunch.

Women weren't plentiful at Groom Lake, but this wasn't the old days when they were desperately scarce either. Not just office and catering personnel, but contractors, scientists, mechanics, and a pilot or two as well.

Many of the women got into the spirit of being locked away from friends and family. Personal privacy was guaranteed by the threat of a military court-martial if anything was said to anyone anywhere about what happened here. It was forbidden, when in the outside world, to even mention who else had been on the base in case it revealed something about what was happening at Groom Lake.

And that threat didn't end upon leaving the military, as a few fools had found out the hard way. A top secret clearance was a commitment for life.

Some of the women, like the aircraft here, were *very* experimental. They tended to be the younger set, but didn't complain as long as he was willing to play along. In that respect it was single guy heaven: hot women and hotter aircraft.

What happened at Groom Lake, stayed at Groom Lake...

but everyone here knew about what went on throughout the base.

Except for this one building.

In a land of open secrets where everyone had top secret clearances, not even rumors escaped Hangar 33B. It had been built in 2014 at the far southern end of the runway, and still no one was talking about why it stood over a mile away from the rest of the base. There'd been a lot of speculation about what was here, but that was all.

Now that he was inside, he saw that none of the theories had come close. The general consensus said that 33B was for trialing the next generation of LRBs. Both Boeing and Lockheed Martin had long-range bombers they were hoping to sell to the Air Force. And now that he saw what was really here, he wished he didn't know.

Groom Lake security's rules of engagement were shoot-to-kill. Patrolled twenty-four/seven by the Camo Dudes—the heavily-armed camouflage-wearing contracted teams in Chevy Suburbans—it was the most secure military base the US had anywhere in the world. Maybe not counting the cryptos and hackers dug down into their deep holes in Fort Belvoir, Virginia. But for people who did real work, this was the place.

Depending on the current projects, five hundred to a thousand people lived and worked inside the Area 51 security bubble. Even so, his entry into Hangar 33B had required an escort just to get him close enough to the guard station to offer his ID. He'd been around enough to recognize the difference as he was validated for future reference. These weren't US Air Force or even Camos—they were heavily-armed and trigger-happy CIA.

"Sir?" He wanted to know why the general had brought him here.

Instead, Harrington remained stoically silent on the mezzanine at parade rest as he too looked down on the newly arrived drone that looked nothing like Harvey's fat Stingray.

The MQ-45 Casper looked like science fiction—missile-thin and mean as hell. Far more lethal than it had looked through his Stingray's camera.

Two people moved in to service it.

He hoped to hell this wasn't about what he thought it was.

11

"A RATHER UNIQUE CRAFT," THE GENERAL REMARKED DRILY. His first words since ordering Harvey to follow him.

At first Harvey had been afraid that Harrington was upset because of Harvey's on-going affair with the general's chief assistant, a full colonel who outranked Harvey by a step. A five-foot-eight, unpresuming brunette who most guys didn't look at twice, unless they were at full attention receiving orders passed on from the general. She'd proved to be exceptionally high-performance for a mom with two teenage kids and a husband on the outside.

She'd surprised him by joining him at a table in the DFAC when he'd been dining alone with a good thriller. They'd started with that. After a few more friendly meals mostly discussing books they'd both read, she'd become the first woman his own age that he'd bedded in some time.

She'd taught Harvey about the advantages of a mature woman with experience and imagination—and a killer body hidden under her fatigues. The sex had quickly turned into

a genuine affection. Not that she'd ever leave her family—
they both knew that from the start—but as their schedules
allowed, they'd now spent most weeknights together for over
three months.

Each Friday night, Helen took the Janet Airlines
commuter flight from Groom Lake to the private and secure
terminal on the west side of McCarran Airport in Las Vegas
built specifically for servicing personnel flights to all of the
secure military bases from Edwards to Groom Lake. After
the weekend with her family, she'd catch the early Monday
morning flight back. Many personnel took the flights daily,
but her role as Harrington's right hand hadn't allowed that.

Being single, Harvey rarely bothered to leave the base.

But as he and the general stood in Hanger 33B and he
saw the drone rolling in under the cover of darkness and
another already parked there, he knew that Helen wasn't
tonight's problem.

"Yes sir. That *is* something special."

The long dagger of the MQ-45 Casper was mostly nose.
The first break in its perfectly smooth shaft of a hull was a
tiny canard wing at the midpoint. Close behind that, a
slender delta wing continued to the very stern like the
spreading section of a smooth-flowing river. There was no
tail empennage. Instead another tiny canard wing, looking
like an afterthought was installed above the main delta
wing's trailing edge. There it could compensate for the
supersonic collapse of the wing's trailing-edge control ability.
The only break in the flow of the entire structure was the
open maw of the air intake scoop for the engine near the
midpoint. The mottled carbon-fiber-gray hull made it hard
to see against the concrete floor.

"Mach 2.9—"

Harvey couldn't hold in his whistle of surprise. "Faster than the Lightning or the Raptor jets?"

Harrington offered a ghost of a smile as he continued. "Range of ten thousand miles with fifty percent of flight time at supercruise of Mach 2.1 and—"

"Which was why it only needed to be refueled over the Bering Sea." Harvey didn't know why he kept interrupting the general, but it was such a magnificent piece of engineering that he couldn't help himself.

Supercruise was the ability for an aircraft to fly faster than the speed of sound without lighting the afterburners that inhaled fuel. Afterburners delivered a serious amount of "go fast." But that meant more fuel usage, which meant bigger tanks, which meant a larger aircraft just to carry the tanks for the fuel the afterburners needed, which then had to be more powerful because the plane was bigger...

A supercruise design had proved to be the answer to that endless growth cycle. The Concorde supersonic passenger plane's design had incorporated sustainable supercruise over long distance flights. Apparently, so did the MQ-45.

"Yes. From the Bering Sea to *their* test range was only eight thousand miles round trip." He didn't say China; he didn't need to. He'd know that Harvey was smart enough to have already figured that out. But what did it mean that the general was confiding in him?

Harvey could only stare at the aircraft. With a reach like that, they could fly over any city in the world. "But why wasn't it detected as it—"

And then he saw why. The F-117 Nighthawks retired from Groom Lake to hangars out at Tonopah Test Range Airport had been only the first step in stealth. The Raptor and Lightning jet fighters had extended that with two very distinct solutions.

But this aircraft was the whole concept taken to another level. The sharp-edged chine ran like a ring around the middle as if the aircraft was sliced in two. The rounded underbelly looked to be from an entirely different vehicle than the more angular bulk of the upper section. The deeply ducted exhaust port would shield the engine's heat signature from both above and below.

A supercruise, stealth UAV.

He wanted— He *needed* to touch it. He *needed* to take back that piece of himself that had been stuck on the ground since being grounded by his ear. The Martin-Baker Club tie (awarded to every ejectee saved by an MB ejection seat) didn't make up for having his ass planted on *terra firma.*

But a supersonic, stealth UAV was the unmanned aerial vehicle to beat them all.

Harvey was a pilot.

The general must need a pilot.

A pilot for...

He tried to speak, to ask, but his throat was too dry. Not knowing it, he'd gripped the mezzanine rail and felt powerful enough to rip it apart.

"It's not as simple a process as flying the MQ-25 Stingray refueling tanker. The control suite is similar, but the maneuvering is more similar to the F-22 Raptor, which is why I'm giving you the option. But I must warn you, for you to control it we have to—"

"I don't care," it seemed that he wasn't done with interrupting a superior officer. "I want in. You're showing me this for a reason and I want it. God damn, General, just give me the chance to crack the sound barrier again and I'll take the fight wherever you send me. I'm all in; just show me where to sign."

General Harrington actually smiled as he clapped a hand on Harvey's shoulder.

Oh god, please let that mean I'm in.

"Helen thinks very highly of you. Said you were pure flier."

It took him a moment to understand that the general knew all about Harvey's affair with his assistant. Is that why she'd joined him for those first dinners? An assessment for the general? Maybe. Probably. But what had happened between them after that was all them. Helen wasn't the sort of woman to sell herself except for affection.

Pure flier?

Hell yeah.

It was all Whitmore men ever dreamed about—and probably talked about too much. At least the declassified parts. Flying was the only thing he'd ever cared about since age four when Dad had let him sit in the cockpit of his F-14 Tomcat. His very first memory was that day, the moment he'd become a jet pilot in all but fact. He'd learned to read from the Tomcat's operations manual.

"Helen is cleared for all aspects of this project. Including myself, there are only six people at Groom Lake who are fully on the inside of this program—others know only small aspects, such as maintenance. If I hear so much as a whisper outside that circle, I'll put the gun to your head myself and claim it was a training accident. We clear, flyboy?" He delivered his threat in a perfectly calm tone and Harvey didn't doubt him for a second.

Saluting seemed too trite a response. Instead he held out his hand, "Fire when ready, sir."

General Harrington's firm grasp was all the answer he needed.

12

CLARISSA LEANED HER ELBOWS BACK ON THE CIA DIRECTOR'S desk and relished the solidity of it. The wide cherrywood surface bearing only a picture of his deceased wife with their two Marine Corps sons. She could feel the strength of it behind her as clearly as the power of the man who sat before it.

Director Clark Winston was a breast man—which was ironic, as breast cancer had killed his wife. Or perhaps that was why. He ran his hands up to grasp hers through blazer, blouse, and bra. Maybe it was affirming to him that Clarissa's were still unsagging and unblemished by disease or nursing a child. Today's red Merino wool pencil skirt had conveniently oversized buttons running up her left thigh that were now undone just enough to hike it over her hips.

Since they'd become lovers, she never wore anything underneath her skirt at the office—a detail she'd only had to point out to Clark once for him to get the idea.

Of course, like everything else in this world, men had it

easy; he'd had to do no more than unzip his pants before she straddled him.

"We lost another pilot," she offered him a groan of pleasure that he always seemed to appreciate. Her putative reason for visiting his office in the late evenings was her end-of-day division director's report.

"Serious consequences?" He used one hand on her butt to keep their hips together as he buried his face by the small ruby heart that dangled in her cleavage. At fifty-seven he still had an enthralling strength from his years as a field agent.

"None. He was unattached per our requirement. And the emergency pilot was able to regain manual control of the drone and land it safely." At the same time one pilot had been performing magnificently over China, another had suffered a mental aberration so severe that he'd never leave a top secret mental clinic again. That they had landed rather than crashed the second drone had been a miracle she wouldn't be bothering Clark with.

"Good," Clark grunted as she shifted her hips in small circles to massage him inside her.

He was far from her best lover and she had yet to see if he'd be the most important one. The best had been a very high-ranking officer in the Bundesnachrichtendienst. Stefon was high inside the German foreign intelligence service. They'd had a very cooperative relationship during much of Clarissa's climb within the CIA, mostly on the political-intel front except on the occasions where one of them found a reason to cross the ocean. On those occasions, Stefon loved Clarissa's hair down and in exchange offered two things: head-spinning orgasms, and far more information than he'd ever received from Clarissa in return.

But Stefon hadn't been careful. He'd entered into an office politics battle, lost, and been assigned to the Africa desk. After that, he'd no longer been of any real use beyond occasional phone sex. Such a pity.

Clarissa let Clark concentrate on her body as she watched the view out the one-way glass of his top-floor eastern-corner office in the Old Headquarters Building. It was the best view in Langley, looking out over the sleeping trees of the CIA's private wooded reserve down to the Potomac. If she was director, she'd have chosen one that looked inward on the campus buildings, overseeing the thousands who worked here to keep the nation safe.

D/CIA was but one of her possible futures.

Clark was a sufficiently political animal that he could probably be talked into the idea of following in George Bush 41's footsteps: Director of Central Intelligence to VP and eventually the 41st President of the United States of America. It wouldn't be that hard to achieve, either. Between the two of them, they knew where most of the skeletons in DC lay.

Clark wasn't some pliable young buck with delusions of grandeur. He was a serious-minded chief spy with a weak spot for tall blondes with sharp minds and shapely bodies. She'd have to be careful to make sure he thought it was his idea.

Then, as she was only twenty years Clark's junior, perhaps she'd become his second wife and eventual First Lady. He was still terribly handsome and she was tall enough that they did look very good together.

Or perhaps D/CIA for herself while he was VP? Then maybe even run as his VP, opening her own path into the Oval Office. Now *that* was an attractive option. Perhaps marriage *after* they held the two highest offices in the land. Keep it all in the family.

She opened the buttons on her blazer, glad she wasn't wearing silk. This fabric wouldn't stain as he teethed her through her blouse and bra. Another groan, not voiced only for his benefit. There were certain things that Clark did very well and breasts was one of them.

For now, she was content to be the Director of Special Research—a position she'd spent years designing for herself since her early days as an agent running Taliban interrogations in Afghanistan. She'd made it to her position without once sleeping with a person key to winning a promotion. Oh, she might have suggested it would happen a time or two, but it hadn't.

She'd, by Jesus, made it with her brains far more than her body.

Actually, completely with her brains. All her body did was level the playing field so biased against women.

By Jesus. One of her father's favorite phrases. *You'll strip and get on your knees right now or, by Jesus, I'll—* As if *that* somehow made his abuse holy. She really had to purge that phrase from her thoughts.

How much had he told the family priest? Had he mentioned that he'd begun making her life hell on the night of Mom's funeral—the single worst night of her life? Bury Mom on the same day that Dad buried himself in her and permanently interred her naive teenage dreams. No, of course, the priest bastard hadn't said a word. Confession: the sanctimonious hole down which girls' lives could be safely flushed. Effortless absolution of sin for the faithful.

Clarissa had held complete control of her own life since

Dad had "unexpectedly" died on the night of her own sixteenth birthday—the age at which she finally wouldn't have been slammed into foster care by social services.

She'd had the satisfaction of feeling him shrivel inside her as he died.

Never even got to shoot your last load, Dad.

She'd cleaned him up and left him in his own bed with a vibrator up his ass, his hand clenched around his withered penis, and enough opiates in his bloodstream to kill a horse. The drug companies gave such cool samples to psychiatrists.

Her alibi had stood the test.

She'd taken the JV quarterback's cherry in his own bed that evening, then slipped him a couple of Dad's sleeping pill samples. A quick trip home to deal with Dear Old Dad for the last time *ever* aside from his funeral, then she'd crawled back into bed with Danny Boy. His parents had been more than a little upset at finding her asleep there in the morning, but he'd been thrilled when she'd cleared the last of his drug hangover with a good-morning fuck after his parents had stormed out of the room. With a little guidance, he threw a better-than-average balling. She'd offered some extra deep groans of pleasure and tossed in a few happy yips for his folks' edification. They'd stayed an item for all of sophomore year.

Since then, she'd made her own way *in* her own way.

She'd already made Division Director before her unplanned liaison with Clark had begun. She hadn't turned from offering him solace for his recently lost wife when the opportunity arose last year.

"I've already arranged for a replacement," she scraped her fingernails over the back of Clark's suit jacket and let him imagine her doing it to his skin this weekend. They were planning a little getaway in a luxury cabin in the Poconos.

"A replacement for what?" Men's minds seemed to have so much trouble maintaining focus during sex. It was useful knowledge even if she didn't understand it. Sex only served to sharpen her own attention as her pulse and respiration rose in autonomic response to Clark's increasing efforts. He wasn't a bad lover—just unskilled—which meant he was trainable once she decided if he was worth the effort.

"The pilot. Don't worry," she shifted over him so that he slid even deeper inside her and then began using her hips to lead him upward in earnest. "Our prize drone program is still completely on track."

D/CIA to VP then President?

Yes, the drone wasn't the only program on track. This weekend she'd begin teaching Clark *exactly* what was possible both in and out of bed. Perhaps she'd finally let her hair down for him this weekend.

This corner office *was* a good choice. By leaning her chest into Clark's eager attentions and looking to the right down the Potomac as his body clenched before his sadly predictable release, she could just see the seven miles to the White House sparkling in the distance—as if she could reach out and touch it.

13

"I SPENT THE NIGHT RUNNING DIFFERENT SCENARIOS," Miranda informed the team over breakfast. "No stall—not even a full-power, high-speed stall—breaks the inherent strength of the C-130's tubular hull section to allow the flattened form we witnessed yesterday. Also, none of the scenarios actually fold the nose of the aircraft back underneath the body of the plane like a broken toe."

"What does?" Holly stopped eating her Western omelet with a side of sausages and English muffins, then thumped her feet to the floor to look more closely at the screen as if the answer was there.

It wasn't.

It was out in the field, but just in a way that no one, including herself, had thought to look at it.

Miranda called up the profile she'd finally found at three a.m. and spent the last several hours refining, then tapped Run.

At full cruise speed of three hundred and thirty-five

miles per hour (Mach 0.447 at this altitude), the graphic of the C-130 Hercules cargo plane suddenly flipped upside down.

Inverted, but still plunging at a steep angle, it dove almost straight down into the ground from an unrecoverable height of five hundred feet—a distance it covered in 1.08 seconds.

Not a peep out of the stall indicator.

"See how the nose folds under," she hit pause, then moved through the rest of the display in tenth-of-a-second frames. "By hitting off center after the nose broke off,"—painfully reminiscent of her parents' last flight aboard TWA 800 but she pushed that to one side—"the hull twisted in the air and slammed into the ground right-side up. Yesterday I spotted a sharp twist in the primary frame members just aft of the cockpit but I couldn't account for it. It must have survived long enough to keep the hull in line as it flipped over. These need to be revisited today." She highlighted the three most likely elements to inspect.

"That would finally explain the hull failure," Holly proved out her knowledge of structural considerations as she nodded her agreement. "The hull slammed down on its belly faster than a barracuda hitting a jackfish. The upper framing would shatter at about three g's, especially with the tearing of the high wings. Once that happens, it wouldn't need more than four g's to flatten the sides like that."

"The model shows that hull impact varies down the length from four-point-seven to six-point-two g's," Miranda confirmed.

"More than plenty," Holly picked up her plate and went back to eating.

No one else spoke, so Miranda resumed her explanation.

"Here, at 1.22 and 1.43 seconds, the tail section broke off and tumbled to land right-side up by chance. I'm hypothesizing that it was the straight-down, vertical impact —crumpling the propellers and the leading edge of the engines where the nacelles extend forward—that buffered the wings enough to not catastrophically shatter the fuel tanks."

"How did you figure that out?" Jeremy was twisting his neck trying to look at it upside down. He had proven himself very insightful as they'd worked over the wreck yesterday, but even he hadn't seen it, which partially compensated for her second sleepless night in a row.

"Bugger me!" Holly exclaimed. "The wings are on the wrong sides of the plane. Why didn't I see that?"

Jeremy began cursing as well. Mike still didn't see it, but he didn't need to. The aircraft itself wasn't his specialty —people were. But she could certainly appreciate that— she hadn't been required to suffer through any more dealings with General Harrington. That alone had immense value.

"It took me half the night to see it, because of the general's one misleading comment. A stall would have landed the plane right side up. A one-wing stall and we'd have expected to see a full roll. His 'solution' biased my perceptions until I recalled that only the wreck mattered. Dead planes don't lie."

"Oh, I like that." Holly repeated it once or twice.

"Miranda invented it," Jeremy jumped in. "One of the instructors told me all about how you proved what had happened to—" He jolted as if...

Miranda checked Holly's smile. As if she'd kicked Jeremy under the table.

Miranda continued, "This plane wasn't flying east to west, but rather west to east. The wings were mostly broken off and landed straight down when the flipping of the hull finally separated them fully. Some force didn't knock the plane from the sky, but rather threw it down. I was unable to simulate sufficient wind shear. I actually overrode the model and replaced the four Allison T56s with a pair of GE90s."

"The engines off a Boeing 777 twinjet."

"Your idea. Or at least the idea I had from you talking about the 777, Holly."

"That would send it down like it had been swatted by a bloody fly whacker," Holly demonstrated by slapping her hand on the table loudly enough to make Mike jump and spill coffee on his pants leg.

"Like spiking a ball in the endzone," Mike replied as if correcting Holly's Ozzie metaphor while he dabbed at his thigh with a napkin.

"Seventy-five... seventy-four-point-seven...four times as much thrust with the engine change," Jeremy looked down from where he'd been staring at the ceiling.

Holly and Mike were staring at him in surprise.

"What? I'm sorry I was so slow, but I wanted to make sure I didn't drop a zero going from kilowatts to Newton meters per second."

Miranda nodded; it confirmed her own calculation last night. She appreciated the precision.

"Football—" Mike tried to turn back to his original topic for some reason.

"*American* football," Holly corrected him. "Football is

either soccer, rugby, or maybe Australian rules football if you're a neo from—"

"A *sports* reference," Mike wasn't to be outdone. "After scoring a touchdown, a *football* player may throw the ball at the ground."

"Why? No, never mind." Miranda narrowed her eyes at the model—which didn't help at all. She set it to loop, less than five seconds from the beginning of the plummet until the last major piece of the wreckage settled in its final resting place. It took so little time to destroy a seventy-thousand-pound aircraft.

"The pilot never stood a chance," Mike sounded grim. Which meant he'd been a pilot, or was one. Or perhaps he just had empathy. Whatever the reason, he was correct. They could definitely cross pilot error off the list. A decision that always made site investigations much more difficult.

"Your analogy has merit, Mike. Some force did indeed throw the plane down very hard. As this Hercules was indeed powered by four T56s and not four GE90s, we need to find that force."

"So, you're saying that it didn't stall?"

The others laughed at Holly's wry tone.

She couldn't find any humor in it herself. All she could see was the plane falling out of the sky. It was so different from what had happened to her parents' plane, but she couldn't look away from the cycling image.

TWA Flight 800 had departed JFK for Paris on the evening of July 17, 1996. Twelve minutes and twelve seconds from wheels-up to the plane-killing explosion eight miles out to sea from East Moriches, Long Island, New York. The detonation had shattered the plane at the leading edge of the wing—so forcibly that the seven hundred and thirty-six confirmed witnesses ashore had reported a sonic boom despite the distance.

A spark from faulty wiring in an overheated and near-empty section of fuel tank had destroyed the 747 in midair.

The nose, including First Class where her parents would have been, broke off from the rest of the plane. While the headless fuselage had burned and climbed another three thousand feet on uncontrolled, runaway engines before stalling and plunging downward, the nose of the 747 had tumbled thirteen thousand feet down to the ocean. The best simulations said it had taken them eighty-three to ninety-seven seconds to fall.

Had they died instantly or survived only to die on impact? Or perhaps they drowned in their seats as the nose sank?

Unlike the 747's occupants, the C-130 pilots plunged to their deaths with too little time to even panic. They'd been dead less than two seconds after LOC-I—loss of control in-flight. They'd been beyond ever feeling pain again within the first tenth of a second after impact.

There. The nose of the C-130 hit top first and crumpled under the thirty-five tons of aircraft that had made certain of their fate. Safely dead.

No question of whether they'd burned on the way down or had time to take each other's hands. Maybe one of her parents had died and the other survived long enough to know.

To understand.

Long enough for regrets?

She knew all about regrets.

Why hadn't she been on that flight?

Because horse riding camp wasn't out. She and her governess, Tanya Daniels, were to fly over to Paris the next week. Horse camp had kept her from dying as she was supposed to. Instead Tanya had become Tante (Yiddish for 'aunt') and raised the grieving child Miranda had become.

Jeremy shut down the looping projection, but still Miranda could only see the broken fuselage of the 747, tumbling from the sky over twenty years ago. End-over-end or nose-first all the way down? All the medical examiner's report had told her was that the initial whiplash of the explosion, which had mercifully broken the necks of all except nineteen of the passengers, hadn't killed her parents. Nor had fire. No other conclusions were possible.

A hand rested on her shoulder and squeezed firmly. She forced herself to shake off the image. Only Tante Daniels knew about her past. Only she...

Except Tante wasn't here at Creech Air Force Base.

Miranda followed the hand on her shoulder up an arm to a face.

"Holly," she managed to breathe it out on a whisper.

"You okay, boss?"

She managed a nod—which was a complete lie.

"Okay," Holly covered for her by breaking up Jeremy's explanations to Mike about force dynamics. "We know what we're looking for now. Mike, start with the general. See if you can cajole the flight data recorder out of him."

"Local airport radar information as well," Miranda managed to find part of her way back from where she'd slid.

"Right," Holly still kept the anchoring comfort of her hand on Miranda's shoulder. "Jeremy, you and I will start on structural evidence to corroborate the model. Miranda—"

"I'm going to Washington."

Jeremy looked surprised, then terribly disappointed that she was leaving so soon.

Miranda should stay and oversee the investigation, but she suspected that Holly could handle it from here as well as she could.

Besides, there were some things this team wasn't cleared for.

Miranda wanted to retreat to her home north of Seattle. She wanted the peace of the quiet island where she could be alone with the eagles who nested there and the reminders of her parents.

But Miranda feared that it was the other Washington where she would have to visit first to find some answers— like what had happened to the flight data recorder, because it was practically guaranteed that Mike wouldn't be able to get it no matter how charming he was.

She wondered what she *herself* wasn't cleared for.

14

"WE STARTED WITH AN fMRI HELMET," THE DOCTOR told him.

He hadn't offered his name and Harvey hadn't asked.

"But were unable to achieve the minimum response times required. Scalp-mounted EEG electrodes lacked the necessary accuracy. Directly implanted electrodes proved to be the solution."

Harvey tried not to squirm. He was sitting in a chair not all that different from an electric chair and he had to hope that he wasn't about to be executed. His arms and legs were fully immobilized in padded clamps. His head was secured against movement in a rig that would be claustrophobic to anyone not used to a modern Air Force pilot's helmet. And the back of his head was bare for the surgeon to access.

He wanted to tell the doc to just shut the hell up and do it before he lost his nerve. But that might disqualify him. He had no idea what the rules were here, and twenty years in the Air Force had taught him that most basic rule: *When in doubt, keep your trap shut.*

Because they needed him conscious for the procedure, he'd thought having Helen present would help—it didn't. She was in her professional Colonel Hard-ass mode—making it hard to lose himself in stray thoughts about her body.

Last night had been different. It hadn't been hot sex or even just an amazing snuggle—Colonel Helen Thomas was the queen of the sexy snuggle.

And it wasn't just sating their bodies either.

Helen had talked, for the first time she'd really talked about herself. Even as she teased him with those fine fingers and quick tongue or settled against him in postcoital bliss, she'd spoken of dreams. Of honoring her father by joining the military. Of the woman who'd been denied combat pilot flight because of her gender and how that had destroyed the girl's dream of becoming an astronaut pilot—they were all former jet jocks.

Her interest in going aloft as a female mission specialist?

Even less than his.

They were both pilots first in their blood; she'd been denied even that.

He hadn't known that space was one of their shared dreams. He'd allowed himself a brief fantasy about meeting her in the astronaut program and getting to be the first couple to do it in space. Not so much. Besides, it had already been done plenty.

Harvey wanted to take her aloft in one of the T-38 trainers and give her that supersonic flight. Maybe even have some hot intercom sex at Mach speeds and a dozen miles up. Except he couldn't do that either because of his ear.

She talked through most of the night as if in a hurry to tell him everything. That worried him some...more than some. But he sure wasn't going to ask what she knew that made her that way.

Harrington had said she was cleared for all aspects of the program.

He rather suspected that he himself wasn't, and he really didn't want to know what that shit was. He just wanted to fly.

Helen had even talked about how her husband was a good, reliable man who'd provided her with a teenage son and daughter and been a good father to both. He was also a jock type with little imagination who thought that the physical act was all there was to sex. Last night there'd been *so* much more that they'd barely slept. Until last night, maybe he hadn't really known either.

But there'd been no wake-up sex this morning. She'd simply held him in silence for a long time before going to the shower alone. The bird colonel had been the woman who'd stepped out of the bathroom. He could respect that, even if he didn't like the thoroughness of the transition—not so much as a good morning kiss.

She'd left while he was in the shower.

As he sat strapped into the chair with his back toward the doctor, Harvey liked Helen's worried look even less.

"Hey," he called out. "It's not like it's brain surgery."

It earned him a half laugh from her. It would have been encouraging if the other half hadn't sounded like a choke of worry.

"Oh, but it is," the doc destroyed the moment. "While I

have developed techniques that allow us to implant the probes without opening your skull, nonetheless, I shall be planting the electrodes directly upon the surface of your cranial folds in such a manner—"

"Just shut the fuck up and do it, okay, doc? I'm not the kind of guy who wants the details."

The man harrumphed at not being allowed to fully explain his brilliant techniques to the nth degree. Pissing off the dude about to fish around inside his brain wasn't smart, but no one had ever accused Harvey of that.

All he knew how to do was fly and that had always been enough.

He'd been told that the brain didn't have the pain-sensing kind of nerves and that they'd given him a local anesthetic for the point of entry at the base of his skull, but he swore that he could feel the hair-thin wires and tiny sensing electrodes being guided into place—scraping along in the inside curve of his skull in arcing trajectories to land all over his brain like one of those nuclear warheads slamming down all over the earth. It was a good thing they had his head clamped into place so that he couldn't twitch and accidentally lobotomize himself.

"Think about turning left. No! Don't move your hands. Just think about the sensation of the turn itself. Good. Good. Now right. Excellent! Up... Down... This is very good; you catch on quickly. The other pilots have not proven so rapidly adaptable."

Other pilots? The general had hurried him along fast enough that he'd given no thought to the other pilots. He probably should have asked to meet them first, not that it would've changed his mind. He had been introduced to the two people maintaining the returned MQ-45 that he'd refueled less than twelve hours ago over the Bering Sea. Their knowledge, and security clearances, were limited to aircraft maintenance.

The moment he'd touched the Casper's skin, Harvey just knew that they were made for each other. The texture was smooth, but it wasn't. It was like very fine sandpaper, the surface broken into a thousand, a million tiny reflective surfaces—none of which lined up. Any radar signal wasn't just deflected by the skin, it scattered with no strong return to the receiver. The hangar lights hadn't been visible as even a brighter spot on the hull, never mind a reflection. It seemed to eat the light as easily as it ate the sky.

The doc kept giving him commands and he continued thinking them until he could feel himself once more in his F-15E Strike Eagle. Not "left rudder" but rather that slightly sickly sliding sensation of uncorrected yaw. Not just "down," but down with that high-in-the-nose fullness like when pulling a negative-g dive that increased the blood pressure to the head.

Helen left as they started working on his optic nerves— bright, dark, spectrum of color, ...—and Harvey could simply give himself to the process.

In between each instruction, while the doc was doing Harvey-didn't-want-to-know-what, he lectured Harvey on the details of his "brilliant" techniques anyway. Polysyllabic nightmares like electrocorticography and intracranial extraoperative electroencephalography swirled together with skin heat (a critical awareness factor in supersonic operations where hull temperatures could easily exceed a thousand degrees Fahrenheit) and "reach down with your toes like when you can't see the next step in a wide-spaced ladder" (for lowering the landing gear).

The last and largest piece that the doc inserted was a one-inch subdermal disk tucked through the tiny incision —"Like a model ship unfolding inside a bottle. Have you ever seen it done? No? A fascinating procedure." He tucked it in the area behind Harvey's right ear.

"This has the same material density and pliability as your skin. You will be convinced that you can feel it like a piece of iron, but you will be wrong. Once the cut heals," he flapped a small Band-Aid in front of Harvey's eyes to make a point of just how fine his work was, "even a lover can press on your skin and won't be able to feel it."

Harvey wondered if the doc knew about Helen and him, and whether or not he'd just earned a sharp punch in that arrogant nose.

"You'll be convinced that you can, but you'll be wrong. This will pass in a few days. Except post-mission sensitivity. It isn't real, it's psychosomatic. The other pilots say that after a flight it feels like there's a 'hole in your body.' I believe that is their crass term. Load of poppycock."

As if the doc would actually know. Harvey would trust his unknown fellow pilots on this one, but even if they were right, anything was worth the price as long as he could again feel like he was flying.

"When you interface with the craft, we will place a small adhesive disk directly over this subdermal implant. It will read your brain pulses accurately through the skin without any pain or sensation."

"When can I fly?"

"The Band-Aid is off to one side and won't interfere,"

General Harrington circled into view while they unstrapped him from the chair.

Had he been there long enough to see the fear that Helen had been so poor at hiding? Perhaps the general had signaled her to leave without Harvey noticing. It made him feel more kindly toward the man.

"Let's go try the simulator before I give you a hundred-million-dollar aircraft," the general's words wiped away all other concerns.

Harvey shoved out of the surgeon's chair. He forced himself to turn and thank the doc, rather than clock him a good one, just in case he needed any more work done on his brain.

A second basic Air Force rule: *Never fuck with The Man, no matter how much of an ass he was.*

15

LAS VEGAS TO DC. IT HAD TAKEN MIRANDA ALMOST EXACTLY twenty-four hours to reach the same place in the sky where the first plane had been turned around—just north of Santa Fe.

This time she was aboard a 737-800 in a standard 162-seat two-class configuration. In seat 2A as she preferred. It was directly in line with the pilot and also the same seat her mother had sat in on TWA 800. Mother had always enjoyed the window seat and it had been a merry game between them about whose turn it was to sit there.

Miranda also liked the idea of riding close behind the captain of the aircraft who would be the one doing everything possible to save the aircraft if there was a problem. And, if she was going to die, she liked the symmetry of doing so in the same seat as her mother.

Miranda struggled to keep her hands calm when the flight attendant approached her seat, but thankfully all she wanted this time was to know if Miranda would like a mimosa with breakfast service. Knowing that it was very unlikely she'd be flying as pilot in the next eight hours, she accepted a glass.

Her seatmate was a slouchy teen in shredded three-hundred-dollar jeans and practically hardwired into her phone. That left Miranda in blessed silence. The clean sound of the engines' roar was her primary accompaniment.

Could a cracked fan blade be heard before it broke free and shredded one of the engines?

How was the creak of the fuselage passing through a temperature gradient or even an air pocket distinct from the squeak-and-squeal of a failing skin seam?

At least with the 787 Dreamliner, Boeing had started working with single-piece-composite fuselage-barrel construction, which vastly reduced the number of possible failure points—though that introduced the new concern of possible delamination of the composite.

But the Dreamliners were mainly deployed on long-range transoceanic routes, which had other issues for her ever since TWA 800 had gone down in the Atlantic.

She resisted the urge to make a decision tree of the dangers versus flight selection in her notebook. Instead, she accepted the orange juice and champagne drink and used that to keep her hands still while she considered her options.

In DC she couldn't approach the Chairman of the NTSB. Like the rest of the five-member board, he was a political appointee and not cleared for military flight investigations. He could know that she was assigned to one, and even where, but Clarence Duffy didn't have sufficient security clearance to know what she did or discovered.

Only two lead investigators had sufficient clearance for her to speak to.

Even though he was ten years her junior, every time she saw Rafe Zachmann, he joked that she must marry him so that they could have little Top Secret Investigator-in-Charge children. At least she assumed it was a tease. Unable to be certain, she did her best not to be in DC at the same time as Rafe.

Terence Graham was old guard. Rafe was always teasing him in meetings to remind them again which of the Ancient Greek wars he'd fought in. Back in the day, he'd probably been the first black IIC, but he never confirmed that any more than his service in the Peloponnesian or Trojan wars. Forty years in, he knew more about how aircraft flew and how they died than most people knew about their own clothes closet.

In 2000 he'd brought over two decades' worth of front-line experience to the first class through the newly founded NTSB training academy—her year to join the National Transportation Safety Board. His courses had been like a ruthless firehose, washing clean the most obscure details that had become so critical. The fine art of tracing the unexpected.

Miranda knew her greatest failing was a need for "elegance of solution" as Terence called it.

"Sometimes the answer is just messy, girl. Gonna have to get used to it."

She never would. Late at night, she'd "come to" pacing up and down the length of the big family house still trying to solve some accident or other whose report had long since been filed and closed despite no clear results. "Unknown cause" was the bane of her sleep.

If Terence couldn't help her, she'd approach her contacts in the US Air Force Aircraft Accident Investigation Board— but she was less certain of them. In the many military aircraft she'd investigated, she'd rarely had the same investigator to work with.

Yes, she'd start with Terence Graham if he was in DC. It had been too long since she'd seen him anyway. Perhaps he'd experienced the mixture of removed recorders and missing military investigation teams.

And she would find time to visit TWA 800. How ironic that an eighty-foot section of reconstructed fuselage was the center of the NTSB Academy's training program. She knew every heartless inch of it. Although it didn't include any of the nosecone section—as it had broken away cleanly and not been a key part of the investigation but rather a consequence—she still visited it at every chance. It was the closest thing she had to a grave marker. The small stone she'd erected on their island after scattering her parents' ashes felt far more empty.

The two-acre memorial on Long Island, New York, near where the plane had plunged into the Atlantic, was stark, beautiful, and meaningless in comparison. Staring at her parents' names etched into the curved granite wall had left her cold.

The remains of the aircraft, as a classroom to herself and other NTSB investigators, had felt real, alive.

What use was memory without action?

She investigated airplanes so that others wouldn't have the memories she did.

As she exited baggage claim at Dulles Airport, she spotted her name on a tablet screen held by young man in a neat suit. She hadn't called for a car, though she usually did. Maybe one of the crew had done it for her.

Mike perhaps? Thinking considerately about people would be his department.

She nodded to the man in greeting, who didn't bother introducing himself. He simply took her site investigation pack and led the way out the automatic doors.

It was only as the black sedan was pulling away from the curb that Miranda spotted a man pushing rapidly toward her through the crowd of debarking passengers.

She didn't recognize him, but he too held a tablet with her name showing brightly on its screen. His haste made her question her unquestioning state until this moment.

Miranda narrowed her eyes to mask her inspection of the driver and his companion. They looked normal.

But would she know if they didn't?

16

"IT'S STILL NOT MAKING SENSE." THE TWISTED BITS OF STEEL that Holly seemed so fascinated by weren't the only thing that wasn't making sense.

Mike had talked to everyone who would speak to him— all three of them. None of them even admitted to knowing a General Harrington.

Three guards still encircled the plane, but the dynamic was different today. Yesterday they'd been facing outward, guarding against possible intruders in the heart of the Nevada Test and Training Range.

Today, they lined the green-flagged perimeter of the debris field and faced inward. Nine heavily-armed mercenaries yesterday—Holly had assured him they were not regular Air Force personnel and he supposed if anyone knew, she would.

So three heavily armed guards to watch three unarmed NTSB agents. The odds were definitely not in the NTSB's favor.

He suspected that it wasn't so much Harrington's doing that he was inaccessible. The two Camo Dudes who'd been awaiting their arrival looked as if they wouldn't admit to knowing their own mothers. The pilot of the tiny four-seater helo had been the third of the silent trio.

Jeremy had been oblivious to the implied threat of the encircling guard, who wouldn't be there if it wasn't for their own crew. He plunged into tracing the plane's systems, or rather the remains of them. He spoke constantly to himself as he worked, so it was easy to track what he was thinking.

"Primary hydraulics. Twelve gallons possible in system, three-point-two still in reserve tank at full capacity. Estimated leakage through five known post-impact severed lines: five-point-six. Still two-point-eight elsewhere in the system. Total loss below two quarts. Far too little loss for a hydraulics-induced failure. Cockpit secondary pumps not turned on by pilots—lack of time or lack of need? Mostly likely, the latter. Okay, fuel system." And he'd started crawling deeper into the plane's wreckage.

Holly wasn't much better, photographing the ends of twisted metal pieces that looked just like every other twisted metal piece to him. At least she did it without the running commentary.

"What are you expecting to find?" He asked her as he folded down one of the few remaining nylon-mesh seats that had once lined the entire hull down either side. Most of the others were crushed down the length of the sandwiched hull off to his right. This was about the only place on the entire site that was out of the blistering sun, also perhaps the only remaining seats that weren't stained brown with dried blood.

He had no intention of moving out of the marginal shade ever again.

To his left, Holly stood where the nose must have once been attached. Instead of more plane, there was an open circle of sky and desert. He couldn't see Groom Lake from here, but it lay there somewhere beyond Holly's left shoulder. An arc of the desert was blocked by the crumpled nose of the plane off her right.

"Not much, really. Look here," she tapped on some piece of metal beam that was as big across as a briefcase. The mangled end looked shattered, like someone had snapped a stick of wood over their knee. Fragments stuck out in various strange angles. The surface looked like a bad attempt at frosting a cake—all lumpy and misshapen.

"So what am I looking at?"

"You're looking at the strongest part of the plane. This is the main keel beam, if you will. It's where all the frames that make the hull tie in together."

"Well it's broken now, Holly."

"I can see that, Mike," she put enough venom in that last word that he decided to keep his mouth shut. "I can even tell you what broke it. Something very rare and strange called ground impact. Based on the deformation angle and the degree that it was a brittle rather than a ductile failure—and no I'm not teaching a Metallurgy 101 class today—I can even estimate the speed and angle of impact once I get back to my computer. You know what that tells us?"

"Sure. That this plane crashed."

"Exactly. All this," she waved a hand at the metal she'd been inspecting, "happened because the plane crashed. What doesn't it tell me?"

Mike thought back to Miranda's simulations this morning. "Uh, what it was that made it crash?" He wished it hadn't come out so tentatively.

"Give the man a Violet Crumble!"

"A what?"

"Best candy bar anywhere; just got to go to Australia to get one. Grab a clue, Mike. I'd kill for one right now," Holly sighed as she leaned back against the remains of a large machine gun that had its barrel almost folded in two.

"Which clue? That you're a lunatic? I already figured that out."

"Won't find an argument from any of my ex-boyos on that point."

"What are you doing here, Holly? Kick-ass Australian SAS soldier to American NTSB? You don't make any sense."

"Another point none of my ex-boyos would argue." She studied the narrow wedge of hull protecting them from the sun. "Needed a change. That kind of mission is a drug. You get crazier and crazier, taking risks you should never take and surviving by skill and luck."

"You survived. I'm guessing that there was a lot of skill involved." Because damn but the woman radiated competence.

"*I* did." Then she swallowed hard and looked sad. He didn't like that expression on her face. It didn't fit with the woman he was starting to like despite all of her bristly edges.

"Oh." Mike didn't know what else to say. He wanted to offer a subject change, but couldn't come up with one.

Holly's expression shifted to a frown and Mike braced himself to be the butt of some new remark.

"You know..." she mumbled it half to herself.

"Many things. I'm a smart guy. Just ask me."

"Miranda."

"She's enough of a loon to make you look sane." Mike wondered how long he'd have to stay out here in the desert.

"Fair dinkum or not, she's also a smart one. She knows the answer isn't here, so she's gone looking."

"Then what the hell are we doing out here in the desert?"

Holly pushed back to her feet and positioned herself to study more crumples of metal. "You and me, mate, we're the distraction."

"Oh great. Don't forget Jeremy."

"Hey, Jeremy," she called out. There was a crash of falling metal, a couple of scrambling sounds, then the man in question popped his head in through where the gun probably used to stick out.

"Guess what I found. You'll never guess. I'll tell you. Unless you want to guess?"

Holly did one of her withering looks.

"Okay, so I'll just tell you." He pulled his head back out of the window and stepped around the one remaining partial hull frame to join them inside the plane. "I know why the plane didn't explode on impact."

"No fuel," Mike guessed.

"No. We could smell it yesterday. That had to be at least fifty ppm."

"PPM?"

Holly, now back to normal, aimed her disgust at Mike, but thankfully he could depend on Jeremy to just barrel straight in.

"Parts per million. So if you have fifty parts of kerosene for every million parts of air, that's a pretty strong smell.

Humans can detect it right down to about half a part per million. Can you imagine what it must smell like to a dog? Most breeds are forty times as sensitive to smells as we are. I think they must—"

"So why didn't we explode?" Mike had been tempted to let Jeremy just keep rambling to irritate Holly, but decided to spare the kid her probable retribution.

"The C-130 Hercules' wings are attached at the very top of the fuselage, right? So they were most exposed to whatever struck from above. I'm guessing whatever it was, it punched right through the wings *and* the fuel tanks. You said that the general said that they were returning from a delivery, so their tanks were probably relatively empty anyway. If the breach was big enough, the bulk of the remaining fuel could have air dumped even in just the one to two seconds that Miranda hypothesized between whatever caused this and the crash. What little was left was mostly in the air by the time the plane hit."

"Which is why we could smell it so strongly but it didn't ignite," Mike was glad that none of them smoked. Who knew what lighting a match would have done.

"No," Holly's twist of a smile said he'd goofed again. "There was a breeze. It would have blown away anything in the air. But if it sprayed over the soil, it would have continued to evaporate."

"Also," Jeremy signaled one of his frequent topic jumps, "did you notice the Camo Dudes get really weird every time I crawl into the aft section of the fuselage?"

He and Holly didn't even have to exchange a glance. They both turned on Jeremy in unison.

"Okay, which part of the hull and how weird were they?"

"Who?"

For half a second Mike considered what he could do to get back at him. Then realized that Jeremy wasn't playing Holly-style games; his brain had simply moved on. Thankfully, he was able to haul it back just as quickly.

"Oh. The Camo Dudes. They always flinch when I get near the hinge point of the rear ramp."

"Anything else?" If Holly was trying to look casual and disinterested, she wasn't doing a very good job of it. She was leaning back comfortably enough, but she'd gone quiet as if preparing for action.

"Not really. Their hands drift to weapons like they're ready to take me down if I find something they don't want found. Crazy, huh? I must be reading that wrong. Anyway, I didn't notice anything weird. Other than the guns I mean. Nothing about the plane."

Mike didn't need Holly's training to know that Jeremy wasn't reading it wrong.

"Look, Jeremy, why don't you just stay away from that part of the wreck for now."

"I'm already done there. Not many important systems that far aft, really. Elevator and rudder control, ramp mechanisms, and stuff. Most of the stuff I'm interested in next will be out in the tail empennage, which broke off. Probably just a lot of sheared wiring, but I want to see if there's anything I wouldn't expect in a crash."

Holly pulled out a handful of plastic sample bags and a marker pen, then held them out.

Mike took them cautiously, "What am I supposed to do with these?"

"Go out fifty feet past the green-flagged edge of the

debris field—that's about twenty-two steps or eleven paces with your typical stride."

Mike looked down at his feet and wondered if *they* even knew what his typical stride was because he certainly didn't. "Why would I do that?"

"I want twelve soil samples in a radial pattern just like a clock around the whole wreck. We can analyze them back in the lab to see if we can spot a pattern of soil contamination so make sure you label them clearly."

"You want me to go out there in the sun with the snakes?" He'd already forgotten about the fuel question.

"Better yet," Holly handed him some more bags and a black duffle to put them in. "Get samples at a hundred feet out as well. That would be another eleven paces in case the higher math is beyond you. Do you need a calculator?"

"But—" Then Mike shut his mouth. He didn't want to be told to venture even farther out into this snake-infested wilderness.

"Oh, and keep your eyes open for anything strange."

"Strange like what? Stranger than you?"

She shot him a radiant smile. "There's naught on God's green Earth stranger than me."

"Hallelujah! That's assuming we don't count our fearless team leader."

"Isn't Miranda amazing? Wow! I can't believe I'm on a first name basis with Miranda Chase." Jeremy disappeared out of sight once more.

"And what exactly are you hoping to learn? That there's fuel in the soil around a crashed plane? Can't we just call the EPA?"

"What I'm hoping for is to have *you* be *my* distraction,"

Holly began pocketing the tools that she'd been using to measure and test the shattered keel beam thing. "Try not to get yourself shot."

"You want me to go out there and deliberately irritate three guys carrying big, mean, nasty rifles?"

"They aren't rifles. They're equipped with M4A1 carbines, which have a shorter barrel and are lighter weight than rifles," Holly was emphatic. "Thirty-round magazine with just Insight optics—not even a Block I upgrade to one of Trijicon's sights, which are a serious improvement."

"They are so going to shoot me."

"Not with a rifle, they aren't, mate. Because they don't have any."

17

"This is an unusual request, sir."

"I'm an unusual man." Drake rocked back in his chair and propped his feet on the desk drawer he always kept pulled out for that purpose.

"Seriously, sir. We don't—"

"You do know who I am, right?" A lieutenant would have just delivered the item. The woman might be one of those ageless Eurasians, but her lapel insignia were shining birds, which said colonel and meant she was mid-forties, which he found hard to believe.

"Yes sir. You're Four-star General Drake Nason, CJCS, Chairman of the Joint Chiefs of Staff. But the NRO is not in the habit of—"

"I don't care what the National Reconnaissance Office is in the habit of."

"—the habit of," Colonel Gray persisted with the stiffest spine since Christ was nailed to a cross, "providing surveillance of high security American sites."

"Yet you *are* standing here, aren't you? In the Pentagon, just across my desk from me? And you are actually here, in case you hadn't noticed."

"Yes sir. I noticed," her dry tone stated that there was actually a person behind that stiff spine.

Drake had always cultivated a casual attitude when he could; it tended to unbalance most lower ranks and make them reveal more than they intended. He'd been tagged with the handle "Renegade" back when he'd joined the Charlie Company, 3rd Battalion of the 75th Ranger Regiment. A Georgia boy serving in Georgia had fit him down to his boots. He no longer had to worry about not ticking off the higher ranks, because with four stars on his office door, there weren't any other than the Commander-in-Chief.

"And since you're here, that tells this old boy that you have the data I requested, which means that you *are* surveilling those sites and you have something to deliver. Otherwise Patrick would have called me up and told me to go suck an egg."

"I'm told he considered it, sir."

"Patrick was always a bit of a prick." The man had been an Air Force puke before shifting over to run the NRO. It wouldn't surprise Drake for a second if Patrick tried to refuse the request just to get back at Drake's own Army heritage.

"Yes sir." For half a second he couldn't tell if the stiff-necked colonel was being agreeable, or privately agreed that her boss *was* an asshole. He checked again, but he still couldn't tell.

Drake waved her forward.

She made a show of reluctance to take the last two steps.

Then she opened her briefcase and handed him a slip of paper over the desk. It had an address on a secure server.

"There's no password here." He flipped it over, nothing there either.

"It's..." and then she blushed. Brilliantly red.

"He insisted on something obscene."

"Not quite, sir." Her voice seemed a little strangled.

"So..."

"Pardon my language, sir. Apparently your opinion of General Patrick is fully reciprocated. It's—" She cleared her throat again, but it didn't seem to work.

"Let me guess: Up yours, asshole."

"Initial caps on each word with no spaces or punctuation. Yes sir," she replied in the tightest of tones. "My apologies, it's not how I wished to address the CJCS, sir."

Drake had to laugh at that. "Tell your boss I said hi and to go fuck himself."

"Yes sir," the blush didn't abate, but there might have been a smile hiding under it. "I must remind you that it's a single-day password and will expire at midnight."

He checked his watch. He still had ten hours.

She saluted smartly, he returned it, and she headed back out the door.

He watched until she was out of sight. Not because she had a cute ass in her full-dress uniform, though now that he was watching, he noticed she did. He must be getting old, because all that did was remind him that she was about ten years older than his eldest and he hoped to god that no man was looking at his daughter and thinking that same thought. Elsie was a doctor and happily-married mother of his first granddaughter—who was old enough to start thinking about college in between thinking about boys who were undoubtedly busy thinking that at sixteen *she* had a cute ass...

Time just moved too damn fast sometimes.

The departing Colonel Gray was mostly reminding him of one of the items he'd discussed with the President before accepting the appointment to be CJCS.

Information inside the intelligence-military establishment needed to be openly shared. The enemy was not in the building next door, but he was having a hell of a battle proving that to many of the agencies. More Colonel Grays and fewer General Patricks were needed, but he still had no idea how to implement that.

He logged on to the indicated secure server, selected the appropriate file folder, and keyed in UpYoursAsshole. "Bastard," he muttered as he inspected the folder's contents.

Drake watched each of the imaging files there.

Visible light was useless because the desert sunrise hadn't reached central Nevada yet at the time of the crash.

Infrared satellite imaging showed a four-engine C-130 Hercules flying. Readouts had been added in the lower right corner: Altitude (est. m.), Ground Speed (est. knots), and Distance to Runway 32 (km). Runway 32 was the compass direction of one end of the Groom Lake runway, without the extra zero. So the Hercules had been flying from the west before turning for a straight-in approach from the south to land on the runway oriented at 320 degrees.

Each image showed the Hercules flying straight and true one moment, then gone the next as if simply wiped from the screen.

For ten minutes he viewed the five ten-second files that the NRO had provided him.

All he got for his troubles was being ten minutes older.

He'd wanted to make his own assessment, but having learned nothing, he opened the one text document in the folder: *NRO Event Analysis*. Two pages of useless chatter finally convinced him that the NRO imagery analysts, the very best and brightest in their field, had learned as little as he had.

Where was that damned woman from the NTSB? She was supposed to be here by now. By the time he'd tracked her down, she'd already been aloft on her way to DC—which was convenient. He wanted to speak to her before he had to go explain just what the Hercules had been carrying when it crashed.

18

MIRANDA WONDERED AT HER OWN NAIVETÉ.

Oh, you have a sign with my name on it? Of course I'll follow you without asking any questions.

Neither the driver nor the man who'd been holding the sign and was now seated in the front passenger seat had been of any help.

"No ma'am. All we know is to pick you up and escort you to a meeting."

"No ma'am. We don't know what meeting or with whom."

"No ma'am. We're not at liberty to say where."

At a stoplight, she surreptitiously tried opening her door. They must have disabled the back door handles as if she was no more than a child.

A child? Or a kidnap victim?

Why would anyone want to kidnap an NTSB agent? That just might be a first.

She'd landed at Dulles, and they were heading east

toward DC, so that was a good sign, but nothing else was. Even grasping her right hand with her left didn't stop her from trying the door handle several more times over the next five minutes.

The vehicle seemed to compress in on her. The air was thick and over-air-conditioned yet it did nothing to evaporate the sweaty feeling.

Then the picture snapped into focus. She never should have had that drink on the flight; it had clouded her thinking. Except it had been four hours ago.

You also haven't slept in over forty-eight hours.

While true, that wasn't typically relevant. The interrupted early flight out of LA yesterday. Then awake all last night working with the modeling software. What it had done was give the alcohol a disproportionate stronghold on her thought processes.

Yes, that was it. Not fear, just lack of care.

Cooperation seemed to be her only option at the moment.

Perhaps if Holly was here, she would do some action-heroine thing, taking out two men who significantly outweighed her and then taking control of the car. As this wasn't the movies and Miranda would never be Holly Harper...

Cooperation implied simply accepting the current circumstances as normal. Well, if they *were* normal—or rather if she was going to *pretend* they were—what would she do next?

She slipped out her phone. This time it connected instantly to the local cell networks.

"I'm just going to check in with my team."

No reactions to her announcement from the front seat.

She dialed Holly's number, which went straight to voicemail as she'd expected because Holly would be in the NTTR dead zone.

"Hi Holly. I made it to DC. I just wanted to check in on your progress. As I told you, I'm going to be in and out of meetings all day." She'd said no such thing and felt a bit like a movie secret agent herself. Holly would know something was up. "I'll keep my phone by me so that you can call. I really need that new data you were working on before the meetings." She even thought to add a 'Thanks' and was pleased with her own dissembling.

Still no reaction from the front seat.

She dialed Terence.

"Hey, girl. Where you hanging out?"

"I just landed in DC. How are you doing?" She decided it would be best if she didn't say why she was here. Her kidnappers—or perhaps escorts?—were bound to report anything she said. Were they tracing this phone call? She didn't see any signs of it, but would she know?

"Whoa, something big must be up if you're asking me civilized questions." He always teased her about such things, which was why she made a point of including them in conversations with him. And she then broke the code, by continuing before he responded. He always answered how he was when she asked.

"I was hoping to catch up with you this afternoon or evening." Hopefully he'd understand her urgency.

"I had plans but, uh, I'll cancel them. Just ring me when you hit town. I'll be in the office." Good. He did understand. "Or did you want to make your pilgrimage to old 800?" He was the only one who knew about her regular visits to the reconstructed wreck at the NTSB Academy.

"Oh, I doubt if I'll have time this trip. And don't wait for me. I may be delayed."

"Yeah, right." He knew that she was far more punctual than any airline. Then he seemed to register her comment. "Right. Well, I'll be waiting for your call," then hung up. It was the closest thing she dared to dialing 911.

If the two men in the front of the car thought anything of her two calls, they weren't showing it.

Or of her sudden unexpected cooperation in accepting the current circumstances as normal. A complete give away.

She'd make a lousy secret agent.

19

"THAT LITTLE BITCH!" CLARISSA SHOUTED INTO HER PHONE.

Miranda Chase was supposed to be sitting in Clarissa's office, not telling the guard that if anyone wanted to meet her, she'd be sitting at the *Kryptos* sculpture down in the CIA's central courtyard.

"I'm sorry, ma'am," the agent who'd fetched her from the airport said. "Unless you want us to physically carry her upstairs, she refused to go beyond the lobby other than to visit *Kryptos*. So, James led her there and I'm calling you."

She slammed down the phone.

CIA division directors did *not* hop to the commands of pissant NTSB investigators.

She stared down at the woman's file on her screen. Frumpy even in her official photo: no makeup, hair in disarray, wearing some kind of a sloppy vest. Yet the citations spoke of her brilliance in the field of crash investigation.

But why had she been called to this investigation? It was supposed to have been quietly swept under the carpet. God damn Harrington. He was in the middle of the fucking Nevada desert and he couldn't even do that right. There was no chance of this woman uncovering the truth, but still Clarissa had to be sure.

Out of options, she took the elevator down to the ground floor and strode out into the courtyard. A few shade trees, a green lawn with a small pool set among rocks, and the incredibly frustrating *Kryptos* sculpture.

A small woman who couldn't be more than five-four stood facing it. Her file hadn't communicated her diminutive stature. In her rumpled clothes and heavy boots, it would be easy to dismiss her as a cleaning woman. She looked even smaller with the two guards looming nearby. Incompetent slugs—she waved them away, back to other duties—they couldn't even get a woman half their size to Clarissa's office.

This? *This* flat-chested excuse for a woman was the best the NTSB had to offer? She shouldn't have worried about a thing. Except her file said that she had a better crash investigation resolution rate than anyone else in NTSB history.

"I've been reviewing your file." Clarissa hadn't intended to start that way, but something about this Miranda Chase she wasn't sure how to handle—and Clarissa *always* knew how to handle people, male or female.

Chase made no response. Either she was too slow to understand the dire implications of a CIA division director reading her file—or she did understand and she was terrified. If she was the latter, she was the best actress Clarissa had ever met; her face didn't show a thing.

"Does that surprise you?"

"I find it...curious. Why were you reading it?"

Most people, decent, normal people, wanted to know *what* was in their files. It placed the subject at an immediate disadvantage to ask so that she would know where the power lay in this meeting. Clarissa could detect no response.

"I like to know the background of anyone I meet with," Clarissa pushed a little harder.

Chase continued to face *Kryptos* for a long moment as if seeking a thought, but kept her silence.

The damn thing bothered Clarissa a little more every time she stood by it. James Sanborn had become *the* name in cryptography. Not some codebreaker, but instead a sculptor who had designed the enigmatic thing. The ten-foot-high side-bending S wave of green-hued copper was...irritating.

Sanborn had encoded cryptographic messages into four sections.

It had taken the CIA five years before they'd cracked the first panel (only to find out that an NSA team had done the first three panels in two years). And nobody had cracked the final panel despite Sanborn's two released clues.

Unless the NSA had and weren't talking about it —bastards.

"My father and I used to work on these codes," Chase reached out to brush a hand over the surface. "He'd be sad to know that it was solved before his death, but that information wasn't released until three years after his death."

"You were trying to solve one of the greatest modern cryptographic puzzles at the age of twelve?"

"No," Chase turned to look at her—almost. Her gaze seemed to glance off the shoulder of Clarissa's Brooks Brothers palest-blue jacquard pantsuit. "We worked codes together from the time I was *five*. For my seventh birthday, he gave me a quarter-scale model of *Kryptos* that still stands in our garden. That's when I began working on it in earnest. I often wonder if he wanted me to become a codebreaker, but I never thought to ask him while I still had the chance. Instead I now choose to solve the hidden codes in the puzzle of aircraft accidents. I haven't worked on the uncracked fourth panel of *Kryptos* in years. Thank you. It's nice to see the original."

"You're welcome," Clarissa managed to keep her tone pleasant. "Now, shall we go up to my office? There are some questions I'd like to ask you."

Chase stepped to one of the slab-stone benches arranged around the sculpture and sat as if it was just as fine as a leather conference chair.

Clarissa inspected the courtyard. Other than the two guards, whom she waved back out of earshot, the courtyard was quiet at the moment; most people hurrying between the New and the Old Headquarters Buildings would be doing so along the connecting wings or underground. Sighing, Clarissa sat on the stone opposite.

"Your lobby," Chase nodded back toward the entrance, "is almost exactly twice the length of the loading bay of a C-5 Galaxy transport jet—the largest one in the military."

"I know what a C-5 Galaxy is." But Chase barely let her say the words before continuing.

"The largest in the US military that is. The Ukrainian Antonov AN-124 and AN-225 are longer. You see, the polished concrete flooring of your lobby is made up of alternating light and dark in four- and two-foot sections respectively. Twenty-eight pairs of flooring from threshold to threshold. Assuming you convert the eight entry stairs to be the twenty-ninth pair and add in the entry and exit door thresholds, makes it one hundred and seventy-six feet. Precisely the same length as the usable portion of two C-5 Galaxy cargo bays. The C-5 has eighteen feet of usable width capacity and your lobby's center section is only sixteen feet from face-of-column to face-of-column. Though your lobby is six feet higher, so that does distort the comparison, but it's intriguing to compare the similar volume of the spaces applied to different purposes."

Clarissa could only stare at the small woman. What part of her supposed genius considered that to be relevant to anything?

"You've read my background. What's yours?" Chase jumped back at least two topics as if there'd been no pause, though she still appeared to be talking to Clarissa's left shoulder.

"I'm Clarissa Reese, Director of Special Projects here at the CIA."

"That's your foreground, not your background."

Chase's gaze focused on Clarissa's other shoulder.

"Why have you sent for an NTSB inspector?" Chase said it like a rote phrase.

20

CLARISSA REESE'S FAILURE TO ANSWER IMMEDIATELY WOULD have told Mike something—all it told Miranda was that she was going to have to wait some more. She allowed her attention to shift back to *Kryptos* while she waited.

Between subtle shading and the absence of light lies the nuance of illusion.

Actually the solution to the first panel ended with *iqlusion,* but the reason for that final misspelling had yet to be revealed. Sanborn had said it was either for artistic balance or to make it harder to solve. Personally, she thought that it would factor in as a deeper clue to the fifth puzzle of *Kryptos*—the one that could only be attempted after the solution of the fourth panel had been found. She knew that subtlety and nuance were not her strengths, but she had made it her life's goal to shed light and battle *iqlusion* whenever possible.

Normally a crash investigation was very straightforward —often complex, but straightforward. The thousands of pieces of TWA 800 had taken four years to salvage from a hundred and sixty-three feet of water, reassemble, and analyze before a definitive finding could be announced. But it had been a process of collection, reassembly, discarding of various possibilities (including a missile strike), and then a result. The exact ignition point of the massive explosion had been identified and all 747s were now updated or redesigned to prevent its recurrence.

The crash of the C-130 in the NTTR would eventually reveal its own truth from the land *between subtle shading and the absence of light.* Just as the third panel had translated to reveal a paraphrasing of Howard Carter's description of his penetration into Tutankhamun's tomb in 1922: *but presently details of the room within emerged from the mist.* So, too would the C-130 eventually reveal its secrets to—

"I'd like to discuss your current investigation."

Miranda blinked in surprise. *Kryptos* was so engaging that she'd briefly forgotten where she was. "My current investigation?"

"Yes."

"Which current investigation would that be?" She decided on caution. She hadn't appreciated being kidnapped as it delayed her speaking with Terence. Also, being kidnapped wasn't exactly a positive turn of events.

"Don't toy with me, Ms. Chase. You wouldn't like it."

"I have three investigations with the reports in final draft and undergoing editing, two presently in peer review. Another which is on hold pending metallurgy and two others on hold for other reasons outside my control."

"I'm speaking of the C-130."

"I'm not at liberty to discuss that with you."

"Do you know who I am?"

"According to your earlier statement, you are the Director of Special Projects for the Central Intelligence Agency. It is a statement that I'm willing to accept at face value."

"And you know what that means?" There was a rising tightness in Clarissa's voice that Miranda had learned to associate with tension. Perhaps even irritation. Curiously enough, Clarissa Reese reminded her of a young Corsican mouflon ram on her island. Even in his first year he was lording his great curved horns over all of the other yearlings and was unflagging in his challenges to the bigger and wilier adult sheep—no matter how many times they thrashed him.

"Why don't you tell me?" Because Miranda had no idea what it meant.

"It means that I have the highest level of security clearance available, so tell me."

"I'm not at liberty to discuss that with you."

"You *what*?" Clarissa's fair skin actually began turning quite red, distinctly offset by her pantsuit. It wasn't a pleasant color for her complexion. Then Clarissa flinched when a hand rested on her shoulder. A tall man with broad shoulders and hair just starting to go salt-and-pepper gray had come up without either of them noticing.

"Something wrong, Clarissa?" He didn't wait for an answer, "Are you coming to our one o'clock meeting with Franklin?" He hadn't removed his hand.

She, in turn, did nothing to make him remove his hand from her shoulder.

He squeezed it sufficiently to ripple the material of her jacket.

If she were to dissect the individual actions of the new arrival and Director Reese, would she be able to unravel their motives? The man's hand on Reese's shoulder was neither restraining nor admonitory. It appeared...casual. As if touching her was a common occurrence. Her reaction said that she too was inured to his contact in this manner.

She herself had had few lovers in her life and had never been comfortable with casual touching.

"This..." Clarissa flapped a hand in her direction (still not dislodging the director's hand), "...*person!* She refuses to disclose information that I need."

"Not many people get away with denying our Clarissa anything she wants." He finally removed his hand and held it out. "Hi, I'm Clark Winston. I'm the Director of the CIA. Perhaps I can help here."

"I'm not at liberty to discuss my current investigation with you either."

The man blinked at her in surprise.

Miranda sighed. It seemed that she was going to have to explain the obvious.

"Per the National Security Act of 1947, the Central Intelligence Agency was formed as a civilian *foreign* intelligence service. My current investigation that Director Reese is inquiring about is regarding a *military* aircraft that has crashed on *domestic* soil. As this occurred inside a restricted military environment and has been code-word classified, I am not at liberty to discuss this with you or your staff. Now, while I appreciate seeing *Kryptos*, there is nothing further I can say. If you wish a copy of my final report on the matter, that will *not* be available through typical NTSB channels. All inquiries should be routed through the proper military authorities at the US Air Force Aircraft Accident Investigation Board."

Miranda rose to her feet and headed back toward the lobby. She had other things she needed to be doing. Hopefully she could get a cab at the front door.

21

"Wow! I'm guessing that didn't go the way you wanted. What was that all about?" His laughter stung.

It took everything Clarissa had to not swat at Clark.

First, for resting his hand on her shoulder in public, as if she was just some woman he was fucking and he didn't care who knew. She had to get that retrained right away.

Second, because she needed someone to strike at.

"*That,*" she spat out the word, "is the lead crash investigator on a small problem we had with our drone project."

"What crash? What the hell aren't you telling me, Clarissa?"

"Not now, Clark."

"That's Director Winston, Ms. Reese, and you'd damn well better remember that."

She kept forgetting that Clark actually had a spine when it suited him. Dangerous mistake. "Nothing important,

Clark. Just a C-130 that went down in a sensitive area that we don't want a civilian investigator poking around in." Which was at least partly true.

"Well, fix it. That's a key project in your portfolio."

She would.

Right now!

Nobody, but nobody just walked away from Clarissa Reese. Miranda Chase had just crossed the wrong woman and was about to find out how painful an experience that could be.

She yanked out her cell phone and dialed.

"Security," a female voice answered.

"There's a woman named Miranda Chase who has just passed through the lobby. Short, frumpy beyond belief—"

"I thought she was kind of cute," Clark mumbled. Clarissa ignored him.

"—carrying a backpack. I need you to stop her."

There was a brief pause, then, "I can't do that, ma'am. Sorry."

"And why *not?*"

"She got into a black Chevy Suburban, not one of ours, and is just now rolling out through the main gate."

"Bitch!" Clarissa ended the call and shoved her phone into her jacket pocket.

Clark started laughing again.

"What? There's nothing funny going on here."

"Sure there is, Clarissa. You've got to lighten up," again that too-familiar hand on her shoulder. Instead of slapping it aside, perhaps she should break it. "You just called one of our top security people a bitch."

"No, I was calling that NTSB woman a bitch."

"I'll bet you a steak dinner at The Capital Grille that I get an 'inappropriate use of language' report on my desk by nine a.m. tomorrow morning."

Clarissa sighed; he was probably right. Clark usually was about people. "No bet."

He laughed again in that easy way of his that charmed staff and senators alike. And how many unsuspecting foreign nationals had he charmed in his decades as a field operative? No reason that skill wouldn't work on the majority of the American people as well.

If she was going to do this, she might as well put her bet down.

"*You* pay for the steaks at The Capital Grille..." Some news hound would chronicle them dining together in public. And that would set the wheels rolling. She could be his lover, his successor at the CIA, his wife when he made President, and then run for the office herself—perhaps set a new precedent of a four-term First Family. Definitely time to consolidate the image. "...and I'll pay for breakfast in bed."

"Deal!" They shook on it right there in the CIA courtyard. He tried to make it a soft, sensual handshake, maybe even tug her forward against him, but Clarissa used all her gym-time strength to keep it as firm as any man's would be.

"Two things, Clark. One, you can have me in private...." After they were photographed at The Capital Grill he could have her in public, at least on his arm. "But you can't have me in public at work. Here you're still my boss." Everywhere else? Well, they'd just have to see who played the stronger hand.

"Right. What's the second thing?"

"Never, ever laugh at the woman you're fucking. Clear?"

His grin was as easy and winning as ever. "Yes ma'am."

22

"THAT WAS...AMAZING!"

"You had better be talking about me," Helen bent down to blow a raspberry against the center of his chest so hard that it tickled. He clamped his hands hard on her hips and leveraged her side to side to rub more tightly against her.

Harvey had come back to Helen's apartment from the simulator, charged up like he'd never been in his life. Sex after a flight had always been an awesome combination—something he'd mostly forgotten in his two years as a refueling UAV pilot. And while he couldn't fly the real drone until after dark, he had synced into the simulator like it was a lost part of himself rediscovered. Every instruction was answered as fast as thought, responding to his merest whim in ways even his own hand couldn't achieve.

He'd greeted Helen with a full-body slam, torn her clothes aside, and feasted upon her like a man reborn. And he was.

The sense of flying the drone wasn't sitting in some ground-based armchair with flight controls and a keyboard.

It had been visceral.

As real as he could imagine.

Well, maybe not as real as burying himself in Helen's raging heat, but it had only been a simulator and she was definitely the genuine article.

They hadn't made it past the throw rug just inside her door and he didn't care. She had squirmed and bucked and egged him on until their final release lit up like a turbocharger on full burn.

Or a supersonic stealth drone.

"Of course I was talking about you. You could short-circuit a man's brains."

At her sudden frown of worry, he could only laugh. Having flown even a simulated MQ-45 Casper allowed no room for doubts. The brain-drone interface had performed seamlessly.

"Fear not, fair Helen," he palmed her breasts. "Wait, that comes from somewhere." He let himself continue to watch and tease her magnificent breasts. Helen, as a mature woman, knew what to do with her body in ways the younger set never imagined. And they were so in tune now that her magnificent hand-full breasts responded to his slightest touch.

"It comes from Helen of Troy," she remarked drily as he raised his head enough to taste one.

"Ah yes, the queen who launched a thousand ships and one lowly jet jock."

"She also destroyed a kingdom."

"Destroyed a *man* is more like it. Being inside you," he

shifted his hips to emphasize his meaning, "is exactly where I want to be." If there was some way to have her *and* fly the ghost drone at the same time, that would be the real ultimate. Maybe a blow job *while* he flew? It might be ridiculous, but he couldn't help imagining it, because that was another thing Helen did better than anyone before her. Such a pity that a crew of three people worked around him for every flight.

"Helen of Troy was young and beautiful." She still didn't understand the mature beauty she possessed. She'd accused him of being infatuated, which was hard to argue with.

"How can I show you what I mean?"

Helen stretched against him in a long, catlike gesture but didn't say a word.

"Pilot's discretion, huh?" He rolled her aside so that now she was the one on her back and he lay on his side beside her.

"Left bank." He nipped her left breast, making her grab it with a protective hand.

"Right bank." Her right. He sucked deeply until she rested her other hand on his cheek to guide him downward.

"Yaw," he mumbled not releasing her right breast. He slipped his fingers through hers from behind, then ran their joined hands along the inside of her right leg, up the thigh, and she opened to his touch. "More yaw," he teased the other leg open.

"Now watch." He slipped his arm behind her head to support it tipped up on his biceps, then rested his cheek on her forehead so that they were both looking down her length.

He took a long time arousing her notch by notch, guiding

her hand with his, only his fingertips between her own touching her skin. Without ever quite touching between her legs, he helped her trace the line of her slender waist, the curve of her hip, the softness of her inner thigh. Her breathing accelerated as together they palmed her soldier-flat belly, then once more up over her chest. She was soon arching her hips, straining against his grasp to guide his hand down.

Once she was beyond speech, groaning in helpless frustration, he leaned down and whispered into her ear, "Keep your eyes open...

"Throttle." And he curled their interlaced fingers around and into her.

Harvey could only watch in fascination as Helen unraveled before him at their shared touch. He could do anything to her in this moment. Anything, and it would only make it better. But all he did was hold her tightly and watch as she crested against their hands.

"Yes, you're that lovely," he whispered into her ear as the release slammed through her again.

Flying Colonel Helen Thomas resulted in an incredible sense of control and power. He watched the tears from such a powerful orgasm slide down her cheeks even as her desperate gasps settled into contented murmurs and sighs. She curled around their joined hands, clasped tightly between her thighs.

Infatuation? The word came back up. No. He'd always enjoyed toying with a woman's body. But watching her had been something more...giving her a release that had made her weep and cling seemed only a part of what had just happened.

What would it be like to take his Casper drone so far aloft?

23

MIRANDA WASN'T SURE IF SHE'D STEPPED OUT OF THE LION'S den and into the lion. But the car had pulled up the moment she'd stepped out of the CIA's front doors and the second man from the airport had been waiting for her.

He'd at least had the decency to introduce himself, Sergeant Oscar Lamont, and ask if she was willing to accompany him to a meeting at the Pentagon. It wasn't where she'd been planning to go, but at least it wasn't being kidnapped. And it was closer to Terence's office in downtown DC than the CIA's Langley headquarters.

She'd stepped in. The speed of their departure seemed startling until she turned and saw one of the CIA guards running out of the lobby and trying to flag them down. Miranda double-checked, but she had her knapsack with her. Nothing left behind.

The midafternoon traffic was already thick and slow. At a stop, she tested the door handle. She could feel the latch mechanism engaging—no rear door lockout—so she released it without opening the door.

Not a prisoner this time, it was easier to settle back in her seat and try to picture the *Kryptos* sculpture again. Instead of the great copper curves, she now considered the tall Director of Special Research. So elegant in her blue pantsuit, poised on her rock bench as if she too was a statue built with perfect care.

And the easy hand of Director Winston upon her shoulder.

Obviously lovers, but she doubted that was relevant.

A lowly C-130 Hercules lay shattered in the Nevada desert, and it was of deep interest to Clarissa Reese.

Why would the CIA possibly care about such a crash?

Because there was something the CIA didn't want anyone to know.

Something they were testing?

But what relevance would that have to the downing of a manned C-130? If they needed a target drone, they could certainly have launched one without personnel aboard. So that didn't fit.

It was something about the aircraft itself.

But she'd seen no unusual radome or radar pod under the wings. No sign of atypical electronics. Anyway, if they were testing a new performance capability, it would be on one of the new generation C-130J Super Hercules, not on a thirty-year-old airframe.

If the CIA's Director of Special Projects was willing to kidnap her and then try to stop Miranda's departure, what might she do to the NTSB team in the NTTR? She wasn't sure, but until she had more information, caution seemed appropriate.

She dialed Holly's number again. It was four o'clock here, one p.m. in Nevada. The team would likely remain in the field for another four hours before they'd be able to check messages. Next time she'd make sure they were all issued satellite phones.

"Be prepared to leave on no notice."

The sergeant glanced at her in the mirror.

She hung up the phone. This time she was able to return to her contemplation of *Kryptos* and the unsolved fourth panel.

24

MIKE MOPPED AGAIN AT THE SWEAT ON HIS FOREHEAD. HE wished it was only due to trudging around in the Nevada heat and the threat of being unexpectedly eaten alive by some desert beast. So far he'd spotted only three sparrows and one lizard as long as his forefinger.

The three perimeter guards had looked bored out of their skulls when he'd first stepped from the aircraft with his fistful of plastic bags and a set of orange flags that Holly had given him as his only defense.

After Mike had decided that the center of the aircraft's wreck should be where the wings had once joined onto the fuselage, he pulled out his tablet computer. The guards had seen them wandering through the wreckage enough yesterday that it apparently didn't raise any alarms.

Now that Miranda had departed, they were all synced to Holly's computer for the master diagram. She knew more about crashes than he did, but he still didn't like having her in charge. The person best at dealing with people should be the leader.

Of course that didn't begin to explain Miranda Chase.

Certainly it was his first investigation for the NTSB, but he *knew* project management and team operations.

Holly was so dismissive of something that he knew accounted for the bulk of crashes—the human factor—that he wondered if she was human or some kind of anti-human alien. She *was* a technical girl, but did she have to keep ramming down his throat how much he didn't know about aircraft? Metallurgy 101 as if he couldn't see that the aluminum beam had been snapped rather that twisted to the point of failure. It seemed that half of her jargon was just to mess with him.

He tipped his head back to glare up at the achingly blue sky. *Dummy!* That's *exactly* what half her jargon was for. Well, two could definitely play that game.

And now she'd sent him out to distract three armed men.

Shit! There's the real issue, Mike. You're allergic to dying.

Forcing his attention to the task, he marked twelve radial lines around the aircraft diagram. Then tagging and numbering points at fifty and a hundred feet past the green-flag perimeter had him all set up. The tablet's GPS would now guide him to the correct position no matter what his paces said.

The moment he'd stepped past the perimeter flags, all three Camo Dudes attention had focused on him like a human magnet for malevolence. Rifles that had been lazily slung over shoulders were swung down into their hands. Stances shifted from bored-shitless to ready-for-action. And despite their sunglasses, they were clearly now tracking him like a target as if he was a bomb-carrying terrorist.

It meant he'd be a good distraction for Holly; he just hoped to hell that her comment about not getting shot had been a joke.

It had surprised him just how wide an area he was covering by circling a hundred feet beyond the debris field. Apparently it surprised the Camo Dudes as well and he soon had a shadow—a six-foot-three shadow in a bulletproof vest and carrying a lot of things that Holly would know what they were, but he'd just call guns.

The CD wore camo pants, a black t-shirt, and camo baseball hat with no logo. His enviable heavy leather boots reached well up his calves and looked decidedly snake proof.

Mike didn't offer him any sunscreen.

"Hi. I'm Mike. Mike Munroe." He'd held out his hand to as little avail as not shaking Miranda's. Not a good start, as no manly handshake ensued. Which was probably just as well; the guy looked as if he could crush bricks with his.

After about five more samples taken and flags left, the guy had finally grunted out, "Shit, man. You do this for a living?" The fast speech, softened vowels, and even the "Shit, man" almost rising like a question at the end pinned him as being from Southern California. A home boy, not that Mike would ever admit to being from there himself.

"Kinda weird, huh?" It still surprised Mike as well that this could somehow be part of his job.

"Fuckin' A."

"I didn't start out with the National Transportation Safety Board."

"You dudes are with the NTSB?"

"What did you think we were?"

"CIA. That's Groom Lake right over there, so we figured you had to be spooks. Kinda freaking us out to be assigned to watch you."

"That's what *we* thought *you* were." And Mike would keep how freaked out he was to himself.

"Nah. Just security. Didn't sign on to spend all day standing around in the fucking desert, but the pay is good. Good pay in the NTSB?"

"Better'n I was getting," Mike had learned early on to ease his language halfway from its carefully studied region-neutral state to match however the person he was speaking with spoke. It was that fine line between being accessible and being patronizing. He'd suffered more than a few poundings in high school before he'd figured that out. Besides, it was only half a lie. At least this time.

He was followed in silence for two more pairs of samples and flags.

"What were you before?" Silence worked wonders when used right.

"Advertising." He kept the answers short, which seemed to fit the guard's patterns.

"Thought there was buttloads of cash there."

"Can be. Wasn't." Had been until the FBI had come in and screwed it all up.

Turned out his little company's best two clients—his *only* two clients at first: a grocery store and a dog groomer—were both fronts for a minor Syrian money laundering scheme. They'd used him to extract information from his clients and, with the success of the ensuing takedown, they'd wiped out his entire client base. But they'd directed him toward new clients: fronts for Chinese gangs, Mexican human smugglers...

Soon he'd been their plug-and-play guy for all those actions.

He'd go in and do the whole advertising-schmooze thing. Gain their confidence, run some good ads, get in deeper, until he stumbled on some actionable intelligence. He'd report it to the FBI as "a private citizen" and they'd swoop in to clean out some rat's nest. It had been a very profitable and mutually beneficial arrangement—he got paid twice, FBI and for the ads—for almost two years.

They'd vetted him and increased his security clearance over time...until a military secrets smuggling bust—run through a French pastry chain—had gone way south through no fault of his own.

One day he'd had a steady stream of work and some very nice cash flow. The next, the FBI had stopped returning his calls and he was the proud owner of an advertising firm with no clients. No backlist. Not even a portfolio of work he could admit to.

However, they had left him with his security clearance.

He'd always liked flying, so he'd signed up for the NTSB to kill some time. Somehow that had equaled a free trip to the NTTR and being faced by paranoid Camo Dudes.

"I'm Don, by the way." *Ding!* Faceless Camo Dude suddenly has a name. Major progress.

"Hey, Don. So what did *you* do before this?"

"Couple tours in Afghanistan. Nothing big, mostly base security down at Bagram. Got a taste for not being dead up in the Korangal Valley. I watched a lot of stretchers and body bags come outta there."

"Not being dead really improves the outlook on your day, doesn't it?"

"Fuckin' A," Don chuckled. *Second ding!*

"What's it like? I mean, you must be good at what you do or they wouldn't put you here at a place as important as this." *Butter him up.* "What makes someone good at doing a job like this one?"

"Well..."

25

"AND FOR THE NEXT HOUR, DON TOLD ME MORE ABOUT ALL the nasty situations he'd faced on base patrol than I ever wanted to know. Apparently drunk Marines are the biggest problem because they're always looking for a fight. Even on a dry base they'd get it shipped in. Once an attack helicopter, I think he said it was a Viper."

"AH-1Z," Holly said, as if that illuminated anything for him. He'd kept an eye out, but never once spotted Holly around the rear of the plane.

"Yes, one of those," Mike covered. "They shipped it into Afghanistan with a fuel tank full of Southern Comfort whiskey."

"Three hundred and seven gallons," Jeremy observed. "Let's see. Whiskey weighs about 7.411 pounds per gallon, so that's one ton, two hundred and seventy-fiv—"

"That's a lot of whiskey. Maybe he wasn't telling tall tales about his dealings with drunken Marines."

"Did you find out anything else?" He and Holly had met

up in the shade of the upright jet engine, as if it couldn't just fall over and squash them at any second. She actually leaned with her back against what had to be the only uncrumpled bit of sheet metal on the whole site. Mike sat where he'd see if it started to fall.

"Yeah, he likes his pizza with just Canadian bacon and pineapple, but doesn't want to look like a wuss to the other guys, so he eats it loaded just like they do. Gives him heartburn."

"Last week," Jeremy leaned up against the engine next to Holly. Mike edged back another half step to the very edge of the shade. "I had this garlicky chicken with white sauce pizza. I'm not even sure that it's technically pizza without tomato sauce and cheese, but man it was tasty."

"Holly?"

"What?" As if she didn't know that he was asking about what she'd found in the rear of the wreck. At least if the engine fell on them, it would crush her first before putting him out of his misery.

Fine, two could play that game. He *wouldn't* be the first to ask what she'd learned while he'd been sweating out his distraction across the Nevada desert. "Favorite pizza?"

"Weren't you paying attention? I ate pizza just last night."

"A loaded, a vegetarian, and two pepperonis."

She only blinked once in surprise that he *had* noticed, then recovered with, "Well there's your answer, mate."

"No. It either means that pepperoni is your favorite with two votes or that if I was to spread refried beans and chocolate mole sauce on a pizza crust and bake it, you'd eat it."

"You should really learn to listen better. I told you, 'There's your answer'."

"All of the above," he sighed. Another round to Holly.

"Mushroom-artichoke-prosciutto for me," Jeremy looked thoughtful for a moment. "Or maybe triple-cheese and mushroom. Thankfully I got Mom's digestive genes; she's Canadian, so I'm not lactose intolerant. Like a lot of Vietnamese, Dad can't eat cheese pizza at all." He fished out an energy bar.

Mike considered throttling Jeremy for being as obtuse as Holly. Jeremy he could deal with.

"What? Do you guys want one?" Jeremy held out the bar. All innocence.

Holly took it and began to unwrap it. Couldn't the woman focus on something other than food for a second, just one lousy... Then Mike sighed as Holly grinned at him. Maybe he understood better why the nuns of Catholic school always threatened to wash out his mouth with soap. He'd try that on Holly if he thought he had a chance of surviving the attempt. Preciseness of language might be the only worthwhile thing he'd learned from the nuns.

"Holly," he finally gave in to his curiosity.

She looked at him with wide-eyed innocence. At least she didn't bat her "baby blues" at him.

"What did you find?"

"Didn't find dingo shit," her humor evaporated. "I crawled all over that section. Nothing stood out. I photographed everything in hopes that Miranda can spot something we didn't. Nothing even half as cool as what you found."

"Wow, Holly! Major concession there. You feeling okay?"

"Kinda nauseous, but only when I look at you." But they all turned to look at the section of wing.

It had broken off from the engine nacelle and flopped to the ground bottom-up. He'd had an idea as he completed gathering his soil samples and recruited Don and his Chevy Suburban to flip over a twenty-foot section of it. The entire top of the wing looked like it had folded inward. The empty fuel tanks had been shattered just as Jeremy had hypothesized. Then Mike and Don had flipped the rest of the fifty-foot wing that stuck out this side. Sure enough, the entire thing had been punched in.

"Not a scratch, scrape, or burn. It can't be an explosion from above or we'd see the scorch marks," Holly glared at it.

"Miranda's unknown force," Mike tried to imagine what could do this, but wasn't having any luck.

They'd already photographed it and talked it over for half an hour without getting any wiser.

"Whatever it was, the C-130 got slapped hard. You learn anything, Jeremy?"

"Well, I kinda did," Jeremy announced as he chewed. "Out under the right horizontal stabilizer, where it broke off from the tail." He took a slug of water and then another bite of his energy bar. "It was—"

Don came running around the engine nacelle, sweat dripping from his forehead. He looked more than a little bit panicked.

26

"I HAVE SOME IMAGES TO SHOW YOU."

Miranda liked the introduction.

The escort through Pentagon security had informed her that the Chairman of the Joint Chiefs of Staff—the highest-ranking officer in the US military—was waiting for her. The sign on his office door stated that he was General Drake Nason. So any repeat of that information would have been a waste of time.

It was said that every office in the Pentagon's vast complex was within a ten-minute walk of every other, and she now believed it. The walk up the ramps and long hallways to his office had indeed taken just seven minutes and nineteen seconds. The concept of five nested pentagons of decreasing size, cross-connected by frequent corridors, was an ingenious feat of architectural engineering.

Once past the lobby, most corridors and ramps were utilitarian with white walls and colored concrete flooring. As they'd reached more important areas, wooden wainscoting had indicated the change. At the general's office, the wainscoting had given away to floor-to-ceiling paneling and finally plush gray carpeting in the general's reception area.

The size of his office—half office-conference room and half comfortable sitting area with couches and wingback armchairs—spoke of his importance as thoroughly as his title. That and the pair of Navy captains and a vice admiral who'd been hustling out of his office just as she'd arrived.

The man himself was lean. His hair almost too short to see its gray color. Any assessment he must be making about her own person was so brief that the color of his eyes remained an unknown. It had been easy to guess what Clarissa thought of her, but not General Drake Nason.

The doors clicked shut behind her.

"I don't need to remind you that these images are top secret."

He didn't, so she didn't comment on it. Her bag was out at the receptionist's desk, so she simply sat and waited.

"I've been over these images several times myself, but I don't see anything unusual. Perhaps as an expert in the field, you can see something. After that I have some questions for you."

From a control at his desk, he dimmed the room lights. Then he turned to a large computer screen hung behind his desk.

She sat unmoving through the ten minutes of video clips.

"Again," her first words seemed to echo strangely in the room as she rose and moved closer to the screen.

Without a word, he restarted the loop.

Radar tracking: she was right about the west-to-east flight. And the speed: three hundred and thirty-one miles per hour, just four below her projection. Altitude she'd been off by over twenty meters, but well within her estimate's confidence interval.

Then as abruptly as if it had been moving across the page screen, it disappeared.

Infrared tracking showed normal flight until the aircraft was directly over the crash coordinates.

"See here, the sudden bright flare of all four engines in the infrared?"

She didn't bother to look to see if the general nodded in the dark.

"That's caused by the plane nosing abruptly downward so that the camera could see the additional heat signature of the engine's exhaust ports. They're typically masked from above because they're under the wings. To get this view implies a down angle over seventy-five degrees. An unrecoverable angle for the one-point-two seconds the pilot had—even if his plane had been fully functioning."

"What do you mean by that?"

"Do you have any other views of this aircraft?"

"Visible light, but there's nothing to see."

"Play it." She waited while the general queued the file.

"Can't say I'm used to being ordered about," he muttered with what sounded like a chuckle. Without the room lights, she couldn't see if that assessment matched his facial expression. She doubted he'd be squinting his eyes in the darkened room.

"It wasn't an order, sir. Simply the next logical step in the investigation."

"Yes ma'am." Again it sounded like humor.

And then the visible-light sequence played back.

Almost perfectly black.

Even though she knew where they must be, she had difficulty spotting the wingtip and taillights as they were only the merest suggestions. There was also a sliver of visible light glowing out the back of the four turboprop engines. The flight continued for several seconds, then the engine glows brightened for an instant as expected before blinking out. She'd anticipated a brighter rear view flare, but not enough so that it surprised her. A second later, there was nothing—just darkness.

"Again."

"There's nothing there, lady."

"Again."

He didn't sound as amused as he reran it.

"Stop! Back up a tenth of second. Another. That's good." Miranda wasn't sure what she'd seen, but it was on the screen—somewhere. "Zoom in."

As soon as he did so, the pixels bloomed to life.

"No good, zoom further out."

"It is zoomed all the way out." He returned it to the initial view.

"That makes no sense. Lights."

"What makes no sense?" He brought them up and she returned to her chair.

"You have a highly segmented view of the terrain. The severe pixilation upon magnification indicates that you are viewing an extremely small segment of a KH-11 Crystal satellite image."

"I never said it was a KH-11."

"Unless you are in cooperation with the Russian or Chinese governments, I can only assume that you contacted the National Reconnaissance Office for these images. The only craft type I'm aware of that has that degree of resolution —able to clarify the heat variations of the pilot's high, side windows as six separate panels rather than a single section —are the KH-11 telescopes. They're directly based on the Hubble Telescope design and have a putative six-centimeter resolution."

"Can't say as I put that together myself, but I reckon you're right. Is this going to happen every time I show something to the NTSB?"

"Exposing national asset capabilities?"

At his nod, she considered his question.

"No. I know of only one other person who could reach that conclusion. He also has the clearance to see these images, the man who trained me. But I don't think he followed optical systems much beyond the SR-71 Blackbird's Hycon TEOC camera. He always preferred film to photo-optical sensors. He calls them 'modern mysticism'."

"So our secrets are safe."

"I have clearance, sir. I assumed you knew that before you brought me here."

"I'm sure my assistant did before you entered the Pentagon. I actually just asked to speak to the lead investigator, but you were already en route from Nevada. Now, what can you tell me?"

Miranda sighed. It seemed that she was going to just keep having this same conversation all day.

"Not a thing, sir."

27

DRAKE COULD ONLY STARE AT THE SMALL WOMAN. "YOU clearly saw something on that screen."

"Yes sir. And I'd appreciate a wider area view of those images, especially the visible light one."

He was halfway through dialing Colonel Gray before he caught himself. She'd shifted this to her own agenda with all the agility of a seasoned political warrior. Something that Drake hated about his job. Too much partisan politics, not enough solution-driven thinking.

"So what did you see?"

"I'm not at liberty to discuss it, sir."

He hung up the phone and stared at her.

The woman stared back without even blinking.

"You care to explain that? Is this some NTSB rule I don't know about?"

"No sir. It's your rule."

"My rule?"

"Well, the US military's. While Groom Lake is not a SCIF —a Sensitive Compartmented Information Facility—"

"I know what a goddamn SCIF is." He was fast losing his sense of humor.

"While Groom Lake is not a SCIF," she continued as if she was lecturing a fifth grader, "it has many of the attributes. It is a highly secure facility. Obviously it breaks the tenet of compartmentalizing information securely from interception or monitoring, as you've proven with the satellite images—"

"That I didn't authorize or know about," and he was going to cut Patrick a brand-new asshole over that one.

"Be that as it may. I'm not at liberty to discuss it with you, sir."

"You think I don't know what goes on in my own damn testing facility?" Unable to help himself, he pushed to his feet and began pacing behind his desk. He'd never shaken all the miles he'd trooped first at West Point and then up and down every hellhole on the planet since. The desk always felt like a trap to him. He could feel the weight of the forty-thousand people crawling through the Pentagon building like ants, each one mining away their tiny bit of information. Gray and Patrick over at the NRO, the National Security Advisor, even the other chiefs of staff. That bastard vice admiral he'd just sliced a new asshole into in front of his captains and—

"CJCSGDN," the woman said quietly.

"What's that?"

"To answer your question: No sir. I don't."

"Which question? You don't what?" He stopped close by her chair and glared down at the NTSB investigator.

"I don't think that you do know what goes on at your 'own damn testing facility'."

"And how did you reach that conclusion?"

"Five distinct points come to mind."

"Oh, do enlighten me." Drake vacillated between kicking her ass out and having her arrested. Instead he waved a hand for her to continue.

"First, it was you who chose to send me to the NTTR with such high priority."

"I just called Duffy and told him to send his best and do it damned fast."

That appeared to surprise the woman.

"You're thinking he doesn't like you? You're right. But you don't have to like someone to know their skills. For a political appointee, he's actually a good administrator."

She looked thoughtful about that for a long moment, then moved on. "Second, there's something wrong with this crash. Something that's worrying you enough to send an NTSB team to assist in what should be a straightforward military investigation. An investigation that the military is *not* proceeding with, I might add."

Not a chance Drake was going to tell anyone why he'd hit the panic switch on this. Certainly not this woman. As to why there were no military investigators out there, he hadn't wanted someone else's team in there uncovering the worst— not that he'd be admitting that either.

"Third, I just realized that you, CJCSGDN—Chairman of the Joint Chiefs of Staff General Drake Nason, are the one who sent the order to General Harrington to cooperate with me. That implies that you didn't expect him to and felt it necessary to force the point."

"So much for hiding that truth." When she looked at him quizzically, he waved for her to continue as he crossed back to his chair and sat.

"Fourth, you are unaware that this investigation has been code-word classified."

"It's been *what?*" He shoved back to his feet and turned the wrong way to get around the desk again. He slammed his shin into the heavy oak of the open drawer. "Ow! *Shit!*"

"And fifth, you are unaware of the CIA's own interest in this crash."

That, and the screaming pain in his barked shin, had him dropping back into his chair once more.

28

"Let's go! We gotta get outta here. Pronto!"

"Hey, Don. What's up? It's only three o'clock, we've still got tons to do." Mike couldn't think of a single thing, but he was sure Holly would find some dirty job for him. Maybe he shouldn't argue.

"We're going, right now," Don grabbed Mike's arm and spun him toward the parked helicopter that had delivered them this morning.

Mike didn't need to check with Holly about what to do when he saw Don's hand slide around the handle of his not-a-rifle rifle.

"Just me?" Christ he hoped not.

"All three of you. Now!"

"Okay." He'd have to tell the nuns at St. Bernardine's that prayer *worked!* If he was ever dumb enough to revisit that particular slice of hell. "Give us a couple more minutes."

"*Now!*" Then Don relented, showing he was human and hopefully not a firing squad. "Incoming wargames. They were supposed to stay over in Coyote A, that's a section of the NTTR. But some tactical shit has shifted or something and we've been ordered to clear out for safety's sake. So unless you want your ass shot up, and I'm not talkin' about by me, get moving."

"Holly! Jeremy! Emergency evacuation!" He yelled even though they were right there. Mike was halfway to the helo when he remembered his knapsack and sample bags. He doubled back for them even though Don was yelling at him.

Don could only shoot him.

Who knew what Holly would do if he left anything behind?

Just like this morning, Jeremy had climbed into the copilot's seat beside the Camo Dude pilot, clutching his oversized gear bag to his chest. He and Holly were in the back of the tiny helicopter with all of their gear pinning their feet in place.

The pilot was starting the helo, which responded with a high whine, and then a slow *whoop* of the rotor turning around the first time.

Don and the other CD on the ground were racing away in their Chevy Suburban, as fast as if there really was a fire —a great dust plume marked their escape route.

"Wargames, huh?" Holly twisted to look out her window, then she lay her body on him to look out the other. "Don't get any ideas."

It would be hard to, even with her lying against him. Holly still wore her vest and there were three different sizes of pliers, a multi-bit screwdriver, and a couple of pens that felt as if they'd been honed to a knife point. She was one very fit and nicely shaped soldier, and he'd always been a fan

of trim and athletic. Of course he was also a big fan of tall
and curvy. But he had a strict policy to never sleep with
women who hated him.

"Do you see anything?" she asked in a whisper.

He turned and got a face full of surprisingly soft
ponytail. "Not much."

Holly dropped back into her seat.

Once his vision cleared of the images she'd managed to
plant in his head—despite all her sharp points—he looked
out the window, but had no idea what he was seeking.

They weren't even off the ground yet.

Glancing back, he could see the whole spread of the
wreck. In the gap between the upright T-56 engine and a
mangled wing strut, he could still see the salt-white smudge
of Groom Lake without a single alien or exotic aircraft
sighting despite two days of keeping a lookout.

"Hey," Holly leaned forward to shout to the pilot. "I left a
bag at the wreck. Can you hang on? I'll be real quick, but it's
awfully important."

"Forget it, lady."

"But it could cost me my job."

In answer, he lifted them off. Apparently the rotors
weren't fully up to speed as they more jostled along the
ground than left it. Guy must be seriously spooked to make
that mistake.

Holly dropped back into her seat. Except she was smiling
this time.

"What did you leave?" Mike leaned in to whisper and
tried not to notice how close he was to her. In the little
helicopter, they started out with the shoulders touching,

leaning close enough to whisper over the loud engine noise practically put him in her lap.

"Is all your data synced?" Holly of course never directly answered a question. Then out of some foreign and wildly unusual thoughtfulness, she actually did. "Not a thing. Just checking."

Her answer didn't make him any wiser about *what* she was checking.

He pulled out his tablet and synced the last update back to Holly's computer. "It is now."

"I just hope that Jeremy is more consistent than you are."

He reached forward to tap Jeremy on the shoulder, but Holly slapped his hand down hard enough to really hurt.

"Hey! I use that on occasion."

"Yeah, and we know exactly what for."

"I get the ladies to do that for me. What ladies do that for you?" It was crass, but something had to put Holly in her place.

"Boyos, mate. And they do plenty of good things for me."

She tapped in some commands, then pulled a sim card out of her tablet. Taking her big knife, she jabbed it into the rubber heel of her boot. Keeping it pried open, she slipped the sim into the gap. When she withdrew the knife, the rubber closed seamlessly. She slid the big knife back into its thigh sheath.

"Why?" Mike mouthed it, suddenly afraid to speak aloud.

"Look casual, but keep an eye out your side," he could feel her breath on his ear. It tickled. They were finally aloft and moving away from the wreck.

"What am I looking for?"

"You'll know it when you see it."

"You really suck at being a big help. You know that, right?"

Holly winked at him, just before she shouted, "Go to hell, Mike Munroe!" Then she landed a painful punch on his arm at the same moment the pilot and Jeremy twisted around in surprise.

"Ow! Goddamn it, Harper!"

But Holly had crossed her arms under those nice breasts covered in sharp objects and turned to glare out the window. He could practically feel her laugh.

And...she now had a perfect reason for them each to look out opposite sides of the helo.

"Well, fuck you too, Harper." He put in all the bravado he could muster, then he turned to glare out the other side. He wished he'd thought of something else to say. By now the sexy Alejandra in Denver would be so steamed at being stood up—and that he'd not thought to call her last night from Creech Air Base—that he'd never get her back. And he certainly didn't want any of that from Holly Harper. Not even if she was offering. Which she wasn't.

Nothing to do but watch the goddamn Nevada desert.

29

"WELL, HARVEY. YOU DID VERY WELL IN THE SIMULATOR."

"Thank you, general." Harvey bit his tongue to not ask the next question. *How fucking soon could he get aloft with the real Casper drone?*

The conference room was perched in a corner of the hangar's mezzanine. Harvey recognized the protective measures: no walls in direct contact with the hangar's walls. The air conditioning unit built into the room would pump air straight into the hangar, but also wouldn't allow any sonic monitoring along the ventilation path. The one door into the room was doubled, one swinging out and the other inward. Everything isolated.

Inside the room were a stand-alone computer, a big wall screen, and a small table. Six people could fit in the room, but there were only the three of them: himself, Harrington, and Helen at the keyboard.

General Harrington nodded to his assistant.

Helen took a deep breath.

Harvey could picture exactly what that would do to her rib cage and breasts, but she was in full-on bird-colonel mode, so he just left that image in his imagination. She punched up an image of a submarine. It was like nothing he'd ever seen.

"Narco-submarines are becoming increasingly sophisticated. Fiberglass hulls to avoid sonar." Helen flashed up various images as she spoke. "Running submerged during daytime, only surfacing at night. Radar allows them to submerge again even if we get near them at night. They can easily carry ten tons of cocaine, with a street value over a billion dollars. If they invest five million in building a single-use submarine, what do they care. They're very hard to track. Even if we come close, they hear our planes or ships and they submerge out of reach. The MQ-45 can arrive almost silently and approach faster than they can submerge."

She left up the final image of a beached fifty-foot sub painted in a mottled camouflage that would look like waves and sun reflections off the sea. A group of Coast Guard stood around the sub, but there was no matching pile of cocaine bricks. They'd gotten away with the cargo before the Coast Guard arrived.

"And you'd like me to see if I can find some." Cruising low over the Pacific at Mach 2. How low would he have to fly to kick up a rooster-tail plume of water behind him? That would be fun to find out.

"Yes. You can make two roundtrips from here down the coast to Colombia and back. We'll have a refueling drone waiting off Baja."

Flown by some poor sap just like Harvey had been just forty-eight hours ago—dreaming of real flying with no hope for the future. And now the future was here and it looked awesome!

The general leaned in. "We haven't tried this type of mission before. We aren't even sure if your side-scanning radar can pick them up. We estimate there are over a hundred a year working along the coast. Our record capture was thirteen of them in a single year. They can now run fully submerged; they even vent their diesel exhaust out the bottom of the hull to help cool it and decrease their heat signature. And if we get alongside them, they scuttle the boat and the evidence goes to the bottom of the sea."

"So what am I supposed to do if I see one?"

The general leaned back and Helen smiled softly. "I believe we call that pilot's discretion."

30

"WHAT THE HELL DID YOU TELL THE CIA?"

Miranda wondered what it was with generals and this project. She hadn't met that many of them over the years, maybe they were all angry by the time they reached this rank.

That didn't seem likely.

Perhaps it was just this incident.

"The same thing you've told me?" General Nason growled when she didn't answer.

"Code-word classified is a rather self-explanatory term in my experience. I told them nothing. One of the departmental directors seemed rather upset about that. The director himself appeared more amused."

"Amused, how could you tell?"

"He appeared to be teasing one of his division directors as he kept his hand on her shoulder."

"On her shoulder?"

"A Ms. Clarissa Reese, Director of Special Projects. It

appeared that he was in an intimate relationship with her; I'm not the best judge of such matters but the indicators were there." Miranda considered that for a moment. Is that how Mike viewed people, the same way she viewed a crash?

The general blinked in surprise. "Clark Winston is sleeping with one of his directors?"

"Yes, I would say the indicators were definitely there." Perhaps it would be worth discussing this novel thought with Mike and receive his input. It still didn't explain either general's anger. She had no prior experience to compare General Harrington's sidearm being aimed at her in juxtaposition with General Nason's angry glare. Yet all three people were undeniably angered by the crashed C-130.

"Well, you didn't talk to them, that's something at least. And what asshole classified a plane crash?"

"I might ask why you assigned me to the investigation without knowing its sensitivity."

"Just answer the damned question, lady."

"You will wish to speak with General Harrington. Until you do so, I haven't slept in over forty-eight hours and that started in a very different time zone. If you'll excuse me." Again, she assumed permission rather than asking it and rose to go.

"Sit your ass back down, woman."

"Am I under arrest?" That would be a new experience; one that she'd rather not investigate. "Or is this some other form of incarceration without my permission—such as the CIA attempted?"

"Just," the general scrubbed at his face, then sighed. "Sit down for a minute. Please." The last looked as if it pained him enough that she sat.

He punched a button on his phone. "Get me General Harrington on the line."

While they waited, he slouched back in his chair and glared at her over steepled fingers.

"General Harrington isn't available, sir," a woman's voice chimed in over the intercom.

"Well, find him before I send in the 1st Armored out of Fort Bliss to roust his ass!" He punched the intercom off and went back to glaring at her across the desk.

Miranda tried to pretend it was her father's neutral expression as he waited for her to solve the latest code puzzle that he posed. By the time she was ten, he no longer offered even the simplest clues. Not, "consider a dice cipher" (one of her first, where the letter was based on the number and orientation of the dice face) or "have you thought about the Playfair cipher" (with its missing letter and substitution matrix).

When she'd still been actively working on the *Kryptos* ciphers, she had prepared her mind by pretending her father still sat across from her and worked her way through the various types of ciphers he'd taught her from the simplest substitution system on up.

Today, having seen *Kryptos* without him beside her, all it did was make her sad.

Sam Chase might have thought his expression was neutral, but Miranda could now see the encouragement behind it. Could see how he had built her knowledge layer upon layer until she could simply see the solution to most basic ciphers and some of the intermediate ones. Until her mind was honed to the challenges of solving puzzles *of any type*.

It hadn't served her well in school though.

She'd seen Terry Smits tinkering with a Rubik's Cube. She should never have said that it looked simple, and certainly should never have proven that it was when he'd tossed it to her. It had been her first insight into three-dimensional coding sequences. Apparently solving it so quickly in front of his friends had been particularly upsetting. The bruise she'd sustained after being shoved hard into a locker had developed an intriguing tessellation.

That was but the first of a dozen examples before she finally learned to keep herself to herself.

Was that the trick to *Kryptos'* fourth panel? Could it be segmented into a multi-dimensional matrix? Fourteen rows. The first of thirty-two characters, the next twelve of thirty-one characters and the last of either twenty-nine characters or thirty with a leading space. Possible index rows of—

The general's phone rang too loudly to focus.

She pulled out her small personal code-reference notebook and added the concept to make sure that she didn't forget it.

The general set the phone to speaker.

"This is Harrington."

"Why did you code-word classify a plane wreck?" General Nason's snarl reminded her of Terry's when she'd tried to explain how she'd solved his Rubik's Cube so fast. He'd snatched it away so hard he'd almost broken one of her fingers—she hadn't been able to hold a pen properly for days. That was before he'd shoved her into the locker.

General Harrington's silence was just as deep as Terry's had been, finally driving her out of both Chess Club and Math Club. She hadn't been much of a joiner since then. For reasons she didn't understand, he'd only become angrier when, for the first time in the three years since she'd joined it, neither club made it past the city-level competitions.

"Harrington," Nason stood, planted his fists on his desk, and glared at the phone as if Harrington could possibly see him. "Unless you want to be in charge of the depot rebuilding captured AK-47s in Libya, you'll give me the goddamn code word. *Now!*"

The silence stretched until it had a thinness that defied all physics in that it still included connection.

"Or would you prefer a court-martial for failure to follow a direct order from a superior officer?"

"You are not in the chain of command."

An astute observation, in Miranda's opinion. The Joint Chiefs of Staff, including the Chairman himself, were actually forbidden by law from direct command. They might be the highest-ranking officers in the military, but their roles were strictly advisory.

"You doubt my ability to ram that last statement down your throat until you choke on it?"

"No sir." Harrington did not sound pleased to Miranda's ear.

"Well?" The next pause was equally long.

"I don't recall it, sir." Holly had been right after all; General Harrington had made it up on the spot.

"Security so effective that even you aren't cleared for it," General Nason almost smiled at that. "Well there's a woman sitting here in my office who obviously has a memory far superior to yours. Perhaps I'll put *her* in your job."

"That NTSB bitch couldn't—"

General Nason cut the connection, then rocked back in

his chair and looked at her over steepled fingers. "He doesn't seem to like you much."

"No, he doesn't." But Miranda already knew that. Another man who relished stating the obvious. Perhaps it was a Y-chromosome trait.

31

THEY WERE NOW A HUNDRED FEET UP, BUT AS THE WRECK WAS dead astern, there wasn't much to see. Mike kept watching the desert intently, wishing his arm would stop throbbing where Holly had punched it.

She was clearly superior physically, so he couldn't get his revenge that way—besides, that wasn't his way, it was hers. He'd think up some other devious trick...later.

For now, he was appreciating her suspicious mind. Being cleared off the crash site with no notice had turned to careful silence, slipping a backup of their data into her boot heel, and now watching behind.

If he knew what he was watching for...

Would he recognize a wargame if he saw one?

But Holly had been suspicious about that, too. If it wasn't a wargame...

He spotted a single plane racing in from the east. It was moving fast and low and would cross close behind them.

He tapped Holly on the thigh in warning—hoping she

wouldn't kill him for presuming—not daring to look away so that he wouldn't lose sight of it. Mike suspected that a wargame wouldn't have a single jet off on its own.

For half a second, her vest full of tools was jabbing into his back as she leaned against him.

"Speed!" Holly shouted loudly enough to blow out his eardrum. "We need more speed!"

The helicopter nosed down and leapt forward.

The jet disappeared behind them. And Holly was gone to look out her side window.

He swung over as well, until he was pressed up against her back. He had a notebook and a small pocket recorder, but that was it. No prickly vengeance would be his.

The jet reappeared from behind her side of the helicopter and moved away. He'd never seen anything go so fast.

"Hang on!" Holly shouted again.

He wished she'd cut that out. They all sat within an arm's length of each other.

A shock wave slammed into them, hard, accompanied by a massive boom even louder than the turbine engine.

The helicopter lurched, as if it had tripped on something in the empty sky.

"Sonic boom," Holly called out. "Now comes the kicker."

"The wha—" Was all the chance he had to get out before there was another blast. This one slammed into them both sonically and physically.

The helicopter seemed to lurch forward for a moment... then stop dead.

It dropped like a lead weight.

As the pilot wrestled to regain control of the aircraft—

which had an alarming number of buzzers and red lights going off—Mike wondered what his last thought would be. He'd rather not have a replay of his life if he had a choice.

Whatever his final thoughts before death were, he didn't have a chance to think about them.

As the helicopter struggled to survive, it twisted sideways.

Past Holly's shoulder, he had a clear view of something that looked right out of a war movie. A roiling cloud of superheated orange and yellow below, with a vast double cloud of smoke above like a pair of massive gray chrysanthemums. It bloomed exactly where they'd spent the last two days.

The next instant he was looking up at the sky.

He looked out his own window—straight into the fast-approaching surface of the Nevada desert.

32

"So it seems that you are the sole keeper of the classified code word on this project."

Miranda wasn't, but she was the team's IIC. Being in charge meant not exposing your team to undue distractions. Holly Harper had also heard the code word and Miranda had no doubts regarding her memory.

Knowing that General Harrington had made it up on the spot, and then forgotten it in the uncontrolled heat of his anger, didn't invalidate its existence. Or perhaps it did.

She rose to walk about the office. Movement was conducive to thought processes involving ciphers and perhaps would be in resolving this particular conundrum. Much of his office was filled with various maps. Some made sense to his current position: central America, Eastern Africa and across the Arabian states, Southwest Asia, and much of Russia's border shared with its former Soviet state protectorates.

Close by the general's desk was a collection of photos that had her circling the large desk.

They were career officer photos.

"Grenada was my first operation back in '83," General Nason rose to stand beside her. "That's me, the cocksure lieutenant who thought he knew some shit." Even then he'd stood out for his lean height, towering several inches over the other members of his squad gathered close in front of a helicopter.

"It's the year I was born."

"Whole lot of miles behind both of us, Ms. Chase."

She looked through the photos.

"My last field op," he tapped the photo of him standing with a team in front of a small UAV drone with a flat nose but the distinctive downward v-tail and rear propeller of the MQ-1 Predator. "Operation Joint Guard in Bosnia. It was '95, I think."

"It was 1996, the month after my parents were killed in TWA 800."

"Sorry, I didn't know that. Though I remember the 747 going down. A whole class of French students went down with that, didn't they?"

"Sixteen students and five adult chaperones. My parents were not part of that."

"Why were they aboard?"

"They were vacationing in France. I was supposed to join them the next week. If only I'd been with them."

"Then you'd be dead."

"That's been pointed out to me. Perhaps if they'd waited until my horse camp was over, but they said they couldn't wait."

"Did they have business over there?"

Miranda could only blink at him in surprise. She'd never questioned *why* they couldn't wait for her. They had left for France and died en route. Never asking the next logical question of why was...confusing. She considered calling Tante Daniels right now, but she suspected that it would be rude and decided against it.

The general harrumphed at her silence. "We were a joint Air Force, Army, CIA team flying the GNAT 750 from Albania, the predecessor to the Predator UAV that offered us satellite control."

"All created from the mind of Abraham Karem, the father of the UAV. He started with the Albatross, then Amber." Miranda felt as if she'd just tripped and fallen.

"What is it?"

Miranda tried to think how to unsay the word she'd just said, but it was now out there. For a moment she imagined being able to gobble up her words once they were spoken and was suddenly transported back to the childhood book *The Phantom Tollbooth* where that was possible. Her mother had given it to her to read at camp. She'd finished it the same night that Tante Daniels had come to tell her the bad news in person. The last book of her childhood.

She could no longer eat her own words—at least not literally.

"What about the Amber?" The general's eyes were slowly narrowing until he was squinting at her.

She squinted back, but all it did was shadow his features with a blurred focus on her eyelashes.

"Ms. Chase?"

"Amber," she managed, picturing the early Unmanned

Aerial Vehicle, "is also a very interesting word." Not *Jurassic Park* at all. Holly would be disappointed to learn that.

"As in a classified code word."

Miranda knew she was no good at hiding such things and sighed. Then gave it one more try, ignoring General Nason's smile, "It is the first full-sized surveillance UAV with a high-reliability factor. In many ways the origin of the species."

"And a classified code word."

Resigned, she gave in. "And a classified code word."

"So tell me what's going on with that crash." The general looked smug as he returned to his chair and waved for her to sit once more across the desk from him.

"I can't, sir. You haven't yet given me the code word."

He actually laughed, "I could get to like you, Ms. Chase."

"You would be among the select few." Other than her mentor Terence and her aunt-in-all-but-blood, she wasn't sure if she actually had any friends.

"What can you tell me about the crash of the C-130 Hercules in the vicinity of Groom Lake that is code-word classified Amber?"

Miranda opened her mouth but the sharp ring of her phone cut her off.

33

"THEY BLEW IT UP."

"They nearly blew us up with it," Miranda could hear Mike call out in the background of Holly's call.

"Blew it up?"

General Nason jolted at her words and she switched her phone to speaker since he was, by whatever method, now cleared for this investigation.

"They sent in an F-35 Lightning II stealth fighter, supersonic, which was kind of cool, and blew the shit out of it. Based on the pressure shock wave around one psi that tumbled our helo, it was probably a pair of GBU-12 Paveway IIs, corroborated by the accuracy with which they struck. At least a thousand pounds of combined explosive and definitely guided in."

The general looked at her in puzzlement. "Hit what?"

"Our bleeding wreck. Weren't you paying attention? First Mike almost pissing himself because—"

"I didn't! Besides we were almost killed!" Mike shouted.

"But you screamed like a little girl. We all heard it, so don't try to change the story. And then getting the full frisk and pat down before they confiscated all our data at Creech," Holly continued.

"I went to Groom Lake and all I got was a rectal probe. I want a goddamn t-shirt that says that!" Mike was still fuming in the background.

"Who would do that?" Miranda couldn't imagine such a thing. Or couldn't have before her visit to the CIA earlier this afternoon.

"Who held a gun to our faces yesterday morning? I'll give you two guesses but neither one was me." Holly sounded completely calm, but with no sense of humor. She was in some strange soldier-efficient mode unfamiliar to Miranda.

The general narrowed his eyes at Miranda in what now appeared to be a question.

"Harrington," she suggested.

He shifted from narrowed eyes to narrowed eyes with a furrowed brow that might just be fury once more. At least she'd guessed right on the question part of his look.

"Don't forget your desk drawer."

"What was that?" He and Holly said in unison.

Then the general looked down to his side and slapped the drawer shut with a curse.

"Who confiscated your data?"

"Depends," Holly answered the general. "Who am I talking to?"

"This is Chairman of the Joint Chiefs of Staff General Drake Nason."

"CJCSGDN," Miranda added to help Holly make the connection.

"Oh, the chap who signed the orders that almost got us shot a second time."

"They *what?*" the general-in-question's face suffused with red.

"Catch a clue, mate. Miranda, I know that you're the Investigator in Charge and all, but you really need to find someone quicker on the uptake. No offense, General." The Holly she knew was now back in place, enjoying an excuse to tease the highest-ranking officer in the US military.

"It was seriously cool," Jeremy chimed in. "Primary buffet from the sonic boom, then the pounder from the double blast off the two bombs. I bet we weren't a thousand feet out. Pilot hit the desert hard enough to bend a skid, but he didn't bust a blade. Awesome flight. I've *got* to learn how to fly a helicopter."

Nason punched his phone. "Get me Harrington again."

"Why would I get him for you? We just got away from his people. Miranda, I got your messages. We decided not to wait and cleared out. We're en route to Vegas by car. You want us in DC?"

She glanced at the general yelling into the phone for someone to find him Harrington and then thought of the CIA who'd been waiting at the airport for her.

"Yes," she picked up her phone and texted a quick message as she spoke. "That would be good. Why don't you meet me here in DC at NTSB headquarters?" Better not to say some things aloud.

"Roger that." She heard Holly's phone ping with a completely different set of instructions. "Got your message loud and clear."

A message pinged back in from Holly. *We saved the data and photos, no samples, but not sure if any of it has meaning.*

"Good," Miranda answered aloud. "I'll catch up with you when you arrive."

"Roger and out." The call ended from Holly's end.

The CIA, seeing *Kryptos*, and now this. They were like secret agents together. Maybe her team (God, she actually had a team?) needed to get matching hats or something.

Nason punched his phone to speaker. "What do you mean you didn't order the flight?"

"I mean that I didn't order the flight," General Harrington answered back.

"Then who the hell flew an F-35 Lightning II within ten klicks of Groom Lake and blew up my plane crash site?"

"Are you sure someone blew up the plane? It was just a wreck, why would anyone do that?"

Miranda could see General Nason was once again rising to his feet. This time, not only were his bunched fists planted firmly on either side of his phone, but his face remained suffused with red.

Was fury an opportunity? The concept had worked once, when she'd managed to get the upper hand with an aged Sikorsky compass dial that General Harrington had inadvertently stepped on.

Before the Chairman of the Joint Chiefs could explode with rage or hang up his phone, Miranda leaned in with her question.

"Perhaps the same person who removed the flight recorders from the crash prior to my arrival, General Harrington?"

"No. That was me. But I didn't order the bombing."

"There were flight recorders on that flight?" Nason snarled. Like a dog, an actual snarl.

"Cockpit and data," Harrington replied after a long hesitation.

"And they were removed?"

"Yes sir." A little faster, like he was finally giving in.

"Well at least he's answering my questions now," the Chairman muttered to her. "Where are they?" he asked aloud.

"It was a single combined unit."

"We call it CVDR—Cockpit Voice and Data Recorder," Miranda explained for General Nason's benefit. "Occasionally an FVDR—Flight Voice and Data Recorder."

"I can't begin to tell you how little I care about that. Where the hell is *it?*"

"It was returned to the crash site, sir. I fear it would have been destroyed in the bombing if that actually occurred."

Holly hadn't mentioned finding a recorder, so it probably was gone. At least that explained why they hadn't been able to find it the prior day.

"Did you listen to them? Did anyone listen to them?" General Nason's voice had turned low and dangerous just as Harrington's had yesterday when she photographed the wreck. Perhaps it was a good thing that Nason didn't have a sidearm at the moment even if Harrington was so far away.

"No sir. They were locked securely in my safe from shortly after the crash until I returned them to the site this morning."

"And the bombing. You don't know if a crash that was your responsibility was bombed within ten kilometers of an airbase that is also your responsibility?" Nason roared.

"It's been a busy day, sir."

"Well get your ass unbusy, get out to that site personally, and see if by some miracle that recorder survived along with your career, or if they both just went to hell! And find out who ordered that damn plane. Start with how it got cleared through NTTR airspace. I expect a full report every thirty minutes until this is resolved."

It was an impressive statement of engineering that General Nason didn't destroy the phone with how hard he cut off the connection.

34

GENERAL ZHANG RU SAT IN HIS PRIVATE OFFICE IN CHEN MEI-Li's apartment. It was one of the few places he could think without interference. He'd even given the girl a thousand yuan to go out—shopping or a movie with girlfriends or whatever girls her age did in the mornings.

Here there was no swarm of investigators pursuing irrelevant and inconsequential information about what had happened to the valuable asset of the Shenyang J-31.

Also no scapegoat hunter asking what had his nephew done wrong. Thankfully, he'd had a substitute personnel file already prepared for Wang Fan. It now reflected that he had recused himself from any promotion decisions concerning the boy from the very beginning.

Even so, the brush with the CDI gave him chills. Thankfully he'd managed to focus the Commission for Discipline Investigation on three-star General Liu Huan, not so much the "fortunate destroyer" as his name had promised. His record of service had already been erased as thoroughly as every other sign of his existence in the Army Air Force. Good! He'd never liked Huan, and no one was better placed for the promotion to replace Huan than himself.

But to cement it, he must understand what had happened to his plane.

If he could be the one to unravel the solution, then he would become untouchable and his climb toward a seat on the Central Military Commission come one step closer. And when he finally achieved that, he could *order* the CDI investigations rather than nearly falling to one.

For the hundredth time, he ran the telemetry and satellite images he had smuggled off the base. At first he'd done it for what he feared they'd reveal—by taking them off base, he could study them even as he prepared to run.

When flight had proven unnecessary, he studied them in hopes of understanding, but no grand illumination shone from the heavens like the Buddhists promised. The girl had latched onto the current cultural permissiveness and several Buddhist icons and images had appeared in her apartment. If she wanted to claim that meditation and studying tantric yoga were the secrets to her prowess in bed, he certainly wouldn't be reporting her.

He'd seen the tapes of the flight so many times that he could feel each motion. His nephew *had* been a highly skilled pilot. His escalating series of maneuvers during the first portion of the flight were very good—unimaginative, but so precise that they could still stir his own desire to climb back in a cockpit and pit himself against the air and the g-forces once again.

But what Wang Fan had achieved in the final minutes of his flight had been nearly miraculous.

At first it had appeared to be chaos.

But the more Ru watched the images as the boy dodged in and out of view among the mountain peaks before his final disappearance, the more Ru became convinced that every movement was deliberate.

There!

No failure of the jet that he could conceive would cause a barrel-roll to snap into a flat-spin and recover with a broken loop. It was more as if Hēidì, the Black Dragon God of Winter, had been chasing his nephew across the sky. Could even the Black Dragon drive Wang Fan to such perfection in flight?

The girl had hinted at Wang Fan's fears about the final day's flight before breaking down in tears while she curled up in his lap. What if Fan's fears hadn't been about the Shenyang J-31 as his words to the girl had implied, but instead been about some imagined meeting with an invisible god? There had been no doubting the girl's sincerity—she'd been nearly broken by Wang Fan's death.

Had a madness descended over his nephew as the analysts had surmised?

If so, it was a madness with an intense brilliance.

Again Ru watched the flight tapes on the screen. But what if Fan's mind hadn't collapsed? What if this was the flight of a pilot discovering his true mastery as his final act?

The g-forces of the loop seemed to drive Ru through the bottom of the chair. The barrel roll slammed his ribcage painfully into the arm before he almost knocked his chair over backward with the weightlessness at the top of an

Immelmann loop—entering fast at the bottom and climbing, past straight up, until flying upside down.

But Fan hadn't corrected by rolling right-side up. Instead, he'd cross-controlled so sharply into a vicious, and notoriously hazardous, inverted flat spin that Ru's bones ached in empathy. Eight *g*'s pulling out of the flat spin before disappearing for six achingly long seconds deep into the chasm cut by the Dadu River.

Each time he watched; Ru was unable to breathe until...

The gyrfalcon jet reappeared under full afterburners, punching straight up into the sky, driving all the blood from his head down into one of the most powerful arousals Ru had ever had.

He heard the girl come in through the front door of the apartment and tentatively call his name.

"In here. Come."

She looked in at the door tentatively. She was never invited into this room; he had the only key to this office and kept it locked at all times. It had little more than a desk, a chair, a computer, and the quiet in which to think. The girl would have called it Zen or something. There were few secrets here, but he didn't want her prettying it up as she seemed to so enjoy doing to the rest of the apartment.

"Here. Now!" Ru managed to bark it out against his desperate need.

"I brought you a gift," she began reaching into one of her bags.

"Later!" He undid his pants and lifted himself enough from the chair to shove them down. "Now!" He couldn't even recall her name through the haze that surrounded him.

When she was close enough, he snagged her wrist and

dragged her to her knees. A fistful of hair, so thick and lush, and she had her mouth upon him.

He watched the screen as she did her work.

From the desperate climb, a full-throttle plunge back down to the mountains. The girl's sharp teeth and wise tongue followed every beat of his racing pulse as he rode the jet with his nephew, down, down toward the waiting earth.

"Did you do this for him?" He didn't release her enough that she could speak; instead he felt her nod as he watched his nephew perform a triple barrel roll with such force that it was amazing the wings didn't snap and fly away on their own.

"Good. More! Harder! More than you did for him." He steered her with her hair just as his nephew had steered the jet, slaloming deeper into the mountains until Ru actually believed the Black Dragon just might have been after Fan in truth—could feel the dragon watching over his own shoulder.

A final satellite image. A final flicker of shadow and light.

Then Wang Fan and the Shenyang J-31 were gone. Gone to whatever fate had awaited him in the mountains, out of sight of satellites and sensors. A fate from which he'd never returned.

Ru let the release hammer through him. His body wasn't so old that it had forgotten how it felt to fly. The girl was worth every yuan he'd paid for her: the apartment, her allowance, using her as a tool to control Wang Fan and others—all of it. He kept her pinned there until the very last of the flight had drained from him and he once again sat in the chair in his private office.

The best analysts in the PLAAF had reviewed this tape

and been unable to tell him what had gone wrong with the plane.

What if nothing had?

And what if his nephew had really been as good a pilot as he'd been a lover? Ru held no illusions that the girl would ever cry over his own death, yet she'd wept over Fan's after a single night together.

Ru had to find someone who could see past the failures they were expecting and find the actual solution. Was it worth using a great favor?

Perhaps it was. Perhaps it was.

He rubbed a soothing hand over the girl's hair, smoothing it back into place, down her back, as she continued to kneel in place and keep him warm with her soft breath and clever fingers.

35

"I HATE DENTIST'S CHAIRS," HARVEY GRUMBLED AS HE LAY
back in the control seat for the MQ-45 Casper UAV. It looked
disconcertingly like one...that had mated with a well-padded
Barcalounger.

Helen had never shown him a picture of her family. Did
her kids look like her? Did the same shy smile shine in their
intelligent eyes? Was their hair the same liquid brown of
flowing dark chocolate like hers, or did they take after their
father with his imagined Teutonic blond good looks and too
many teeth when he smiled?

"How do you feel about electric chairs?" Helen teased
him as the technician strapped him to the contraption:
ankles, wrists, and forehead.

"Never met one, but I'm wagering that I'd like it better
than a dentist's chair."

"The mighty pilot afraid of a little man with a drill. My
fantasy is ruined." It wasn't like Helen to tease him in front
of others.

A simulator was not a hundred-million-dollar bird of prey and he was so mortified that he might screw up and never get to fly again. But he'd never show that, so he gave her the laugh she'd earned.

The techs ran broad Velcro bands around his thighs as well.

"Hey!"

"The actual UAV connection is far more visceral than we can achieve in the simulator. We'd rather you didn't come back from your flight all black-and-blue."

He looked at the thick padding all around him and wondered just what he'd be putting his body through while he was aloft.

"Take it easy at first," she got serious—just a little too serious for him to joke that's how they'd started out making love earlier today. "We have a standby pilot at the manual console who can recover the craft from most circumstances. If you need to, just stop trying and he'll try to take over."

"Try." Harvey considered the word. He considered quoting Yoda from *Star Wars,* "Do or do not. There is no try." Instead he saw that the techs were busy checking readouts just out of earshot and offered her a hungry leer. "Try is *not* what I just did to you in your bed. I *do*—a hundred percent."

Her blush only served to confirm that he'd absolutely done a hundred percent for her.

"Tell your backup pilot to go home; I won't be needing him."

One of the techs returned and smeared a small patch of salve behind his right ear—a salve that he now knew would rapidly harden into a sticky glue. They pressed the pickup sensor into the glue and began running him through alignment tests.

"Up. Down. Left. Right. Level flight..." As they said each one, he pictured the accompanying sensations. Covering his eyes with soft pads, then blackout goggles, they soon moved to visual cues. As they calibrated the alignment of the patches both under and on top of his skin, the drone's visuals began coming online.

"Brightness. Focus. Near. Far. Look up. Look left..." A bright target had been carefully aligned exactly in front of the drone sitting in the hangar, just the other side of the thin wall beyond his feet. He was just finishing the calibration of the spectrum when an object as large as an unexpected moon shifted into his range of view. He shifted to the nearest focus he could, but it wasn't enough. Still, the outline was familiar. The curve of Helen's chin, blurry, but well known.

He reached out to touch her, but the restraints kept his hand in place. Instead, the drone jolted forward an uncertain foot as he twisted the front wheel and it dropped out of its chock. The image of Helen greeting him through the drone's camera jumped aside.

"Sorry." Some voice half remembered echoed back to him through the open hangar door. Then he blocked her out.

All that existed now was the drone. He could feel their connection through the patch behind his ear as if it was a hole. No, not a hole. The doc had it wrong: life didn't drain out through the connection. Nor was it pumped in. It was a wide-open conduit to a new world.

"Engine start," he thought of the heat in his gut and let the warmth build. A heads-up display of data screened across his optic nerves. Temperature rising in the engine. He could almost feel the last disconnections of fuel and electrical umbilicals.

The visual alignment target split in two down the middle when the hangar bay doors rolled aside to reveal the night.

There was so much data overlay that he could barely see the stars. It was like a night out in New York City: you knew the stars were there, but spotting more than a few dozen beyond the streetlights, restaurant neon, and towering apartment buildings was a rarity. Night had fallen over the Nevada desert and it was time to prowl.

36

MIRANDA JOLTED AWAKE. "WHERE AM I?"

"Exactly where you requested, ma'am."

She could only blink uncertainly. It was an inconspicuous house in the backwaters of Georgetown. It was familiar, even if how she came to be here wasn't.

General Nason had finally called a car for her. For hours they'd puzzled over what little she knew of the crash.

It wouldn't have taken nearly as long if he wasn't constantly interrupted by a whole series of calls and people coming in to discuss some global crisis she wasn't cleared for. Her legs ached from how often she'd had to rise and go to the outer office, only to be called back in minutes later.

She showed him the crash profile that she'd calculated and then, as he wasn't a flier, had to explain why it was so anomalous. At her request, he'd showed her the NRO images from the crash site again and again but she'd gained little more insight.

They had both studied the single image that included the stray flicker of unfocused light where none should be.

It had made no sense that it was present in neither the preceding nor following frame.

Only that one tiny flicker, then gone.

All she could compare it to was the Challenger Space Shuttle crash. Inconspicuous little puffs of smoke leaking past a frozen O-ring at launch—that fifty-seven seconds later became a massive flare that had shredded the shuttle.

In the visible-spectrum footage of the C-130's crash, there had been the tiniest flare of light, but what did it indicate? It had appeared well past the outer edge of the Hercules' wingtip and couldn't have originated from the plane.

She'd reiterated that they'd been shown too little—a surveillance area covered barely twice the size of the Hercules aircraft itself. "A KH-11's imaging capabilities wouldn't have been tracking just the plane, it would have been surveilling an area of a dozen square miles or more. We need the wider view, not just the tiny section they've given you."

Finally exhaustion had triumphed and she'd nearly fallen asleep with her head on the general's desk while he called the NRO for new images.

A car.

He'd had her escorted to a car to take her wherever she wanted to go.

She'd mumbled an address, this address, and passed out in the back seat.

Pulling herself together, she managed to climb out of the back seat with some semblance of dignity. The orderly handed her knapsack over, which almost took her to the ground. The porch light was on and she followed it like a plane following glide slope indicator lights on short final. Up the path beneath rose arbors, thick with leaves and buds but yet to show the first bloom. Terence's wife had always loved roses and had planted them shortly before she left him. Now they made great lush arches, each of which seemed to peel off a layer of her worries and exhaustion.

She raised the brass door knocker just as the door opened. Unable to release her grip soon enough, it pulled her stumbling forward. Terence caught her before she face-planted on the hall rug.

37

"COLONEL GRAY, WE REALLY MUST STOP MEETING LIKE THIS." Drake unintentionally punctuated it with a large yawn. "Syria is being a royal pain in the ass tonight." Regrettably, the C-130 crash wasn't the greatest of his worries at the moment—but it was close.

"Yes sir."

"I apologize for the hour, Gray."

She shrugged, "It's past midnight. Just the start to another fine day at the NRO. And apparently at the office of the CJCS." Her flicker of a smile offered a touch of commiseration and a surprising amount of humanity.

Drake decided that he could get to like her. He was so sick of the people who cowered before his desk or tried to curry favor. Gray was apparently simply herself.

He waved her to a seat and, somewhat to his surprise, she actually took it this time.

"Why are you here again and not some shift officer?"

"It's my duty to serve."

"Right. Now try answering the question."

She rubbed at her eyes for a moment, then sighed. "I'm head of the domestic imaging division, reporting directly to General Patrick."

"Which means you get the crap job of dealing with me at two in the morning."

"Yes sir."

Drake liked an officer who didn't pass on their responsibilities to subordinates. There was a respect for his office there that he really appreciated. "So, what do you have for me?"

Again, she handed over a slip of paper with a secure address.

"Same password?"

"Our system doesn't allow duplication of passwords."

Drake could only smile. "What's he calling me this time?"

Again, the sigh. "'Fuck you twice, asshole!' Sir. Including the exclamation point, only the entire second word capitalized."

If that bastard didn't control twenty percent of the US intelligence budget, Drake just might take him on. He still might.

He keyed in the password and the files opened. He dimmed the office lights and began running the clips.

"Movies at two a.m. Shouldn't we have popcorn?"

He appreciated the humor, but was too tired to do more than offer a brief smile in the dark.

He started with the visible-light view that had so interested the Chase woman.

It was such a wide area that it took him some time to

even find the doomed C-130 Hercules—identifiable by its blinking navigation lights. He lost it twice when he tried to zoom in.

"May I?"

"Why not? You're the imagery specialist in the room, after all. I'm just the lowly Chairman of the Joint Chiefs and don't know shit." Drake shoved the keyboard and mouse across the desk.

Gray made no comment. In moments, she had the C-130 centered and the invisible nighttime landscape sliding by, indicated only by the changing latitude and longitude readouts in the corner of the screen. There were no lights in the middle of the Nevada Test and Training Range other than at the few scattered airfields themselves.

She began zooming in.

"Not too close," he called out.

She stopped the zoom at about ten times the view he'd had before.

One moment the Hercules was dead center on the screen: red and green wingtip lights, white taillight, and red anti-collision beacon on top.

The next moment it was gone.

"Back up slowly, frame by frame." Wasn't that what Chase had done? Yes, it was.

As she scrolled backward in time, she reached the crash —all of the Hercules' lights blinking into being. The white tail and rear-side wingtip lights said he was looking almost directly down on the stern of the aircraft as it plunged nose-first into the ground.

"Continue going back."

Instant by instant, the alignment of the lights changed as

the plane spent the one-point-something seconds Chase had designated as its transition from flight to crash.

Just as it achieved regular flight in a way that he recognized from the zoomed-in images the NRO had released earlier, there was the tiniest flash of light off the tip of the wing.

"There. What's that?"

"What is what, sir?"

"Drop the sir, Gray. Name's Drake. Go forward one frame. There. I'm talking about that small flash off the port wing."

She zoomed in, but the faint smudge simply became a larger smudge.

"How did I miss that? It isn't there on the prior...or the following frame," she flickered some control back and forth with bright clicks of the keyboard.

"Maybe you all dismissed it as a stray signal. I didn't even see it until it was pointed out to me. That's why I wanted the wider area view."

But no matter what they did, neither of them could see how it impacted the wreck or what its point of origin was.

"What can we tell from the shape of the flare?"

"If that's what it is, sir, nothing. It doesn't fit any profile that I'm familiar with."

Drake was wishing he hadn't let Miranda Chase leave, even if she was out on her feet. "Go back one frame."

The flare disappeared.

"Zoom back." The plane grew smaller.

"More."

"Again." Nothing.

"Goddamn it, how far could it travel between frames?"

"That would be based upon the speed of whatever caused the flare. A railgun projectile that fires a round at two-point-four kilometers per second, about Mach 7, would travel approximately four hundred meters between image frames, but it would leave a hot streak of light behind as it burned the air around it. This image is broad enough to cover even that."

"Could it have come from the aircraft? No, Chase told me it wasn't."

"Who is Chase, sir?"

"Miranda Chase, NTSB. Clearly knows her aircraft."

"Implying we at the NRO don't. May I remind you that I started as a combat pilot, then spent fifteen years as a line officer specializing in tactics for the US Air Force before joining the NRO, sir."

"You can remind me all you want, but you've never met anyone like that NTSB woman. Stand down, Gray. I'm not impugning you. The woman probably couldn't command her way out of a paper sack, but she knows her planes bolt for bolt. She's also the one who spotted that damn flare or whatever the hell it is."

"Yes sir." She didn't sound happy about it and there was no expression to read as they sat in the dark.

Drake turned on the desk lamp, which had them both blinking like confused owls. He slouched in his chair, folded his hands over his belly, and inspected her.

"Fifteen years on the line?"

"Yes sir."

"If I recall, your boss spent less than two."

"He never was a line officer—never eligible for combat command. He flew as a RIO in an F-14 Tomcat, but didn't see any action either. He screwed up his knee in a motorcycle accident. Rumor is that it's even less glamorous than it sounds. Apparently he knocked over someone else's motorcycle, staggering out of a bar, and it landed on him. That's why he still limps."

"Radar Intercept Officer, a backseat driver. An NFO." Technically a "non-flying officer"—Radar Intercept Officers weren't pilots—but everyone knew the second definition of "no future occupation" so there was no need to say it aloud. NFO as much as meant the person wasn't qualified to do *any* job except their present one. Too injured to be a RIO, he'd played politics instead.

Gray's lips curved slightly, "Yes sir. A total NFO." He'd bet she had a good smile if she ever relaxed that ramrod spine of hers.

"Let me guess, he has a big F-14 poster by his desk."

"No sir," and then she did flash that smile and it was a shocker. "But he does have a two-foot-scale die-cast model of it right down to his name painted on the side. It even has its own accent spotlight."

They shared an easy laugh. "So he's not going to be of any help on this. Any other suggestions?"

"It would help, sir, if I knew why this crash was of such interest to you. I'm surprised that—"

"That it's receiving so much of my attention on a busy night like this," Drake sighed. He wished to hell it wasn't and he could only pray he was wrong about what had happened out there in the Nevada desert. And why.

38

MIRANDA LAY IN TERENCE'S GUEST BEDROOM BUT COULDN'T sleep no matter how badly she needed to. Being awake for two nights and three days should have knocked her out as well.

She and Terence usually got together when she came to Washington—which wasn't all that often. She did her best to work from the Seattle office when she had to report in at all. She mostly lived out in the field or on the family island in Washington State.

His wife had left him twenty years ago, before Miranda had even joined the NTSB, and he seemed to appreciate the company. She appreciated coming to a safe and familiar place whenever she was in DC.

The life of a top NTSB investigator, by its very nature, included a great deal of unpredictable travel that happened with no notice and continued for an unguessable duration. His wife had tolerated it until the kids were teens, then broken it off, hard.

Terence didn't speak about it much. He'd ended up with the house when she eventually settled in with a law professor at Howard University.

Miranda did her best to get home every night, and succeeded less than half the time. She knew Terence's schedule must have been the same—though he was doing more instruction than investigation now.

He'd be retiring soon, which she didn't like, but was staying in Washington, DC, to be near his kids: one in college, the other clerking to a US Senator. Terence said he was looking forward to being home.

Her own shortest assignment had been a nose-over loss-of-control event at the Tacoma Narrows Airport near the NTSB's West Coast office where she kept her own plane.

A two-seat Piper Tomahawk trainer had come in on a crosswind landing, missed the edge of the runway, and planted a wheel firmly in the muddy median after a typical Pacific Northwest rain dump. The plane had nosed over, bent the propeller, and flipped onto its back to perch balanced on its canopy and high T-tail.

She'd been headed home from work, but the runway had been closed while they tipped the plane enough to open the door and let the uninjured pilot out. By the time they had it flipped back over and towed to the service hangar, she'd already interviewed the pilot and the control tower operator. They both confirmed that he'd been properly notified of wind conditions.

Pilot error in failure to plan properly for reported crosswind.

The fact that a gentle breeze could easily brush the tiny plane aside had also been a factor, but not relevant as it was the only plane type the pilot had ever flown and he should have known better.

She'd only been an hour late in climbing into her jet for the ninety-mile flight home. The next shortest had been three days because they saved the simple ones for the newer IICs, something they'd never done with her. Her longest had taken months of work to resolve.

Over the years, Miranda's relationship with Terence had shifted from mentee / mentor to colleagues. A few years after she'd graduated, he'd offered her the guest bedroom. She supposed it meant they were friends—her only real one.

"Thinking mighty hard there, Mirrie." Terence knocked lightly on the door, then stepped into the room carrying a large mug of hot chocolate. He always kept the kind with marshmallows for her—the same mix her mom had always kept.

As he set it down on the nightstand, he tugged on a lock of her hair as if lightly ringing a bell pull. She must have slept some, because she hadn't noticed the arrival of daylight.

He'd called her Mirrie since the very first day at the NTSB. Back then he'd been an aged and wise forty-five to her twenty-two. She was the only female student of twenty there—fresh from her double masters at the University of Washington in materials and aerospace engineering with a bachelor's in mechanical engineering. She was also the only one he'd ever bestowed a nickname on.

"I've been thinking about my parents."

"Must be some bad juju going on if you're going back to that."

"For one of the most well-educated men I know, you

make a curious choice about when to regress to Jamaican roots your people left behind a century and a half ago."

"West African roots we left behind more like three centuries gone, girl, and we never really leave those behind. Just trying to tease you some."

Teasing as a form of endearment. Holly certainly teased Mike a great deal in the short time Miranda had known both of them, but they didn't appear to be endearing themselves much to each other. She dropped the subject.

"There's something going on with this crash that has me thinking about my parents a lot."

"Tell me about it."

"I can't. I shouldn't. They code-word classified the investigation, but not really."

"Huh," he sat on the foot of the bed. "That's a new one on me."

"Me too. I was hoping you knew what to do about that."

"Is that why you came to DC, to talk to me?"

"Yes. There's something about this crash that is upsetting a lot of people."

"Victims' families—"

"No. It's a military flight with only five aboard. I suppose with your clearance, and the general faking the code word, it doesn't really matter." She sipped at the hot cocoa and scorched her tongue just the right amount on a half-melted marshmallow. "A C-130 went down unusually hard in the NTTR."

"And the Air Force investigators called you in?"

"The Chairman of the Joint Chiefs of Staff. He's one of the upset ones." He'd pounded his desk enough times in frustration for her to be very sure of that.

"Whoa, Mirrie. That's way above this old boy's pay grade. That makes no sense."

Miranda sagged. She'd so hoped on Terence having some answers.

"Have a cause yet?"

She could only shake her head. "Nighttime crash. I have a flicker of light, perhaps a meter square and twenty meters away from the wingtip, from a satellite image. A flicker with no discernable radar or infrared signature."

Terence stared quietly out the window while he contemplated that. He always made her think of a preacher when he did that—suddenly so quiet and wise. She could always count on—

"Nope. Not a clue. Who else is hot under the collar on this besides the chairman?"

"The commander of Groom Lake and a division director at the CIA who had me kidnapped."

"Kidnapped?" He jolted to his feet, then looked down at her. "You okay?" His dark eyes were narrowed with worry. How many emotions were accompanied by narrowed eyes?

"They didn't use force. And I got to see *Kryptos*. You know how long I've wanted to do that. But I could never get permission to enter the CIA's grounds."

"Kidnapped? You had me on the phone and you didn't just say that? I'd have raised the cavalry." He looked upset enough that he might just have done such a thing.

"I was fine. Maybe 'escorted to a meeting against my will' would be more accurate. Though I did take some comfort in knowing that you'd be expecting me. I was able to depart at a time of my choosing. Though in retrospect, I'm surprised that my tactic worked. It might not have if the Army hadn't been waiting for me. They then took me to a meeting with Drake."

"You're on a first-name basis with the Chairman of the Joint Chiefs?"

"Yes. His request. He's the one who assigned me to this crash. I can handle the wreck myself. But there's something else going on about it and you know how bad I am at political things."

"Yep, you do suck at it." Again he gazed out the window. "Only been in the Nevada Test and Training Range once myself."

"It's my third."

"You always were hot shit." A phrase that she'd always meant to look up the etymology of because—the literal interpretation was so...unsavory.

She went on to describe the wrangling that had occurred over the wreck: the CIA, the CJCS, and now the bombing of the wreck.

"They blew up the wreck before your investigation was done."

"Yes, apparently by someone other than the Groom Lake commander who was in charge of it. He sounded quite surprised that it had happened."

"So, there were aliens on board and they wanted to destroy all of the evidence." Terence laughed aloud.

It was a good, deep sound, which made her feel much better.

"Mirrie," he was still chuckling. "You've got some serious problems."

"Is it a male trait to repeatedly state the obvious?"

"Don't be changing the subject, honey. You've got the CIA

and the Chairman of the Joint Chiefs both interested in this wreck. You have some unknown third party blowing shit up in the desert. Anything else I don't know about what's going on?"

"Don't forget your aliens."

Again that surprising burst of laughter. "That must have been a hell of a wreck."

"It had a very atypical final flight profile. Like a big hand had reached down and wiped it from the sky."

He harrumphed at that, then turned to her.

"My suggestion, Mirrie? Don't chase the what. You're the best there is at that, but that's not going to help you here. Follow the who; then you can figure out the why."

"I was never very good at the who."

"I know," he ran a soothing hand down her hair and over her back. He kissed her gently on top of her head. "I know, girl. It's okay. You'll figure it out."

39

HARVEY PUNCHED OVER THE CALIFORNIA COAST AT HARMONY. The town boasted eighteen people, a bankrupt dairy, and a chapel that belonged in Hobbiton far more than southern California. He'd grown up there.

They never found Dad after he went down in his F-14 off Honolulu. No ashes for him. Probably shark food.

Mom was there...her ashes as fertilizer in a rose garden, but not really counted as a resident anymore. He hadn't been back in twenty years.

Harvey waggled his wings in a wave anyway. Not that she'd have heard him pass by at sixty thousand feet running at Mach 0.99 anyway.

Once clear of the shore, he dropped and turned south. He didn't even need to think about it—his desires and the drone were one. The night sea rushed to greet him as he dove down to a mere hundred meters above the surface.

At Mach 2.1 supercruise, he raced by oil rigs and supertankers, container ships and cruise liners. He'd never appreciated the amount of sea traffic moving along the California coast until he had to be careful to keep at least two kilometers from any surface vessel.

The wingtip vortices spinning off behind him, like sideways tornados, could be as much hazard to surface vehicles as they were to other airplanes in flight. After his passage created them, they would sink through the air at a hundred meters a minute. As long as the circular wind currents he generated hit the water and dissipated before any surface vehicle could stumble into them, everything should be okay.

He watched astern as he dragged two glorious spirals of water along the surface behind him. Invisible in the night, to anything other than his carefully crafted radar, it was a thing of beauty.

A glance aloft revealed stars of the radiance that could only be seen through night vision.

Helen had tried to explain to him that flying the drone was very different from piloting a jet. But as a non-pilot, there was no way for her to explain it.

Harvey wasn't *flying* the drone.

Harvey *was* the drone.

It was the ultimate hand job: his slightest whim was answered by the UAV with unbelievable perfection.

Not a drone.

Definitely not a drone.

An unmanned aerial vehicle.

Except it wasn't unmanned because he was here, one with the aircraft, flying far more surely than some piece of meat in a chair back in Nevada. Or even than some piece of meat in an F-35 Lightning II's cockpit. All those brother pilots he'd so envied for their ability to fly were like mud on the ground.

This was a future.

Here he ruled the sky.

Holding a hundred meters above the sea, the horizon lay over thirty kilometers to either side. His "vision" included everything big enough to throw back a radar signature.

Off the US–Mexico border, mapped like a red line across his vision, the sea traffic dropped significantly. Now the main surface craft were the massive container ships bringing produce from Chile to the western US.

All the way down along Baja he saw nothing unusual. Along the coast to Colombia, he even swung the extra eight hundred miles down to Ecuador. Narco-subs hadn't been spotted that far south, but it didn't mean they weren't there. It turned out to be a waste of an extra half hour of his time.

But on his sweep north, he spotted a trio of very deep-sea fishing boats driving out to sea in a loose formation a few kilometers apart. On a whim, he spiraled upward, taking his time as he climbed to sixty thousand feet and watched them slide west. Three fishing boats headed to sea in the dead of night.

He imagined a plot of where their courses might converge, then began searching the area. It wasn't long before he spotted the anomaly—a straight line radar pattern with no vessel to make it.

Someone had told him that nature abhorred straight lines. Probably Old Man Tucker, who helped run the round-doored Harmony Wedding Chapel. Of course, he might have been talking about Harvey's mom, as single women in Harmony could be counted on two fingers. If he was, Harvey didn't want to know—imagining the old guy and his mom ever doing the dirty was far too weird.

The straight line below was a reflection from his radar. He made three passes over it and determined that it was actually below the surface of the water. It was the line of air bubbles from the diesel engine exhaust reflecting aloft the turbulence it was causing underwater.

"Well, isn't that convenient?"

"Isn't what convenient?"

Harvey almost stumbled in the air. He'd forgotten about how communication worked.

There was no radio—no need for it with a drone.

All he had to do was speak aloud and the operator sitting next to him at Groom Lake could respond immediately without any missed words or radio interference. They were just talking person-to-person two thousand miles away from the rest of his consciousness.

For a second it broke the illusion and he could feel the padded chair in the bunker and the pressure of the blackout goggles on his face. Suddenly the conduit of information through the contact behind his right ear ached. He reached up to rub it and felt the pressure of the arm straps as his beautiful UAV tumbled sharply.

He forced himself back down the conduit. Could feel himself moving up to the satellite in orbit and finally back down to the tumbling Casper. Almost viciously he grabbed control and righted the aircraft.

"Do *not* talk to me while I'm flying unless I specifically ask something."

He heard only silence in the Groom Lake bunker.

Good.

Damn, but the situation was convenient, even if he wasn't going to be explaining why out loud.

For half an hour, he circled and waited.

No other vessels in the area—they'd found a place far from the shipping lanes.

At some signal, the submarine surfaced just as the three deep-sea fishing boats arrived. According to Harvey's briefing, they would unload the submarine and then scuttle it in deep water. Throw away a four-million-dollar vessel after a single use of moving a billion dollars of cocaine. The three fishing boats would then return by three different routes to three different ports.

He tipped his nose over and pointed straight down at the clustered boats and submarine.

Just killing them was too easy.

He let the speed build in the silence of an unpowered dive.

At five thousand feet, he dumped a set of flares and began pulling up into a loop. The flares burst to life at a thousand feet and the boats were suddenly in a vast halo of light. In moments, they were firing weapons aloft at the drifting flares.

But he now had the Casper down at sea level, still silent, cruising at just below the speed of sound, in a sweeping arc around them. He imaged boat names, ports of call, and the faces of every man aboard.

They were firing nowhere near him and his speed was bleeding off. He was below six hundred miles an hour as he turned directly toward them.

A hundred meters before he passed over the group, he lit full afterburners and aimed his nose straight up. Forty-five thousand pounds of thrust punched straight down onto the gathered boats.

In the rearview, he could see that the three fishing boats were immediately capsized. He dumped an AGM-114 Hellfire set to fire astern and lased the submarine. Before the missile had time to accelerate to Mach 1.3, it impacted the sub.

It didn't even matter that it was a direct hit, the eighteen pounds of explosive would kill everyone in the water with just the blast shock.

But it *did* hit the submarine dead on. The warhead punched through the sub's Kevlar skin and detonated inside. Twenty meters of narco-sub and probably ten tons of cocaine unfolded like flower petals blown open from inside.

He wished he could shut off his hearing; the techs back at Groom Lake were applauding.

Harvey ignored them, spread his metaphorical wings, and went searching for another target.

MEL DAVIS TURNED HIS FORD F-150 PICKUP OFF SE Covington Sawyer Road onto 179th Ave SE just as his brother gutted out an off-key falsetto to match Carrie Underwood's high note. She was belting out *Cowboy Casanova* on KMPS radio.

Danny didn't get that she was singing about assholes-to-all-women like him, or maybe he did but didn't care. Thankfully his brother was a better aircraft mechanic than he was a man...or a singer. Besides, he was blood. Just no way was Mel going to be introducing him to any more eligible women—at least not ones that he or his wife ever wanted to be friends with again.

Left onto 179th, he reminded himself again to fix the small green-and-white Airport sign that was listing badly after the winter rains had softened the ground at the turn. Crest Airpark lay up the narrow one-lane that climbed to the airfield between the thick Douglas fir trees. They had to get an early start today; they had lessons scheduled, and the

Cessna 152 still needed an oil change before the flight. Then he needed to order parts for Erin's Piper—shit, he should have done that yesterday.

Clearly the DJ was having a "Danny retrospective" as he spun up Little Big Town's *Better Man,* even if all the wishing in the world wouldn't make Danny into one.

Up over the rise, Mel was halfway to the first hangar before he jolted the truck to a halt.

"What?" Danny broke off in mid A-just-a-little-flat about how he enjoyed talking down to women.

Mel could only stare out at the runway.

Parked close by the tall trees at the north end of the lone runway, not even pulled over onto the taxiway, was what had to be the biggest plane ever to land at Crest.

"Is that..." Mel just couldn't wrap his mind around what he was seeing.

"Isn't that one of those new fighter jets?"

"The F-35 Lightning II," some part of Mel's brain coughed up. He could see across the way that a couple of the folks who had houses along the far side of the airport were out in their yards. Despite it being just past sunrise, some were dressed for work, some in bathrobes. And Tom Jenks stood with his fists on his big hips, wearing nothing but a pair of tighty-whities that were a real eyesore on his bulbous frame. He looked like a Goodyear blimp with all that gray chest hair on display.

But that didn't change what was sitting in the middle of his runway. A hundred-million-dollar jet had been parked at his airport with the canopy popped open.

He drove over the grass verge, cut between Simon's Beech Bonanza and Tammy's Cessna 172 and pulled up close beside the jet. It wasn't all that much taller than his truck, so he eased up close beside the cockpit, then climbed out and into the bed of his pickup. It placed him high enough to see that the cockpit was unoccupied.

"Think the keys are still in it?" Danny was looking over his shoulder.

"No! Just...no!" Danny could drive women crazy and cost Mel friends, but no way was he letting his brother wreck a hundred million dollars of government fighter jet.

Besides, with his luck, Danny would drop a bomb or shoot half the airpark with some stealth machine gun.

"Who the fuck do I even call?"

41

"You really are hot shit, Mirrie."

Terence was no longer looking down at her. Instead, he was standing at the window peeking out between the curtains.

"It appears that there are people waiting for you."

"What people?"

"Wait for it..." He held up a finger as he watched someone out front, then swung his arm down just as there was a sharp knock on the front door downstairs. "Don't know who they are. Some in uniforms, some not so much. I don't think I have that kind of popularity."

The knock sounded again as Terence headed for the stairs.

Then her phone rang with a number she didn't recognize and a text message buzzed in before she could even answer it.

"Wait a minute! Just everyone stop!"

"I'll get the door. You better answer...something."

"But I'm not even dressed!" She tucked her sheet and blanket more tightly around her.

"You can answer a phone naked, you know. Text messages, too. Either way, better hustle along, girl. Doesn't seem like the day is going to do any more waiting for the queen to put in an appearance." He closed the door as he left.

The text was from Holly. *We're here.*

Miranda answered the call with a, "Hold a moment please." Then texted the six-digit code Holly would need.

She could hear voices downstairs as Terence dealt with whoever was at the door.

"Thanks for holding." Rote politeness had its purposes. "How can I help you?"

"I have a problem." General Drake Nason's voice sounded rough with exhaustion. "I think I found the jet that bombed your wreck."

"Oh." She wasn't sure what else she was supposed to say.

"It ended up in the Pacific Northwest."

"Oh?" That didn't seem likely. "At JBLM?" It was the only major military airfield in the area.

"Someplace called Crest Airpark."

"No. Really, where?"

"Crest Airpark," the general repeated as if he was enjoying himself.

"But..." She'd flown in there a couple of times. It was a tiny one-runway field tucked awkwardly in among tall trees in the hills above Kent, Washington. A training field for beginner pilots and a convenient countryside strip for people to keep their private planes or take private lessons. "So you have the pilot."

"Nope. It was a dead-stick landing. Means no power."

"I know what it means."

"Oh, of course you do. No power, gliding in. Takes a really exceptional pilot to do that in an F-35 Lightning II."

The voices downstairs were becoming rather heated and Miranda was still naked.

"Why is someone downstairs? Are they your people?"

"Downstairs? No. I don't even know where you went last night."

"Well, someone is here," she scooted over to the window and peeked out, misjudging the flexibility of the curtain material and momentarily revealing a bare breast to the people looking up at her. She spotted one man's wide grin before she let the material drop back into place. "Four Chevy Suburbans. Two police cars. And a lot of people in dark suits."

"What the hell?" General Nason didn't sound happy at all. "Delay as long as you can. I'll try to get people there. Give me the address." As soon as she did, he was gone.

Heavy footsteps on the stairs.

She scooped up her clothes and knapsack, then retreated to the bathroom and locked the door.

There was a knock on the door, "Ms. Chase. I've been asked to escort you to a meeting."

She yanked on her underwear as she scanned her options. She flushed the toilet in between yanking up her slacks and lacing her boots. She was still naked from the waist up, but that seemed to buy her a moment.

Her options, other than flushing the toilet again, were quite limited but they did include a window.

Opening it, she looked down into Terence's small back

garden where they sometimes shared a quiet dinner beneath the blooming magnolia. To the side was a lip of the roof.

The pounding renewed and quickly became more insistent.

With a moment of inspiration, she dropped a towel and one of her t-shirts out the window before pulling on another one. They fluttered down to land on one of the patio chairs and the wrought iron table.

Swinging out the window, she placed a foot on the roof's edge. By clutching onto the corner trim, she eased onto the shingles and managed to edge her way up the steep slope until she'd reached the peak.

There was a crashing sound of the bathroom door being broken open. Didn't people understand the purpose of the little hole in bathroom doorknobs? All it took was sticking a slender object into the hole to unlock the door.

The man fell for the ruse and shouted out that she'd jumped out the back window. People began running around the house. Except this was Georgetown and yards were very private. Someone climbed over a gate, the next person kicked it down.

She edged up to the peak and looked down at the street out front just in time to see a SWAT team truck roll up.

Her phone rang again. She answered it quickly, but every face turned to look up at her.

"*What?*" She didn't even look at who had called and ruined her ploy.

"Transport is almost there." It was the general. "They'll deliver you to the Pentagon."

"What about these other people? There's a newly arrived SWAT team as well."

"Apparently the CIA has declared you as a suspect in a terrorist bombing incident and enlisted local forces to capture you. Anything you want to be telling me?" He offered a chuckle that was wholly inappropriate for the moment.

The police had weapons aimed up at her as did members of the CIA—because she assumed that's what the men in black suits were. The ones streaming out of the SWAT van were heavily armed and armored.

Someone grabbed her ankle. She tightened her grip on the roof's peak and kicked out instinctively. She contacted with something.

A male voice cried out and he released her ankle.

She turned in time to see a man with blood gushing from his nose sliding toward the edge of the roof. Before she could so much as call out a warning, he was over the edge.

He stopped himself for a moment by grabbing the rain gutter. She could see by the flexion of the material that Terence had stout steel gutters rather than the aluminum ones.

For a moment, the man's white-knuckled grip remained in view.

Then the gutter itself separated from the edge of the roof. The man cursed as his knuckles disappeared from view, then a grunt as he landed in the back yard. The CIA now owed Terence a new gutter.

When she peeked back over the rooftop, she saw that the SWAT team had a sniper perched behind his van; his long rifle zeroed so exactly on her face that she imagined she could see her own reflection in the end of the scope.

"Still with me, Miranda?" She'd forgotten about the general on the phone.

"There's a sniper out there. And the SWAT team is now racing into my friend's house."

"I hope your friend relocked his front door when he closed it."

"You *what?*" Even as she protested, she saw the SWAT team scatter across the front yard and duck for cover. There was a hard explosion as they blew up Terence's front door.

"Look to your left."

Down the street, Miranda could see a television van slewed across the street. A cameraman and a reporter were squatting in the open doorway clearly filming her.

"So my demise is to be on national television."

"I'd suggest that you wave, but I can see you need your free hand to stay on the roof. It's making some great footage, by the way."

Miranda didn't like her current perch even one-handed, but she had to hold the phone somehow.

"They're presently reporting about the police and CIA invading Georgetown. Right now the reporter is announcing that they are attacking two unarmed and highly respected NTSB officers. Oh, here comes the best part," Drake was practically chortling, which sounded odd coming from a grown general.

Miranda, perched on a rooftop in the center of Georgetown, tried not to feel self-conscious that everyone was looking at her. Then she glanced at the big camera and ducked lower behind the roof edge. *Everyone!*

"Apparently a General Patrick," the general continued happily, "he's the director of the NRO by the way and a complete jerk, has targeted the two of you in a personal vendetta, thereby dangerously exposing your top secret-classified investigation for the highest levels of government —unnamed, but that's me. It is so surprising that such information leaked in this day and age when secrets are so well kept."

Was that sarcasm? It was one of her weakest areas. It sounded like Terence when he was teasing her so she'd assume that's what it was.

"It seems that someone gave the local station an anonymous insider tip, which also might have been me but I'm not telling, that the raid is based on bad information illegally obtained and released by the aforementioned General Patrick with neither proper vetting nor due process. He's going to be in a world of hurt before the day is out. Now look to your right."

She spotted four black dots that rapidly resolved into helicopters racing in her direction. They were painted dark green with gold tops.

"Just a little QRF—that's Quick Reaction Force to you—that we keep handy. The US Army's 12th Aviation Battalion are tasked to evacuate senior political personnel in the event of a terrorist attack on DC, but I improvised."

She could barely hear him over the roar of the slowing helicopters.

"Though you seem to enjoy semantics and as you are a significant intelligence source in an on-going investigation, who is falsely accused of being a terrorist, I think my use of the QRF is justified."

Three of the helicopters slewed to a hover high above the tree-lined street. Right at eye level from her position atop the roof, she could see the pilots and the gunners who sat directly behind them. Their massive, six-barreled Gatling machine guns looked so close she felt she could reach out and touch them, but they were aimed down at the startled people in the street—even the SWAT team appeared to be paralyzed in their surprise. Ropes were kicked out either side of the hovering helicopters and Army Rangers began sliding down the ropes.

"I remanded a Ranger squadron to the 12th for this action. This really looks great on TV; I should have taped it for you. Though I'm sure it will be on the news for days. Tree-lined street. Just a block from the Speaker of the House's home. You know the guys love a chance to do this kind of thing. If there's an investigation, I'll claim that it was a readiness training exercise. But I don't see any problems." The general was enjoying the situation far too much in her opinion.

He might be right about their enjoyment, but they were very effective at what they did. The Army Rangers were brandishing weapons and subduing the teams that had attacked Terence's house with the casual ease of long practice.

Less than thirty seconds after their arrival, everyone was lying on the ground, including the SWAT team.

A black sedan tried to drive away, but the Rangers shot out its tires almost casually.

It tried to drive away on its rims.

Someone pumped a few rounds into the engine.

It lurched to a stop close in front of the news van and a burst of steam came out around the edges of the hood.

A fourth helicopter came to hover beside her, moving in

until it was almost resting on the other side of the roof's peak, just a foot from her fingertips.

The copilot opened his door, but didn't raise the visor that hid most of his face as he looked down at her. "Ms. Chase?"

"Yes?" She managed to shout.

"General Nason asks if you'd care to join him?"

"Say yes," the phone still by her ear advised.

"What about my friend?"

"The Rangers already have him safe. Now say yes."

"Yes," she echoed, then the copilot waved her to open the back door and climb aboard.

As the big green-and-gold Black Hawk helicopter moved away from the roof and turned for the Pentagon, Miranda could see the Rangers pulling the driver from the broken sedan. Then they yanked a passenger out of the back seat.

A tall woman with long blonde hair in a disordered ponytail glared up at her.

Clarissa looked beyond furious as the camera and reporter moved in for a close-up.

42

"WHAT THE HELL?" MIKE LOOKED AROUND THE SNUG HANGAR at the end of the totally Podunk-nowhere Tacoma Narrows Airport and wished he was anywhere else. "Why did Miranda send us here?"

Though it was definitely the right place, as the code she'd sent with no explanation had unlocked the door.

The sunrise sent a narrow beam of blinding light through the cracked-open outer door. Dust motes danced in the air, and not much else. The hangar was immaculately clean and just big enough for two planes: a sweet Mooney M20V Ultra—the fastest single-engine light plane out there —and a small jet plane made of shiny aluminum that he didn't recognize.

There was a small work area and two old couches.

"She sent us here because no one in their right mind would look for us here. Can't imagine anyone choosing to bomb this place." Holly's observation sent a shiver up his spine. He'd never come so close to death as that tumbling descent of the helicopter in the explosion's wake.

"Will you look at that?" Jeremy sounded like he always did, delighted past all human possibility. He had rushed over to the shiny aluminum jet and looked at it as if he was going to drop to his knees and start to pray.

"What's the big deal? Looks like it belongs in a museum. Maybe in a *History of Flight* display." He looked at Holly, who for once didn't have the answers to everything that happened under the sun.

"It does, that's what so amazing about it. Don't you recognize it?" Jeremy didn't wait for an answer. "It's a Canadair CL-13. In the US it was called the F-86 Sabrejet. It's the single most produced military jet in history. Between the US and Canada, they built almost ten thousand of them for the Korean and early Vietnam Wars. Why it even...oh!" Jeremy sounded like he'd just died and gone to heaven.

"What?" He and Holly said in unison.

It really didn't look like much. It was all rounded where modern fighter jets were angular. The skin was bright aluminum rather than gray or black, and instead of a nose cone, it just had the hole like a hungry maw for an air intake. The rear had a single exhaust port. It had swept-back wings and one of those bubble canopies. It wasn't even very big, not much longer than the Chevy Suburban Holly had rented to drive them down from SeaTac airport—apparently such mundane things as a comfortable sedan weren't proper for "normal folks with half a brain."

"Guess!" Jeremy turned to face them.

"It came as a prize in a Cracker Jack box?"

"No. What are those?"

Holly clearly didn't know either.

"Oh my god, I'm surrounded by heathens!"

"In 1952," Jeremy couldn't help himself and answered the question he himself had asked, "Jacqueline Cochran became the first woman to break the sound barrier. She did it in a Canadair Mark 3, which had been modified specifically for her and was the only one of its kind. Her wingman for the tests was Chuck Yeager. You do know that he was the guy who broke the sound barrier first ever, right? This plane," he patted it like it was a puppy dog, "is the Mark 5! It's the closest production plane there is to the one Jackie Cochran flew."

"Which means?"

"Which means that this has to be Miranda Chase's own personal jet. Jackie Cochran was the most accomplished female pilot of her day—actually, I guess she still is. She holds a ton of records that no one has broken yet. She was even in the first female astronaut program, which she helped organize—not that NASA would accept them even though they passed the same rigorous tests as the Mercury guys."

"And that makes Miranda..."

"Too cool for words!" Jeremy sighed happily before disappearing behind it to inspect the plane further.

"You know what I need?" Mike turned to Holly.

"What?"

"A drink."

"I need breakfast."

"The two aren't mutually exclusive; a bloody Mary sounds pretty good right now. Where the hell are we? Tacoma, Washington? Do you even know what's near Tacoma, Washington?"

"Actually I do," Holly stepped into the slice of sunlight, which made her appear to glow.

"Well, what?" Mike couldn't help asking when she didn't continue.

"Seattle-Tacoma airport, the busiest civilian field in the Pacific Northwest. JBLM, Joint Base Lewis-McChord, one of the largest military fields in the country and top ten in both area and personnel of all US military bases. Three airports —Boeing Field, Renton, and Paine Field not far north—are where all of the Boeing airplanes are built and tested. Plus a half dozen municipal fields like this one. And the NTSB office for all of the western US is just across town."

"I'm from New Jersey." (Because Mike was never admitting to his SoCal childhood).

He considered. The Denver office covered everything from Colorado to Ohio and Minnesota to Louisiana. The West Coast office covered Washington to California and Montana to...

"Does that include Hawaii?"

"It does. And don't even think it, mate."

"If you hadn't said anything, I wouldn't have." Though Holly Harper in a bikini *would* be an amazing sight. But he'd been thinking about assignments to the lush pickings of Santa Monica, Waikiki, and Sun Valley, Idaho, ski bunnies. "Do you ski?"

Holly simply scoffed at him.

"Shouldn't we be going to the NTSB offices?"

"Miranda said to come here."

"Oh, hey!" Jeremy called out at some new discovery. "This is majorly serious."

They moved over to join him. The cupboards around the

small workbench opened to reveal a whole array of very high-tech equipment.

"Miranda Chase is so *awesome!* I thought we were going to have to wait to get to DC for this. Guess not." He hauled over his equipment bag and began emptying it on the other end of the bench. Meters, saws, measuring instruments from micrometers to hundred-foot tapes, laser levels, and a vast array of other tools were unearthed.

"How much shit do you carry Jeremy?"

"Just the stuff I really need."

Still more surfaced: drills, sample bottles and bags, and, at the very last, he pulled out a bright orange machine about eighteen inches long and less than a foot in the other two dimensions.

A large label on the side announced, "Do Not Open."

"What the hell is that?"

Holly knew but was too surprised to rub it in. "You recovered the Black Box and didn't think to tell us?"

"Well, it was weird. I mean, I was all over that tail section the first day. No recorder. Yesterday afternoon, just before they evacuated us, there it was. I put it at the bottom of my pack because I wanted access to my other tools. I was going to tell you, I really was, but then they rushed us off the site and confiscated all our data. They took out about half my gear, then stuffed it all back into the pack; never went deep enough."

Mike handed him his things to reload his pack.

"I figured it was best to keep my mouth shut. But Miranda has all the gear here to read one. Only the lab in Washington, DC, is supposed to have that. But this investigation is so weird, I figure what the hell." Even as he spoke, he was unscrewing plates and pulling out wires.

There was a low thrumming sound from outside that built until it seemed to rattle the nearly vacant hangar.

"Mike, go see what that is."

"Yeah, yeah. That's all I'm good for and don't I know it." Outside the narrow opening in the hangar door, he saw a helicopter coming in to land at their small civilian airport— except it was big, black, and looked very military. A nasty itch told him where they'd be landing.

"We got company! Unmarked military," he called back into the hangar.

He heard a muffled, "Oh shit!" behind him. He turned and saw them stuffing the pieces of the bright-orange Black Box into one of the cargo spaces of the silver jet and closing cupboards as fast as they could.

Figuring Jeremy and Holly needed a moment, he stepped out to lean back against the door to buy them what little breathing space he could.

Another great day, Mike. Once again you're the freaking decoy.

43

MIKE SURVEYED THE LANDSCAPE AS THE HELICOPTER FLEW THE airport's approach pattern, then came hovering down the length of the runway. He never understood why they did that since a helicopter could just land wherever it wanted to, but they always did.

Not sure what was coming, he did his normal routine of completely ignoring the situation until it arrived in front of him. All the worrying in the world never achieved anything. And clients could always tell.

Be casual.

Think about other things.

The sun was actually shining. He wondered if that was as unusual as he'd heard or if the Pacific Northwest inhabitants spread rumors of how awful the rain here was to keep the hordes away.

The view to the east was magnificent. Close beyond the airport, the graceful double span of the Tacoma Narrows Bridge arced high over the eponymous waterway lost to view far below. The island-dotted waters of Puget Sound stretched north and south off either end of the hidden Narrows. The city of Tacoma lay on the other side with a bright blue bubble of a sports dome visible at the far edge of the small city.

In the background, the Cascade Mountains rose in sharp peaks of abrupt icy edges reminiscent of the Colorado Rockies. There was definitely some good skiing up there. And then dominant over all of it towered the dormant volcanic pinnacle of Mount Rainier, at least twice as high as all other peaks. To the south he could see the blasted-out top, also snow-covered, of Mount St. Helens.

The temperatures here were mild. Sailboats cruised down on the island-dotted waters and planes of all sizes plied the air. Even as he watched, a small plane buzzed in to land on the airport's runway. Overhead, commercial airliners were climbing up out of SeaTac and a big military jet burned all four engines hard as it climbed out to the south from what must be Joint Base Lewis-McChord.

Could do worse, Mike. Could definitely do worse. He was sure as hell never going back to New Jersey, where his advertising firm had been elevated, then killed by the FBI. Denver had been a nice assignment, even if it was damn cold in the winters. He decided it wasn't a bad gamble to ride this situation out for a bit and see how well it paid off.

The unmarked black helo settled close in front of him. One of the pilots jumped down just as Holly joined him.

"One of you named Holly?" The pilot called out over the roar of the still-running engines and beating rotor.

Why did that make a horrible kind of sense? Here he was

thinking that the future might finally be taking a turn for the better, yet suddenly Holly was in charge.

"Give you a clue, mate," Holly hooked a thumb in Mike's direction. "It's not him. His name is Evelyn."

Mike sighed.

"What can I do for the Night Stalkers?"

"Who are the Night Stalkers?" Mike really needed to learn when to keep his mouth shut.

Holly rolled her eyes at him just as Jeremy came up and answered. "They're the Army's secret helicopter regiment, the 160th Special Operations Aviation Regiment, or SOAR. They fly around SEALs, Delta Force, and US Rangers into all kinds of places that no one else can go. The 4th Battalion is stationed right here at JBLM. They're the ultimate in cool."

The pilot gave Jeremy a friendly thump on the shoulder as if he was the second coolest person there after Holly. *Crap!*

"Are they cooler than Miranda Chase?" Mike teased him.

"*Nobody's* cooler than she is." At least the kid was dedicated in his hero worship.

"How can I help you, chief warrant?" Mike wasn't going to let Holly keep one-upping him forever. Learning rank insignias had been very useful on occasion. He'd made it one of the first things to memorize about the military. The pilot wore a silver bar almost completely covered by four green squares. Chief Warrant Four meant he was very senior and a particular specialist in rotorcraft.

"They found something and want you three to look at it."

"Some *thing?*" Mike kept his tone amused and friendly.

"Hey, today I'm just the errand boy. All I know is that someone up the command tree wants you three taken to a little airport over that way. I'm to be at your disposal."

"That doesn't sound like a usual Night Stalkers' mission," he took a wild stab in the dark. Jeremy had made it sound as if these were awfully high-end guys.

"No shit, Sherlock. You coming, or can I get back to my real life?"

Mike waved him ahead, not even checking with Holly before climbing aboard the helo. She closed and locked the hangar door before following him.

Once they were in the back and the two crew chiefs had secured the side door before returning to sit by their side-mounted machine guns, Holly showed him a message on her phone.

Trust no one. It was from Miranda.

"Then why didn't you stop me?" he whispered to her as softly as the whining engines and beating rotors allowed.

"Sometimes you just have to play out the scenario and see where it leads."

She was right...which was exactly how he'd lost his advertising business to the whims of the FBI.

Maybe it wasn't too late to transfer back to Denver.

44

DRAKE FELT THE BLOOD DRAIN FROM HIS FACE AS HE STARED AT his phone. There were some calls that were never supposed to happen.

His personal cell phone was a holdover from a happier time when he'd trade hot and heavy texts with his wife from wherever they each were. A Doctor Without Borders wasn't supposed to be struck down by one of the diseases she was chasing, and she hadn't been. Instead an Al-Qaeda murder squad had done it for vaccinating a bunch of kids. Both his boys were far more likely to reach out from their ever-changing selection of video face-to-face apps—he'd installed about a dozen and just answered any of them that buzzed at him.

There were only four other people who had his personal number rather than the one issued by the government. That the incoming number was blocked told him precisely who it was.

"Are you okay, sir?" Colonel Gray leaned forward in quick concern.

"Could you give me a minute?" They were both strung out on coffee and a box of Krispy Kreme donuts someone had left in the nearby break room and they'd wiped out hours ago.

He was too distracted to even pay attention to her cute ass as she stepped from his office and closed the door. For all their crash-footage review, including getting Harrington to send them the radar tracking records from Groom Lake, they'd learned little more. Drake had been on the verge of sending Gray home when they'd found the missing F-35 fighter jet in Washington State followed closely by his call reaching Chase during her panicked rooftop flight.

And Syria, as usual, after a whole night deciding whether or not to recommend launching a massive strike from a carrier, had turned out to be another Russian-manufactured fiasco that everyone was backing down from.

"Yes?" Drake answered the phone, but there was no need for names.

"I have a problem. I much need your best image analyst." The voice spoke in thickly Mandarin-accented English.

"To do what?"

"There is a flight that you cannot be allowed to see, but I must know what went wrong. My people think it was plane or pilot. They are wrong. I know this. But I must explain what happen."

Drake scrambled for a way to say no, but it was a chink in the armor of the Chinese military.

He'd met then military attaché Colonel Commandant Zhang Ru by chance almost twenty years ago at a Geneva shish kebab joint during a G-20 meeting. He was as aware of Zhang's climb to power as Zhang was of his own.

It was impossible not to respect the man's skills.

They were also both rabid patriots.

In the decade since the one time they'd met, it was only the fifth time they had been in contact. The last one had been to warn off the Chinese from interfering with a political takedown just beyond the Burmese border. The one before that had been from Zhang to warn off a US battle group from entering an area commanded by a Chinese general who wanted an excuse to start World War III. By delaying the group's passage of the Taiwan Strait by a single week, Zhang had time to have the man disgraced.

But this time Drake was being asked to offer technical assistance. The question was, did this kind of help constitute a serious danger to the safety of the United States?

This was supposed to be CIA shit. No one trained Joint Chiefs on how to run a double agent without becoming a double agent yourself. Where was that line drawn? On the other hand, his job wasn't only to win wars, but also to avoid them.

"You must not look at this," Zhang repeated into Drake's silence. "Only analyst. You may not read report. We must both be clear of this."

Drake wondered at the "of." Zhang's English was poor enough that he may have meant "on" to confirm clarity. But perhaps his language skills were accurate and they both needed deniability, which meant this was an even more delicate request.

"That's a hell of an ask."

"Yes." Zhang's flat statement told Drake just how important this was.

Drake hoped that Zhang knew what the hell he was doing and didn't end both of their careers. Or both of their lives.

"Why?" Drake needed *something* more.

"Because there are moments when even the most cautious person must gamble big. This is..."

Drake grunted. He hadn't made Chairman of the Joint Chiefs by playing it safe. Zhang was a step away from the CDI. To have a connection, even one as tenuous as their own, into the Commission for Discipline Investigation was an unobtainable card, even if it was a wild card.

"*This* is my gamble. Are you remembering the name of the restaurant?" Zhang asked into his own silence.

Drake did. That must be the password. For the first time he regretted going anywhere near the place even if it had been damn good shish kebab. "Send it!"

His phone beeped with a message. It was a link to an online secure file transfer site, the kind meant for grandma's dirty photos, not international military secrets. Maybe low profile was best in this case. Even as he glared at the address, he could see that the call had been ended from the other end.

At a soft knock, he snapped out, "Come!"

His assistant looked in. "Ms. Chase is here, sir."

45

You're going to love this! Holly's text was followed by an overhead video of an F-35A Lightning II parked at a very small airfield surrounded by thick conifers.

Miranda recognized Crest Airpark right away. At least once a year someone misjudged how short a thousand-meter runway really was when surrounded by tall trees. Both landing and taking off at Crest required a higher-than-normal level of situational awareness.

No one heard it come in last night.

Really dead-stick? Miranda sent back. Accurately landing an F-35 without power on a field as short as Crest Airpark would require an exceptional pilot. Or one with a death wish.

Apparently. Jeremy opened the bomb bay and there are two empty hardpoints. Which confirmed that this was the jet that had bombed their C-130 out of existence.

Grab recorders.

*Already got them aboard a Night Stalkers Black Hawk. As
well as the QAR.*

Good job. The quick access recorder in the cockpit often
captured information not included in the data recorder. It
was intended to be easily downloaded and reviewed, unlike
the heavily protected voice and data recorders. And she
supposed that trusting the Night Stalkers was a reasonable
choice. Certainly better them than the CIA.

Cockpit clean. Too clean.

Miranda was puzzling at the meaning of that when she
ran into the back of a woman her own height and size but
wearing an Air Force uniform. The woman's reaction was
excessive, stumbling forward to land awkwardly in a heavy
chair in Drake's waiting area.

"Uh, sorry."

"It's okay," the woman managed to turn and sit. "Asleep
on my feet. Almost literally, I'm afraid. I didn't see you
coming."

Miranda held up her cell phone in apology as it pinged
again.

Nothing else to learn here, we're going back to TNA.

Good. Tacoma Narrows Airport should be well off the
CIA's radar.

"You're her."

Miranda looked up from her phone, trying to decide if
there was some other instruction she should send, but
couldn't think of how to explain this morning. "I'm her
who?"

"You're the one..." she glanced around to make sure no
one was near them, "...who spotted the flare off the wingtip."

"I think flare may be a misnomer. There was an

unquestionable light source. It didn't follow the patterns I would expect if it was other interference on a camera's lens."

The officer smiled wryly, "Not on this camera. Trust me. It's at the source."

"We only know that horizontally. There could be a vertical displacement. A passing airliner or—"

"It wasn't. I've already checked all of the air traffic and lower orbits."

"Orbits." It hadn't really sunk in before, perhaps because she'd been so tired. They had looked down from space, yet the individual navigation lights on the plane had been very clear and distinct. "Your KH-11 cameras have exceptional resolution, sub-ten-centimeter from three hundred kilometers."

The Air Force colonel nodded as if confirming something to herself. "They do. And you're definitely her. I'm Colonel Elizabeth Gray from the NRO."

Miranda shook the offered hand.

When Elizabeth released it, Miranda inspected her own hand. The camera had the ability to resolve that width from orbit.

"My hands are clean," Elizabeth said in a strange tone.

"So are mine," Miranda answered for lack of a better answer.

Drake's assistant came out of Drake's office. "The general is ready for you, Ms. Chase, Colonel Gray." He waved them toward the door.

"Yet your KH-11," Miranda continued looking at her hand, "which can see the width of my palm, was unable to clearly resolve a light source that might have measured as much as a meter in diameter. I find that very interesting."

46

"Hang on." Mike wasn't ready to leave Crest Airpark just yet.

There was something happening here, even if neither Holly nor Jeremy seemed interested in anything other than the plane.

"Mike! I want out of here before they send over the replacement pilot."

"Tell them they need to send an inspection team to make sure there's no boobytraps."

Holly narrowed her eyes at him in question.

"I'm not saying there are but it will slow them down. We weren't blown to hell when we grabbed the flight recorders and checked the bomb bay. Luck, or is the plane clean? Do you know how many ways there must be to sabotage a plane that complex?" He didn't, but she probably did.

This time she nodded sharply and, thank God, kept her mouth shut as she went to talk with the Night Stalker pilots. It seemed unlikely that there was a trap; it would have been easier to have blown up the plane before leaving. Or perhaps even ejected over the ocean after doing the bombing rather than leaving the plane to be discovered.

No, it wasn't boobytrapped. Whoever had flown it had just needed it to be out of the way for a while.

It didn't matter; Mike only needed a couple minutes with no distractions from Holly or Jeremy.

He started out striding toward the airport's owner, but then caught on that the people around him seemed to have a Sunday picnic sense of time—there was curiosity, but no hurry. He slowed his walk and gait to match.

"Hey, Mel. How's it going?" He eased up beside the airport owner who'd called in the find.

"You mean other than having a military jet parked in the middle of my runway? Are you sure I can't tow this thing aside?"

"Well, I wouldn't be the one to bill you for a hundred mil if the tow screws up. Do you even know where the parking brake is?"

Mel rocked back on his heels for a moment and gazed at the jet. "Maybe I can tow it and, if I screw something up, make it my brother's fault."

"Always worth a shot." Danny Davis had already tried to hit on Holly twice, both times earning him a laugh right in his face. But it was clear that the guy was a total dog and Holly *was* very fine to look at.

Even as Mike glanced over at him, Danny set up on his third run at her while she was talking to the Night Stalker pilots.

Mike didn't quite see what happened—Holly was too fast.

One moment Danny was walking toward her with an easy confident swagger more appropriate for a dive-bar dance floor than an hour past sunrise in the wilderness of the Pacific Northwest.

The next he was stumbling the other way, holding his nose as it gushed blood, yet Holly had barely appeared to move.

"Think he learned his lesson?" Mike asked Mel.

"Knowing my brother as well as I'm ashamed to say I do, no." They shared a laugh.

"You could get some serious mileage on social media to more than make up for the inconvenience." Mike nodded toward the jet, redirecting the conversation.

"Damn. I always forget that kind of stuff. The wife usually takes care of it for me."

Mike took a picture of Mel smiling in front of the F-35 Lightning II. He captioned it with, "Come to Crest Airpark if you *really* want to learn to fly!" Mel posted it to Crest's social media site.

"So, Mel, can you explain something to me?"

The guy shrugged.

"I'm no flier, but how can someone land a jet like that and have no one hear anything?"

"Hell if I know; I live down the road a piece. Hey, Tom," he called out to a grizzled man with a scraggly beard. He wore a bathrobe that didn't quite meet in the front of his big gut. "Come here and tell this guy how you slept through that jet landing. There had to be tire squeal and some seriously hard braking if he didn't have power to the thrust reversers. He didn't even use the whole runway."

"Cold night so we all had our windows closed. If it came

in just after sunset, I was watching one of the Star Wars movies. You know how I like my Star Wars, Mel."

Mel nodded his confirmation, then explained to Mike. "Mel has a killer sound system that can really shake the place. He likes his star destroyers to rattle the building. Neighbors are farther down the runway and might have just thought Tom had his windows open."

"If I heard it, I probably thought the noise fit the movie." Tom gazed off into the distance for a moment. "Something odd though. I did hear a motorcycle."

"No motorcycles in Star Wars movies," Mike stuck his hands in his pockets to mimic Mel's lazy thumbs-hooked-in-pockets stance.

"Nope," Tom agreed. "The Star Trek reboot, but not Star Wars."

"The new Kirk and the babe," Mike acknowledged.

"Jaylah," Tom sighed happily.

"Always more of a Beverly Crusher guy myself." Mike had found that choice also earned him the most Trekkie creds in guy conversations. Especially in women Trekkie conversations. The coolly intellectual Next Generation doctor—who *hadn't* been cast for her breast size or her kick-ass body. Long and sleek, like Holly without the muscles, with brains and red hair as a bonus—to go with Dana Scully. Beverly was the "thoughtful" choice.

He went silent and waited to see if Tom brought up the motorcycle sound again.

"Hey. Doesn't Danny have a bike that he keeps here?"

Mel almost choked on a laugh. "If someone hijacked his Yamaha R6, he's gonna have a coronary to go with that bloody nose. He loves that thing more than any woman." He turned and yelled out to his brother. "Danny! Bet your bike has gone missing."

He didn't have to say anything else. Despite holding a bloody towel to his face, Danny sprinted over toward the hangars. His roar of anger sounding across the airfield moments later answered that question.

That told Mike what he'd been wondering about. Someone hadn't been waiting for the pilot's arrival. It was a single perpetrator—like those super-undercover guys sent out on a solo mission in a movie. It had that feel to it. One guy, one hundred-million-dollar jet, and a stolen motorcycle at the end. Untraceable and very cool.

Mel was laughing. "Bike is lipstick red. License is a custom one: 'Magnet,' as in a self-proclaimed 'Babe Magnet'."

"Thanks, buddy." Before he turned to go, he glanced at Tom, trying to think of how to thank him without thanking him. "Bet you're old school."

Tom grinned in happy acknowledgement.

"Uhura all the way," Mike guessed.

"Oh yeah. Nichelle Nichols? Hot stuff. You seen how that woman aged? That's seriously fine."

"Mighta noticed that," Mike offered them a nod and an informal salute before he turned to the waiting helicopter. He gave Holly a let's-get-going sign.

They were airborne before he had both feet inside.

He wondered if Miranda already knew that it was the CIA who'd blown up their plane.

"Hey Holly? I've got something new for you to send to Miranda."

47

THEY'D HAD TO REMIND HARVEY THREE TIMES TO RETURN TO Groom Lake before dawn. It was still dark out over the Pacific, but Nevada would get the sunrise an hour earlier and he had to tuck the Casper drone in the hangar before then.

He'd picked up another submarine just departing Ecuador—estimates said that there was at least one en route to the US almost any day of the year. He didn't want to risk losing it overnight, so he jammed their radios and tried a different tactic.

They must have thought they'd hit the worst storm ever as he ran close by them time after time in varying directions, chewing up the waves at full throttle in between rolls, loops, and hard-banked turns. His Casper remote was even more fun than the F-18 Hornet from the front seat.

When the sub tried to submerge to get clear of the artificial turbulence he'd created, he dropped a nice little pair of two hundred and fifty-pound SDBs. The small diameter bombs had fallen to either side of the diving sub, squashing it flat like a pancake.

Sorry, guys. That'll teach you to be asshole drug runners.

No Coast Guard. No expensive trials. No evidence except for some seriously stoned deep-sea critters.

Disconnecting from the Casper, all neatly parked and chocked in the hangar, was like...hell.

Like the morning after he'd tried to drink a whole bottle of Jack Daniels to celebrate graduating from the Air Force Academy. Eyes so scratchy, they must be bloodshot as the devil's. The moment he sat up, he began barfing his guts out. The techs had clearly been expecting that: bucket, towel, and a glass of fresh water were all waiting. Even a breath mint.

He wanted to cry as they peeled off the interface contact —like they were extracting a long, thin thread of his soul. God damn the doctor to hell for being right about the post-flight reaction.

Helen wasn't there, but Harrington was.

The general held out his hand.

Harvey managed to blink his eyes clear enough to shake it.

"That was some damn fine flying, son."

Harvey gasped with relief. That gave him back a piece of himself. If the general was pleased, he'd get to fly again. The aftereffects were completely worth it.

"Most pilots have to rotate out every three hours. You were under for nine, but the techs assured me you were sufficiently well adapted. Glad you had the guts to ride it out."

"Never felt a thing until they just pulled the plug."

The general's expression said there might be something else he was referring to. No, he must mean the mission.

Harvey was already feeling a little better already.

"I was thinking, sir. If I lurked particularly close to the Colombian coast, I should be able to find at least a few subs' point of departure. The Casper could blow the shit out of the manufacturing sites just as neatly as..."

The general's shrug stopped him. As if killing those subs was only practice...or a test for him.

Then Harvey remembered refueling a Casper flight over the Bering Sea on its way to China.

He whistled, to himself, in surprise.

With the Casper he could dust targets in Beijing *and* Moscow in a single night. Then deep-six a sub off Polyarny, Russia's main Arctic submarine base on the way home over the North Pole with no one the wiser.

Damn but that was an amazing thing.

48

"YOU'VE HAD AN *INTERESTING* MORNING, MS. CHASE."

"You have a very strange view of my morning then, General Nason."

He watched Colonel Gray—he really had to learn her first name at some point—assessing Miranda Chase. The two women had done one of those simpatico things women did during the brief moments he'd been on the phone with Zhang Ru.

Curiously, he found himself valuing Colonel Gray's positive assessment of the curious woman who seemed to be at the center of so much trouble.

He'd been considering asking Gray to help him with Zhang Ru's assessment, but he didn't like the idea of putting her military career at risk along with his own.

He could offer Miranda Chase a level of deniability though, not telling her the source of whatever files Zhang had sent. And she had spotted the obscure flare.

For now, he'd hold off.

So, he summarized. "We have an upset CIA director staging a home invasion on domestic soil without involving the FBI. We have a wrecked Air Force C-130, down in a highly secure flight area."

"Not just downed," Chase corrected him.

"What do you mean?" Gray leaned forward.

"No reasonable projection explains what occurred. The flight profile doesn't even match the tail falling off, which it didn't, and the engines being at full throttle, which they weren't, and power diving straight into the ground, which it did but with a force all out of proportion to the controllable elements of flight. It didn't merely crash. As I believe I mentioned before, it was slapped out of the sky."

"Slapped?" Drake slammed a hand down on a piece of paper on his desk. "Like that?"

"More precisely," Chase held her left hand above his desk. She studied it for a moment, then stood to place her hand higher above the surface, facing palm down, and stretched out her thumb and pinkie finger. "Here's the Hercules, at approximately one-two-hundredth scale. My hand is six inches long and my pinkie-to-thumb reach is eight-and-a-quarter inches. Think of my wrist as the nose and my fingertips as the tail."

Drake looked down at his own hand. He didn't know what his hand's dimensions were. He caught Gray making the same consideration of her own hand and they traded quick smiles as Chase continued.

"So we have a reasonable facsimile of the plane's ninety-seven-foot length with one hundred and thirty-seven-foot wingspan conveniently to an accuracy of one-point-nine percent. At that ratio, the curiously low flight level of five hundred feet would be thirty inches above your desk."

Drake nodded for her to continue and did his best to keep his smile off his face. Gray didn't even try.

"If I crash my plane by controlling the elevator angle and driving the tail upward," Chase bent her fingertips which would cause an airflow change, making her fingers rise up.

She cocked her wrist to illustrate—then accelerated her hand nearly straight downward to thump the heel of her hand on his desk.

"We would see the wings break off, the nose crumple, but the plane would ultimately remain right-side up based on our first estimate of soil-type analysis."

Drake checked in with Gray, but she was now watching Chase closely.

"However," she returned her hand to its initial height above his desk. "If we have an outside force acting on the Hercules like a slap from above," she slapped her left wrist with her right hand.

She didn't first tip her fingers toward the ceiling, instead she pushed the heel of her hand downward, then paused a third of the way down.

"Note that the nose was pushed down, rather than the tail being raised to cause the descent. An abrupt and severe downward acceleration. Whatever force it was, it acted on the wings of the plane, but not the tail."

Then, without warming, she finished the gesture, slamming the heel of her hand down hard enough to make him and the picture of his wife jump.

Then she sat down as calmly as if she'd never moved.

"The nose folded under. It broke free as the plane landed on its back."

She twisted her arm to demonstrate.

"The wings sheared off and fell to either side. My team reports that they flipped one wing over yesterday and the entire upper surface had been drastically deformed inwards with no sign of a nearby explosion. It was just," she shrugged and folded her hands in her lap, "a slap. The fuselage struck the ground so hard that it bounced up and rolled over so that it only appears to have hit right-side up. I surmise that the tail broke off before ground impact as it appeared to follow too similar a trajectory."

"The people?" Gray asked softly.

"Any personnel aboard would have died instantaneously upon impact. The downward vertical acceleration was so severe at altitude, they may have been dead well before impact."

Drake was aghast at how easily she seemed to talk about such things. Those were his men. They might be Air Force, but he was Chairman of the Joint Chiefs and that transcended military branch.

"Don't you feel anything, Ms. Chase?"

"Yes. I'm glad that they were spared the possible question of whether they survived the eighty-three to ninety-seven second fall that my parents suffered during the destruction of TWA Flight 800." She said it with a near robotic self-control but Drake could see the pain, the real pain in her eyes. She might not admit to feelings, but he could see that, despite his initial assessment, she had them.

"I'm sorry. I didn't know."

"How would you? You said it was your assistant who

would have reviewed my file. And it wasn't your fault, so there is no reason to apologize."

Drake had no answer to that.

"They were in First Class. So it was unlikely that they were killed in the initial explosion. Possible, but unlikely. Were they conscious? I'll never know. At the time I was in Washington State taking a horse-riding lesson."

"Were you able to estimate the downward force necessary to cause such a course change?" Gray changed the subject back to the C-130, which Chase seemed to accept easily.

"It would require approximately seventy thousand pounds of thrust. Roughly the weight of an additional Hercules C-130 striking against it."

"But there was only the one plane involved in the crash."

"Yes, there was. The source of that force is what we're seeking. A force that leaves a one-meter halo of light that lasts under the length of two frames of the KH-11's camera."

Gray glanced quickly at Drake, but he shook his head. "I didn't tell her what took the images."

"It wasn't difficult to surmise," Miranda stated flatly. She'd apparently re-compartmentalized her parents' loss.

Gray might be trying to hide it, but Drake could see that she was impressed.

Miranda Chase continued as if they hadn't spoken, as if she couldn't stop until she completed her thought. "At an apparent frame-rate of six frames per second based on the speed of the C-130 over ground, that means that the effect in question was visible for less than a third of a second—the frame it was visible in and the time between the frame back and the next one forward."

Drake studied his desk for a long moment before making his decision.

"Do you have your computer with you, Ms. Chase?"

At her nod, he showed her his phone with the message from Zhang Ru.

"Copy down this address."

"I don't need to."

He looked at it himself. It was a complex mix of some fifteen letters and characters. Drake hating feeling outclassed, but at the moment...

"The password is AliHaydar," he spelled it out.

He almost told her the restrictions about what she saw, but changed his mind at the last moment. He knew that if he instructed her to never reveal the file's contents, he'd probably never be able to convince her to ignore that instruction.

"Please view it without showing it to either of us. I have an...associate who is interested in your conclusions."

49

"THIS IS NEW, CLARISSA," CIA DIRECTOR CLARK WINSTON grinned down at her.

"Go to hell, Clark." The US Army 75th Rangers had been kind, courteous, and handled her with steel-strong hands as if she was a Taliban terrorist.

A pair of utterly imposing Rangers fully dressed in battle gear had marched her into the CIA lobby with her wrists zip-tied together—perhaps she shouldn't have tried to scratch out the master sergeant's eyes. They refused to release her without a hand-written receipt from the director.

He wasn't laughing anymore, "Who do I make the receipt out to?"

"I've been instructed to request the receipt be made to the name of General Fitzgerald Patrick," the sergeant stated.

"Fitz?" Clark sounded surprised.

"That's what I was told to ask for, sir," that perfectly polite Ranger thing still firmly in place. Now she wished she *had* gotten his eyes.

But Clarissa didn't say a word. She didn't care if Clark and Fitz *were* old drinking buddies. She was going to find the most sensitive information on any project from the NRO—that wasn't one of hers—and leak it earmarked from his office. Or perhaps have him leak the details of the prior President's most flagrant affairs—he'd had a taste in women as low as his taste in fast food. Whatever, she had a personal hacker in her department who would just love to hack an e-mail server at the NRO for her. General Fitzgerald Patrick was going down for this.

It was so demeaning to be traded in like a piece of lost luggage. And then, after the Rangers took their bit of paper and strode away like the Special Operations soldiers they were, she had to ask the security desk to cut her bonds because Clark didn't even carry a penknife. The woman in charge of the shift was definitely smirking as she cut the ties.

Bitch!

Though Clarissa kept the thought to herself this time.

Clark took her by the arm and escorted her out of the lobby and through the courtyard to *Kryptos*.

"I'd rather go clean up." She tried to walk off, but he merely tightened his grip. She was so sick of being manhandled, but before she could retaliate, he pushed her down on one of the stone benches in front of the cryptographic sculpture.

"You look perfect as always."

Men were so blind. She could feel that her skirt was askew. She had a long run in her stockings, and her hair was spread across her shoulders—her scrunchie had been a fatality of the failed operation to grab and silence that NTSB woman.

"Now tell me why I woke up alone this morning." He remained standing, which left his crotch at nearly face height. He was lucky that *she* didn't carry a penknife. A glance down revealed a deep slice in the toe of her favorite Rejina Pyo high heels. Would Clark feel the damage on her shoe if she kicked him in the balls with it?

"You didn't wake alone. I fucked your brains out before breakfast. You're the one who fell back asleep." Men loved sex first thing in the morning, she knew that, and Clark was no exception. Was it her fault if he fell back asleep when there were things to be done? She'd also let him have her after the steak dinner they'd shared—and yes, been photographed at—exactly according to plan. *Remember the plan.* She managed a deep breath but it did little to calm her.

He gazed around the courtyard as if considering. It was midmorning and, thankfully, the foot traffic through the courtyard was minimal and here by *Kryptos* it was nonexistent.

"I like your hair down," he refocused on her.

"Fine. Whatever." At least he knew better than to try and grab her father's favorite handhold when they were in bed together. He was a considerate lover if not a skilled one. She'd definitely need to work on the latter if she was going to choose him for the rest of her life—she'd seen too many careers ended due to wandering libidos so she'd have to be true to him. And Clark was definitely a one-woman man.

He finally sat, just where Miranda Chase had perched yesterday on the granite bench. "Now, explain to me what was going on this morning."

"That Miranda Chase is on the verge of exposing the Casper drone project."

"How is that possible? I thought she was investigating a downed C-130?"

Clarissa felt ill. "She was."

"But how are the two tied together?"

50

Jeremy had hunched over the flight recorders for an hour before calling the team in.

They'd both offered to help, but it wasn't even clear if Jeremy had heard them while he worked.

Instead, Mike had spent the time sitting shoulder to shoulder with Holly, going through the photos she'd saved in her boot heel...and learning nothing new.

"The voice recorder is surprisingly uninformative," Jeremy pointed at the squiggling lines of an audio file on his computer screen. "There's what sounds like a whoosh of a door opening in flight and letting the wind in, then a loud bang that I interpret as shredding metal, but all in an instant. There was a single, incomplete curse from the copilot, and then the sound of the plane's crash itself just a second later."

It had all happened so fast that Mike wasn't surprised at the lack of information. "So the pilots can't tell us anything from their graves."

"What about the data?" Holly leaned over to peer at Jeremy's screen. Mike didn't even bother because it wouldn't mean much to him.

"That's where it gets interesting. This data set shows a low-speed stall and a crash."

"Bullshit!" Even Mike knew that was wrong.

"It's good, even well done, but it's not internally consistent."

"What does that mean?"

"It means," Holly studied it more closely. "That someone faked the data on this recorder."

"Why would they— Oh, so what did they want to hide?"

"Thankfully, they're also not very smart," Jeremy tapped a few keys and all of the numbers changed. "A CVDR is intended to record thirty minutes of voice and two hours of data, overwriting itself in a loop. But what they did here was paste in their crash scenario before deleting the other data. Then they went back and deleted the actual crash data, without scrubbing it."

"So you just what...undeleted it?"

"Yep!" Jeremy said that as if such things were normal. "I had to rebuild the disk file system mapping table, which is what took so long, but I got it."

"You just outsmarted the programmers at Groom Lake?"

Jeremy shrugged, but Holly pulled him into a sideways hug. "We're so proud!" She kissed him on the temple and he practically glowed with delight. A delight he instantly buried by turning to the screen.

"See here? The transition from level flight to an off-the-scale rate of descent was a matter of a few hundredths of a second. Most of the data ended at that time. I'm guessing the tail was snapped off when the main fuselage transitioned from horizontal flight to vertical descent so abruptly. One data cable, which runs along the main beam at the bottom of the hull, survived another three hundredths of a second and recorded an airspeed of almost Mach 2."

"No way!" Holly stopped glaring at the screen to glare at Jeremy. "A C-130 can't go Mach 2. It's not aerodynamically possible."

"It's right there," Jeremy redirected her attention back to the screen.

"What if whatever struck it was going Mach 2?" Mike suggested.

They both turned to look at him.

"There *was* only the one wreck..." Jeremy pointed out.

"You know those wings that I had to circle around to collect the soil samples?" Mike could still see them stretched out, shimmering in the midday heat. "Remember that wing I flipped over. The tops were punched in and peeled open like an orange zester had been run over the surface. What if that zester was something supersonic and very, very close?"

Now surprise showed on their faces.

"I have a brain, goddamn it."

"So does an emu. It weighs almost a whole ounce. Way outta your league." But Holly didn't really put her heart into the insult. She was clearly thinking about his idea and she looked as if she'd bit down on a lemon.

"That would explain the whoosh-and-bang sound on the cockpit voice recorder."

Holly was nodding her agreement...and he'd bet she hated that.

"To cause that kind of structural damage, it would have to pass within..." Jeremy pulled up some modeling software on his computer and quickly tapped in some numbers before whistling softly. "It would have to pass within three meters at Mach 2. It would be well below the height of the C-130's tail. Now that's some flying."

51

UNABLE TO SHAKE OFF THE FEELING THAT HIS BODY WAS STILL parked in the Groom Lake hangar, perched on its wheels, Harvey decided to try doing something normal.

Helen was busy doing her job and he couldn't sleep.

Not thinking particularly clearly, he wandered out to the ball field.

"There he is!" Hinkle called out as he came around the corner of the DFC—Harvey hadn't felt hungry. "Took your time, buddy. Game's just about to start."

Game? Harvey had just been hoping that someone was around for a game of catch. He shook his head to clear it and scanned the field. The *Fire Heads* were just taking the field—the munitions specialists. "Uh, where am I in the order?"

"Put you at cleanup, just behind me."

Harvey nodded and went to pick out a bat and start stretching. Fourth up gave him a couple minutes. He tossed his glove down on the bench and, picking up a thirty-four-inch aluminum, laid it across his shoulders to start working out the kinks from eleven hours wired into the Casper.

He had to stop and rub the spot behind his right ear.

Goddamn quack of doctor was right—it felt like a steel plate from the inside, but he couldn't find it with his fingertips.

He went back to stretching. Maxwelton was watching him strangely. Maxie kept mostly to himself. He'd been on the *Remotes* for a while, almost as good a hitter as Harvey but he played deep left field to Harvey's first base so they didn't have much to do with each other on the field.

"Hey," Harvey acknowledged him, but he kept staring.

Then he reached up and rubbed behind his own right ear.

"No shit!"

"No shit."

Harvey couldn't think of what else to say. Harrington hadn't introduced him to any other Casper pilots. Had that been on purpose?

He turned at the crack of a bat followed by a hard slap of a ball striking a glove. Hinkle had just been caught out. Only Smitty had made it on base, standing out at second all alone. So much for the big advantage of batting cleanup. Two outs at the top of the first—not a good start.

He exchanged a last look with Maxie before stepping up to the plate. Low and outside, why the hell did he fall for the first pitch? He popped it up to right field and they were done.

It was the fifth inning before he ended up sitting in the dugout by Maxie with no one else close by.

"Six-one," he sighed as he sat down with a bottle of water. "The *Fire Heads* really suck."

"Yeah, too bad we suck even worse."

"Yeah, too bad," Harvey agreed. He tried to resist rubbing his ear, but couldn't.

"It's habit forming," Maxie acknowledged.

That's when Harvey noticed Maxie had his own hands tightly clasped in his lap, trying to resist the urge.

"It's The Rip, man."

"The Rip?"

Maxie glanced at him quickly. "How long you been plugged in?"

"First flight."

"Shit! Goddamn Harrington."

"What's The Rip?"

Maxie shrugged it off, but Harvey didn't want him walking away either so he changed subjects.

"How many others are there of us?"

"A couple others, I think. Jefferson lost it two days back."

"Lost it?" Harvey hoped that didn't mean what he thought it meant, but Maxie tapped his temple.

"Coming back from a run over Brazil, I think, started hotdogging. Rumor is he knocked a couple of small planes out of the sky way down south. Heard the techs whispering about a dozen tourists on an island hopper that went down in the Caribbean off the Yucatan. They started talking about one of ours going down close by," he nodded to the south, "but they shut up real quick when they noticed me listening. They forget that we can hear them even when we're flying."

"That big explosion yesterday afternoon?" Harvey had been surprised that they were doing bombing tests so close to Groom Lake. That was highly unusual. But if it was a drone—

"Nah. That wasn't us. Flew over it last night on my way out to...well...out—to see what was worth seeing. Nothing but shreds. Hercules, maybe a C-17, not enough left to really tell."

Jefferson lost it? Harvey didn't like that idea at all as Hinkle struck out and they returned to the field. He recalled that the guy had been acting pretty weird lately, then stopped showing up for the games.

Where was he now? Some ugly debrief room? Or a padded cell?

Or worse?

Harvey felt a cold shiver despite the morning's heat.

52

Miranda downloaded the files and glanced through them quickly.

A fifth-generation Shenyang J-31 Gyrfalcon fighter jet.

She glanced up at Drake, but he merely shook his head so she kept her mouth shut. Perhaps he didn't want Colonel Elizabeth Gray to know the content. But it would have been easy to send her from the room.

Perhaps he didn't want to know what they contained himself.

It was odd, but that felt right, even if she was less rather than more successful making instinctual conclusions.

She couldn't read the labels on the various data streams, but the numbers told her what she was looking at: altitude, air speed, g-force, engine temperatures, and so on.

Arranging the several feeds about her screen, she synchronized them and hit Play. Satellite imagery, two full screens of data feeds from the aircraft itself, and limited radar coverage. Curiously there was no audio track.

The flight appeared normal. The pilot was good, but made no maneuvers she couldn't have duplicated at lower speeds in her own Sabrejet.

He dove out of sight into a mountain range.

The pilot who emerged might have been another person entirely. He flew combinations she'd never seen even at the most extreme aerobatic shows. Something had changed back there, out of sight among the mountains.

There was a very active aerobatic club on just the next island over from her own. She would often fly over to San Juan Island in an unremarkable Beech C23 Sundowner to watch their competitions out of the Friday Harbor Airport.

Were these extreme maneuvers captured in recordings as exceptional when performed in an advanced military aircraft? She thought so, but wasn't positive.

Again she almost asked Drake the question, then reconsidered when she saw his flat stare. No squinted eyes, no emotion at all that she could interpret.

Colonel Gray was watching him with what appeared to be curiosity: the same way she'd looked at Miranda when they first met.

Miranda returned to the images and readouts.

There was nothing wrong with the aircraft and the pilot was showing masterful control.

The aircraft disappeared behind the mountains and didn't reemerge.

The data feed ended abruptly. At the last moment, there was a severe downward acceleration.

As severe as what had hit the Hercules.

She ran the multi-screen feed again.

There was something wrong.

Miranda found it on the third replay. There was a reflection off the Shenyang's canopy. But the reflection didn't vary with the angle of the plane's twisting track to the sun. It hugged the aircraft like a mirror.

At Mach 1.9.

Only on two occasions did its position vary by even a few meters from the Shenyang's side.

She pulled out her phone and texted Holly, as it was the only number she had for the team.

Is it possible that a high-speed, close-proximity aircraft knocked down the C-130?

The answer came back in seconds. *We're just checking that model now. Per recovered CVDR data, we think ~Mach 2 passage above Hercules, crossing at right angles. 3 meters max separation?!?!?!?*

Miranda pictured the Hercules wreckage and made her own conclusions.

Yes, that force would be sufficient to explain the damage and abrupt directional change of the Hercules.

"We know why your Hercules crashed." She spoke without looking up. She ignored the commotion that statement caused in the room. Restarting the Chinese satellite feed, she zoomed in to the resolution limit— significantly lower than Colonel Gray's KH-11. What if the odd reflection off the Shenyang J-31 was indeed another aircraft?

What if it was a supersonic aircraft that the J-31 pilot was trying to escape but couldn't? An ability to fly so close that it had shredded the C-130 Hercules at Groom Lake.

She closed her laptop and considered the problem.

If the J-31 pilot was not working *with* the "reflection"

aircraft, then it was shadowing his every maneuver. The more desperate the flight became, the closer it moved. She could feel his panic as assuredly as she'd always imagined her parents had in their long fall into the ocean. In some ways, it was the one emotion she truly understood.

"The control maneuvers..."

"What was that?" Drake barked at her.

"Sorry, I shouldn't have spoken aloud."

"Speak anyway."

Miranda could only blink at him in surprise. "I understood that you specifically didn't want me to speak about this," she patted her hand on her laptop.

"I didn't. I do. Uh... Perhaps in general terms."

"You wish me to discuss specifics in general terms?"

He offered a chilly smile. "Precisely."

She stared down at the laptop. "That's not something I do well." There were so many things she didn't do well.

"Try."

Miranda could feel a little of the pilot's panic sweat on her own palms.

"Please," he asked as softly as when he'd asked her to stay earlier. Or was it yesterday? Everything was blurring together.

She was still bothered about unintentionally revealing the code word "Amber" and didn't wish to get caught out again.

"An...exceptionally maneuverable aircraft flew over your Hercules C-130 at a distance closer than you and I are now seated."

"But that—"

She held up a finger to silence him. "It did this at ninety-degrees to the C-130's flight path, without impacting the upright vertical stabilizer of the tail's empennage while traveling at Mach 2. An exceptional display of precise control."

"But none of the radar imaging shows a second aircraft," Colonel Gray leaned in.

"Don't forget the flare on the one image," Miranda decided that if both the flash source and the KH-11 satellite's recording hardware were taken into consideration, that it formed a reasonable hypothesis. "Perhaps a narrowed exhaust port, blurred by its speed of motion, moving faster than the CCD's image capture rate. Charge-coupled devices, the photo-reactive part of any digital camera, have an image capture rate of—" Drake's gesture cut her off. She always hated not being able to complete a sentence. *—of one-sixth of a second,* she completed for herself.

"A narrowed..." Drake looked puzzled.

"Stealth," Gray whispered in surprise.

"Precisely," Miranda agreed. "A narrowed exhaust port on a stealth aircraft would only be visible from a small angle of view, making its track effectively invisible in darkness at all other angles. It's the only possibility that fits the known data. Once you eliminate the impossible, whatever remains, no matter how improbable, must be the truth."

"Now you're quoting Sherlock Holmes at us."

"Sir Arthur Conan Doyle, actually. But yes." Miranda had always felt a kinship with Doyle's mad detective. There were many things wrong with his fictional choices (both in drugs and Irene Adler), but not with his cerebral agility. "Now, in general terms, General Nason, your associate is confronted with a similar dilemma. An aircraft of apparently impossible maneuverability was captured in his images. It flew with a precision and response time that is unlike anything I have ever seen. My first instinct was to dismiss it as no more than a curious reflection."

"But if it was a highly maneuverable stealth aircraft..." Drake stared at the ceiling as he drawled out the idea slowly. She glanced up, half expecting to see an aircraft there as if he was studying it.

"Not merely maneuverable. It's responsiveness is nearly robotic in perfection."

"Nearly?"

"I spoke most carefully, Drake."

53

HE WANTED THE WORLD TO SLOW DOWN FOR A MINUTE. DRAKE was due to report to the President in under an hour about what had been lost in the desert out at Groom Lake aboard the Hercules.

A stealth aircraft that could reach into Groom Lake *and* somewhere in China? That had to be the Russians, but his intelligence reports hinted at no such craft. How was he supposed to—

"Do you think it was the same aircraft?"

Drake knew there was a reason he liked Colonel Gray. Woman kept her head in a crisis.

Chase tipped her head one way and then the other. "At least the same conceptual design—I cannot speak to the likelihood of it being the same frame number with the evidence I have. It's a reasonable supposition as both observed maneuvers were of such exceptional caliber that it would seem unlikely that such finesse of technological advance would be achieved simultaneously in two distinct aircraft. This is definitely something very new. At least in my experience."

Definitely Russian.

Drake rubbed at his forehead. They'd been done with the Cold War thirty years ago. He'd been there, a fresh-minted major in the 75th Ranger Regiment and so proud of his oak leaves, on the ground in Berlin the day the Wall came down.

War was done.

Over.

Except there'd been Somalia, Iraq, Afghanistan, Libya, Syria, and enough other hellholes to make him retire if the President hadn't personally asked him to stay. And now the Cold War was back with phrases that had never even existed when his career had begun: cyberattack, social media disinformation campaigns, drones, the Internet itself...

Hell!

...JSOC, The Night Stalkers, even stealth aircraft had been less than five years old when he'd joined. And Delta Force less than ten.

"Could I see the wider area imaging at Groom Lake?" Miranda asked in that strangely passionless way of hers.

Colonel Gray took care of setting it up for Chase while Drake contemplated how bad it would be to show up blind drunk for a White House meeting.

Chase kept asking for different views and replays.

He began gathering what he'd need by the dim light from the screen that mostly glowed with nighttime darkness.

"There it is."

54

"WHAT?" GRAY SAID AT THE SAME MOMENT HE DID. SO AT least he wasn't the only one in the dark.

"Run it back. Here," Chase reached out and took the keyboard from Gray. "Watch the upper right quadrant." Her control of the imaging easily matched Gray's. The runway lights of Groom Lake, along with some spill from the other buildings, marked the base. The clock in the lower right corner showed time flowing ahead.

"What are we looking for..." his voice petered out as the runway lights blinked off. The base was still visible, so it wasn't the camera. Something was landing on the runway that no one wanted to be seen, not even in the middle of the Nevada desert in the hour before dawn at a base manned only by personnel with top secret or better clearance. Something that didn't care about the lack of runway lights.

"Now watch the lower right quadrant," Miranda zoomed in rapidly.

A vague outline of a hangar stood at the south end of the

runway. Suddenly a light spilled out into the night. A long sleek delta-winged aircraft slipped off the end of the darkened runway, then turned gracefully into the light spilling out of the hangar's doors. For a brief instant, it was perfectly lit.

Chase stopped the video and zoomed in until the aircraft filled the screen.

"No markings," Chase noted. "Just camouflage coloring."

"No cockpit," Gray added. "A drone."

That's what it was. What it *had* to be. A drone that had downed a C-130 Hercules and whatever had upset Zhang Ru enough to call for his help interpreting his images. That had implications he'd have to think about later.

"Shit! It's ours."

55

IT WAS PROBABLY EVEN A WORSE CONCLUSION THAN IT BEING Russian.

The US services weren't just hiding things from one another; they were creating secret aircraft and carrying out secret missions against foreign assets without informing each other. He was the Chairman of the Joint Chiefs and should know about anything the President or the National Security Advisor knew.

But what if he didn't? Maybe they had shut him out of the loop, in which case it was definitely time to retire.

Or worse yet, what if the President and even the NSA didn't know?

That would leave...the CIA.

"Gray. Find out where that F-35 Lightning II that bombed our Hercules came from."

"I already did. Luke Air Force Base in Glendale, Arizona is missing one."

"Let me guess. The plane went missing, but all of the pilots are accounted for."

Gray nodded. "But who outside the Air Force is trained to fly the F-35?"

"A few pilots in the Air National Guard and..."

Her gasp was quite satisfying.

"My team postulates the CIA," Miranda spoke up before Gray could.

"Yes, their Special Operations Group has three pilots who've been through our training programs."

Our. Drake liked that Gray still honored the service she'd come from rather than using *their* as if the Air Force's problems were now someone else's. There was an awful lot to like about Colonel Gray. Nothing wrong with her mind either.

"The same people who tried to kidnap me this morning," Chase observed quietly.

"They didn't want you to solve this. You'll be safe as soon as we let them know that you already have. Then it will be out of your hands."

"Why would the CIA bomb a wrecked Air Force plane on a secret military base?"

"To hide the damage that they did to that US military airplane."

"Perhaps..." He didn't want to argue with Gray's conclusion. He wanted that to be all that there was to this. But what if it was more?

What if the CIA had decided to declare war on the US military? There had been two people undercover on that flight. And the loss of one of those people could be potentially devastating.

If this was a CIA *attack?*

Because they knew about the passenger?

Then the nation was on the verge of an interagency war.

56

DRAKE WAS AMUSED TO SEE THAT CIA DIRECTOR CLARK Winston had brought along the blonde woman from this morning's fiasco.

His Rangers had definitely enjoyed telling him of Clarissa Reese's poor attitude about being treated as a prisoner of war. When he'd shredded Clark Winston's receipt made out to General Fitzgerald Patrick, they hadn't said a word.

"Rangers lead the way, boys." He'd shaken both their hands and offered them friendly slaps on the back. The 75th Rangers were brutally tough and it was a hard slog meant for younger men, but a part of him still missed the camaraderie. Didn't get much of that at his level. They'd stridden out of his office with the well-deserved pride of the fine soldiers they were.

General Fitzgerald Patrick had brought Colonel Gray. Probably as protection against the bad publicity from the news reporting that he'd declared war on Georgetown.

Drake did his best to restrain his friendly greeting so as not to get her in trouble with her boss. As he shook hands with her, she slipped him a note.

He couldn't help smiling when he glanced at it.

Drake had provided the Chase woman transport to wherever she wanted to go—a flight home. He'd like to have kept her, or even brought her here to the Situation Room in the White House's ground floor, but couldn't justify either one so he'd let her go. He had routed her on a military flight that was headed out of Andrews Air Force Base to JBLM in Tacoma, Washington, to keep her name off the passenger manifests until he'd had a chance to deal with the CIA.

No time like the present.

While people were still settling at the Sit Room conference table, he went over to Clark Winston and Clarissa Reese at the coffee station.

"Call your dogs off the NTSB woman. We've already got the information on your drone project."

"You don't know shit." She was smart enough to keep her voice down, but didn't yet know that smart and ruthless didn't win every battle.

"Fine." He handed over the note that Gray had given him. "I know the President loves a good movie."

The woman's skin went sharply whiter than her white-blonde hair as she read it.

CIA attempted erasure of NRO satellite feed. All conclusions of MC confirmed.

"Who's MC?" Clark read the note over Reese's shoulder.

"The woman that your Assistant Director Clarissa Reese here attempted to kidnap in Georgetown this morning.

Kidnap attempt, and made national news for blowing up a portion of a civilian's house."

"The CIA attacked Georgetown? No shit?" Clark did his best to look surprised, but didn't quite pull it off.

He could have, if he wanted to. After all those years in the field, he could lie with a dead-straight face.

But not the blonde.

Reese cast a quick sideways glance of surprise at her boss.

It was obvious that Miranda Chase had been right; they were definitely sleeping together. And Reese had shown Drake that Clark knew about the attack anyway.

Drake considered. He'd never understood the man, but liked him despite that. CIA directors were a notoriously humorless breed and Clark Winston was a breath of fresh air. But he was apparently very good at hiding things with that sense of humor.

He decided against trying to knock Clarissa Reese out of place just so that he could maintain some window into Clark's thinking. If he wanted to play with someone barely half his age, let him.

"Just let Chase alone. She's already told us all she knows." Drake addressed this to Reese, who watched him steadily with her dazzling blue eyes for a long moment before nodding her assent. He had a daughter and hoped his assessment of Reese's actual agreement was accurate. There was more in her look, as if she was assessing his own viability for something.

He was definitely getting too old for this shit and took his coffee to the table. He selected a chair across from Gray. Her dark eyes held none of the cold calculation of Reese's.

Caffeine-boosted alertness shone, just as his probably did after the long night, but no games. Definitely needed her first name; he already had her phone number.

"So, what the hell have you been up to, Patrick?" President Roy Cole breezed into the room, flanked by his Chief of Staff and the Secretary of Defense, with his usual no-nonsense attitude. They all jolted to their feet even as the President made his usual patting motion. Cole took his chair at the head of the table.

"I don't know what you're—" Patrick sputtered.

"You know. I've always felt that you saw the NRO as your own personal fiefdom. Disinformation leading to military action in Georgetown? Really? Now there's a new leak of classified surveillance of the Russian President's private compound that I'm informed just hit the *Washington Post* from your own e-mail account."

"I never—"

He waved a hand at his Chief of Staff who'd come in with him. Nora Farber pulled out a sheet of paper and began speaking, "The *Post* sent us your e-mail as a courtesy heads-up. We've confirmed that the IP address matches your latest e-mail to the President this morning regarding the imagery for the takedown of the head of Iranian intelligence."

"Please tell me you didn't leak that as well," Cole sat bolt upright like the ex-Green Beret he was.

"I never leaked any of it," Patrick thumped a fist on the table.

Drake spotted a flicker of a smile on Clarissa Reese's face. Definitely a dangerous woman to keep an eye on. Maybe Clark was playing with fire, or maybe he didn't even realize what the woman was doing.

Still, better the shark he knew about than the one he didn't.

"I'll bet it was this asshole's doing." Patrick jabbed a finger in his direction and Drake could only laugh.

"Wish I'd thought of it," though he *had* thought of the first parts. Patrick had also clearly aggravated the CIA because they had to be behind the e-mail leak. It didn't matter; Drake had fought on too many battlefields and played far too much politics over the years to be caught out so easily.

"And you need a broader vocabulary of insults, General Patrick. The two passwords you so reluctantly gave me, for data that I legitimately requested—UpYoursAsshole and FuckYouTwiceAsshole!—have a repeated common text string, which cryptanalysts tell me is bad form."

Cole scowled down the table for a moment before speaking. "I've never liked you, Patrick. You've always been an arrogant prick. And I now realize that I've never trusted you either. You," he aimed a finger at Gray. "Who are you?"

"Colonel Elizabeth Gray, sir."

Score. Drake finally had her first name. Well, perhaps that thought was more suitable for a fifteen-year-old, but when this was over, he was definitely asking her out to dinner.

"I'm head of domestic imaging. Though I assist Director Patrick on numerous other projects, both foreign and in space."

Patrick sent her a bitter look of betrayal. Hard to blame him, even if he deserved whatever was coming to him.

Cole glanced at him. "Drake, you worked with her?"

"Just the last twenty hours, but almost all of those. Exceptionally competent, sir."

"Patrick, you're hereby relieved pending investigations."

"But you can't! I'm not appointed by you. I'm—"

"Appointed by me and I can dismiss you," Secretary of Defense McCann spoke for the first time. "And I'm glad to finally do it. I can also state that Gray has been an exceptional asset, one I use myself rather than Director Patrick whenever possible."

"Get out of my house," President Cole commanded. "And leave your NRO security pass with McCann right now. If you'd rather retire quietly, we'll take that into consideration. No promises. Gray, you're Acting Director until McCann and I figure out what is going on over there. McCann, see that I get a recommendation for a rank bump to general for her before you announce her new role by end of day. Can't have her overseeing people who outrank her; that place is enough of a nightmare without that burden."

Drake watched Elizabeth Gray swallow hard, one of her few tells about the state of her nerves. That and her occasional electric smile. Nobody was watching Patrick as he slinked out of the room.

"Sir, either of the deputy directors—" Gray started.

"They don't have the imagination necessary to run the NRO in the way it must be going into the future," McCann spoke up, but not unkindly. "I've worked with both of them since back when you were still a line officer flying combat. They're highly competent in their roles, but unimaginative. She's the best recommendation I have, sir." He addressed the last to the President.

Cole stared at her in silence until Drake was impressed that she didn't simply melt under his gaze.

"Drake? She fit in with what you were talking about right after I took office?" Cole asked without looking at him.

"Interagency cooperation rather than competition? Absolutely." Rather than looking at the President, he turned to face the pair from the CIA. No, the woman. Clark might have the personality to draw the spotlight and his share of savvy and secrets, but Drake expected that Clarissa Reese had the power, or soon would. "It's the essential element we *must* have going forward."

He held her gaze until she offered an infinitesimal nod of acknowledgement.

Not that he'd trust her. But it was a start.

57

"SO, ARE WE DONE?" MIKE PRAYED THEY WERE.

The three of them sat on high stools around a stainless-steel table. The deck of The Hub restaurant overlooked the Tacoma Narrows Airport runway. Every five or ten minutes some small plane flitted along the single runway.

The number of them increased significantly around lunchtime and were all parked just beyond the windbreak of glass that ringed the deck. Soon The Hub was half full of people who apparently just flew in for lunch. He liked the familiar feeling of seeing so much iced tea and lemonade.

The three of them were still technically at work, but any pilots also had to follow the FAA's eight-hours-from-bottle-to-throttle rule. Only passengers were lucky enough to have a beer at lunch.

It was frustrating, because he could see that it was a local microbrew, and they'd looked good when he read over the beer menu.

The Hub had a good feel. And it wasn't just the logo of a silhouetted naked lady with long billowing hair, seeming to fly from her handhold on a bicycle's handlebars. People appeared to be glad to be here.

It took him back to the "Good Old Days," which weren't so old and hadn't been so good, but had included lunchtime flying. When the FBI's and the thug-clients' advertising dollars had really been flowing, he'd gotten licensed and picked up a zippy little Beech Bonanza.

With its distinctive v-tail and Mike's leopard logo, it had been a hit with the clients. He'd taken any number of them out on a flight to a rural airport on a "pie quest"—a common excuse among pilots to go flying to various airport diners like this place—and do the business deals with ad campaign sketches rolled out right on the wing of the plane.

Seeing Miranda's Mooney sitting in the hangar made him itch to fly again. However strange she might be, the woman had taste in her planes. The Mooney was sweet, going seventy-five miles an hour faster than his Bonanza— the very last sliver of his business assets that he'd sold.

He kept marginally current in a rental plane, but it wasn't the same.

The Reuben sandwich was better than average, though Mike didn't know why he kept ordering them wherever he went. Nothing would ever match Katz's Delicatessen in lower Manhattan, but he kept trying.

Holly had opted for something called a Kona pizza that boasted porter BBQ sauce, roast chicken, caramelized onion, and grilled pineapple. Next time, if there was a next time in this rinky-dink corner of civilization, that's what he'd get.

He'd tried to get a taste of it and almost gotten a fork through the back of his hand for his trouble.

Jeremy had a bacon, mushroom, cheese Hangar Smashed Burger with a massive pile of tater tots, but wasn't looking up at all from his computer.

"I don't know," Holly had ordered a large pizza, but was still making strong headway through it. Of course they'd all missed breakfast because of the fighter jet parked out at Crest. "Boss hasn't called us off. Her text did say she was coming into JBLM in about five hours. I figure that we can wait that long."

"I suppose," Mike surveyed the bar, but there weren't a lot of single women here. Mostly it was couples or guys with planes. A low-target environment. Maybe it livened up in the evenings. Though at this point he'd be glad to just chat about planes.

Small, general aviation planes. He'd had enough of exploding C-130 military transports and plummeting helicopters to last him for quite a while.

"We're not done," Jeremy said without looking up.

"Why not?"

"There was a lot more on that flight recorder."

"Such as?" Holly lounged back after snagging the second-to-last slice of her pizza. Her light blonde hair, freed from her Australian Matildas ball cap, fluttered about in the afternoon sunlight. He could see that it was just killing the guy pilots who were trying to focus on their lunches with a low success rate.

"The C-130's prior stop was on a beach in Baja California, Mexico. No record of any contact with Mexican authorities."

"But that doesn't involve us."

"No, but the other voices do."

"Other voices?"

"Normal crew is five people: two pilots, flight engineer, loadmaster, and navigator. Right? That's even what that General Harrington told Mike they had removed from the plane."

Mike nodded to confirm that. Then he took another bite of his Reuben to curtail his ability to make any statement that Holly might want to attack.

"Except this C-130 received the AMP upgrade through the Avionics Modernization Program, meaning it had been upgraded to a glass cockpit. So, their minimum crew is two pilots and a loadmaster. That's three people."

"Even I can count that high, Jeremy," Mike set down his sandwich. "Minimum crew doesn't mean that's all that were there."

"No, except I only get those three voices in the cockpit—two guys and a female copilot. The fourth audio channel was a general pickup in the cargo bay. It's intended to record any crash-relevant atypical airframe noises, shouts by passengers, and the like. Instead, it picked up snatches of a conversation."

"Why is that a big deal?"

Mike was happy to let Holly fall on the sword of one of Jeremy's winding explanations for a change.

"Because they weren't Air Force crew members. They may have been dressed like them so that the general would think that's what he unloaded into the Groom Lake morgue, but they weren't on board before that Mexico beach landing and I can filter enough snippets out of the background noise to know that they're talking about meetings at Groom Lake."

"I'm sure lots of people have meetings at Groom Lake," Mike would take the fall on this one.

"Probably not ones speaking in Mandarin."

Mike considered. Probably not.

58

"Now, what about our other little problem?"

President Cole had chased everyone else out to the waiting room.

Now it was just him and the President. Even the CIA and the Secretary of Defense had been sent away.

Drake sighed.

"Two things about that, sir. First, we've learned what happened to the Hercules C-130 transport as it approached Groom Lake. It was downed by a CIA drone for reasons that are still unclear."

The President scowled but held his peace, awaiting more information.

"Also, a second drone, probably from the same series, downed a Chinese aircraft at roughly the same time three days ago. Though I only heard about it today."

"Shit! Where did this happen?" There was no faking his surprise. Drake felt better about feeling bad. It wasn't only him that the CIA had kept out of the loop.

"Central China."

Cole opened his mouth...then shut it again.

"The Chinese have *not* figured this out, but they know something's wrong."

Cole grunted, "And you know all of this for reasons that I don't want to know the details about."

He didn't make it a question, so Drake didn't bother answering.

Drake still hadn't figured out what to tell Zhang Ru about Miranda's conclusion that his jet had been attacked by an American CIA drone.

And he hoped to God that who he thought were on that Hercules when it crashed weren't on that Hercules.

Even if he *knew* they were.

"Are the Chinese going to be a problem?"

"I'm not sure yet, Mr. President."

"Don't let them become one."

"Yes sir, Mr. President."

Once Miranda had provided longitude, latitude, and time from Zhang Ru's videos, Gray had looked at the NRO's satellite recordings of the area.

So he hadn't quite broken his word to Zhang; Miranda was the only analyst to look at the imagery Zhang had provided. And he himself had inspected neither.

The CIA drone now parked at Groom Lake had mounted an attack against a foreign power deep in the heart of China. What in the world *had* the CIA built out in the middle of his military reserve?

Even worse, what the hell had those crackers been thinking?

The only way to stop an interagency war, if that's what they were brewing, was to see it for himself.

"The second thing—you know I was within minutes of departure for Groom Lake when the C-130 went down."

The President nodded.

"There is no clear reporting on this, but the flight had a crew of three when it departed Edwards Air Force Base, yet five were reported as deceased at Groom Lake."

"Hell and damnation," Cole whispered softly.

"Sir, between the two problems—our two extra people and whatever the hell the CIA is up to—I'm going to depart within the hour for Groom Lake, both to confirm our information and to straighten this out."

"You mean confirm our worst goddamn fears." President Roy Cole was Ex-Special Forces himself; he always preferred men of action.

And as the Green Berets were as much about relationship building as fighting, the President appreciated men willing to do the task themselves—a way of thinking he and Drake shared despite Drake coming from those "Special Operations ass-kickers of the 75th Ranger Regiment" that the President was always teasing him about.

"Take whoever you need. Get me some answers. Preferably today."

"Yes sir."

Cole was halfway to the door before he stopped and asked without turning. "Anything that I want to know about why a SWAT team was taken down by a combined 75th Rangers / Army 12th Aviation element less than two miles from this house?"

"No sir. Not a thing."

"Good," the President left the room. He was chuckling softly as he left.

59

GRAY HAD ASKED TO ACCOMPANY HIM FOR HIS RIDE OUT TO Andrews Air Force Base even though she wasn't needed in Nevada.

From the first second in the car, she'd asked him a whole series of questions about the NRO's best-practice communications with both his office and the President's that showed she'd been thinking hard since the very moment of her new appointment. Only a few minutes from the airport, her questions had finally run down and she looked as exhausted as he felt.

No, she didn't, at least not to his eye.

"Tell me about your life, Elizabeth Gray." He liked the way her name felt when he said it.

"Or Lizzy. I was named for Elizabeth Bennett." At his blank look, she thankfully explained. "She was sort of the first great romance heroine in novels. Mom loves Jane Austen books."

"You're a romance heroine turned Air Force colonel?"

"No," she smiled over at him. "I'm a romance heroine turned Air Force *general* and Acting Director of the National Reconnaissance Office. And don't think that I won't hold it against you if I make a disaster of the whole situation."

"Yes sir, ma'am," he saluted her. "Anything you say, ma'am, sir."

"Go to hell, General Nason."

"Probably." Which wouldn't surprise him. There were so many things that could go wrong in the next twenty-four hours that it made his head hurt. One reason he didn't want General Gray along, so she'd be clear of this mess. "I bet you a hundred bucks that you'll be great."

"I made general for my forty-ninth birthday," she let out a startled breath.

"When's that?"

"We're celebrating it right now with a car ride to the airport. I was supposed to have it with Mom. I think. I've been awake so long that I don't even know what day it is."

"Your birthday."

"Oh right."

Forty-nine? Just nine years his junior.

"I'll tell you what, General Elizabeth Gray," he spoke as the car rolled to a stop close by a C-37B Gulfstream VIP business jet.

Clark and Reese were already waiting for him. He might need Clarissa Reese—it was her project after all—but he also didn't trust her. Clark would be his hammer, plenty ticked at being forced to fly out to Nevada with him.

Drake climbed out of the car, then leaned down to look back in, "When I get back and have gotten some sleep, I'd like to take you out to dinner to celebrate."

She didn't even hesitate before she hit him with one of those electric smiles of hers.

"That would be lovely, Drake."

"That's General Drake to you." He closed the door before she could respond, slapped the roof of the car, and spoke to the driver, "Take the general to the NRO where she belongs."

60

"No ma'am. I can't divert this flight. You've seen our cargo."

Miranda considered handing the radio call from General Nason over to him anyway. But she didn't. She pulled the headset that the copilot had handed her back on.

"I'll be there with my team as soon as I can, Drake."

"How soon is that? I'm just departing Andrews."

"I'll be there with my team as soon as I can, Drake." What else was she supposed to say?

"Hurry," and he was gone.

The pilot was right, nothing should divert a Dignified Transfer flight.

"May I place a call or text to my team?"

"If you use the plane's wi-fi, you can text all you want. If I patch you through our system, I can't guarantee that the call will be private. In fact, I can pretty much guarantee it won't be if you're cross-patching to a civilian line."

She descended the steep ladder back into the cargo bay

of the massive C-17 Globemaster III cargo jet. It was almost twice the length and nearly four times the carrying capacity of a C-130 Hercules.

Imagining the possibility of the mystery drone flashing by overhead and shattering the big plane was not a comforting thought. Though it was only early afternoon and she suspected the drone didn't come out during daylight hours.

She sat in one of the jump seats along the side of the aircraft.

Two officers sat at the tail end of the cargo bay, watching the rows of flag-draped coffins. She'd asked and been answered politely, but the officers hadn't looked up to continuing the discussion. Yet another Marine Corps CH-53E Super Stallion helicopter had fallen out of the sky. Twenty-seven Marines had gone down with the five-person crew, and the officers were keeping their people company for their final ride home. Of the thirty-two dead, twenty-four coffins were headed back to the Pacific Northwest.

Need you at Groom Lake.

Mike shouting with joy, Holly texted back. *Don't know why. Don't care. When?*

How soon can you get there?

With or without being shot down? Holly included a smiley-faced emoji, which Miranda appreciated as it told her the message was meant as a tease.

Without = preferred, she sent back with her own smiley. Emotions were so much easier to understand when they were labeled.

Mike asks if we can borrow the Mooney?

That would place them there in about four hours. She

glanced out a tiny inspection port in a personnel hatch—a C-17 didn't bother with such trivia as passenger windows. She'd flown over this section of the Rockies so many times over the last twenty years that she knew they were just twenty minutes east of Missoula, Montana.

Keys in the third drawer down, left-hand cupboard.

You trust him with your plane?!?!?

No wide-eyed emoji, but she'd assume it was pretend shock on Holly's part.

And you expect me to board an aircraft he's piloting???!

Okay, maybe not so pretend. How was she supposed to tell?

I'll be in JBLM in just under two hours.

Should we wait for you? Rather have you as pilot. This time Holly sent another smiley, so the rest of it must have been a tease.

No. Get moving. I'll catch up in my jet. Clearance will be waiting for you.

On the hoof. If we arrive dead, blame that dingo-head Mike.

I promise.

While she waited for the flight to arrive in Tacoma, she sat with the dead and wondered why General Nason had called them back in.

61

"YOU LET THE *FIRE HEADS* BEAT YOU?"

Harvey kept Helen spooned lazily against him as he nuzzled her hair. "Didn't *let* them do anything. They beat us fair and square."

"More like they kicked your asses," she reached around to slap his ass to make her point. "Seventeen-three? Who loses a seven-inning softball game by fourteen runs?"

"Ease up, woman. That stung."

"Awe. Poor little pilot who can't play ball to save his skin."

He decided to ignore that.

"You know, we need to talk about The Rip. It—"

"I can't tell you how good it feels to be a pilot again. It's like... like... I don't know, but it's just like that."

Her silence went deep.

"What? I cut you off. What were you going to say?"

She shook her head no.

The Rip. Someone else had mentioned The Rip. Who? He couldn't seem to grasp onto it. Maybe it wasn't important.

So, was her silence his cue to probe deeper or to let it go by? It was one of those women cues that never seemed to be the same twice.

"Harvey..."

"Uh huh."

She ducked and turned her face into where her head rested on his arm as if hiding her face. Again her silence stretched out and twice she started to turn to him but didn't.

"It's Friday. Don't you have to catch a flight soon?"

"I...called home to say that I couldn't get away this weekend."

"Really, why?"

That earned him an elbow in the ribs. Helen had sharp elbows.

"Oh." For him? "Whoa!"

"Don't get all *Whoa!* on me. I'm not staying for a superior sexual experience, though I fully expect to have at least a couple of them."

"That's a guarantee. Then you're staying because..."

She didn't answer. Her silence was so deafening that her answer was definitely *way* out in major *Whoa!* territory and then some.

"...because I have another flight coming up and you're all worried about me?" Harvey covered.

"Yeah. That's it." But she sounded awfully sad—like he'd really missed the mark. Not even a little hint of sarcasm in her words. Helen wasn't the sort of woman who got sad.

Pointing out that she had a husband and a life on the outside didn't seem like the right move. Escorting her to the Janet Airlines plane to Vegas in an hour so that she *would* go home this weekend would be the right move, no matter how much he didn't want to.

Other than flying, she was the best thing that had ever happened to him.

He was a goddamn Air Force pilot, and he had the best lover of his life in his arms. A lover who'd just as much said what...? That she *did* love him?

Really serious *Whoa!* territory!

Harvey didn't know if he'd ever have the right words for it, but he pulled her back tight against him until she gasped in surprise.

"I feel about you," he whispered in her ear, "the same way I feel about flying. If it was up to me, I'd never give up either one."

"Oh, Harvey." She kept her hands wrapped tightly over where his rested on her breast as her hot tears spilled onto his arm. "I just can't say it."

"It's okay, babe. It's all okay." He didn't want the L-word coming at him anyway, not even from Helen.

She shook her head fiercely, but didn't say another word.

62

"IT MAKES ME WANT TO SING!"

"Please don't," Holly and Jeremy called in unison.

"Off we go into the wild blue yonder, Climbing high into the sun."

"Aaaaa! Kill me now!"

He glanced into the back seat to see her pretend to stab a knife into her gut, slice it open *hari-kari* style, and then flop over dead. At least by being in the back, she didn't die onto the Mooney's flight controls.

If it got this kind of response, he'd definitely have to learn more than the first two lines of the official Air Force song.

But he still felt like singing.

The Mooney passenger plane, once he'd worked his way through the checklist, was an absolute dream to fly. Fast, agile, and forgiving on the controls—which was good as he'd never flown such a powerful airplane before. Thank God for checklists. He'd had Holly carefully read out every one to make sure that he didn't screw up Miranda's plane.

And that woman flew a Sabrejet? What was *that* like?

At least he didn't have to worry about its condition; Miranda kept both her aircraft absolutely immaculate. He supposed that shouldn't be a surprise anymore. The woman had a precision that was unique in his experience. Even Jeremy didn't see and observe the kind of details that she did.

Her view of the big picture sucked, which he supposed was what Holly did for her. And Jeremy was just a Miranda in training—Mr. Super Geek.

They were most of the way across Oregon, California, and Nevada while he wondered what the hell he could do.

And came up with squat.

A glance at Jeremy showed the guy was passed out against the passenger door. Mike switched him out of the headsets' intercom circuit.

"Hey, Holly?"

"What? You're not going to start singing again, are you?"

"Maybe later. Special concert just for you. I do a good Elvis impersonation." He put on his best John Wayne accent and tried a rendition of: *"You ain't nothin' but a hound dog, pardner. Why in Sam Hill are you cryin' anyway, son?"*

Holly made a death-gargle sound.

"Have a question though."

"Keep your day job."

"Actually, that was kind of my question. What in the world *is* my day job?"

"Straight up, mate?" It was one of the first times her tone was serious.

"Straight up."

"Well, you're good with people."

"Sure. Any time you ladies piss off a two-star general or want to distract a mercenary, I'm your guy."

"This one was technical. When we get into people—"

"Yeah, yeah. Interview folks. I'm good at it, but where's the home run in that?"

"Seriously, Mike? You don't see it?"

"See what?"

"And I thought I was the one who'd be from Back o' Bourke in this American crowd."

"Goddamn it, Holly. I—"

"Shit, Mike. Miranda needs someone who's good with people so that she can *function*. She's scared to death of everything. Her past, her present, her own ruddy shadow. She's the best there is; just ask Jeremy. Me, I'd never have come up with the cause to that crash in a year and she did it in a single night. The solution? She uncovered some serious CIA shit and found it in another day. I can try to keep her safe, but you're her buffer to all the scary shit of having a team and having people around her. If you'd step up to the goddamn plate, she could do her job without melting down like she did."

"She had a meltdown?"

Even as Holly cursed him, he could see it. Her paralysis after she'd demoed the real flight profile after working on it all night. She'd never said why, but she'd clearly panicked—panicked by shutting down entirely. All the signs had been there, but only Holly had been paying attention.

"Crap! I didn't see it. How did I miss that?"

"Well, open your bleeding eyes, mate! Now don't get us all killed."

They were just coming up on southern Nevada. The electronic flight charts, displayed on a high-visibility screen at the center of the console, showed they would be intersecting the wide, comb-toothed blue line of restricted military operations area shortly. Specifically the airspace boundary of the Nevada Test and Training Range where he'd probably be shot for intruding *before* they bothered asking any questions. Inside that, Groom Lake itself was surrounded by a heavy-dashed blue line that simply meant "Prohibited."

There wasn't anything obvious out the window to mark where they were. Looking ahead (or to either side for that matter), they were back in the land of lumpy brown landscape: desert, scrub, sharp hills, and plenty of beige sand.

He hated beige.

It was like the ad designer's nemesis. Every client was comfortable with beige, and no other color, not even gray or white, carried so *little* emotional impact. Of course, he was no longer an ad designer but rather an NTSB human operations guy. Like he was doing such a bang-up job of that.

Still, God or whoever had put down his paintbrush a little early when it came to the Nevada countryside.

Maybe if he—

A silver jet blasted by them.

"Shit! I knew it. They're going to shoot us down." He grabbed for the radio, but Holly already had hit the switch on her headset.

"Hi, Miranda. That's a mighty shiny jet you have there."

"It is shiny."

Holly laughed as Miranda came looping back around and took up station just off his left wingtip.

"I have the base control tower on another channel. They're expecting us. Stay just above and to the right of me so that you don't catch my wake turbulence."

The Mooney was fast, but it couldn't fly even half the speed of sound. He glanced over and down at Miranda. She wore a full pilot's helmet, and to match his speed must feel as if she was suddenly crawling. The four-hour flight in their plane would have been an hour and a half in hers.

Mike did his best to ignore the sweat on his palms as the flight map showed him entering some of the most restricted-access flight space in the country. But he didn't think that's why he was sweating.

What the hell was he doing here? Flying into the NTTR with an NTSB team?

A team? He'd never managed a team in his life.

That was enough to worry him out of the sky...

Until the twin-tail F-18 Hornet fighter jet—with a full array of weapons hanging from its wings—showed up less than fifty meters away on his other side.

"General Nason," Harrington's salute was sharp as Drake deplaned at Groom Lake.

Last time they'd met had been four years ago at a strategy conference. Then they'd shaken hands rather than saluting. But it had been a tense couple of days and he hadn't been the CJCS at that point.

And that meeting hadn't been at the center of Groom Lake. He hadn't been out here in years. It still had the long, salt bed runway that he recalled. There were more buildings, but not many. Two-story, concrete block structures and vast hangars. The place was like a faded watercolor painting titled "Boring."

"General Harrington," he delayed returning the salute long enough to let the man know he was treading on very thin ice. "If I find that you are still holding back a single thing, you'll be in Leavenworth Penitentiary before sunrise."

Harrington gave him the standard "Yeah, right" look that came from overconfidence.

Drake was running out of humor with this whole situation; he'd been up for two days and his assistant had been burning up the secure comm channel about a devolving situation in Hong Kong and another in Azerbaijan. And he was in Nevada with a pissed off CIA director and his uncontrollable lover.

"Failure to inform a superior officer of developing situations. Attacking a friendly foreign national—China *is* still on the friendly list."

"I didn't know what they intended—"

"Interference with an official crash investigation."

"I didn't blow up the goddamn—"

"I was referring to the removal and return of the flight recorders, which were not destroyed in the bombing as someone hoped, by the way." He wondered what Clarissa Reese's reaction to that bit of news might be. "Confiscation of the NTSB's data and samples."

"Wait, what? That wasn't me."

Then it was the CIA, whom he'd deal with later. "At the moment you should just be glad I don't want you hung, Harrington. I'd give you three-to-one odds that it wouldn't be hard to prove treason if I put my mind to it."

Winston and Reese came down the plane's steps.

"These are CIA Director Clark Winston and Director of Special Projects for him, Clarissa Reese."

Harrington didn't return Reese's haughty nod. Clearly they already knew each other; only time would tell how well. Maybe Harrington was finally being careful.

Director Clark Winston did his man-of-the-people thing and made a shot at getting Harrington started on baseball, "Spotted the field as we came in."

Drake cut him off. "Where's the rest of my team?"

Harrington just pointed aloft.

The desert sunset was moving fast, but the last of the sunlight aloft illuminated a small cluster of aircraft. A small general aviation plane entered the field's flight pattern, closely followed by...

"Is that an F-86 Sabrejet?"

"That's what my escort pilot tells me." An F-18 trailed along, close behind the pair.

"These are not military combatants. They're members of the NTSB team."

"Who I've already met, yes sir. They come onto my base in a fighter jet, I'm going to damn well be ready to shoot them out of the sky."

Which Drake had to admit made sense even if the jet was over sixty years old. Air Force thinking rather than his more deeply ingrained Army thinking? He'd have to talk to now-General Gray about that and see if he was shortchanging the other military branches in ways he didn't even realize.

He almost laughed. How fast had she earned his trust and respect? "Pretty damn!" as his granddaughter was fond of saying. He was definitely looking forward to that dinner.

They all stood and waited until the others had joined them. The pilot of the light plane made a respectable if not elegant landing. The Sabrejet smacked down on the numbers as neatly as any seasoned fighter jock nailing a carrier landing—a skill he'd always marveled at whenever he was in a position to witness it. Who on Miranda's team...

Then Miranda Chase glided the Sabrejet to a stop close beside them and popped the canopy.

He stepped over to help her down. "You fly well, Miranda."

"Yes, I do. General Harrington, I'm ready to see the drone now."

Drake had learned to just go with the flow around Miranda. She was one *very* focused woman.

"No you're not. That's classified. What drone?"

"Last warning, Harrington," Drake was really sick of the man. "We're not here for a dog-and-pony show about aliens." The man finally sagged.

"There are aliens here?" The pilot from the other plane stepped up. Despite having landed first, he was much less adroit at taxiing and had only just parked. "Hi, I'm Mike Munroe. Human operations investigator for Miranda. My dad and I were really hooked on Area 51 stuff."

"Get a grip, Mikey. We're in the real world now." A lovely blonde with a bright Aussie accent stepped up beside him. She was everything that Clarissa Reese wasn't. Casual, unstudied, and she radiated an easy confidence. "Holly Harper. Formerly in the Oz SAS, now in the Queen's service," she bowed deeply to Miranda. Which earned her a laugh from everyone—except Miranda, who shuffled uncertainly from foot to foot, and Clarissa, who just looked as if she hated everyone.

"Guys," the young Vietnamese man practically shouted. "Do you realize the kind of gear they've prototyped and based here? Not just nuclear bombs, but the U-2, the SR-71 Blackbird. Can you imagine the sound of those rolling right down this runway on their way to go spy on Russia? Pow! Right over the North Pole at a hundred thousand feet going Mach 3. And that's before planes went Mach 3 like it was something normal. The F-117 Nighthawk, the first-ever stealth bird, and—"

"You have to forgive him. Jeremy's our local genius," Holly cut him off. "He's cute, so we keep him around and feed him doggie biscuits and pat him on the head." She then did just that, though Jeremy didn't appear to notice.

"Is that the new Ultra-wideband Synthetic-aperture radar I saw at the head of the dry lake? Have you gotten around the power limitations compared to multi-baseline interferometry? Oh, an acoustic weapons testing platform, sweet. I'd love to check that out if you'd let me. Acoustics is fascinating from a weather dynamics perspective. I've read all of the available public information on those and I think that you guys are really missing some tricks."

At first, Drake had let him and the others prattle on because he wanted to get a feel for Miranda's team. Reese and Winston's eyes were glazing over with frustration, another bonus. But he suddenly had the feeling that he should be taking notes.

"It's not just directed sonics. There's untapped capacity in phase manipulation. You guys should really get into that; I wrote a couple papers on it in college. Do you have a railgun out here? Always wanted to see one fire. Did you know the air around the projectiles actually burns from the heat of passage? I've forgotten where you're testing those. Oh wait, that's the Navy in Virginia. Never mind."

"Down, boy. Down," Holly made as if to reach for his arm.

For some reason, Jeremy snatched it to his chest protectively.

"See? He can learn."

Jeremy started to speak again, but Holly reached toward him once more.

"Cut that out, will you?"

Again she made a show of patting him on the head as he clutched his arm protectively.

Drake found it easy to like Miranda's people.

Then they went silent as Miranda repeated her first words from before all the merry mayhem.

"General Harrington, I'm ready to see the drone now."

MIRANDA SAT IN THE BACK OF THE VAN WITH HOLLY AS THEY drove down the empty stretch of the field.

They'd parked their jets and the Mooney by one of the hangars near the main base that ran from midfield, then north along the west side of the runway. Even as they were driving away, the aircraft were being rolled out of sight into a big hangar despite the descending darkness.

The van was currently driving their group over a mile to a lone hangar at the far south end of the field.

"Here," Holly pulled out her tablet and began whispering to her quickly. "Here's the data they loaded onto the CVDR."

"They tampered with—" Miranda couldn't even speak. Nobody tampered with black boxes. That defeated the whole purpose of gathering the information in the first place. The displayed profile was the already disproven Stall Scenario.

"Jeremy was a good boy and found this deleted profile." Holly flicked to the next screen.

Miranda didn't even need to scan it. She could see by the pattern of the numbers that it was almost exactly as she'd predicted and witnessed on the tapes. She nodded for Holly to keep moving; they were already halfway to the remote hangar.

Mike was making a point of having a loud conversation about aliens with Jeremy, who sat immediately ahead of her and Holly. An eighty-decibel noise masker. Well done.

"And this," Holly flashed to the next screen.

The route out of Mexico was of no consequence to her.

"Before the stop on a Mexico beach, there were only three voices aboard."

Miranda wondered why Holly was bringing it up. No amount of sand ingestion could have resulted in the flight profile caused by the passage of the drone.

"After the pickup, there were *five* voices, two of whom spoke in Mandarin."

She hadn't told Holly anything about the Chinese flight imagery that she still had on her own computer.

"The guards became very itchy whenever any of us explored the rear of the aircraft just forward of the loading ramp hinge point. Here are a series of images I took there."

Miranda flicked through them quickly. The damage was remarkable. It was so severe that she'd lost a clear impression of it in just the last thirty-six hours. Holly's records brought it back with stark clarity.

"I can't take all the credit. Jeremy did a bunch of this."

"And what did Mike do?"

"He kept the guards off our backs. Even made friends

with one of them, which may have saved our lives. Wouldn't have been too surprised if they would have just cleared out and left us there to be blown to shit otherwise. He also helped us figure out what was going on in the recording."

Miranda pulled up the Chinese image sequence and started the playback, holding the tablet so that only Holly could see it. Miranda traced the drone's path until Holly whistled softly in surprise.

"They thought it was a reflection."

"Why don't you?"

"It doesn't shift with the sun."

Holly watched a while longer, then nudged her shoulder into Miranda's. "Serious fair dinkum, girlfriend. Serious."

Miranda already knew she was right, but Holly didn't seem to be stating the obvious either. A compliment perhaps?

"So, this drone can do some serious shit," Holly shut down and stowed her tablet as they pulled up to the massive hangar. "Can't wait to see the little bugger."

Miranda didn't share her enthusiasm.

She'd seen the faulty wiring harness that had killed TWA 800, both the rebuilt shreds and the new one Boeing had supplied as part of the investigation. Seeing the final thing that killed planes always brought up a deep churn of sadness that she only held back with a hard struggle.

As the van drove up to the hangar, the massive doors parted sideways like a set of shark jaws preparing to eat them alive.

65

"You're just in time to see this." Rather than rolling into the hangar, Harrington stopped the van.

A long thin needle of an aircraft slipped out into the night—at the first moment it could take off unobserved.

Miranda, along with the others, pressed her face to the window, trying to see it better as it rolled by.

"That's seriously next-level," Jeremy was the first to recover his voice.

"Yes," Clarissa Reese sounded pleased. "Mach 2.9 capable. Supercruise at 2.1. Ten-thousand-mile range and that includes fifty percent of the flight at supercruise. Up to twenty-four hour loiter time on site at subsonic speeds. We can—"

"Shut up, Clarissa." Director Clark Winston's tone was flat and harsh.

Miranda glanced at Holly, who, with a barely visible shrug, suggested she didn't know what to make of it either.

Again, Mike would, but she couldn't ask with everyone right there in the van.

"And the reason that I don't know about this?" General Nason snapped out.

Clarissa started to speak, but Clark cut her off again.

Harrington finally spoke as they watched the drone disappear into the dark. There was only the softest rumble as it took off. "Compartmentalized need-to-know. It's DARPA work."

"And because I'm just the Chairman of the Joint Chiefs of Staff, I don't need to know what the Defense Advanced Research Projects Agency is up to. Internet, stealth, killer drones, and now stealth killer drones. One step closer to the edge, Harrington."

From the back, Miranda couldn't see Drake's face but, silhouetted by the light spilling from the still open hangar door, she could tell he was facing the CIA people. "You two have a great deal to answer for."

"Not to you, we don't!" Clarissa snapped out.

Clark's sigh was audible.

"No, Clark," Clarissa rounded on him. "We don't reveal our sources when we have a spy undercover. Not to the press and not to Army generals with delusions of grandeur."

"Clark," Drake said calmly. "Tell your division director that if she speaks to me again without a specific instruction, I'll have her rendered into one of the torture centers she used to run and see how she enjoys what they hand out."

He paused for a long moment, but no one else spoke.

"Clark, your undercover spies don't cost a hundred million dollars of military assets and threaten to destabilize global peace."

"Peace? You call this peace? This isn't even détente anymore," Clarissa refused to be silenced, raising her voice until it rang in the van. "This is asymmetric technologic warfare. If we aren't at the cutting edge, we're dead. Why do you think DARPA was founded?"

While she wasn't wrong, Miranda would never have said it in so antagonistic a way to a four-star general.

Drake opened the passenger door and stepped out. Sliding open the side door, he grabbed Clarissa's arm and yanked her from the van. She struggled, but was ineffective as he marched her over to the two armed guards standing by the hangar door, watching the night.

Through the open van door, she could hear Drake's instructions.

"Take Ms. Reese to a secure conference room. Do not speak to her. Do not let her make any phone calls or speak to anyone else. If she won't behave, you have my permission to tie her to a chair and gag her." He pushed her into their arms and turned his back on her.

As they dragged her off, he waved the van into the hangar. The big door-jaws closed behind them and they climbed out onto the hangar floor.

He snapped at Harrington, "Show us this damn thing."

66

ZHANG RU SAT WITH CHEN MEI-LI IN THE CHRYSANTHEMUM courtyard of the Mei Fu restaurant in Beijing. As it was one of the finest restaurants in the entire capital, he'd told her to purchase a dress of classic elegance.

She had exceeded his expectations.

Ru found his eyes returning to her time after time.

A high-necked black dress was elegantly embroidered with scenes of imperial-era serenity. Her long hair, up in a simple swirled bun pinned in place by meticulously inlaid chopsticks. The teardrop of skin exposed just below her clavicle made him want to grab there and tear the dress from her body to take her.

Yet in another way, she was so sophisticated that she almost looked untouchable.

Seated here in the converted royal home of a Qing Dynasty prince's wife, she...belonged. The home was decorated throughout with the art and belongings of the greatest opera *dan* singer of them all, Mei Lanfang. The man had portrayed women for over forty years, refused to perform for the Japanese despite their harsh punishments during the WWII occupation, then ultimately became master of the Beijing Opera itself. Waterfalls and fluttering velvet drapes separated the four courtyards.

All the elegance of a time that had not survived Mao's Great Leap Forward was embodied in the girl in this place.

"You are perfect."

She tipped her head in a regal nod.

"The man who is joining us for lunch, you must impress him, Mei-Li. It's important."

"Yes, Uncle Ru." She even said the title dutifully as if she truly was his kin. The barest flicker of her eyes warned him of Zuocheng's approach.

"And how are your computer studies going?" He'd let her enroll in university as long as it didn't interfere with his schedule.

"I am at the top of my class, Uncle Ru," she replied loudly enough to be overheard, but with a humbleness that was indeed admirable.

"As you should be. As you should be. Ah," he turned to Zuocheng as he reached the table. "Greetings, my old friend. It's been too long. I'm so glad you could join me. I hope you don't mind that I asked my niece along. She works hard at school and I fear my second cousin does too little to reward her efforts. Perhaps because she is the youngest."

He'd risen to shake Zuocheng's hand like an equal, but kept his words about the girl.

"Mei-Li, this is the great General Li Zuocheng of whom I have told you so much."

He'd told her every detail he could recall through the

night, starting with him and Zuocheng bunking together during in-flight training and both flying in the Sino-Vietnamese War. It had created a bond that had lasted through the four decades since.

The girl had asked many probing questions, indicating that she was as thoughtful as she was beautiful.

Mei-Li had risen from her chair and, keeping her hands clasped low in front of her, a position that emphasized her form and the beauty of her dress, she bowed her head in a greeting that flowed from her natural grace.

Her trainers at the national gymnastics center had taught her well.

He hadn't decided yet whether to let Zuocheng have her or to withhold her services as a tantalizing toy to dangle in front of him. That was but one thing of the many that would depend on how the lunch went.

Zuocheng bowed respectfully in greeting rather than merely nodding before taking his seat at the table.

They exchanged pleasantries as the waiters served seaweed- and black sesame seed-encrusted tofu, steamed peanuts in chili sauce, and pork *baozi* dumplings for an appetizer. Mei-Li served them, not taking a *baozi* for herself. He made a show of serving her himself, "She really must eat more." But she didn't touch it.

He and Zuocheng may have started flying together but, after the war, Zuocheng's superior family connections had elevated him more quickly. He was one of two vice chairmen of the Central Military Commission. Not technically in direct line to power but certainly a major voice in the military as one of the President's two main assistants in his presidential role as chairman of the CMC.

"Did you hear about Huan?" Zhang broached the central topic of the meal as casually as he could over steamed perch with ginger and spring onion, stuffed with spicy crab.

"I did. Fuck that useless garbage's family to the eighteenth generation," he practically spit out the worst of all ritual insults. "He let us down on the J-31 program by choosing that Wang Fan boy as the test pilot. Nephew of yours, wasn't he?"

Zuocheng looked across the table at Mei-Li as he'd been doing much of the meal.

"Your brother?" He asked in a much kinder tone.

Ru decided he would keep Mei-Li for himself for now and merely let Zuocheng dream of her.

"No sir. He is from another side of my uncle's family." She ate a tiny flake of the fish with her chopsticks and smiled sadly. "Still, a terrible thing. My uncle was most upset about the loss of such an important aircraft to the incompetence of such an opportunist; one who had married into his family in hopes of getting unwarranted advancement."

A nice touch. The girl definitely had a mind, which he'd have to make more use of in the future. She performed exceptionally with Wang Fan and was now charming Zuocheng.

"That wasn't you who promoted him, Ru?"

"Oh no. I recused myself from his career. I think that former General Huan advanced the boy so quickly in hopes of currying favor with me. He knows that I work very hard on developing our next-generation aircraft. He so often strove to cut corners in order to report cost savings to his superiors that I feared he would place our pilots at risk. Or perhaps he was going to claim credit for my work before his corruption was discovered."

It was a risky speech.

To claim one's own importance was *baizuo*—arrogant as a Western liberal elitist. But a fighter pilot had a certain bravura, a justified ego because he *knew* he was better than those around him. A trait that he and Zuocheng shared.

Ru decided he was safe to have spoken so.

But would Zuocheng?

In for a little, in for a full measure of rice.

"Huan wasn't even a pilot. He was an administrator," yet another reason Ru hadn't liked him and he let his disgust enter his tone. That it hadn't been Huan's choice, a bad inner ear from a childhood infection had kept him out of the air, was a fact that few other than Ru had ever unearthed.

"Yes, he must be replaced with someone who was a pilot," Zuocheng agreed.

It was within reach! Ru kept his pleasure from his face and struggled to not get his hopes too high. *Perhaps, just perhaps he would be chosen to lead in General Huan's place.*

"What's his mission?"

Miranda felt uncomfortable looking at the pilot strapped into the chair. Their party stood in an observation room, looking at the strapped-down pilot and the operations team through a one-way window.

She'd lost her own team at the second drone sitting on the hangar floor.

Holly had tried to follow her to the observation room, but Drake had waved her off. Now it was just her, CIA Director Clark Winston, and the two generals.

With the pilot on the other side of the window, three technicians were in the space: a med tech who looked bored out of her skull, a guy slouched in front of a set of flight controls reading a novel supposedly ready to take over if anything went wrong with the neural connection, and a commander who was observing the tactical screens.

"Major Carl Maxwelton is patrolling boat drug-traffic routes out of South America into Southern Mexico. Most of what makes it into the US is via land routes over the Mexican border. Tonight we're trying to move upstream, patrolling the Venezuelan coast," Harrington announced.

"What was the planned mission prior to our arrival?" Drake asked with an insight that Miranda knew she lacked. Mike might well have asked the same question. He saw when people were hiding things—a very valuable skill.

Harrington stood stiffly. "We were going to shred some of Syria's front lines."

"Waging war without—"

"Ease up, Drake," Clark spoke up. "We don't report to the same people you do. The Senate Select Committee on Intelligence has stamped Syria as a go-to proposition for application of CIA forces."

"Does the committee know what it is that you're flying or even what you had planned?" Nason turned back to stare into the room.

"Only in the most general terms," Clark stuffed his hands in his pockets, even though the room wasn't cold. "We told them that we weren't putting our people at risk due to remote operations."

"Not putting—" General Harrington finally sputtered to life, shedding his carefully stiff demeanor. "Do you know what that thing is doing to him right now? It's ripping out his mind. Just like it did to a lot of good pilots before him."

Harrington spun to face Miranda. She'd have taken a step back, but bumped into the closed door when she tried.

"You want to know what happened to your precious C-130 Hercules and the five good people who flew on her? I'll fucking tell you. I'm so goddamn sick of the lies. One of your precious pilots..."

He spun back to Clark and jabbed a finger inches from the director's face so closely that he stumbled back and fell into a chair.

"...had his brains scrambled by 'The Rip'—that's what the pilots call it. Cal Jefferson was a good man and a better pilot. The Rip fried him, burned him out, just like the other basket cases I've got in lockup."

He began pacing up and down the cramped space.

Harrington became more and more agitated until he began speaking as he paced. "On the flight home from destabilizing a Brazilian dam project, he downed a tourist flight crossing from Cancún to Cozumel—killed a dozen people just for the hell of it. Then—almost home safe but before we realized what was happening—he strafed that C-130 just to see how close he could get at supercruise speeds."

"Exactly as you surmised, Miranda," Drake nodded.

"Less than three meters," Miranda agreed. "And he must have avoided clipping the tail section by less than that."

There were some things she didn't like being right about.

Miranda imagined she could feel Holly's firm grasp squeezing one of her shoulders and took strength from it. Her last team, who'd been with her for five years, had never understood her as effortlessly as Holly did.

"Poor bastard," Harrington was muttering. "Didn't think about the consequences until he circled back around and saw the destruction. If his mind had still been functioning, he would have known better, but he was too deep in The Rip by then. The C-130's copilot had been his lover. He almost succeeded in committing suicide by drone, ramming it into this building, before we were able to wrest control from him. Unless we drug the shit out of him, he does nothing but cry the whole time. We haven't gotten a coherent word out of him in three days."

Harrington waved helplessly toward the main section of the base.

"There," he again stepped toe-to-toe with her. "Now you know what really happened to your damned plane, Ms. Chase. Hope you can live with it. Don't know if I can."

He finally turned away from her to face General Drake Nason.

"The whole program is fucked. Nothing we do can protect the pilot. It's like normal drone pilot burnout, but it is hugely accelerated—months instead of years. Good men. Just gone," he snapped his fingers.

Drake rested a hand on Harrington's shoulder until he calmed and once again stood upright. "Recall the pilot while you still can."

Harrington nodded once, twice, then stepped through the door out of the observation room and into the flight control space.

68

"MAJOR MAXWELTON. WE HAVE A TECHNICAL ISSUE AND NEED to cancel this mission. Please return to base immediately." Harrington appeared to be speaking in a normal tone in the room.

The pilot made no acknowledgement from where he was strapped into the padded chair.

"Maxie? That's an order."

Still no response.

Harrington shook his shoulder.

"I don't think he can hear you," the med tech was studying her instruments. "According to my instruments, his own hearing is no longer registering in his auditory cortex. Maybe he's become so bonded with his machine that he can no longer hear us."

"Radio him. Call the drone." Drake snapped out the order.

"Uh, sir." The backup pilot had dumped his novel on the floor and jolted up to stand at attention on the general's entry. "It's a drone, sir. There's no radio on the aircraft. Not directly. There's frequency monitoring equipment, but that's routed back to here. We always just speak to the pilot."

Miranda stepped through the door and Director Winston followed her in.

She pointed to the pilot's console.

"Then do what you're here for. Take control of the flight and return it here." No one else should die. If she had her way, not a single person would ever die in an aircraft ever again.

"I can...try." The pilot sat down at his console and flicked a switch, which lit up a Controls Active sign above his station, but he didn't put his hands on the controls.

"Do it!" Harrington shouted while glaring at her, but whether it was anger at her or at the situation, she couldn't tell. Then he turned back to the displays.

They watched the emergency pilot "try." They all did.

"He's fighting me. He doesn't want to release control."

"Cut the goddamn connection," Drake suggested.

"Sir, you can't—"

Harrington took the two steps to the chair and pulled the plug.

Major Maxwelton screamed.

Not some cry of rage.

Not fear.

It was the unholy scream of a doomed man, knowing he was going to hell.

Miranda had heard it most nights in her dreams for over twenty years.

It was the cry of her parents as they fell from the sky.

Her nerves knew every note of that sound, cut straight from her own soul.

Her father's name ripped at her throat. Unable to contain it, Miranda echoed the major's scream—as she lost her parents all over again.

69

"MIRANDA? COME ON, MATE. IT'S OKAY. COME ON BACK."

Miranda opened her eyes and looked up into Holly's. She lay in a sterile, uninviting office on a hard sofa.

"You still with us?"

"I seem to be. What happened?" And then she remembered, all too clearly. "The pilot. Did we..." Holly's expression said they hadn't.

"They sedated him," Mike leaned over Holly's shoulder.

"Never heard a sound like that in my life," Jeremy sat perched on the sofa arm by her feet. "One of you was bad, but the two of you together? It was like some kind of psycho harmony. We could hear you both right out on the hangar floor. You screamed your dad Sam's name before you fainted. Was it because they died in that crash?"

"Your parents went down in a plane?" Holly looked at her. "Harsh. No wonder you're such a smashing NTSB investigator."

"TWA 800," Jeremy answered for her before she could speak.

Miranda sat up to see Clark Winston sitting in one of the office chairs. Neither of the generals were around.

"Where..."

"They're debriefing Clarissa. Finding out what missions she's done," Clark answered. "Nason has grounded the program. Permanently, I expect."

"And you don't know what she did?"

"I find it works for me to surround myself with the very best people and then trust them."

Miranda assimilated that as she inspected Mike, Holly, and Jeremy. How to know who to trust? She had no information to go on; perhaps because she'd asked no questions.

"How were you all assigned to my team?"

Holly shrugged. "I'm guessing I was the closest structural specialist with sufficient clearance."

"It just came through as a standard call-up for me, too," Mike held up his phone.

"Because dreams can come true," Jeremy said completely seriously.

"Aww! I knew you were sweet on me," Holly hugged him sideways.

"No, I meant..." but he was blushing too brightly to speak further.

Clark was leaning forward to study her intently. "TWA 800 was a major loss," he spoke as if testing the words.

"A 747's worth of loss," Miranda managed and gratefully took the cold can of Coke that Mike offered her. She cooled her forehead against the chill metal before opening it to drink.

"Damn. You're Sam Chase's kid? I never connected that you were their daughter. The major loss I'm referring to was your parents."

She bobbled the can and only Holly's quick grab kept her from pouring it all over herself.

"What are you talking about?"

"Most of this," Clark waved a hand about them, "is their doing."

Miranda could usually collate and organize disparate facts quickly and accurately in her mind; it was a survival mechanism. At the moment she was having trouble classifying what Clark was saying as individual words.

"Were they able to save the drone?" It was the most relevant question she could formulate.

Holly shook her head. "Apparently, when the local pilot attempted to grab control, there was a struggle. Broke something at high Mach speeds. The remote setup on this is pretty dicey anyway as they didn't load it up with a lot of the autonomous controls. They really depended on the wired-in pilot's autonomic nervous system. The remote pilot was able to dump it in the Cayman Trough. Water's about five klicks deep there and he was still supersonic when he punched the water, so not much left to find even if anyone ever went down there to look."

"Oh. Okay." She filed that piece of information to the side. There was still one other drone, but it was parked safely in the hangar. She could see it out the office window.

Mike was looking at her strangely, but she ignored him.

"My parents?" Miranda turned back to Clark, finally able to face the words.

"Fine agents. They—"

"No. Not agents. They were consultants for..." except she didn't know who for. "Some university...like MIT?" Why didn't she know this?

"That would be MITRE Corporation. It was formed out of Lincoln Laboratory at MIT. They're one of the top consulting firms on military safety technologies. MITRE designed and built the nation's air traffic control system. A bunch of other projects. Your parents ultimately came over to the CIA. They were part of the team working with Abraham Karem."

"The father of drone technology," Jeremy said with awe. "The Predator was his. It grew right out of Amber. The first reliably functional drone."

"Her parents," Clark nodded to Jeremy, "were running field tests for him on developing the Predator. I did a rotation through there, but never had a chance to really know them. I was just security then, whereas they were the heart of a CIA team that had been running the Gnat-750—"

"The successor to the Amber," Jeremy shoehorned in.

"—over Bosnia," Clark continued unflappably. "By the time your parents went down, I was embedded in the Middle East as a ground scout for the drone teams. They were flying over to review possible Israeli secure launch facilities for deploying the Predators into the area, and I was supposed to meet up with them."

"No," the word came out. It was a short, simple word. Two letters and she no longer understood its meaning even though she'd spoken it herself.

"No," she tried it again.

Miranda could feel the scream building inside her once more, but fought it back down by pure willpower.

She was losing her parents all over again.

Not to some memory dredged up by the pilot's scream.

This time, to them not being who she'd always thought, always *known* they were.

"My parents were going to Paris early. I was to follow a week later." Her voice hurt as she spoke.

"They went early to spend a week scouting in Israel with me before you flew in to join them," Clark added.

"Israel? No." There was that word again that didn't seem to have as much power as she'd always thought it had. "Paris."

But had there been a through-ticket to Tel Aviv? Why would she know? Tante Daniels, her governess, would have handled those kinds of details. *We'll fly over to join your parents,* she'd said. *First stop, Paris.*

Miranda had always assumed that had meant they'd all meet up there. Stay in France. Apparently not. With her parents dead off the shores of Long Island, there was no need for Tante Daniels to say more. With her parents dead on TWA 800, there'd been no need to ask.

"MITRE?"

"Originally. We all three ended up in the CIA."

"*Kryptos.*" No wonder her father had been so fascinated by *Kryptos*. He'd seen it. He'd *worked* there. As had Mother. Her mother didn't have the head for codes, so that had been something her father shared with his daughter.

"Yes. First thing he talked about when I met him. Guess he spent a lot of his spare time trying to solve it."

"No, *we* did. It was a constant game for us." And Miranda missed it now more than ever. "I still work on the unsolved fourth panel when I have time."

"Ms. Chase. I'll see that you get a security pass to study the original anytime you wish."

She looked around the room.

"If we have the drone secured and we know about the C-130's crash, why are we all still here?"

"You mean aside from you fainting?"

She ignored Mike's comment and turned to Holly, who sighed.

"Nobody's told us dinkum, but I'm betting that we have another problem."

THROUGH THE PEKING DUCK AND, ULTIMATELY, EVEN OVER red bean paste sesame balls with honeyed Tieguanyin tea, Zuocheng remained cagey over Huan's replacement. Instead he spoke mostly to Mei-Li about his own granddaughters, who would soon be going to university—unless they could be married off advantageously of course.

Then, just at the end of the meal, Zuocheng lounged back in his chair and turned back to Ru.

"This hasn't been mentioned outside of the CMC, so you didn't hear it from me, Ru. It's most worrying, but Peng Yan has gone missing."

Even with all of his years of political maneuvering, Ru was unable to repress his astonishment.

"Shit!" Drake looked down at the last two bodies in the Groom Lake morgue, lying side by side and dressed in US Air Force flightsuits.

"We weren't able to identify this man and woman. They have no identification, no dog tags." Harrington waved a hand at them. "They were at the rear of the aircraft, separate from the rest of the crew. The impact broke their necks. I had my team scour the area several times, but we found nothing else. I even had my men watching the NTSB team closely in case they found something we missed."

Clarissa stood to the other side of the corpses. Humbled, at least for the moment, she'd divulged a complete list of drone operations—and Drake tried not to be sick when he thought of the cost to the pilots. Thankfully, the program was very new, so only a few pilots had gone through The Rip, but Harrington's descriptions of their status were horrific.

He'd insisted that she accompany them to the morgue—

to her credit, she had looked ill at the barely recognizable remains of the three crew members.

But neither she nor Harrington knew about the true identities of the other two passengers aboard the plane.

Neither would even suspect.

Or ever could know.

Drake knew, and felt like the murderer who'd broken their necks with his own hands. He couldn't wipe off the feeling against his slacks and finally had to brace himself on the edge of the table to stop the motion.

So close.

Peng Yan and his wife had been the highest-placed contacts the US had ever made in China's Central Military Commission.

Peng Yan, in his role as the department head of the Equipment Development Department, was at the leading edge of Chinese military innovation.

Drake's ultimate hook on Yan had been via the man's wife; she was an avid UFO buff.

Yan had made a trip to Groom Lake the price of his becoming a double agent.

His demand had been very carefully couched.

"I wish to see the innovation that *has* happened. I do not expect you to trust me to see your new works. But our friends the Pakistanis delivered to us the tail section of your stealth helicopter that crashed in bin Laden's compound. I wish to see a complete one. I wish to sit in an SR-71 Blackbird and fly an F-117 Nighthawk because I love the history; I know you keep those original stealth planes nearby and ready for service. And my wife wants to visit where the UFOs are kept."

Drake's protests that there weren't any UFOs had earned him a tolerant smile.

"Yes, we both know that. But she wishes to visit Groom Lake anyway. Perhaps even eat in the Little A'Le'Inn restaurant along the famous Extraterrestrial Highway."

"Their roast beef is better than their 'Alien burger'," Drake had sealed the deal at the last G20 meeting.

The Intelligence Support Activity, typically known as either 'The Activity' or 'The Army of Northern Virginia'— the elite intelligence and action service of US Special Operations—had overseen smuggling the Chinese couple in through Mexico. And now there was nothing to smuggle back out except a pair of unfortunate corpses.

Shit!

"Bury them very privately and with full honors," he looked at Harrington across the table. "No pictures. No DNA. No names."

72

UNABLE TO GET MORE OUT OF ZUOCHENG ABOUT THE disappearance of Peng Yan without directly asking, which would have been unimaginably rude, Ru surreptitiously signaled the girl before he excused himself for the toilet.

Peng Yan. *Peng Yan?*

Gone missing?

The Director of the Equipment Development Department of the Central Military Commission had gone missing?

If Yan had merely gone on an unannounced holiday with his mistress—such things were not unheard of—he still would have answered a summons.

But if the leadership had him removed, as quietly as they'd erased Ru's former commander General Huan's existence...

For Zuocheng to announce he was missing, something had gone very wrong. Unless he resurfaced soon and with some unassailable proof—such as a secret mission for the President—he would never be trusted again.

An opening in the CMC? The specific opening he was perhaps the most qualified for in all of China. Such dreams never came true.

His signal to Mei-Li had been to go with Zuocheng and perform for him in any way he desired. To buy a position on the CMC, he'd sell far more than her pretty little body.

If only he could discover what had happened to the J-31 and Wang Fan. His nephew had been many things, but incompetent was not one of them. If Ru could answer that, he would know how to play the card.

With the right kind of information, he could leap past the CDI and straight onto the CMC—with or without Mei-Li spreading her legs for Zuocheng.

Yes, if chosen, Ru would be bound to all of Zuocheng's agenda, anything he asked for going forward. But that too was a price Ru was willing to pay.

The instant he was out of the Chrysanthemum courtyard, he texted General Nason.

73

DRAKE RUSHED INTO THE OFFICE WHERE HE'D LEFT THE others, Clark and Clarissa in his wake.

Except it was empty.

Then he spotted them gathered around the remaining MQ-45 Casper in the deeply shadowed hangar.

As he hurried to join them, he saw that Miranda was conscious. Wide-eyed with some shock, but he didn't have time to address that. The other three stood well back.

Drake rushed up to her.

"I need an answer. We have less than two minutes."

"An answer to what?" Several of them asked in unison.

But not Miranda. She stood with her fingertips resting lightly on the long nose of the low drone. It was shoulder-height on her.

He hadn't actually stood close to one yet and it felt sleek, cold, and as if it was watching him. He wasn't a fanciful man, but he could feel death sitting there.

Without removing her hand, she simply watched him.

"Well?"

"We already know the cause of the problem." Miranda brushed her fingers along the first hard chine of the nose.

"Problem?" Clark stepped forward. At least Clarissa kept her trap shut. She'd been much subdued by her brief incarceration.

"Shut up, Clark. A minute forty-five. I don't have time to deal with you." He didn't know what would happen if he didn't answer Ru's desperate text, but he didn't like the various scenarios that came to mind.

He might not like the CIA's methods or their lack of oversight, but they had made exceptionally effective use of their newest weapon.

Weapon? Damn thing looked like it was grinning at him. The drone could easily end all of their careers if any of this was mishandled in the slightest.

Holly stepped forward.

He didn't want to shut her down, then realized he didn't have to. She wasn't talking to him; she was facing Miranda.

"You can't tell them the truth."

74

HARVEY LOOKED EVERYWHERE FOR MAXIE.

It had taken him half the afternoon to track down the memory before he'd found it.

Helen had said, "The Rip."

...and so had Major Maxwelton.

The DFAC, the ball field, the dorms.

The dorms.

He still couldn't make sense of it.

Maxie's room wasn't just empty—it was barren.

No two-dollar plastic baseball trophies standing on the dresser. No glove that Maxie's father had given to him and he still used though it was a little too tight.

Photos of his dead sister—the reason Maxie had joined up in the first place fifteen years ago.

Clothes in the closet and drawers.

Spit-shined shoes and white dress uniforms.

All gone.

"What the hell?"

The empty room didn't answer back.

"*What the hell?*"

"Hey, Harvey," it was barely a whisper.

He spun to face Helen and found her in Colonel Helen Thomas mode.

She stood in the doorway, immaculate in her dark blue service uniform. So beautiful and perfect and austere that he wouldn't dare approach her, even if they hadn't agreed to show nothing in public. She'd never even used his first name outside the bedroom.

"Where's Maxie? Major Maxwelton?"

She didn't answer. She just stayed at the threshold with her service cap tucked under her arm. It was rare to see anyone in dress blues at Groom Lake.

"His gear is..." Gone.

"My condolences, Lt. Colonel Whitmore."

Harvey stumbled back against the chair at the small desk, all that propped him upright.

"How? He flies from the ground. Like me. That's safe, right? Isn't it?"

Helen closed her eyes long enough for his pulse to pound five times in his ears.

"The Rip. I tried to tell you before. But I couldn't bring myself to. I thought...by putting on the uniform...I hoped that I'd find the strength."

"I thought you were trying to say you loved me."

Again she went silent. The pain in her eyes answered that question as well.

"More than you wanted to."

An infinitesimal nod.

"I should have escorted you to the Janet flight. Sent you home to your family this weekend."

She had to clear her throat twice. "I would have stayed anyway. Until we'd spoken. Even before Major Maxwelton's...difficulties."

"Difficulties?"

"He exited the flight precipitously. It was too much. We sedated him, but he found a way to kill himself. I...didn't want that to happen to you, Lt. Colonel Whitmore." She finished the last in a rush.

"Oh." He still didn't know how to respond to that.

"You'll be safe now. I've just been informed that they've cancelled the program."

"Safe?"

"Yes. I'm sorry, I have to go. I have a meeting with the Chairman of the Joint Chiefs of Staff that I need to be ready for. That's the other reason for this," she almost smiled as she indicated her uniform.

Someone banged a door out in the hall and voices drifted in.

"I'm sorry. But I'm glad you're safe now...Harvey."

She saluted.

Only instinct had him returning the gesture before she was gone.

Safe?

Stuck on the ground with the disk of impossible iron still throbbing from The Rip pulling at him. Even when he wasn't connected to the Casper.

What part of safe was that?

75

MIRANDA HATED BEING THE CENTER OF ATTENTION FOR EVEN two people. Being faced by two generals, two CIA directors, and her own team was way too much.

She couldn't think.

Couldn't see past the drone that lay beside her. The cause of so much trouble, but also the closest tie to her parents that she'd had in years.

How was she supposed to get past that to think about this problem?

Her parents weren't who she thought they were. But did that *change* who they were? Did the hundreds of hours spent on *Kryptos* and dozens of other cryptographic puzzles become any less because they were CIA agents?

Did—

"A minute thirty, Ms. Chase. I need an answer now."

Miranda couldn't focus. Couldn't see past the betrayal...if that's what it was.

How was she supposed to answer the general? She barely

understood what he was saying through the jumble of her thoughts.

"You can't," Holly repeated. "Every advance, every generational leap ahead made by our defense technology is only a leap as long as it remains secret. Once a concept is created, once that idea is known to our enemies, we can't put the genie back in the bottle. It will be out in the world for others to use. This," she rapped her knuckles at the drone, creating a surprisingly pleasant bell-like sound. "This will slip out of our control. We must delay that as long as we can. Our enemies may be willing to ruthlessly expend the pilots. We must block that scenario."

"A minute fifteen," Drake reminded her as if stating the obvious limitations would aid her thoughts.

Miranda had to stop the barrage of words. She couldn't think through them.

She couldn't.

But just maybe...

"There was something Director Winston said."

"What was that?" Drake barked out.

He'd said to surround herself with good people, then trust them.

She had trusted no one and nothing since a wiring fault in an air conditioning system had shorted into a fuel sensor, creating a spark that had blown her parents from the sky.

But just maybe...

"Excuse me," she ducked under the long nose of the Casper and waved Holly to follow her to where Mike and Jeremy had been hanging back.

She led them a few meters farther away—then huddled them together and began speaking quickly.

76

Ru almost pissed himself in the men's room. At his age, his bladder no longer emptied all at once, and he didn't have time to be patient right now.

But he must be.

He had to give Mei-Li a chance to convince Li Zuocheng to take her home. In the unlikely event that she failed, he needed to have an answer from Nason. But he couldn't hold off much longer.

Zuocheng had obviously laid down the gauntlet and was waiting to see how fast Ru picked it up. If Mei-Li couldn't distract him, Ru needed to be ready.

Nason had promised him an answer in two minutes. No, he had texted Nason that was all the time that Ru had and the man had frustratingly replied "OK" like he was some American cowboy.

There was less than one minute left.

Where was that American bastard?

Why couldn't he have answered before this meeting?

Ru double-checked that he hadn't stained his pants, and then tried not to grind his teeth.

77

"HOLLY IS RIGHT," MIKE STATED ONCE MIRANDA HAD explained the situation. "You can't reveal the real cause to the Chinese of why their Shenyang J-31 jet went down. It would be a disaster. Perhaps even war."

"But it's what happened." Miranda felt miserable. Now *she* was the one stating the obvious. Did the predilection cross genders?

"What if that wasn't what happened?" Mike was staring at something over her head, but when she turned, all she saw was the hangar's wall.

"Another reason!" Holly jumped in. "You said that to their imaging, the MQ-45 Casper drone looked like nothing more than a reflection. Let them think it was a reflection and that something else brought it down."

She wanted to say, "But it didn't!" Suppressing the reaction was hard.

"Right. You said dead planes didn't lie," Jeremy seemed to particularly like her phrase. "But what if they did?"

"Some other reason the plane went down," Holly was now studying the wall just like Mike, but Miranda still couldn't see anything.

She knew she was even worse at lying than trusting others, but she tried. "The plane performed magnificently. The pilot was exceptionally skilled. His attempts to survive the attack should be in a textbook." Still, all she had so far was the truth.

"So, we need something else to distract them with..."

"...even if only marginally plausible, but something for them to latch on to."

Now Mike and Holly were completing each other's sentences.

Rather than staring at the wall, Jeremy had been staring at the concrete floor with squinted eyes. Did narrowing of eyes help one's mental processes? Miranda tried it but felt no smarter.

"A Russian conspiracy would be convenient." How Mike sounded so casual was beyond her. But then nothing seemed to ever fluster him...other than Holly.

Jeremy kept squinting at the floor. "They copied the airframe from us, but much of the electronics in the Shenyang J-31 are rumored to be Russian. There must be something we can do with that."

"Why would the Russians want to destroy a Chinese jet fighter?" Holly asked.

"We..." Miranda could feel the edge of an idea. Something that someone had said about how she approached a crash. "We... *Oh!* We found the who, just as Terence said I would."

"Who's Terence?" Mike asked.

Miranda ignored the question. "He said to follow the who to figure out the why. We have the real who—the CIA—and we now know the why."

"But," Mike looked suddenly excited, "if we change the *who* to the Russians, what could be their *why?*"

"Dead planes don't lie," Miranda couldn't quite let that go.

"Yes, but we don't have a dead plane this time," Holly pointed out.

Mike nodded. Apparently he and Holly agreed, which was definitely a valid test from two very different perspectives.

He continued, "We have an image of a live one that's now dead. All we have to do is find something that fits the facts. We figured out how the C-130 Hercules went down. It is up to the generals and the CIA to resolve why and what to do about it."

"You're saying that we just need to provide a plausible mechanism to match the Russian *who?*" Miranda's head felt as if it was going to explode.

"It would have been easier if they'd accepted the first *who* of that poor shmuck of a pilot in the J-31 screwing up, but they didn't." Holly pointed west in the direction of China. "So the reason for the crash must be either the US' or the Russians' fault—and my vote is put it in those buggers' lap. So all we need is some plausible mechanism, some Russian *what* that would cause a pilot to appear to be fighting for control of his own plane. Then let the Chinese figure out their own why."

"The RQ-170," Jeremy's eyes returned to normal size as he looked at her suddenly.

Of course. Of course! Miranda knew that Jeremy was absolutely right.

78

Out of time, Zhang Ru returned to the Chrysanthemum Courtyard. He jolted to a halt when he saw that Mei-Li and Li Zuocheng still sat at the table. The little bitch still sat with that icy, untouchable perfection, rather than leading Zuocheng out of here by his dick.

Ru forced himself to step forward with a smile on his face.

Damn the girl! And damn you to hell, Nason! Next time you need help, you can go suck on a thousand-year egg!

Zuocheng handed Mei-Li a slip of paper just as Ru reached the table, then pushed to his feet.

"I too shall return in a moment. You took long enough, Ru, I was half afraid I'd be embarrassing myself in front of the young lady. But we don't leave one such as her untended," then he strode off toward the Men's Room.

"What did he give you?"

She showed him a phone number.

"You were supposed to be taking him to a hotel, not taking his number." He knew he did a poor job of hiding his frustration.

The girl studied him briefly, like he might study a materials requisition for an order of printer paper, before tucking away the number and speaking softly. "It is the number of his favorite granddaughter. He feels that we would be friends and hopes that I will be a good influence on her more modern ways."

Ru had never imagined such a ploy. If Mei-Li became friend and mentor to Zuocheng's favorite, that was better than her sleeping with him.

Wasn't it?

There were too many factors to calculate. Did being "his favorite" imply that he kept a constant eye on her activities and happiness, or that he sent her a present for her birthday? Or bedded her regularly?

"How close are they?"

"They're spending a week together at the Duanwu Dragon Boat Festival next month."

Ru hissed between his teeth in pleasure, then smiled at the girl. "How convenient that we are as well."

"Yes, Uncle Ru," she nodded with an imperial grace that even the Empress Wu Zetian would have found difficult to achieve.

His phone buzzed. He snatched it from his pocket and read the brief message. Then he began to smile in earnest and sent a quick response.

It was exactly what he needed to tell Zuocheng. It would place the Shenyang J-31 project back on track with no more than a six-month lapse. Not the plane's fault, simply the failure to anticipate one particular weakness in the command-and-control system.

He, Zhang Ru, would be the one who had solved what so many analysts and commanders hadn't been able to unravel.

Why?

He needed to prove *why* he had solved it himself.

Ah! Because the technicians and analysts had believed the fault lay with the pilot or the plane. The analysts had assumed that just because China copied the technology of others that it was suspect for that reason alone.

But he and Zuocheng were both men of the world.

They had both *been* pilots!

It was up to thinkers like them to see the greater picture —such as an attack by their supposed Russian allies.

With this and Zuocheng's favoritism for Chen Mei-Li— who Ru supposed he must now treat as if she really was a most-favored niece—he himself would be the obvious person to replace Peng Yan on the Central Military Commission.

It was a pity to no longer have the use of the girl's services; she was such an artist in the bedroom. But that didn't mean she couldn't be used in other ways.

Perhaps Mei-Li should be placed as his assistant.

She did observe people as clearly as himself—a rare trait indeed. With her beauty, poise, and more training, she could become formidable.

Yes, that was very good. At his side, but not too close, she would make an exceptional political asset if not a technical one.

And maybe he would even redeem his true niece now that she was freed from the husband she'd never liked.

Wang Fan? Best to let him rest unrepented in whatever uncomfortable grave he'd found.

79

"Okay, I've sent it. Now would you care to explain?" Drake jammed the phone back in his pocket after reading Zhang Ru's message: *Deeply in your debt.* It was not a phrase a Chinese person used lightly.

Miranda simply waved to Holly.

"Jeremy thought it up."

"From your comment," Jeremy answered her.

"Which I based on Holly's observation."

"Which was based on your statement."

"Because I was trying to answer Mike's question about—"

"Cut the goddamn commentary. What the hell does what I just sent mean?"

"The RQ-170 Sentinel," Clark was the one to answer the question, "was a flying-wing drone that the CIA was operating over Iran when—"

"Like I don't already know that. Get on with it, man."

"Then you know that the Iranians managed to mimic

and eventually take over command of the aircraft. We still don't know how they—"

Jeremy spoke up.

"They overpowered the command frequencies from our distant satellite signals with a high-power focused array. The drone's software rejected our own weaker signals as spurious data and the Iranians landed it with all of its equipment and surveillance data intact. It was actually a brilliant piece of work to take over and successfully land an aircraft they were wholly unfamiliar with. We've, of course, since modified our drones to function only on encrypted and code-validated communications, but we didn't have that back in 2011. The Chinese were among the parties invited to inspect the aircraft. So I felt there would be a high likelihood that a high-level Chinese contact would know about that."

"What he said," Holly confirmed.

Drake considered the message Miranda had given him to send. *Remember RQ-170 takedown by Iranians. Think about Russia interfacing through imported control systems into Chinese jet.*

"So, you didn't actually lie. You simply told them to *think* it was a control takeover by the Russians through their electronics. It is a plausible *who* and *how*. The *why,* as is typical, is beyond the scope of the crash investigation itself. The CIA pilot destroyed the C-130 by flying so close. The pilot having a mental aberration is of no relevance to the situation," Miranda concluded.

Drake knew better. Perhaps not for the crash investigator, but he knew that the *why* was essential.

"They'll think the Russians deliberately crashed the Chinese fifth-generation jet," Clark looked well pleased. "It will lead to a distinct cooling of Sino-Russian relations, at least in military cooperation. That's been a problem since they normalized relations back in 1992 and formalized it in 2001. I like it."

Yes. Clark understood the importance of the *why*.

Clarissa was being smart enough to keep her trap shut. Harrington had leveled several complaints against her as they'd discussed to-date operations—enough that she'd know her fate was in the balance.

The fact that Drake was going to force Harrington's immediate retirement, for his failure to act sooner in the interest of his men, was a different issue. *That* was the first duty of any commanding officer.

There was a long silence as everyone contemplated the solution.

"Are we done?" Jeremy asked softly.

Drake turned to Clark. "My order stands. The MQ-45 Casper is grounded. No future missions. I will not have a machine that kills pilots in my arsenal. How many pilots are there on the list still?"

"Realistically?" Harrington shrugged. "There's one left. He's the best yet. He flies like—"

"I don't give a shit. He's done."

Drake bemoaned the loss of Peng Yan, but couldn't think what to do about it. Unless... Was there a chance that Zhang Ru would replace him? If so, how could he use that? He sighed. Not in any way that he could imagine. Peng Yan was a casual traitor; Zhang Ru, a staunch patriot.

"You two," he jabbed a finger at Clark and Clarissa, "are on probation. And don't start spouting about my not having the authority or I'll ram President Roy Cole down your throats. I'm not saying don't pursue innovative projects. I'm saying that if they touch any military asset in any way and you don't inform me, I will have you drawn and quartered for treason before sundown."

"It's already nighttime," Miranda stated in that strange way of hers.

80

MIRANDA WAS LAST OFF THE RUNWAY AND UP INTO THE FIRST light of morning. The long salt bed of Groom Lake fell rapidly astern. She flew over the remains of the C-130's wreckage, observing a moment of silence. No accident report would ever be filed. Holly and Jeremy had given over all of their data and it had been destroyed.

General Drake Nason flew east in the government Gulfstream along with the two CIA directors. General Harrington had been removed from command and was aboard as well. A Colonel Helen Thomas had been given temporary command. She, too, had known about the devastating effect of the program on the pilots, but had only been following a superior's orders.

Miranda wasn't sure about the meaning of that; the military operated by rules she'd never thought to learn. Perhaps it was time for research on military culture. Drake had thanked her and the team most profusely and said he would call on them again if he ever needed help.

She wished that was never, but as long as planes flew, they'd keep coming out of the sky.

The other three members of her NTSB team were aloft in her Mooney M20V and headed back to the Tacoma airport.

Past the remains of the C-130, she slid the throttle forward and the F-86 Sabrejet roared to life beneath her fingertips. Turning northwest toward her family's island, she flew by the Mooney and rocked her wings to wave hello.

It was an odd gesture.

Waving.

It was something done with friends.

Bye. See you next time.

And she would. They'd all agreed to remain on her team for now. That was as far ahead as she ever looked.

From Groom Lake to the edge of the NTTR, she took advantage of the military test range and managed to nudge the Sabrejet to just over Mach 1. This was no longer the era of Jackie Cochran and even at this instant there might be another woman pilot or two breaking the sound barrier in a military jet...but not many.

"Fastest woman in the world," she told herself and even if it might not be true at this instant, the feeling never diminished. There was a glory in riding out the transition to supersonic flight—little more than a hard buffet in the Sabrejet. It was flight at its purest, at least the purest for a human.

What bird had the purest flight? She'd never before considered whether a Peregrine falcon diving at two hundred and forty miles an hour might be having more fun than a gull soaring below thirty.

At the edge of the NTTR—which she reached all too soon—she eased back to subsonic speeds. By law, supersonic speeds were illegal over civilian land throughout the US. But she stayed up near the limit. She wanted, she *needed* to get home. Mach 0.98 was subsonic and she rode the edge north.

As she passed east of Reno, Nevada—riding the air currents at forty-five thousand feet above the dry and tortured mountains of the northeast corner of California—a shadow slid over her cockpit, blocking the sun.

81

THE NEEDLE LENGTH OF THE MQ-45 CASPER, HALOED BY THE rising sun, seemed to float effortlessly beside her. Miranda marveled at the contrast between her sixty-year-old F-86 and the most advanced aircraft in the world. There had been almost ten thousand of the former and there would never be more than this last one of the latter. Someday soon there would be a replacement—another new breakthrough—but the Casper's days were done.

She knew who flew it.

She and the last MQ-45 pilot ever had sat together for over an hour. A tall, handsome man. His obvious love for his aircraft—he touched it the way she sometimes touched the model of *Kryptos* in her garden—had her feeling an instant bond with him.

They'd spoken only a few words; instead watching the video of his one flight against the narco-submarines. His desperate sadness at the program's closure had reached out to her own sadness.

Miranda had never liked being touched—each contact felt as if it was erasing her mother's and father's final hugs.

But that clear understanding of shared pain had led her to embrace Lt. Colonel Harvey Whitmore. He returned it with all the silent anguish in his heart.

And now they flew, side by side.

Neither moved from formation flight.

If he lost his mind like other pilots and moved in to kill her, there was nothing she could do about it. But his flight, so close that they almost touched wingtips, didn't feel aggressive.

He had no radio, no frequency that could reach him.

So instead, they simply flew.

Together they dropped down to circle the peaks of the Cascade Range, once each: Crater Lake, Mount Hood near Portland, Mount St. Helens and Rainier, and finally Mount Baker north of Seattle.

When she turned for her home island, he followed along beside her, so close that he was no more than a shadow—a reflection. He mimicked her every maneuver as instinctively as she followed the spheres at a crash site.

Harvey was a magnificent pilot.

She'd seen enough in the videos to know that he was the very best of them all. Even better than the pilot on the China flight.

She descended in a lazy spiral centered on her parents' island. On her island.

Maybe it was time she left them dead in the Atlantic. What had been found of their remains were now ashes scattered on the island.

Director Clark Winston had offered to point out their

stars on the CIA Memorial Wall at her next trip to DC. They'd been deemed to have died in the line of service and had numbered—but unnamed—stars there; a tradition for every agent who died in the line of duty.

The Casper circled with her. The runway was too short for his aircraft. That worried her for a moment, then she realized that Harvey would never land here. His body was in Las Vegas and he was taking an *unauthorized* last flight.

Oh, a *final* flight.

A thousand feet above the runway, he waggled his wings.

Friend.

She waggled hers in reply.

Friend.

Then the Casper peeled aside with a suddenness that had her yelping in surprise.

In moments, the Casper turned west toward the trackless vastness of the Pacific Ocean and went transonic.

The last glint of sunlight she saw off the drone showed it was punching toward the heavens on full afterburners.

82

HELEN FOUND HARVEY.

Alone.

In the flight chair.

He no longer needed straps to hold him in place. He'd managed to power up the systems and connect himself in. She hadn't thought to look for him here until she'd noticed the open hangar door from far down the field.

By the time she'd arrived, the drone was long gone.

There was nothing to say, even if he was still capable of responding.

Instead she sat and took his hand.

He squeezed her hand, once. But she held on and watched the command screens.

Harvey flew. Loops, rolls, Immelmanns—maneuver after maneuver in a beautiful flight of such joy and such sadness. She didn't know what she'd expected once he found the woman who had exposed and caused the ending of the Casper program, but it wasn't the flight that followed.

The tears burned hot on her cheeks as the two pilots in craft of such different eras flew over some of the most beautiful scenery in the world. Mountainscape to mountainscape as only a pilot could see them, finally circling above the San Juan Islands she'd never been to and now knew she could never stand to go see.

He waved goodbye to the woman.

Did he also reach back down the fading connections of his body to twitch his hand in her own or was it just a reflexive response to the maneuver—a question she would ask herself a thousand times in the years to come.

He opened the engine wide.

Mach 1.

Mach 2.

Two-five.

Two-seven.

Harvey still had some connection to his body; he grunted at the g-force that must have slammed the craft as he sent the Casper aloft.

It was rated to seventy thousand feet. But rating wasn't capability.

He drove for space with everything the Casper could deliver. Maybe he even did it partly for her. Maybe for both of their lost dreams of space.

He didn't begin bleeding speed until ninety-seven thousand feet. With no munitions and a partial remaining load of fuel, the aircraft was light and powerful. It was still above Mach 2 at a hundred and twenty thousand feet. Even though the engines were starving for lack of oxygen, Harvey kept pushing aloft.

One forty.

One fifty.

At one hundred and sixty-seven thousand feet, he reached the Casper's limits.

With a degree of control possible to only the most exceptional pilot, he balanced nearly a full minute, more than halfway to space. He hovered at thirty-one-point-six miles up, but an astronaut badge lay at sixty-two—still far out of his reach.

Helen couldn't tell if the plane finally tumbled or Harvey simply gave up.

He let the nose swing vertically until it was pointed straight down.

Doing nothing to abate the engines, he gained speed quickly.

At a hundred thousand feet he once more crossed Mach 2.

At fifty he punched through Mach 3.

The wings sheared off at Mach 4.5.

Now, little more than a fuselage with an engine, Harvey continued his downward dive at full power.

He hit the water at Mach 5.8.

If there was anything left to sink, it would settle in the depths of the Alaska trench. In a half million years, the motion of the tectonic plates would drag those scraps down into the mantle. Maybe another quarter million years after that, some few atoms would resurface in the Alaskan volcanoes.

Helen went around shutting off the equipment.

If they didn't jail her along with Harrington, she would hang up her uniform as soon as a replacement could be named to command Groom Lake.

She stood last at the med station.

His affinity for the mind-link must have made him more susceptible to The Rip than any other pilot. Or perhaps he simply refused to keep living without flight.

She watched the last beat of his heart, the last hint of a brainwave fade away, before shutting the equipment down.

She'd go back to her family and see if she could salvage anything of her own life. Of her own heart.

"You really flew, Harvey. Gods but you really flew."

83

CHEN MEI-LI SAT CLOSE BESIDE CHANG MUI—GENERAL LI Zuocheng's favorite granddaughter—as they shared a coconut ice cream upon the grassy bank of the Shunyi Water Park in Beijing. The Duanwu Dragon Boat Festival races were being battled out before enormous crowds who had flooded into the former Olympic Park.

The clusters of the smallest three-meter boats, each with a dragon's eye painted on the prow, made for a colorful and joyous race, all jostling together, and everyone simply glad to be there on a warm, sunny June day.

The ten-paddler class were more serious, but still were clearly enjoying themselves. These had small carved dragon heads at the front.

The great dragon boats of twenty paddlers, a steerer at the stern, and a drummer in the front to keep time were splendid to watch, especially where the longer races required the teams to turn their boats through long sweeping arcs to race back down the course.

An incautious turn caused a boat to capsize and toss its paddlers into the water. The crowd sighed with disappointment, then cheered them as they waved their paddles over their heads even as they tread water.

Mei-Li's favorites were the traditional boats. These were far longer than the "twenty" boats.

She and Mui shared a friendly debate over which boat was prettiest. Which paddlers were the strongest. Which drummer had the best flourishes.

Unlike the fiberglass and even composite-built racers, these boats were built of traditional woods. Teak shone, mahogany shimmered.

As many as fifty rowers wore brightly traditional clothes rather than a team shirt. Gold shirts matched one boat's gold detail work and red matched another's.

Flags fluttered fore and aft—red with golden calligraphy—announcing the dragon's name or calling for blessings from the gods.

The drummer didn't beat upon some tom-tom, but rather a vast drum over a meter wide that boomed across the water like the footsteps of the Jade Emperor himself, coming down from heaven to watch the show.

Their ornate dragon heads reached high out of the water, far above the paddlers' heads, seeming to strive forward even when they sat still. Everyone hushed as Daoist priests "awakened the dragons" by dotting their eyes with a fine paintbrush moments before their first race.

They looked perfect as they slid along the water, ready to fly from the water and soar freely to the heavens.

In the short time since that bastard Wang Fan's death, Mei-Li had begun to glimpse a new life—to look beyond just surviving each day. Listening to Li Zuocheng speak of his granddaughter with love and admiration had shifted her worldview in the course of a single meal.

Yes, it was time she became a dragon herself and raised her own head high. Until now, petty revenge had been sufficient, but her new-born eyes saw that so much more was possible.

Mui giggled at a particularly flamboyant drummer who danced and twirled as he beat a paddler's rhythm against his big drum.

Mei-Li let herself join in the giggle.

Giggling was not permitted at her first Youth Amateur Athletic School. Instead, poise, grace, and perfect control had been the watchwords of her youth. She'd never discovered any reason to laugh.

Until now.

Ever since the moment she'd shared her first kiss with Mui she'd felt it might be possible to laugh. And now it was easy. Mui, just a year younger, was so splendidly unspoiled. Not cynical, not abused, not bitter despite also being a great beauty. Mei-Li was drawn to her in surprising ways.

How little "Dear Uncle Ru" and "Beloved Grandfather Zuocheng" knew of what modern girls did. How easy it was to slip their very loose leash and make their own rules. She and Mui were anonymous in the crowds and no one paid attention to them. If they had walked arm in arm, the boys might bother them. But they walked holding hands in the modern, Western way that said they were a couple with no interest in penises, and the boys left them alone.

To Mei-Li, sex was simply sex.

But Mui had made it very clear what her preferences

were from the first moment they'd met. Mei-Li had thought that her experience and bitter disappointments would make her the dominant one. But Mui treated her as if *she* was the one who needed nurturing. Their first full night together—dining, dancing, then making love until dawn—had shown Mei-Li how much she had to learn.

She *did* matter. As much as she was teaching Mui about navigating the political and military world, Mui was teaching her—about the idea of hope.

Now that she had started, Mei-Li couldn't stop giggling. How little their precious guardians understood. Mui's burning desire to throw off the realm of their patriarchy and become truly Western arced through her like a shining light.

They were so perfect together.

Time would be needed. But Mei-Li would do as Mui's grandfather Zuocheng hoped and teach her how to be mature, sophisticated, and, most of all, to observe.

Between her own role as her newly-elevated uncle's assistant and Mui's insights from her grandfather, there was so much more they could gather for the Americans than a plane's flight schedule or the next design change. That was as high as she'd ever looked while under Uncle Ru's thumb.

Now she would look so much higher.

And someday, after they had destroyed their ancestors and everyone associated with them, she would get them both out and they'd be free in the West.

Yes, Mui had opened Mei-Li's eyes to finding joyfulness.

It came wrapped like a spring roll in a thin sheet of hope she'd never had before.

Adorned with a coconut-ice-cream-flavored kiss.

84

MIRANDA'S NERVES WOULDN'T LET HER SIT STILL.

As it was a lovely September morning, she went for a long walk on the island to pass the time. Spieden was two miles long, less than a half mile across, and lay on the northwest edge of the lovely San Juan Islands of Washington State.

The San Juans were actually the remaining peaks of a drowned mountain range, sticking up steep rocky heads, crowned in thick conifers.

In the 1970s, Spieden had been stocked for big game hunting—none of the predators, but gnu, zebra, several breeds of deer, and over two thousand exotic birds had abounded. The park had collapsed under the pressure of animal cruelty protests and complaints from nearby San Juan Island where stray bullets had been known to cross the half-mile channel.

John Wayne had enjoyed hunting here, and for that

reason, Miranda could never bring herself to watch any of his movies.

Long after the park's collapse, the "Great Roundup" of the 1980s had gathered most of the animals, but not quite all. Her family had bought the island a few years after that. Corsican mouflon sheep and Asian sika deer were among the most successful remainder species.

As a little girl, she'd wandered among them happily. With no natural predators—now that John Wayne and his ilk were gone—they were quite fearless. She'd often been able to hold a newborn kid or pet a fawn.

The family home had once been the grand hunting lodge. Indoor pool, sauna, a kitchen and dining room capable of seating twenty that now only rarely held more than one.

Today, Tante Daniels—after pushing at her for a month, practically forcing her into an action that was the root of all her nerves—had declined to come to the island at the last minute.

"You'll be fine, Mirrie," she'd said over the phone this morning.

"But—"

"Enough already, Mirrie. We buried them over twenty years ago. You're no longer thirteen. Move on."

"I'm—"

"Yes, you're ready. It will be amazing. You'll see. I'll send you good energy, but you won't need it." And she'd been gone.

Miranda sat for a while at her father's *Kryptos* garden sculpture. She couldn't lose herself in the contemplation of its hidden code, but it was a comfortable place to sit.

Director Winston had been true to his word and in the last month she'd twice visited the real sculpture at the CIA when she'd had to return to NTSB's headquarters. Terence had a new front door and roof gutter.

She'd tried inviting him out to the island.

"Not my dance, Mirrie. I'm fine here in DC. You just keep on a doin' that dance you're doin'. It looks damn fine on you, Mirrie."

There was a bright buzz overhead, distant but growing.

A lot of planes buzzed the island, curiosity seekers trying to spot game or the island's residents...resident. Spieden was a closed, private island and landings were prohibited. It didn't stop the tour boats from circling close, but at least they respected the landing prohibition. The boathouse and cottage were down by the water, but the main house was up in the center of the island, well shielded by towering conifers in most directions, except for a long view to the east across the length of the island.

She knew most of the plane sounds.

The Cessna's Lycoming four cylinder—a flat four in the 152 and 172 produced a distinct note from the McCauley 69" or Sensenich 72" propellers, respectively.

The Piper Tomahawk also ran the flat-four, but sounded more like an irritated mosquito. The Piper Cherokee sounded a little more practical with the deeper note of its Sensenich 74" prop.

The Mooney's Continental flat-six with the three-bladed Hartzell Scimitar prop had an aggressive, "I'm fast, get out of my way" tone that she'd always liked.

Forcing herself to her feet, she walked up the path to the

field just as her Mooney M20V turned from the crosswind leg onto final.

Mike had gotten better at flying it over the few months.

She could see Jeremy waving at her through the windshield.

Holly was easy to imagine, slouched casually in the back seat, teasing Mike and keeping some handle on Jeremy's flights of fancy.

Since joining her, they'd handled two commercial aviation crashes: a severe taxiing error that had cost two lives and over a hundred thousand dollars of damage to two aircraft, and the complete hull loss of an Embraer ERJ135 that killed the two pilots and all thirty-seven passengers. Yet the one flight attendant, sitting in the broken-away tail section, had walked away with her hair barely mussed. There had also been at least a dozen general aviation mishaps of varying severity involving small, general aviation planes.

Through it all, they'd been a staunch and reliable team. There was something more. They were also... Miranda wasn't exactly sure what.

The plane landed cleanly on the grass-strip runway that she'd mowed yesterday especially for their visit. Mike rolled it easily into the hangar she'd left open for him. She arrived as he shut it down close beside her Sabrejet.

"Miranda!" Holly hopped down. "You can *not* ever do that to me again. Next time, just girls on the island. Men are way more trouble than they're worth."

"That's not fair." Mike came over and gave Miranda a surprising hug. "If I wasn't here, who would you be complaining about?"

Miranda gave him the t-shirt she'd had made. As soon as he unrolled it, he yanked off his own shirt and pulled the new on. She noticed that Holly didn't look away for a single instant until Mike was done with the change.

He looked down at it again with a huge smile, then hugged her hard. It said, *I went to Groom Lake and all I got was a rectal probe*, just as he'd demanded during the investigation of the C-130 wreck.

Good. She'd been fairly sure that it was funny.

Jeremy came around from the other side of the plane. He, like Mike and herself, wore the Matildas women's soccer team hats that Holly had given them and insisted they all wear.

"If she wasn't complaining about you, Mike, she'd be complaining about:" Jeremy began ticking them off on his fingers, "the miserable season that the Australian Matildas are having. The quality or lack of pizza available at remote crash sites. The men—"

Holly punched his arm.

"Hey! Ow! You're always complaining about men."

"Don't worry, Jeremy, I don't count you among them."

"That's good," then he squinted his eyes at her in a way that Miranda now knew was a mixture of surprise and puzzlement. "Now hold on just a minute!"

Holly belly laughed at his consternation and Mike was definitely smiling.

Miranda marveled that Tante Daniels was right after all. The first visitors she'd allowed on the island since her parents' funeral absolutely belonged.

They weren't just her team.

They were her friends.

It was going to be a good day.

———

If you enjoyed this, keep reading for an excerpt from a book you're going to love.

..and a review is always welcome (it really helps)...

MIRANDA CHASE RETURNS

COMING SOON!

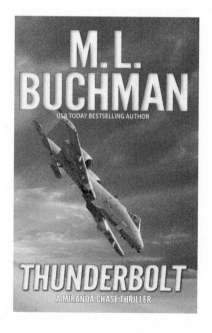

THUNDERBOLT (EXCERPT)

MIRANDA CHASE #2

Spieden Island, Washington, USA
Elevation: 137'

MIRANDA CHASE SHOOED A COUPLE OF SIKA DEER OFF THE
runway. It was a chill December morning only a few degrees
above freezing, so she didn't spend long about it.

A slow wave of sea fog was rolling in from Vancouver and
the Canadian Gulf Islands, adding a thick dampness to the
chill. The first of the US San Juan islands, Stuart and Johns,
were disappearing fast. If she didn't get aloft in the next
fifteen minutes, she'd be trapped here on Spieden Island
until the weak December sun burned it off.

The call from the National Transportation Safety Board
said that a new crash had been classified as urgent.

As if she would lag when there was a crash to investigate.

She opened the hangar door and began her pre-flight
checklist at the pilot's ladder and circling the plane counterclockwise. Tires inflated and clear of obstructions. No

leakage from the shock absorbers, brakes, or gear handling systems. No dings on the leading edge of the wing. All rote by now, but she never missed a step. She was her own ground crew, so it was up to her to make everything perfect.

Because of the frequent fog, she'd thought about installing an instrument landing system on her island. She liked that it would make Spieden one of the only grass strips in the world to have an ILS. The problem was that the outer and inner markers would have to be placed offshore in the deep waters of Puget Sound because, at two miles long and a half-mile wide, her island was too small to support the four-mile long system. Besides, her plane couldn't handle the Cat III equipment that would allow her to land in the exasperating near-zero visibility.

Her F-86 Sabrejet was neither pure North American F-86 Sabrejet nor the Canadair CL-13 Sabre Mk.5 variant anymore. One of the last ever produced before the line ended in 1958, she had tinkered with it over the years, including upgrading to the Mk.6's more powerful Orenda 14 engine. She'd also had to make a few modifications so that she could start the plane herself.

But even with the upgrades it was still all authentically a Sabrejet, and old jet fighters didn't boast modern electronic suites. To shoehorn them in, she'd have to get a custom-designed cockpit—which was never going to happen. She loved the feel and familiarity of the old "steam" dial gauges mounted in the classic cockpit.

The preflight checks only took minutes. She rolled out onto the winter-dead grass as the first tendrils of fog began slipping across the field. Her time was shorter than she'd anticipated. She taxied ahead and punched the garage controller to close the hangar door. Normally, even though she lived alone on the island, she'd get down and padlock it from the outside. But this morning the fog was moving in fast.

Isolate.

Focus.

The island would be uninhabited by humans as soon as she was aloft.

You're taxiing the airplane. Work the checklist.

Fuel tanks full.

Canopy Unsafe alarm dark.

Speed brakes retracted.

The sika deer were back, grazing along the runway as if antique fighter jets rolled by them all the time. They'd never yet run across the runway during a takeoff or landing, but she did hate disturbing their quiet island existence. They were always startled by the full-throttle roar of her turbojet engine.

She loved the deer. They were among the island's many survivors from when Spieden had been set up as a big-game-hunter resort decades ago. Some of the other remaining wildlife she was less pleased about. The incredibly territorial wild turkeys really needed to be cleared out.

There was also a rooster named Dillinger who particularly liked the acoustics of her front porch—at two in the morning. So far, he had eluded her efforts at capture or kill.

Perhaps she'd throw a hunting party. Which would include herself and...

"*You really need some friends,*" Miranda could hear Tante Daniels teasing her. She been doing that since she had been

Miranda's governess, even more so since Miranda's parents had gone down on flight TWA 800 and she'd become the then thirteen-year-old Miranda's guardian. Quite why Tante Daniels so enjoyed a gentle tease, despite knowing better than anyone how much it confused Miranda, was beyond her. At least Miranda found teasing to be more easily identifiable than sarcasm, but not by much.

At the end of the runway, she turned her jet around to face up the runway and performed the final checks.

Flaps to takeoff.

Trim two percent nose-up attitude.

Altimeter to one hundred and thirty-seven feet to match the height of the northwest end of the runway.

Winds calm.

She snapped in the oxygen mask, as she would be flying high, and tucked the tail of her helmet strap inside the chin strap so that it wouldn't tap against her cheek every time her jet hit an air pocket.

She called out her departure on the Unicom frequency in case anyone was in the area.

"Spieden Traffic. Sabrejet N19353 VFR departing to the southeast."

Miranda a satisfying sense of rightness with her custom tail number.

Airplane identifier N numbers painted on a plane's tail only had five characters—of which the first three had to be numeric. So, she'd started with the first five letters of the *Kryptos* sculpture in the CIA headquarters courtyard that she and her father had spent much of her childhood years trying to decrypt. She'd applied the Vigenère cipher (the same one used by the NSA and the CIA to decode the first two panels of the sculpture) using the word "*Kryptos*" itself just as the artist had when he'd initially encoded it.

KRYPT had become UIWEM once enciphered.

Rather than re-encoding that with a second word —"palimpsest" and "abscissa" respectively on the sculpture's first two panels—she'd applied the first alphanumeric encryption method her father had ever taught her. By using only the last number of each letter's position in the alphabet, 21-9-23-5-13, UIWEM had become 19353.

The custom N number was available from the FAA and she'd gladly paid the ten-dollar custom-number fee. The accompanying 20201 decryption key, for the number string of 21-09-23-05-13, she'd ordered as a custom license plate for the island's tractor which she mainly used for mowing the runway. Sometimes it worried her that someone would decode the two together, not that it would cause any problems if they did.

Her radio announcement was only a little unusual, as no other traffic ever flew here—except the one time she'd invited her team to visit. But it was in the FAR, and even if she was the only person she'd ever met who regularly read the complete Federal Aviation Regulations, she did her best to follow them at all times.

Rules were comfortable.

She liked rules.

They gave a structure to the chaotic world.

Miranda paused for five seconds to listen for a response from some other flier stating that her departure might be a problem for them. There was no recommended waiting time, not even in the recent *Non-towered Airport Flight Operation* advisory circular AC 90-66B. It was the first update since 1993 and she found it uncomfortable that it had no listening duration mentioned, just like its predecessor 66A.

Uncomfortable? Perhaps annoying was a better word. She was getting better at identifying emotions. The labels made them more tolerable.

She found it *annoying* that, as one of the lead NTSB accident investigators, she had reported on three separate accidents caused by a pilot who failed to allow sufficient time between an announcement and its action. Three separate times she'd recommended that the FAA change their rules to include the five-second pause, but the National Transportation Safety Board only had the power to recommend, not to enforce.

Hearing nothing, she pressed her toes hard on the footbrakes and slid the throttle forward. As the Orenda 14 engine crossed twenty percent power, she released the footbrakes and the Sabrejet instantly began to roll.

The deer looked up in alarm and bolted for the Doug fir woods as always.

A male turkey scowled at her from a low hedgerow she'd recently planted near the hangar.

Dillinger was, as usual, nowhere to be seen. Maybe her rooster had a stealth coating.

At a hundred and forty-five knots (a hundred and sixty miles an hour), she let the nose wheel lift. At one-fifty, she was wheels-up ahead of the first bank of fog prowling in through the conifers to the west. She tapped the brakes to stop the wheels from spinning then retracted the landing gear.

Aloft, she was in clear blue skies.

Contacting Seattle Air Route Traffic Control Center, she

initiated her filed flight plan and arranged for a fast climb to her best cruise height of thirty-one thousand feet. Now the only question was how fast could she get to Davis-Monthan Air Force Base outside Tucson, Arizona. It was illegal to fly over US soil at greater than Mach 1—an ability just within the performance envelope for her aircraft—but the law didn't say anything about flying at ninety-nine percent of the speed of sound.

She would cross from Washington to Arizona in under two hours. Once again, her team would unavoidably follow hours behind.

The wreck awaited and the NTSB team was on its way.

————

Achin, Nangarhar Province, Afghanistan
Elevation: 25,000'

"MC-SQUARED HEADING DOWN."

Major Carl Carmichael said it aloud in the cockpit just to see how it sounded. He still wasn't used to his new name —"MC-squared" had replaced his "Three-C" nickname almost overnight after his promotion from captain to major two weeks ago. Most guys just got one nickname in a career, but his seemed to keep changing and needed some rethinking each time.

Riding the edge of the never exceed speed, he dove his A-10 Thunderbolt "Warthog" down from Flight Level Two-five-zero.

The chill December sky over the Afghan mountains was a hard, crystalline blue that looked as if it would crack where the sharp glaciated peaks jammed against it. It had that dark purity that happened just before the sun set.

Light in the sky, dark in the valleys. Real dark for some assholes once he showed up.

Down, boy. Head on down.

Twenty-five thousand feet at four hundred and fifty knots (five hundred and eighteen miles an hour) meant thirty-five seconds to target. Actually thirty-one seconds as the ground elevation in the rugged front range of the Safēd Kōh Mountains was above three thousand feet.

A full dive in a Warthog was the best ride there ever was.

The design was fifty years old and his plane was forty. It was still the most kick-ass jet ever. The only plane in the US arsenal dedicated to close air support for ground troops.

Nothing touched it.

"Light is lazy, moving at one-half MC-squared according to old Einstein. We're going full-on MC-squared, Nancy."

The action figure perched on the top of his flight console didn't reply; she just grinned as he worked on how best to use his new nickname.

The hop from Bagram Airfield a hundred kilometers away had taken only seven minutes and he was almost there. He'd crossed the desert flats and the tortured gray lands of the east.

As usual, command had ignored the unofficial Warthog motto: *Go ugly early.* The A-10 was a seriously homely plane, but it totally rocked. And the best way to help ground troops was to get a hog there *before* they were getting their asses kicked.

If they'd called him in before the squad of 75th Rangers had gotten pinned down and cornered in the brutal mountains outside the Afghani village of Achin, they wouldn't be in such desperate straits now.

Total airworthy F-35 Lightning II's at Bagram who could get there in a third the time he could? Zero. He'd be sure to rub that in at the DFAC tonight over steak and baked potatoes.

Medevac helos had launched at the same time he had but, even slower than a Hog, were still twelve minutes-forty out. In twelve minutes there wouldn't be any need for the helos because there'd be no one left for the medical teams to rescue.

...If those rotorboys even dared fly into the valley filled with Taliban.

His high-res thermal tracker let him catalog the situation quickly.

The Talis were dug in on two different hilltops, pinning down the Rangers in the crossfire while their pals chased the good guys up the dead-end valley.

A cliff wall behind the Rangers and a platoon-size phalanx of Afghanis ragheads coming at them fast couldn't be a comfortable place to be.

"Ug-ly! That's the only word for it, Nancy. The only word. Ug-ly!"

A line of three broken US Army vehicles scattered in between the two ground forces said that the Rangers were probably now on foot whereas the Taliban were still mostly mounted.

Technicals—pickups with heavy machine guns and even artillery mounted in the back—totally sucked. They had six of those, almost as many as there were Rangers.

"Twelve minutes to get it all cleaned up, Nancy."

His sister was a bestselling romance novelist who worshipped Nancy Pearl—a major Seattle librarian who had encouraged Patsy since early in her career.

When Carl had graduated from the Air Force Academy, Patty had given him the Nancy Pearl figurine. Ever since, he and Nancy had flown together. With short graying hair, big glasses, and a bigger smile, she was kinda sexy in her tight plastic top and red cape.

She'd flown facing forward at first, but when he'd found himself wondering about her ass hidden by the flowing cape, he figured it was better if she kept an eye on him.

At fifteen thousand feet up, he lased one hilltop gun emplacement and fired off a laser-guided AGM-65 Maverick air-to-surface missile. It would take care of that group in another fifteen seconds.

At ten thousand, he lased the other hilltop and kicked off his other Maverick.

Now he was getting some attention from the ground. The bad kind of attention, but he was ready for it.

"Time to do our dance, Nancy."

He jinked sideways and flipped through a hard wing-over-wing twist as he dove around the back side of the western ridge. From above he'd seen that the valley along the back of the ridge turned and led back up the valley the Rangers were pinned down in.

The two hilltops blew simultaneously.

"Ranger Ground to A-10. Nice shooting."

"Hold tight, boys, Nancy and I are on the way."

An A-10 Warthog's real strength wasn't its heavy armor—though Carl appreciated the well-fortified cockpit every time someone got a bead on him. Nor was it in the variety of bombs and missiles hanging from the eleven hardpoints on the hog's wings and fuselage.

The plane rocked the ground assault role because it had been built starting with a gun.

A damned big gun.

At its heart, the A-10 was two tons of 30 mm GAU-8/A Avenger rotary cannon that just happened to have a tough-as-hell twin-engine jet built around it. Each second it could deliver seventy inch-and-a-quarter by four-inch, high-explosive rounds at three times the speed of sound.

The Tali were about to have their line shredded.

"Ready, Nancy?"

He carved a hard turn at the valley junction over the crap town of Achin—half-a-hundred homes squatting among steeply terraced fields. Anybody who wasn't Taliban was probably ISIS.

Sucky as shit place to be a farmer.

Nancy flashed her big smile as the sun shifted over her face through the cockpit canopy.

Most pilots sighted the Avenger cannon by eye.

Aim the nose.

Pull the trigger.

Ker-pow!

The head's up display would show the gun's aiming point at different distances, but no real hog jockey used it, except at night...maybe. Carl had made the cut to qualify in the A-10 Warthog straight out of flight school. Adding in a decade of tours in Iraq, Afghanistan, and Syria had made it automatic for him to aim and fire the jet's primary weapon.

Practice...and Nancy's head.

When her smile blocked the exact center of the A-10 canopy, the target was perfectly aligned in the gun's sights.

Flipping up the safety, he rested his thumb on the trigger.

Nancy's head was just lining up with the tail of the Taliban column. He could see that the soon-to-be total losers were still looking upward for his return from above after blasting the hilltop gun nests.

Instead, he had the throttle wide open and was cruising along at thirty feet above the ground from directly behind.

"Shoulda checked your six. Gonna ram it up your asses, dudes."

Steep valley walls to either side and an abrupt mountain wall at the head of the valley bounded his play area. He'd have a four-second, two hundred and eighty-round pass, then he'd climb out and see what sort of mood they were in after that. Maybe drop a pair of Mark 80 iron bombs just to chew them up a bit as he went by.

"MC-squared. Faster than lightning."

Damn straight!

He returned Nancy's smile and pulled the trigger.

———

Achin, Nangarhar Province, Afghanistan
Elevation: 3,943'

STAFF SERGEANT JASPER KENNING OF THE 3RD RANGER Battalion, Charlie Company dropped his radio but couldn't look down as it bounced off the rocks.

He could only watch through his rifle scope as the A-10 Warthog came apart in mid-air.

There'd been no incoming round.

One moment, their salvation had been racing up the valley toward them.

The nose cannon— ready to spit death from where it reached out between the Warthog's painted teeth and pissed-off scowl design—had started to spin.

Rather than a lethal stream of punishment for the Taliban column, the three missiles mounted directly to the underside of the main fuselage—ignited.

Without releasing first.

They blew the shit out of the middle of the Warthog's belly.

The plane flipped on edge and plummeted toward the ground. Catching a wingtip on a boulder, it cartwheeled up the valley.

The pilot never had a chance to eject.

The fireball climbed high in the sky and the narrow valley echoed with the explosion as its load of bombs and fifteen hundred 30 mm rounds cooked off from the center of the blaze.

For thirty seconds it was impossible to hear or think anywhere in the area until the explosives spent themselves.

Then the valley echoed with the silence.

The Taliban troops remained hunkered in position. They hadn't even seen the Warthog coming up behind them, and there hadn't been time for them to do more than freeze where they were.

Stunned silence.

No victorious cheer came from the massed troops celebrating a successful takedown.

Just shock.

His own troops were just as frozen.

Happiness is a warm gun. His drill sergeant had a thing about quoting Beatles' lyrics like he was some fossil left over from the Stone Age.

Kenning's rifle wasn't warm, it was blazing hot from all the rounds he'd pumped out of it during their retreat, but the enemy had just kept on coming no matter how many they put down.

He was the very first to shake off the shock.

Looking aloft offered no solace. There hadn't been a spare Reaper drone to circle over their position for this operation, so no Hellfire missile was going to come down and shred the Taliban like God's mighty hand striking from above.

The A-10 unleashed another spate of explosions.

This time the cloud was black with the JP-8 jet fuel from the breached mid-line tanks.

"Rangers!" Kenning called out.

"Hooah!" The responses were few and weak, but they were there.

Three of his men were dead—including Lieutenant Bailey—their remains still back in the blown-up MRAP they'd had to abandon. A glance behind him showed that two more were never going to lift their rifles again.

The remains of his squad began forming up behind the scattered boulders that were going to shield their last stand.

The Talis shook off their surprise. They looked side to

side at each other. Then—close enough that Kenning could easily see—they smiled.

A unison war cry in Pashto declaring "God is great!" shook the valley. Like they needed to thank God for their bloodthirsty ways.

The Beatles tune *When I'm Sixty-Four* took a swing through his head because Drill Sergeant McCluskey had said that's how old they'd be by the time he could make them into even marginally acceptable soldiers.

Sixty-four.

Yeah, that so wasn't going to happen.

────────

US Air Force Air Combat Command
Directorate of Simulation
Site C-3, Elgin Air Force Base, Florida
Elevation: Subbasement 2

A LOOP OF CODE TESTED THE GLOBAL R14A10ACH VARIABLE every three milliseconds as it had been since it was invoked seventeen minutes earlier by a higher-level process.

The test loop resided on a Cray XC50 supercomputer—one small section of which was running a group of fourteen pilots in flight simulators currently battling it out two stories above.

USAF Air Combat Command's Cray was four ranks of computing cabinets. Each cabinet stood six-and-a-half feet wide, six feet deep, and a yard wide. Each cabinet was water-cooled by a blower cabinet the same size but half as wide.

Three sets made a rank. Four ranks created a twelve peta-flop computer—twelve quadrillion operations per second.

Fifty-seven thousand test cycles later—a hundred and seventy-one seconds and a compute load so trivial as to be wholly inconsequential—the R14A10ACH variable tested true.

The subroutine proceeded through the next four hundred and nineteen lines of code in a cascading cycle lasting almost two full seconds.

In that time, the invoked process carried out just four steps:

It generated a one-word message.

Delivered the word to three separate secure cellphones.

After all three phones provided a delivery confirmation —over ninety-eight percent of the total elapsed processing time—it dropped the external connection.

Finally, the subroutine erased both itself and the program that had called it—a load of barely ten thousand operations requiring approximately a billionth of a second compute time.

———

Keep reading Thunderbolt at fine retailers everywhere.
...and don't forget that review. It really helps me out.

ABOUT THE AUTHOR

USA Today and Amazon #1 Bestseller M. L. "Matt" Buchman started writing on a flight south from Japan to ride his bicycle across the Australian Outback. Just part of a solo around-the-world trip that ultimately launched his writing career.

From the very beginning, his powerful female heroines insisted on putting character first, *then* a great adventure. He's since written over 60 action-adventure thrillers and military romantic suspense novels. And just for the fun of it: 100 short stories, and a fast-growing pile of read-by-author audiobooks.

Booklist says: "3X Top 10 of the Year." PW says: "Tom Clancy fans open to a strong female lead will clamor for more." His fans say: "I want more now...of everything." That his characters are even more insistent than his fans is a hoot.

As a 30-year project manager with a geophysics degree who has designed and built houses, flown and jumped out of planes, and solo-sailed a 50' ketch, he is awed by what is possible. More at: www.mlbuchman.com.

Other works by M. L. Buchman: *(* - also in audio)*

Thrillers

Dead Chef
One Chef!
Two Chef!

Miranda Chase
Drone*
Thunderbolt*
Condor*
Ghostrider*

Romantic Suspense

Delta Force
Target Engaged*
Heart Strike*
Wild Justice*
Midnight Trust*

Firehawks
MAIN FLIGHT
Pure Heat
Full Blaze
Hot Point*
Flash of Fire*
Wild Fire
SMOKEJUMPERS
Wildfire at Dawn*
Wildfire at Larch Creek*
Wildfire on the Skagit*

The Night Stalkers
MAIN FLIGHT
The Night Is Mine
I Own the Dawn
Wait Until Dark
Take Over at Midnight
Light Up the Night
Bring On the Dusk
By Break of Day

AND THE NAVY
Christmas at Steel Beach
Christmas at Peleliu Cove
WHITE HOUSE HOLIDAY
Daniel's Christmas*
Frank's Independence Day*
Peter's Christmas*
Zachary's Christmas*
Roy's Independence Day*
Damien's Christmas*
5E
Target of the Heart
Target Lock on Love
Target of Mine
Target of One's Own

Shadow Force: Psi
At the Slightest Sound*
At the Quietest Word*

White House Protection Force
Off the Leash*
On Your Mark*
In the Weeds*

Contemporary Romance

Eagle Cove
Return to Eagle Cove
Recipe for Eagle Cove
Longing for Eagle Cove
Keepsake for Eagle Cove

Henderson's Ranch
Nathan's Big Sky*
Big Sky, Loyal Heart*
Big Sky Dog Whisperer*

Love Abroad
Heart of the Cotswolds: England
Path of Love: Cinque Terre, Italy

Other works by M. L. Buchman:

Contemporary Romance (cont)

Where Dreams
Where Dreams are Born
Where Dreams Reside
Where Dreams Are of Christmas
Where Dreams Unfold
Where Dreams Are Written

Science Fiction / Fantasy

Deities Anonymous
Cookbook from Hell: Reheated
Saviors 101

Single Titles
The Nara Reaction
Monk's Maze
the Me and Elsie Chronicles

Non-Fiction

Strategies for Success
Managing Your Inner Artist/Writer
Estate Planning for Authors
Character Voice

Short Story Series by M. L. Buchman:

Romantic Suspense

Delta Force
Delta Force

Firehawks
The Firehawks Lookouts
The Firehawks Hotshots
The Firebirds

The Night Stalkers
The Night Stalkers
The Night Stalkers 5E
The Night Stalkers CSAR
The Night Stalkers Wedding Stories

US Coast Guard
US Coast Guard

White House Protection Force
White House Protection Force

Contemporary Romance

Eagle Cove
Eagle Cove

Henderson's Ranch
Henderson's Ranch

Where Dreams
Where Dreams

Thrillers

Dead Chef
Dead Chef

Science Fiction / Fantasy

Deities Anonymous
Deities Anonymous

Other
The Future Night Stalkers
Single Titles

SIGN UP FOR M. L. BUCHMAN'S NEWSLETTER TODAY

and receive:
Release News
Free Short Stories
a Free Book

Get your free book today. Do it now.
free-book.mlbuchman.com

Made in the USA
Coppell, TX
27 July 2020